JOIA CITY SERIES

CODE
Of Heart

T.M. POLAK

Independently published

First edition: 2025

Print ISBN: 979-8-9987943-1-5
eBook ISBN: 979-8-9987943-0-8

For inquiries or permissions, please contact: tmpolak.author@gmail.com

CONTENT WARNING

This book discusses and includes sensitive topics such as terminal illnesses (Cancer), sexual assault, domestic abuse, homicide, kidnapping, and learning disabilities (Dyslexia).

DEDICATION

I channeled my inner Elle Woods in December 2024 the day I woke up and said, "I think I'm going to write a book today."

This is for all the dreamers out there with spicy brains like me who have had a version of Warner Huntington III tell them they weren't good enough for something...or a Vivian Kensington who made them feel like they didn't belong...

Because seriously, fuck these people.
You should totally do it anyway (unless it's super illegal).

CHAPTER 1

Aurelia

Aurelia Douro was alone again.

She sat on the dock behind her modest home, her feet dangling over the water. With her hands splayed flat against the weathered planks and arms locked rigid, her shoulders curled inward in a protective hunch. Her whole body leaned forward, as if bracing against a weight no one else could see.

A warm mid-summer breeze caressed her tear-stained face, the moonlight casting a glow on her weary expression. Her thoughts drifted through a lifetime of memories. The first time she sat on this dock was right after she bought the property, officially a homeowner. Eleanor had been beside her—bare feet in the water, laughing at something Aurelia said.

The dock creaked beneath her as Aurelia shifted her weight, the cool wood pressing into her palms. Now it was just her...again.

Things had been going great for the first time in Aurelia's life, and she genuinely enjoyed her job and Eleanor's company. She had finally begun to feel happy, and it was all thanks to her.

Then Eleanor's headaches started, and those feelings Aurelia had come to cherish evaporated, replaced by worry and fear.

The persistent shortness of breath quickly followed. Eleanor became so fatigued that everyday activities were too taxing and painful.

Over several weeks, her health had rapidly deteriorated, with Aurelia begging Eleanor to go to the doctor for a full evaluation. After initially protesting, Eleanor eventually gave in and agreed. That single appointment swiftly evolved into multiple rounds of testing before it yielded a culprit.

Cancer.

It had spread throughout her frail ninety-two-year-old frame, the prognosis bleak.

Aurelia remembered that day and moment vividly.

"I've been on this planet for ninety-two goddamn years, living life on my terms. Like hell will I spend whatever time I have left strapped to a bed with needles jabbed in me, losing all my beautiful locks," Eleanor said when presented with the choice to try chemotherapy.

Despite the devastating news, Aurelia had laughed because it was a typical Eleanor response. She faced every situation with her own set of rules, so it was fitting that she approached her end the same way.

The laughter didn't last long; everything she saw now seemed tinged with gray and edged with a chill that she couldn't shake.

The ride back to the estate following that appointment had begun somberly. Eleanor stared out the window, deep in thought, while Aurelia summoned every kernel of willpower within herself to keep the tears at bay.

Eleanor had eventually turned to her with a mischievous sparkle in her eyes and declared, "Time for us to start planning my farewell party. Let's make sure it's as unforgettable as I am!"

Which was why today's loss felt like the final blow.

Because Eleanor Greaves—her mentor, boss, and the closest thing she had ever had to a mother throughout her thirty years of existence—had passed away. Aurelia knew this day would come, and tried to prepare, but nothing lessened the ache.

No breakup in her messy dating history had ever hurt like this. When she had been living out of her car, Eleanor took a chance on her, giving her hope and a purpose she hadn't known she needed. For five years, Aurelia thanked every god in existence for that chance, vowing never to waste it.

Everything she worked for over the last few months was in preparation for today...but she still hadn't been ready for it.

Per Eleanor's final request, they were to host a grand affair at Starhaven Manor that would be both a celebration of the socialite's life and an opportunity to air grievances with certain attendees.

Aurelia recounted the events that had unfolded earlier that day as she gazed up at the sky, openly mourning the absence of such vitality.

They held a private service for Eleanor's closest friends and family. She was laid to rest in the Greaves family mausoleum at Starhaven Manor, the last of her line reunited with her ancestors.

Rumors began swirling in the social circles about who would inherit the Greaves fortune. As Eleanor's personal assistant, Aurelia knew exactly how vast that fortune was...enough to sustain many generations for years to come. Eleanor wasn't yet cold in the ground before the scavengers started circling.

Aurelia drowned out the gossip by focusing on her work, as she was given three days to execute the farewell party according to plan. If anyone noticed her tearful eyes or wavering voice during this time, they wisely kept it to themselves. She didn't know how she would handle confronting her grief in front of them.

In the end, the event sparkled in all its opulent glory. The ballroom glowed with crystal chandeliers, satin tablecloths in various jewel tones, towering floral arrangements, and a dance floor like a living painting. The scent of jasmine and amber filled the air, while projector screens ensured every guest had a view of the presentation.

Charcuterie boards teased the guests before the multicourse meal, as a string quartet played near the patio overlooking the gardens. Eleanor's farewell was a true reflection of her larger-than-life persona and was no less extravagant, whimsical, and unapologetically grand as she had been.

Guests, handpicked by Eleanor, trickled in; all dressed in dark mourning attire that contrasted with the vibrant space. Dramatic sniffles and silken handkerchiefs dabbed at imaginary tears, but no one noticed Aurelia's quiet observations. She knew Eleanor would have cackled with glee at the show, loving every second of the spectacle.

This was her final act of rebellion.

Aurelia's hands trembled slightly as she thought of what was still to come. She wanted to honor her friend by wearing something bright and chose a royal purple sleeveless maxi dress, accented with a large gold belt and matching sandals. Her usual makeup was light and efficient, consisting of mascara, tinted moisturizer, and lip gloss, but today, she added a touch of bronze eyeshadow.

Selene Vinter, Starhaven Manor's Chief of Staff, approached Aurelia. Selene oversaw the management of Starhaven Manor's daily operations. Her level of authority was second only to Eleanor's. She was serious, direct, and demanded perfection from the staff. She wore a gray variation of her usual pantsuit, hair in its trademark tight bun, and the ever-present earpiece.

Aurelia had known Selene since they were twelve. Placed in the same foster home, their friendship began and extended beyond their time in care.

Selene had worked hard over the years to earn her ultimate promotion to Chief of Staff in the Greaves household. Eleanor had gone through more personal assistants than one could count, usually over something minuscule.

When Selene had encouraged her to apply to be Eleanor's personal assistant, Aurelia was hesitant. The required skills and experience were daunting enough to stop her from sending an application, but she had done it anyway to make her friend happy, and Eleanor hired her on the spot. For the last five years, Aurelia had worked tirelessly to prove she was the right choice.

Selene surveyed the room and said softly, "This is exactly the kind of circus Eleanor would have loved. How are you holding up?"

Aurelia exhaled. "Part of me wants it over, and the other part doesn't want it to end because it means she's really gone. What about you?"

Selene nodded, eyes downcast. "Same. Unfortunately, Eleanor's still holding us to a timeline from beyond." She checked her watch and cursed. "It's time for the first course." She turned to the Master of Ceremonies to start the event.

Guests moved to their seats as he welcomed them to the celebration. His voice rang through the speakers and every projector screen.

"It was Eleanor Greaves' final wish that we gather here today to celebrate her life rather than mourn her passing," he announced. "We will soon begin the meal, followed by a cinematic tribute with personal stories from her closest friends. To close the celebration, we also have a final video from Eleanor herself."

A chorus of gasps and some not-so-subtle—borderline obnoxious—tears rippled through the room. Aurelia rolled her eyes at the theatrics as the video began, and the first course was served.

Too nervous to eat, Aurelia stayed in her corner, eyes fixed on the screen. She didn't notice Charles Pierce approach until he spoke beside her.

"Eleanor was one of a kind," he said softly.

Charles had been Eleanor's attorney since the day he graduated from law school decades ago. Now in his early eighties with silver hair, warm but sharp brown eyes, Charles looked like he had aged significantly these last two months as well. He was Eleanor's friend just as much as he was her attorney, in mourning like Aurelia.

"Only she would demand a farewell party instead of a normal funeral," Aurelia said wryly.

Charles laughed. "And she was anything but normal."

Comfortable in each other's company, they stood quietly for a few moments as they waited to watch the video before Charles broke the silence. "While I don't wish to talk business during an event like this, I need to ask that you come back here tomorrow at 9:00 AM along with the rest of the staff."

He hedged, choosing his next words carefully. "There are...matters within her final will that affect her staff, in addition to other items you and I must discuss privately."

Aurelia's stomach sank. "9:00 AM is fine with me, my schedule's suddenly wide open," she replied with a slow nod.

"See you tomorrow morning then. In the meantime, I need another drink before Act Two of this production gets underway," Charles said with resignation before walking away. Aurelia broke out into a small grin before deciding to follow his lead to grab herself a diet soda.

Calling what came next a production was putting it mildly. Had anyone asked Aurelia, she would have shamelessly classified it as a bona fide shit show.

It started with community members offering heartfelt condolences and stories about how wonderful it had been to work with Eleanor. Aurelia fought to keep her composure as they shared tales of Eleanor's generosity and larger-than-life spirit.

Then the tone shifted. A group of elderly socialites gathered by the podium, forming a line. Each looked virtually identical: petite, silver-haired, draped in proper funeral attire, wearing black orthopedic shoes. The leader of this senior gang, Gladys Heringsworth, went first.

"There are no words worthy enough to express my sorrow for the passing of our dear Eleanor. She was as close to me as a sister could be, and now I find myself bereft—*bereft* without my friend," Gladys blubbered. "My annual holiday party will be a little less lively, but no less sublime," she clarified, "without Eleanor this year." She looked up at the ceiling as she waved a small, frail fist in the air while the other rested over her heart. "I'll have a slice of my Pistachio Custard Pie in your memory, my sweet angel," she cried dramatically.

The sniffling across the room intensified as Gladys left the stage, handkerchief in hand. Margaret Carrington followed, carefully dabbing her eyes as she spoke with conviction.

"Oh, my stars! Eleanor's departure is a loss I'll feel forever," she declared. "She was always such a...*unique* presence. Even when she wore those questionably ostentatious outfits or said such unfiltered things, she did it with such confidence, you almost *had* to admire her audacity. We may not have always agreed, but she certainly...*existed*."

The MC gently ushered Margaret offstage, but not before she scowled at him. Aurelia cringed as Nancy Fitzwalter swiftly took Margaret's space on stage.

"Eleanor...our beloved Eleanor," Nancy sobbed. "She truly was one of a kind. No one else could manage to show up an hour late to every event and still demand the best seat in the house. She had the sort of charm that would make you simultaneously roll your eyes and pour her another glass of champagne. She may be gone, but that unmistakable perfume of hers will haunt my cashmere for years to come."

Nancy exited the stage, outwardly overcome with grief as Gertrude Pavendish began to make her way forward...but was cut off by a speed walking Judith Vanderlyn. Aurelia couldn't contain her surprise over how quickly Judith was able to squeak by. Judging by the ruinous look on Gertrude's face, this was a slight that wouldn't be forgotten any time soon.

"I don't even know where to begin to truly express what a special person Eleanor was. As her best friend—" Gertrude snorted loudly, prompting Judith to glower at her, "—I can honestly say that she was a beacon of grace...after a few martinis. Always perfectly coiffed, even when she got names wrong at charity galas. But oh, how we loved her. She may not have remembered anyone's birthday, but she certainly remembered every single grudge..." she cut another look at Gertrude, "*Truly* unforgettable."

The MC edged closer to the podium, sensing the tension. Gertrude stormed up next, hate-filled eyes still trained on Judith.

"What can I say about our precious Eleanor that hasn't already been whispered at lunch?" She seethed. "She was a master at creating drama. Always the life of the party...but we adored her for it, didn't we? After all, she taught us one important lesson: sometimes, it's better to forgive than to dwell on her antics." She glared pointedly at Judith as she said, "Too bad *some of us* can't always live by these words."

Judith bristled in her seat. The MC quickly intervened to introduce Ophelia Draycott. Aurelia sent a silent prayer to the universe to let this be the last of Eleanor's friends.

Ophelia stood there for a moment, surveying the crowd with beady yet shrewd eyes before she spoke. "I have so many wonderful memories of Eleanor that I will always cherish," she sighed theatrically, bowing her head before looking up at the crowd again.

"What a vivacious spirit she had! She lived life to the fullest—sometimes *too* full. Remember the time she tried to outbid me for that antique vase? *Hilarious!*" Ophelia forced a laugh. "She was a woman of contradictions: so generous with her opinions, even when no one asked, and so humble about her achievements that she never quite mentioned any. But truthfully, she was a friend. Well, a friendly rival, really. I will always treasure the way she made me feel better about myself...by comparison. She had a way of making every room a little louder and every evening a bit more unpredictable. In a world of dull politeness, she was a...*colorful* reminder that chaos can be entertaining."

Aurelia was dumbfounded. At least she had Selene as a real friend. She would rather have a small group of *genuine* friends than what these six impostors purported to be. She couldn't fathom how Eleanor tolerated these women.

Then Bertrand Dallingford shuffled to the podium, cane in hand. Aurelia knew him as Eleanor's sworn enemy. When she had once asked about their relationship, Eleanor had waved it off as "another man jealous of my brilliance."

Bertrand's deep, gravelly voice cut through the room.

"I've known Eleanor all my life, and she kept secrets from all of you," he bellowed. "The biggest secret that old spindly cactus kept was of her torrid love affair with me. Right up until the end, she couldn't keep her fossilized fingers off me. There is not a room in this estate, and that includes the closets and pantries, where she didn't have her way with me. Only three weeks ago, she propositioned me right here—"

"How could you do this to me, Bertrand!" A shrill voice from somewhere on the left interrupted. "You told me that your affair with Eleanor ended years ago and that I was the only woman you had eyes for! I cannot *believe* I ever gave you and your sour pickle the time of day!" All eyes were fixed on Gladys, the source of the ear-piercing wail.

"I cannot control my animal magnetism, Gladys," he shouted back as more women stood, shrieking. Bertrand, despite his limited mobility brought forth by his age, had been remarkably busy indeed.

Dinner rolls and silverware started flying. Aurelia met Selene's eyes. They shared a look that silently begged for ear bleach. Selene began discreetly giving orders over her earpiece, while Aurelia signaled the MC to intercede. He hurried to the stage and guided Bertrand away as security stepped in.

The MC leaned into the microphone and thanked everyone for their "spirited" tributes before wrapping up the segment. Dessert and coffee followed, with murmurs about the final video message Eleanor prepared.

Aurelia then realized she had never seen the video herself. She was as clueless as everyone else in the room, which made her very uneasy.

She looked for Charles before spotting him at the bar, right as he threw back the contents of another drink. He slowly shook his head and faced the nearest screen. With an eerie sense of foreboding, she did the same as the final video began to play.

There was Eleanor, perched upon her favorite silver, gray, and blue leopard print chaise in her personal study. Her white hair was perfectly styled in an elaborate French pompadour with a large peacock feather protruding from the back. Her cerulean eyes bored into the camera as she donned her favorite sequined peacock-patterned pantsuit, large pearl necklace, and bone-colored loafers.

She peered at each person through the screen as if physically here before speaking.

"If this video is playing, I suppose we can agree I'm long gone from this world. My only regret in life is that I couldn't see what kind of sorry-looking lot showed up for my farewell party." Her voice echoed through the silent ballroom.

"For everyone out there wondering where my money is going, if Charles Pierce hasn't contacted you within forty-eight hours, *then you're not getting a dime*. I'm dead, not stupid. I know you've all been talking about it."

She paused, her eyes raking over the camera.

"To my devoted staff members, please report to work tomorrow morning as usual—and *on time*. Just because I'm dead doesn't mean we slack off."

She leaned forward, eyes twinkling with mischief.

"Lastly, I have some things to confess. Bertrand...my beloved Bertrand. There is not a single person here who believes that the thing atop your head you refer to as your hair is real. Now I'm in the afterlife, still *absolutely baffled* as to how someone so filthy rich was duped into wearing a piece of roadkill on his head." Bertrand emitted a strangled sound of indignation while guests snickered.

"But more importantly," Eleanor continued, "I wanted everyone to know about the intimate relationship Bertrand and I continued all these years. When I found out he was putting that limp noodle in my dear friend Gladys's rusty pasta pot, I was ready to beat him with that unkempt head rug of his."

Gasps rang out through the crowd.

"Instead, I strung you along all this time, Bertrand, pretending like I knew nothing." She cackled darkly. "The deliciously scandalous secrets you spilled about anyone and anything after every one of our dalliances...my god, your lips are as loose as you are. *That's* the reason, my one-and-only Bertrand, I kept you so close."

The maniacal glint in her eyes raised Aurelia's hackles, and she braced herself for whatever Eleanor was going to say next.

"And *that's* the reason why my death is the perfect excuse to gather you all together in one room...just so I could say that I know it wasn't only Gladys, but also *Margaret, Nancy, Judith, Gertrude, and Ophelia who kept sampling that tiny cocktail wiener!*"

The room erupted into chatter that got louder and louder, but our precious Eleanor wasn't done yet. No, instead she aggressively pointed a finger at the left side of the ballroom and yelled her last words before the video abruptly ended, "...and Gladys, I will *never* forgive you for stealing my family's secret Pistachio Custard Pie recipe decades ago and pawning it off as your own at your annual holiday party! I hope you rot in hell right along with Bertrand and his saggy harem, you porch-sitting gargoyle!"

The ballroom descended into chaos. Bertrand was carried off by security as dinner rolls and curses flew. Aurelia met Selene's wild eyes while another two security guards tried to hold the line against the mass of angry elderly lovers hobbling in Bertrand's direction, looking for their pound of flesh.

Aurelia looked at Charles, who was still seated at the bar with a new drink in hand. He winked at her before raising his glass in a silent toast and again gulping it down in one go.

It took hours to clean up the mess in the ballroom and even longer for the police to complete their investigation, after several guests activated their medical alert necklaces to call for help.

Eight guests were arrested and charged with disorderly conduct, assault, and even assault and battery on a police officer. It turned out Gladys had used Bertrand's cane to strike an officer who was trying to handcuff her.

As soon as she got home, Aurelia swapped her long purple maxi dress and sandals for a tank top and shorts. She pulled her long, brown, wavy hair into a messy bun, grabbed a bottle of water, and walked out onto the dock.

She had been there ever since, grieving and reflecting on how alone she felt. Despite her closeness with Selene, Aurelia never felt completely comfortable sharing her deepest feelings with her. They both carried their own scars. Eleanor was the only person she had ever truly opened up to—and she was gone.

"I already miss you so much," she whispered to the night sky. "I hope wherever you are now, you're pain-free and haunting someone." A warm, gentle breeze brushed her cheek, like phantom fingers offering reassurance.

A small smile tugged at her lips. Perhaps it was the grief talking, but she chose to take it as a sign that Eleanor was still with her in some way.

Wiping her eyes, Aurelia stood and headed back into the house. She still had to report to work on time tomorrow.

CHAPTER 2

Aurelia

Aurelia jolted upright, breath shallow, the nightmare still gripping her.

It took a minute before she recognized her bedroom and not *that* apartment. Scattered throw pillows lay on the floor, a visual echo of her unrest. She dragged a trembling hand down her face and exhaled a shaky breath. Her tank top clung to her damp skin.

The second her head hit the pillow last night, exhaustion took over and quickly pulled her under. Sleep was usually nonexistent...the nightmares of past events were forever haunting. Rubbing her eyes, she tried to calm her racing heart.

The view out of her window, normally a source of comfort, didn't settle her nerves. The lagoon shimmered beyond the glass, reminding her of why she had fought so hard to restore this once-crumbling cottage.

She had seen its potential the way she hoped someone might one day see hers. Worn, yes, but worth saving.

There would be no peace today. A knot sat heavy in her stomach. She cursed, remembering her conversation with Charles at Eleanor's farewell celebration, turning frantically to check the clock on her nightstand.

It was 7:52 AM.

Groaning, she jumped out of bed. The 9:00 AM staff meeting at Starhaven wasn't optional, and being late was unacceptable.

She wasn't about to start that habit now.

Darting into her bathroom, she flew through a rushed shower beneath shimmering fish-scale tiles, barely pausing to dry off before heading to the closet she had once dreamed of having.

She dressed as quickly as possible, throwing on brown leggings that passed as slacks, a cream tunic, and a coral cardigan embroidered with beads and metallic leaves. Earrings in, favorite nude flats on, and hair twisted into a high bun, she applied a quick sweep of neutral makeup and mascara, forever thankful for her naturally thick lashes.

Grabbing her phone, keys, and bag, she dashed out the door.

She would make it. Just barely.

By the time Aurelia reached Starhaven, everyone was in the ballroom. Selene stood composed and collected at the entrance, dressed in a navy pantsuit, leveling her typical cool gaze at each person passing through.

Having spotted Aurelia, her expression shifted imperceptibly.

"Where have you been?" Selene quietly asked.

Caught off guard, Aurelia replied, "What do you mean? I'm right on time for the 9:00 meeting. Was I supposed to be here earlier?"

"Well, I would've expected you to help me get everything ready for this meeting. I'm only one person, and having an extra set of hands to help herd everyone would have been nice," Selene huffed.

Aurelia blinked. She hadn't received any messages or calls. She tried to sympathize with her long-time friend.

"I'm sorry, I didn't realize you needed my help. You should've called me; I would have been here," Aurelia said.

"Don't be sorry...you're right," Selene sighed ruefully with a slight shake of her head. "I'm taking my stress out on you. You're usually here earlier than most, and I assumed you could help, that's all," she explained. "Let's head in, they're starting promptly at 9:00, and I don't want to miss a thing," Selene said as she looped her arm around Aurelia's.

They entered the now spotless ballroom and found their seats. The audio-visual equipment set up for the farewell event was still there. Charles Pierce stood at the podium with a laptop and a thick folder. While Aurelia sat down, Selene remained standing in front of her seat to call the room to order so that Charles could begin.

After briefly introducing himself as Eleanor Greaves's attorney, Charles explained that he was executing her will—and it required the staff to view the final message she had recorded.

Unnatural silence filled the ballroom.

He then tapped a few keys on his laptop to begin the video presentation before stepping aside, ensuring he wasn't blocking the screen behind him.

Like last night, the screens came to life with Eleanor front and center, wearing the same outfit in yesterday's video and sitting on her favorite chaise lounge. The look directed at the crowd in this recording was drastically different than that of the farewell party. It was softer, more like the Eleanor we loved.

After what felt like a lifetime, Eleanor began to speak.

"My dearest household staff. Words cannot express how much I appreciated all your hard work that ensured Starhaven Manor, the Greaves legacy, and my personal affairs were the epitome of excellence. Know that I will miss you dearly."

Aurelia couldn't stop the wave of emotion that washed over her. She swallowed hard once, then twice, her attention fixed on the screen before her. Hearing Eleanor's voice again helped take the edge off her pain. Selene reached over and gave her hand a comforting squeeze.

"By this time, my farewell party should have taken place last night, and I'm confident it went off without a hitch...and if it didn't, then Bertrand and Gladys had it coming. I can rest easily knowing that I said what needed to be said." Eleanor chuckled and waved a hand in the air.

"But back to more important things. As I was saying...I again cannot thank you all enough for the great care you have shown to my estate, my events, and me through to the end. You have continued to be exceptional, always catering to my every whim, especially knowing what a cranky old biddy I can be."

Aurelia heard a handful of quiet chuckles, no doubt agreeing with Eleanor's description of her disposition.

"Most of you are wondering what will happen to you now that I'm gone. It's no secret that I didn't have any children of my own, and it is my biggest regret in life to have the Greaves legacy end with me. But don't worry, death won't stop me from taking care of you...Well, at least for the next two years anyway."

The air in the room suddenly became charged, and the staff sat up taller and paid more attention.

"Everyone will receive the same salary and benefits as they do now, as well as an annual merit increase as planned. Charles will take over the oversight of general operations, while Aurelia will remain in her position, helping him with my affairs as she normally would with me. The day-to-day will continue under the purview of our current Chief of Staff, Selene Vinter."

Aurelia snuck a glance at Selene, but her expression was unreadable.

Eleanor continued, "Going forward with business as usual: I expect you all to report to work on time and perform your duties as if I were still here—maintain the estate, support my annual events that will carry on at Starhaven.

Additionally, everyone will receive a $50,000 bonus at once, followed by a $100,000 bonus each year for the next two years." There was an explosion of animated whispers, "...assuming you are still employed by the estate for the first and second anniversaries of my passing. This totals $250,000, and I must reiterate that it is contingent upon your continued employment here."

The excitement was impossible to ignore—even Aurelia was surprised, her mouth slack and eyes wide. She glanced at Selene again...her features still carefully schooled and keenly focused on the screen.

"While I have no heir by blood, I've taken measures to name someone as the beneficiary to take over my estate and assets. At the end of the two-year window, it will be at their discretion whether they want to keep the current staff or not. If any of you choose not to stay on long-term beyond that, then you still have a two-year window to find alternative employment. The last thing that I want is for any member of my household to be stressed about losing their job."

There were a few members openly weeping about her generous offer...it even affected Aurelia.

"As my attorney Charles Pierce has hopefully said, *like I told him to*," Charles rolled his eyes, "he will be meeting with you individually to review documents and discuss the terms of this employment agreement. Expect to hear from him and Aurelia within the next couple of weeks as they work out the details."

Aurelia quickly pulled out her phone, adding these meetings to her task list.

Eleanor's eyes glittered with unshed tears. "When you look back on my passing, I hope it's with fondness. I know exactly how crazy and pigheaded I can be, and while I wouldn't change a damn thing about it, I care more about you than you may think," she said thickly.

Eleanor then straightened her spine, and the utmost regal expression she could muster slipped over her face. "Now get back to work! You've had a long enough break, and I can already see black mold forming on the seat where Bertrand's putrid butt parked itself last night."

The video abruptly ended, a reflection of the way Eleanor both entered and exited this world—a disruptive force.

Everything Eleanor did in life followed her personal moral code and rules of etiquette. Dressed to the nines in her signature eccentric style, she was direct and didn't mince words in her messages, preferring to "tell it like it is."

Aurelia wasn't surprised by it, though.

If there was one thing Eleanor hated most, it would be those who hid behind false niceties and disingenuous smiles. It's why she was so generous with her fortune; she truly enjoyed helping others who were less fortunate. Eleanor often sought opportunities to help others anonymously, whether it was through a donation or even paying off mortgages on a whim.

Around her, whispers of shock and gratitude spread. She touched Selene's arm; her friend jumped slightly, then finally turned to her.

"Well, Eleanor was never one to shy away from dramatics," Selene eventually said with a dry chuckle.

Aurelia studied her friend closely. She hadn't been her usual self these last few weeks, but Aurelia attributed it to the stress of Eleanor's failing health. She hadn't been as attentive to her friend as she should have been.

That old familiar feeling of guilt ripped through her for being so selfishly lost in her feelings.

"It's been a rough few weeks, Selene. We're long overdue for a girl's night out," Aurelia suggested compassionately.

Selene smiled brightly and agreed. "I don't remember the last time we had one of those. Text me later, and we can figure out the details." They both glanced over and saw that Charles was heading toward them, manila folder in hand.

A small, satisfied smile crept onto Selene's face, her hands smoothing out imaginary wrinkles in her blazer as she whispered, "I bet Charles wants to meet with me after hearing what Eleanor said in her video," her eyes tracking his every move as he approached.

Aurelia didn't have time to respond before Charles reached them. "That was quite a bit for the staff to process. How are you two doing?"

Despite his role as Eleanor's attorney, she always liked him. Charles gave off the same warm and comforting vibe that Eleanor did—what she imagined having a grandfather would be like. She managed to give a small smile. "Thanks, we—"

"I am humbled by Eleanor's generosity," Selene interrupted. "Of course, my focus is still on upholding my duties as Chief of Staff. I must remain steadfast to keep a strong level of continuity with our employees during this transition."

Face impassive, he carefully assessed Selene, and Charles slowly nodded. "Good...I'm glad to hear that. I'd like to begin scheduling employment agreement meetings today. Selene, if I give you a list of names, can you share the work schedules with Aurelia?"

"Absolutely! I can start on that now if you have it," she enthusiastically replied.

"Excellent," Charles said as he pulled a sheet of paper from his manila folder and handed it to Selene. Then he turned to face Aurelia. "If now's a good time, I'd like to discuss a few things with you in Eleanor's study."

Aurelia could have sworn Selene's smile faltered briefly before quickly regaining composure. She shrugged it off and said, "I'll catch up with you later, I promise."

Selene simply nodded, arms crossed, as Aurelia followed Charles out.

Charles led Aurelia into Eleanor's private study. He was dressed down in jeans and a lightweight button-down shirt, a stark contrast to the suits he normally wore. After closing the doors for privacy, he gestured for her to sit.

As Charles organized his papers, Aurelia silently took in the ivory room she used to love. It felt dimmer without Eleanor in it.

It was a majestic, sun-drenched room with walls adorned with highly collectible artwork. A large floor-to-ceiling window with a glass door framed the background of the stately hardwood desk. Charles sat in the plush, caramel leather executive chair behind the desk, while Aurelia chose one of the two cream-colored armchairs opposite the desk.

The complimentary towering shelves were filled with both antique leather-bound tomes and more contemporary literature, with a few carefully placed but no less exquisite vases and accessories interspersed amongst them. The gilded moldings framed the textured ivory brocade wallpaper, allowing it to absorb and reflect the natural light across the space.

"How have you *really* been doing these past few days? Especially since the farewell party turned out to be a bigger event than we all predicted." His somber eyes searched her face.

Aurelia snorted. "Understatement of the year," she said. "I now know way more about Bertrand's kinks than anyone should. I can't unhear what was said."

Relieved, Charles shared in her amusement. The corners of his eyes crinkled as he sat back in the chair and laughed. Then he instantly sobered and said, "Well, it's about to get more interesting...for you at least. Hopefully, the good kind."

"I'm so nervous right now, there's a *very* good chance I'll throw up everywhere...you've always been so great to me, so I'm just letting you know so you can get out of the way."

With a small smile, he turned his laptop screen toward her. "Let's see how you feel after you watch this message that Eleanor recorded for your eyes only."

That got Aurelia's attention. She straightened. "She left me a personalized message? Why didn't you lead with that?"

Charles chuckled and pressed play. For the third time in less than twenty-four hours, Eleanor was sitting on that chaise. She couldn't help but feel haunted by a ghost, a notion that would have delighted Eleanor.

This version of her was relaxed and far less cantankerous, which helped calm some of Aurelia's nerves.

That relief was short-lived, however, as she took in the impish glint in Eleanor's eyes and her wide grin. As much as she loved Eleanor, the woman was also as predictable as a squirrel after an espresso—erratic, unexpected, and very likely to cause a major traffic accident.

"Well, my darling Aurelia, if you're watching this, then let's pray I'm in heaven...but who knows with some of the crap I've pulled. I hope you've spent the last few days woefully crying over me—enough to be flattering—but not too much. Wallowing isn't a good look on your beautiful face." Aurelia let out an exasperated sigh.

"I'm finally free of my cancer, the constant pain I felt throughout my body, that dirty slug Bertrand and old hag Gladys, and those dreadful kale smoothies you insisted were 'good for me.' So, dry your tears and crack a smile. I'm, finally, utterly pain-free, and frankly, still looking fabulous in the afterlife."

She paused, her expression softening and growing more subdued. Aurelia's instincts were on high alert now, only having seen this version of Eleanor only a handful of times.

"You know, my dear, I've had an exceptionally long life...long enough to know what I'm doing *most* of the time, and yet—somehow, I went through more personal assistants than I did IRS audits. And let me tell you, that's saying something. But the truth is, I never really needed a personal assistant."

Aurelia's breath caught.

"I wasn't looking for someone to file my papers or fluff my pillows—I had plenty of people already working for me that could have done that. Hell, *Selene* could have done that...what I was looking for was *you*."

Knowing how Aurelia would react, Eleanor reaffirmed her statement. "Yes, *you*. Out of all the people I could have picked, *you* are the one I wish to carry my legacy forward. And if you're wondering why, well...it's simple. You're family. Not by blood, but you've been the daughter I never had, the light in my otherwise delightfully chaotic life...and you're so much stronger than you give yourself credit for."

Her tone turned serious, her gaze piercing through the screen as she sat forward, leaning closer to the camera, her irises now a moving entity unto themselves, swirling as if another world existed in their depths—a storm raging within them.

Aurelia's eyes shot to Charles, the silent question churning in her mind and written on her face: *I'm her heir?*

When he slowly and hesitantly nodded, she almost fell out of her chair in disbelief. Aurelia's heart was pounding so hard against her chest that it risked bursting through it.

"...I know about Kyle, that sorry excuse for a man you dated."

That name made Aurelia freeze.

"No, it's the one thing you never told me—you never needed to. But those bruises on your face that you tried to mask with artfully applied cosmetics, or the scratches on your arms you tried to cover up with long sleeves during unseasonably warm weather, told me more than enough."

Aurelia unconsciously rubbed her arms as an uncontrollable shiver wracked her body.

"You've been walking around a shell of yourself ever since. It reminded me of when you were living in your car when we first met, and frankly, I do *not* approve. That man is gone from your life. You're not just a survivor; you're a *warrior* capable of forging her destiny and more...and you have far too much life ahead of you to let anyone dim your sparkle."

Eleanor tilted her head, her tone conspiratorial. "Now, let me give you one last piece of advice from an old woman who has seen it all: people aren't always what they seem. Some friends will prove to be foes, while others, who may be prickly at first, are the ones who will stand by you through thick and thin. Keep your eyes open, your ears sharp, and always trust that sixth sense. It's rarely wrong."

Sitting back with a proud smile, Eleanor sipped some tea. Aurelia frowned at the cryptic message. *What did she mean by that?*

"This inheritance isn't simply money, my darling. It's a gift and a foundation to help you become the fierce, unstoppable woman I always knew you were meant to be. Everything you've endured, every hardship, is a thread in the tapestry of who you are today. Embrace it. Own it. And don't just live—*thrive*."

More memories, some darker than others, slipped into her mind unbidden as she stayed rooted to her chair.

"Oh, and by the way..." Eleanor said casually—*too casually*—as she picked at her fingernails, "...you no longer owe me a penny for that condemned shack that you transformed into such a lovely home on the lagoon. It's yours, free and clear. Title, debts, everything—all taken care of. You're starting with a clean slate."

Aurelia's jaw dropped.

"Now, before you get too excited, there *are* stipulations. First, you'll need to take over Starhaven Manor and at least continue holding the annual events my family has hosted for decades. Don't roll your eyes! They aren't traditions; *they are legacies.* The property and the money are yours. Spend it however you want. Promise me you'll do something good with it—something that would make *yourself* proud."

Aurelia didn't know how to handle all this information.

"Oh, speaking of Charles, he should've told everyone about their staff bonuses by now. Lovely man, isn't he? But for you, my dear, there's an extra surprise: two million dollars upfront. Right now. However, the rest of your inheritance is in a trust with one final teensy condition to access it."

Well, that doesn't sound too bad, Aurelia thought to herself.

"You can't disclose to anyone that you're my heir until after you've been married for a little while, unless legally required, and only with the approval of Charles, *our* trusted attorney. You'll have a challenging time telling who your real friends are when all the leeches come out of the woodwork, so it's best to keep it quiet."

Married? Aurelia thought to herself, confused by Eleanor's words. *I'm not even close to being married.*

Eleanor's eyes twinkled with amusement as she paused dramatically. This was it; this was the moment that would explain why Aurelia had been nervous all day. She was undeniably confident about it.

"You need to get married. Yes, you heard me. *Married.* But don't worry, I've already arranged everything. I've hired the most sought-after matchmaker in the world, who happens to be right here in Joia City—one hundred percent success rate, no less. She'll find you someone wonderful to help shoulder life's burdens. Now, there's no requirement to stay married forever—this isn't a fairy tale—but you *do* need to put in an honest effort. Charles will be the judge of that. Oh, don't even think about trying to outsmart him—he's tougher than I ever was."

There it was—the panic-inducing moment she had been anxiously waiting for.

A matchmaker?!

Eleanor chuckled softly, leaning back with a satisfied smile.

"My darling, this isn't merely about finding someone to love; it's about opening yourself up to the possibilities of life again. You've been through so much, but there is joy ahead—*real* joy. Your husband, god bless his soul, is going to have a heart attack when he finds out what a knockout you are and smart to boot."

Aurelia couldn't breathe or stave off the waterfall of tears threatening to be unleashed.

Eleanor ended with a heartfelt goodbye. "I love you. I trust you. I believe in you. Now go flaunt your assets. I'll be watching...and judging. Always judging."

The screen went dark.

Aurelia sat frozen as she tried to process everything that was just thrown at her, the weight of it all crushing her.

Then, overwhelmed, she bolted for the door...only to crash straight into Selene.

CHAPTER 3

Levi

There was yet another Neuronix, Inc. Board of Directors meeting scheduled for today, and Levi Lockwood was trying to find a way out of it. As the CEO, he knew nothing short of being in the hospital could get him out of it—and even that was a strong maybe.

Though faking a coma did cross his mind.

He sighed heavily, resisting the urge to run his hands through his wavy dark chocolate hair, as he sat behind his hunter green executive desk. He had been going over his notes in preparation for this meeting for the past few hours.

Levi had been up before sunrise despite going to bed late last night, trying to absorb everything. It was extremely important to be ready for any questions that came up.

It took him longer than the average person to go through documents like this, often requiring him to be up exceedingly early after a late night. The document text was blurring more than usual, his dyslexia amplified by his exhaustion.

The lack of sleep, among other things, was starting to catch up with him. The dark circles under his green eyes were extremely noticeable, despite his bronzed skin. There was no time for a full shave this morning either, so that didn't help.

Attention buried in the financial report on his laptop, he was interrupted when one of his best friends, co-founder of the company, and Chief Technology Officer, Isaac Nolan, walked into his office, carrying a drink tray with two tall steaming coffees on it in one hand, and his tablet in the other.

Levi perked up and looked longingly at the coffees. "Please tell me at least *one* of those is for me," he pleaded.

Isaac set them down on the desk and cast his deep blue eyes at his watch, frowning. "What time did you get here? The workday has barely begun, and you're already whining for more coffee."

"Too early," Levi grumbled as he reached for his coffee. "Every time Tyler calls for one of these useless Board meetings, I end up having to prepare more just to make it through them. Is it me, or have they become unbearable?"

Isaac sat in a chair across from his desk and took a sip from his coffee before replying. "He's an ass, so no, it's not only you." His expression darkened. "Speaking of Tyler, yesterday, I found out that the development team was working on changes to Project DL that weren't authorized by me or any of my direct reports."

Levi furrowed his brow, "What do you mean by 'changes'?"

"Oh, you know...just the Chairman of the Board somehow convincing one of my employees to make changes to the underlying code without approval from *literally* anyone," Isaac casually said with an edge to his voice.

Levi completely stilled as the severity of Isaac's message settled over him.

Neuronix was born when he was still a computer science major in college, sharing a dorm room with Isaac and his Chief Security Officer and childhood friend, Owen Voss. It was there that Isaac met the love of his life, and now wife Grace, who had been studying marketing and communications. She dragged her best friend, Ivy Blake, into their group. Ivy served as both Levi's Executive Assistant and Chief Operations Officer, and together they founded and built the company from the ground up.

Levi was no stranger to struggle and how cruel people could be to those they didn't understand. This small group of friends witnessed many of those situations firsthand. They channeled their anger by pooling their talents to not only build a successful company, but one that created technology to help others like Levi.

Since then, Neuronix has been at the forefront of developing state-of-the-art assistive technologies that provide life-changing support for individuals with disabilities, especially those with dyslexia. Many of their applications and software aim to make reading, writing, and learning more accessible and efficient.

The company grew exponentially, finally satisfying a desperate need in the disability services market. This growth took them from being a small private company run out of someone's dorm room to a large publicly traded global company. Answering to a Board of Directors took some getting used to, but after a time, it became second nature.

At least until Tyler Faulkner joined the Board a little less than a year ago.

After Tyler somehow managed to earn enough votes to become the Chair of the Board, the other members forgot they were allowed to have opinions and a voice...or that they had equal decision-making power as Tyler.

Tyler had become more emboldened since amassing thousands of company shares during the last couple of months. The added increase to the stake he previously owned positioned him as one of the majority shareholders in the company. Then he gradually began inserting himself where he shouldn't, single-handedly trying to run the company.

Yet the rest of the members had remained silent, turning a blind eye as they allowed it to happen instead of intervening.

Just the thought of Tyler having this much individual control over the company Levi co-founded grated on his nerves.

Levi had always been a hands-on CEO. When time allowed, he often took part in the development and quality assurance processes of any of their software products before launch. Being in the trenches with the developers helped him stay grounded and connected to the team. Interacting with the team made Levi happy, particularly because the majority were exactly like him.

Neuronix was dedicated to hiring the best talent, with a focus on creating employment opportunities for individuals of all abilities. He believed it to be a key differentiator that set the company apart from the competition while making it a safe place for people to grow and innovate.

However, he never used his status as CEO to do whatever he wanted and would go through the proper channels with Isaac's approval. While they were all friends, keeping strict professional boundaries was critical to ensure smooth company operations.

As CTO, this was technically Isaac's domain, and Levi felt it was important that everyone—including himself—respected and enforced this. *Especially* in front of Isaac's team. Otherwise, it undermined Isaac's authority as a leader. He was too important to Levi as a friend and as the CTO of Neuronix to disrespect him or any of his other friends like that.

So, to learn that the Chair of the Board himself was acting outside the scope of his authority like this made Levi's blood boil.

It was probably because Tyler seemed to have an opinion about *everything*...and had made it clear that he could do a better job of running the company than Levi.

"I'll address this during today's Board meeting. You know he's going to bring Project DL up again, right?" Levi asked. A headache was taking shape behind his eyes.

It's way too early for this shit.

Isaac nodded his head slowly, his jaw clenched beneath the thin beard coating his ebony chin. "I've already reprimanded Harris Wilkerson, the director who took instructions from Tyler, and made it clear that unless there is a communication specifically from me, they are *not* to deviate from the project plan. I put him on a leave of absence while we conduct an internal investigation. Based on the seriousness of the findings, it'll be grounds for immediate termination...I'm sure you can imagine how well he took that news."

Levi angrily shook his head and gripped the armrest of his chair. "If you haven't already, schedule a mandatory meeting with your entire team this afternoon about it. I can attend to reiterate the message if you need me."

"Consider it done," Isaac said. He whipped out his phone and sent a message to his administrative assistant asking him to prioritize scheduling the meeting.

"We need to tighten security here. Board members shouldn't have access to freely roam the building, especially in any area where proprietary code is openly worked on. Please work with Owen on that," Levi added.

"Already on it. I dragged him into my office yesterday right after I tore Harris a new one," Isaac said, taking another casual sip of his coffee. Of all his friends, Isaac was the most logical and put together...and also why Owen often called him a robot. In times like these, Levi sometimes envied his ability to be so levelheaded.

Levi sat back in his chair. "What's the project status now? Hopefully, we caught Harris's interference before they implemented anything."

Isaac visibly tensed, "The project itself is on track, but the problem is we don't know the full extent of what changes Harris made. I've removed his access to everything so he can't do it again, but this is also why I haven't terminated him yet. We're actively investigating exactly what happened."

Levi raised both eyebrows.

"My understanding so far is that Tyler somehow followed Harris down to that area after the meeting last month. According to other team members, Tyler was asking questions about the progress and certain confidential solution attributes...but the part that caught my attention, and *really* concerns me, is how focused he was on the type of data it would capture from the user."

Levi narrowed his eyes and tilted his head as he thought through the potential implications of this.

"On top of that, the team is reporting various issues in the code that continue to pop up," Isaac continued with a frown. "My gut is telling me that he's been modifying it for a while, and there's a lot buried within layers and layers that we need to uncover."

"*Shit*," Levi whispered, leaning against the back of his chair and pinching the bridge of his nose. *This is really bad.*

Project DL was focused on deep learning for text prediction to integrate artificial intelligence into their existing text solutions. This would revolutionize their product offering because it learns how dyslexia uniquely affects each user based on the type of mistakes they make, allowing them to more accurately predict the text they are trying to type with fewer mistakes.

Neuronix was also conducting ongoing research in brain-computer interface (BCI) technologies, which would enable dyslexic individuals to interact with computers using thought patterns, bypassing reading and writing challenges altogether. There was still so much work to be done in this space, but they were leading the charge.

The biggest issue with Harris and Tyler's interference with the project was the impact on the user's personally identifiable information, or PII.

This type of highly customized technology creates a need for a lot of PII, and not only to differentiate between each user, but because it's directly tied to their medical history. With identity theft and data breaches increasing, Levi couldn't help but wonder why Tyler was so interested to learn what PII would be collected with this new solution.

Levi looked at his watch and grimaced. "Well, unfortunately, it's time for the meeting. Let's see what Tyler has to say about it." Isaac schooled his features back into that impenetrable wall he was skilled at building.

Together they stood, collected their things, and left for the Board meeting.

CHAPTER 4

Aurelia

Selene picked herself up off the floor and made quick work of straightening out her pantsuit and her hair, her features still twisted in confusion. Aurelia was a little slower to rise but managed to get to her feet and right herself. There was a good chance she would develop a bump on the crown of her head based on the radiating pain.

She glanced at Selene apologetically and said, "I'm so sorry, I didn't see you there! Only I would manage to pick the exact moment you were about to knock on the door," she rambled. "Are you okay?"

"Yes, I'm fine. These things always seem to happen to you," Selene said with a half-smile.

Charles loudly cleared his throat. Having completely forgotten why she had been in such a rush out the door, it came flooding back into Aurelia's mind with a vengeance. Her newly acquired headache wasn't helping the situation.

"I apologize for the interruption, Mr. Pierce. I didn't realize you were still meeting with each other," Selene stated, first looking at Aurelia, then Charles. "Staff members are asking if they will be getting paid this payroll cycle as usual or if there will be any delays because of the changeover in the estate. I said I'd ask quickly since we get paid at the end of the week."

Charles observed her for an extra breath before confirming a normal pay cycle. "Could you have refreshments and whatever is on the menu for lunch today sent over for me and Aurelia? She was about to take a quick break from our meeting to request it when she opened the door."

Aurelia tried not to look surprised. She was about to do no such thing when she opened that door, and Charles knew it. Instead, she kept her mouth shut and nodded mutely in agreement, wincing as the movement made her head throb even more. "Please include a few tablets of ibuprofen with it, too."

"Of course! And thank you for the clarification, it will ease the minds of our staff, me included."

Selene turned to walk away, but stopped dead in her tracks when Charles added, "Please have it left outside of the sitting room entrance on a cart. Have whoever delivers it call the study's extension to let us know it's there. Our meeting is not yet over, and we have additional privileged items to discuss. Going forward, I'd like to follow the same protocol for all meetings with the staff due to the nature of these conversations. Ensuring that we have a secure place to have confidential discussions is critical."

Selene dipped her head in acknowledgement before leaving. Charles stood directly outside the study doorway, watching contemplatively as Selene shut the sitting room doors behind her. Aurelia debated whether she should reattempt her escape or get to the bottom of the strange exchange she witnessed.

Being ever curious, she chose the latter and interrupted Charles's thoughts as she made her way back into the study, resigned to continuing their discussion. "I assume your lunch request was your way of telling me that escaping this conversation is impossible."

Charles snapped to attention and followed her in, a crease in his brow as he sat back down.

Before Aurelia could speak, Charles turned those wise brown eyes on her and asked, "How long have you and Selene known each other? If memory serves me correctly, I recall Eleanor mentioning it was she who had first recommended you for the personal assistant position."

"Quite a long time, actually," she scrunched her nose as she sorted through her memories. "I first went into foster care when I was eight years old, but I didn't meet her until I was twelve, after being moved into the same home that she was in. We started as enemies...being the same age and having to fight for the same limited resources kind of enables that sort of competition. Eventually, we became friends and have been ever since."

She peered at him quizzically. "Why do you ask?"

Charles paused briefly. "My perceptions are immaterial. As your new personal attorney that you inherited with the estate," he smiled and winked at her when she rolled her eyes, "I would strongly advise that you do not divulge any portion of our conversation today with anyone, including your closest friends."

That sucks...but makes sense, Aurelia reluctantly thought to herself.

But then he added, "Specifically not with Selene per Eleanor's final request." Aurelia's eyebrows shot up hearing that.

"Why would she say that?" As eccentric as Eleanor was, she was highly intelligent and an excellent judge of character. Aurelia didn't know what to make of it.

"She understood how close you both are, yet stressed that no one, not even Selene, knows about the inheritance or its stipulations. Money changes people, for better or for worse, even those closest to us." Charles patiently waited for Aurelia to internalize the information and acknowledge her understanding before moving on to the next topic.

With a furrowed brow, Aurelia nodded and waved her hand to continue. He pulled out a *very* large stack of files and piled them on the desk.

"These documents contain everything you need to know regarding your employment, bonuses, upfront inheritance payment, final will, financial documents, clear deed and title to your home, and most importantly, your conditions of marriage," he said matter-of-factly.

The sheer volume of information packed within those pages made her head spin. Yet her mind zeroed in on the most terrifying file of them all.

"Ah, yes," she squeaked, "the marriage conditions. You know what? I'm absolutely *famished*. Let me check to see if lunch has been delivered yet. Just a quick, not suspicious, walk through those doors to look." She began to stand up as the very urgent need to escape the room reared its ugly head again.

"Aurelia," Charles warned, "take a deep breath."

She plopped back down in her seat and took five of them...and certainly didn't feel any better.

"I don't know much about your past," he said gently, "but I do know Eleanor loved you as her own daughter. She shared little tidbits about your prior romantic partners with me, as well as her reasoning for marriage."

That did *nothing* to make Aurelia feel better.

"The purpose is to open up and rediscover yourself. You will never be in a successful relationship if you don't understand and take care of yourself first. The matchmaker's profiling and compatibility process will help you figure it out."

She couldn't argue with that logic...and she hated it.

"You always have a choice, Aurelia, remember that. You can choose not to do this right now and put it off until you are ready, or you can choose not to do it at all and forfeit the entire fortune. But the point," Charles emphasized, "is to step out of your comfort zone, learn who you are and what you want, and hopefully find your other half in the process."

Aurelia stilled, weighing her options.

"What do you have to lose, Aurelia?" Charles asked softly.

Aurelia silently averted her attention from Charles to the small glass door built into the window, allowing the study to open up to a private terrace overlooking the manor's lush gardens.

Though in its place, all Aurelia saw was a wide chasm of uncertainty—one she would have to leap across without knowing what waited on the other side. Charles's question reverberated in the silence of her mind.

What do I have to lose?

She could lose her freedom...by marrying someone as awful as the last person she was with. The possibility alone made her shiver with discomfort.

What do I have to lose?

She could lose whatever sense of self she managed to build up over the last year.

What do I have to lose? She asked herself again, her blank stare still focused on the windows.

The answer hit her like a freight train—fast, unexpected, and utterly crushing—because the answer was *nothing*.

She couldn't even tell Selene—not legally anyway—so what was there to stop her from jumping in headfirst and seeing this matchmaker?

Aurelia squared her shoulders, sat up in her chair, and seriously considered Charles's question. With unwavering confidence, she stated, "Nothing. So, which one of these outrageously thick file folders holds the key to my future betrothal?"

CHAPTER 5

Levi

The walk towards the executive conference room felt like a death march.

Coming into work used to be exciting; something he was passionate about. Now it weighed him down, having turned into a chore and a burden...and Levi was about to face one of the key reasons for it head-on. He and Isaac stepped through the door to the conference room, bracing themselves for a battle they knew was looming on the horizon.

Located in a secluded corner on the same level as his office, the room was large and spacious. It was full of contradictions, managing to feel both vast and intimate all at once. Two walls were encased in sleek glass panels that gave a beautiful, picturesque view of Joia City.

The skyline shimmered under the morning sky, a breathtaking contrast to the gravity of the discussions that would be taking place shortly within this room. The beauty beyond the windows was ignored by most of the occupants as they entered, an unspoken heaviness settling over the space.

Levi strode over to his seat at the head of the long, meticulously polished white oak table, positioned near the windows to capitalize on the daylight pouring in. The table itself was a statement—an expanse of wood capable of seating a dozen decision-makers with the possibility to accommodate another ten more if needed.

As he passed, he offered curt nods to members of the Board, his presence commanding silent tribute. Behind him, Isaac followed, seamlessly taking his place to Levi's right, a quiet testament to their alliance.

One of the solid walls was dominated by a state-of-the-art screen panel, its surface already queued with a presentation, waiting for the deliberations to begin. Along the adjacent wall, steaming carafes of coffee and assorted continental breakfast items were carefully arranged on the buffet counter.

Members of the Board were hovering over the selection of buttery croissants, neatly sliced fruit, and delicate pastries before the meeting began.

Levi hadn't yet set his coffee down on the table before a deep rasp sounded behind him.

"How kind of you to finally grace us with your presence, Mr. Lockwood," said Tyler Faulkner, his voice slithering. The way it scraped against Levi's eardrums always left him feeling somewhat violated.

He discreetly clenched his teeth and forced his temper back. He made a show of setting his things down and looking at his watch before slowly spinning around and responding. "It looks like I'm right on time, give or take a couple of minutes," Levi said, smiling broadly.

He stared into Tyler's beady eyes, the color almost as black as the man's soul, and the only noteworthy feature—aside from his bulbous nose—in his otherwise sunken and wrinkled face.

The Chair of the Board was covered in liver spots, rotund, and short enough that Levi could see his reflection peer back at him from the shiny bald cap of skin atop his head. The only hair he managed to retain was gray and hung limply as it snaked around the sides of his skull.

The audacity this man had was larger than he was.

Tyler scowled up at him. "It'd be more professional if you *at least* attempted to show up earlier and engage with the rest of the Board members before the meeting. Or are you too good to entertain the likes of us?" he challenged.

Not missing a beat, Levi retorted, "If you wanted me here earlier, then you should've *at least* scheduled the meeting to start earlier. Or are you too good to follow scheduling etiquette?"

Tyler's face and neck turned a bright shade of red as it filled with rage. He sputtered, "Who do you think you are, you—"

But Levi cut him off, his smile unwavering. "Now, now, Tyler," he crooned, "let's not get ourselves worked up when you're supposed to be calling the meeting to order. While I find this back and forth adorable, it's not very respectful to the rest of the attendees. If you want to hang out with me so badly, all you have to do is ask."

Tyler clamped his slimy mouth shut as pure unadulterated hate emanated from him. Not breaking his stare, Levi smiled wider, knowing it would piss him off even further.

Abruptly turning on his heel, Tyler stalked over to the other end of the conference table. Unceremoniously dropping himself down in the chair, he ignored the looks the other members exchanged.

Levi casually sat down, making himself comfortable as he laid out his paperwork and set his tablet up on the table, ready for the meeting to begin. He noticed the glint of malice in Isaac's eyes as he glared in Tyler's direction.

Once everyone was seated, the designated clerk started the audio recording used in drafting the meeting minutes. Tyler called the meeting to order and went through the standard procedural housekeeping items listed on every agenda: roll call, confirming that there was a quorum, and voting to approve the minutes submitted by the clerk from the last meeting.

The agenda topics were *exactly the same* as the last seven meetings...Levi wanted to claw his eyes out.

Evidently, it was beneath Tyler to bother consulting with Levi on the agenda like he was supposed to; instead, he found out at the same time as every other member—only when notified that a meeting was scheduled. It was another entry on what was becoming an extraordinarily long list of Levi's grievances against him.

After what felt like a lifetime, he stopped droning on about the overall goals for today's discussion (which were no different from the last three meetings) and turned it over to Levi for his CEO and management reports.

This was the moment he had been getting ready for early that morning. The documentation before him held the information needed, but it was for appearances only—Levi memorized it so he could speak with ease.

Preparing for this moment wasn't easy.

It never was.

His morning had started hours before dawn, long before the rest of the city stirred. With his coffee growing cold beside him, Levi sat in his home office surrounded by color-coded notecards, each one breaking down dense financial reports into digestible, visual chunks. Complex figures and jargon became sketches and bullet points, the important metrics highlighted in bold colors to anchor them in his mind.

Memorization wasn't a preference; it was critical to his survival. He couldn't rely on reading smoothly from a report without stumbling over the words, and he refused to give Tyler or anyone else that kind of satisfaction.

Except it was never really such an issue until Tyler joined the Board.

So, like every major presentation before this one, he mapped the numbers to patterns and stories he could recall when standing before the Board. It was grueling, time-consuming work, but it was how he turned a perceived weakness into one of his greatest strengths.

He dove right in with a quick operational update, discussing the performance of all business units while a variety of charts, statistics, and data visualizations were displayed on the large screen before them. Revenue, profitability, and cash flow continue to rise steadily in line with their forecasted projections for the quarter.

There was virtually no change in this information from the last time he presented it a month ago. The only thing the Board members cared about was sustaining market share and seeing the value of their stock and bank accounts trending upwards.

Finally, Levi had one topic left to cover—the one he and Isaac had been stewing over in his office.

"Regarding strategic initiatives," Levi said, drumming his fingers on the table, "there isn't anything new to report in terms of ongoing projects and research since our last meeting. We continue to make headway on the BCI front with our initial research, and exploratory data analysis has yielded preliminary but promising results."

Levi paused briefly, gauging the mood of the room. "Regarding Project DL, however, I do have a new development since we last met."

The Board members perked up and shared shrewd glances, eager to hear more about this game-changing initiative. Even Tyler seemed momentarily surprised, leaning forward in his chair somewhat, before quickly slipping on a stony mask of indifference.

Having their undivided attention, Levi continued. "It was brought to my attention that we had a security breach. It involved an unauthorized party gaining access to the software development and research department in the building."

Gasps and murmurs erupted as Levi shifted directly to Tyler and said, "Chairman Faulkner, I'll defer to you to explain to me and the members of the Board how you violated physical security protocol by following an employee off the elevator to access that department right after our last meeting."

Tyler's eyes grew wide, his mouth working like a fish out of water as every head in the room snapped in his direction. A predatory smile worked its way onto Levi's face as he motioned to Isaac and added, "While our internal investigation isn't yet concluded, my understanding is that you used that opportunity to *once again* insert yourself directly into day-to-day operations and influenced that same employee into making significant changes to the software code. I'm *very* curious to hear your explanation."

Before Tyler could reply, Isaac added icily, "As CTO, I'm even more curious to know what project changes were pushed forward without my knowledge or consent, given how horrifically it failed in quality assurance. This little stunt of yours resulted in an employee receiving disciplinary action, jeopardizing their employment here."

Levi raised both arms toward the rest of the room as he said, "So please, regale us with the details of this wildly rebellious situation that you have created for yourself."

He knew it was a dick move, but watching the look of absolute panic on Tyler's face made it worth it.

Sitting back in his chair, hands folded across his stomach, he patiently waited for Tyler to respond.

CHAPTER 6

Aurelia

After meeting with Charles about the inheritance and its possibilities, a tired but more carefree version of Aurelia emerged. The fear remained, but realizing she had nothing left to lose, not even her sanity, made it less overwhelming.

After Selene left, lunch was delivered, and Aurelia and Charles spent hours reviewing documents. Even with her love of reading, the fine print escalated her headache into a migraine that only a nap could cure.

Selene had also sent over the staff schedules, allowing her to shift her attention to coordinating meetings for a little while. It was a much-needed respite that brought a sense of normalcy. Then Charles dropped another bomb, shattering that illusion.

"Eleanor paid for the full-service fee in advance and shared her perspective on your personality with the matchmaker. Her name is Estrella Vale, and she is eager to meet you whenever you are ready."

Shoulders slumping, Aurelia internally groaned.

"She's also aware of Eleanor's confidentiality requirements," Charles added. "If you have a match that leads to marriage, I've drafted an ironclad prenuptial agreement to protect you. It'll be at your discretion down the line when to tell your spouse about everything."

Spouse. She bit the inside of her cheek, the word foreign on her tongue.

She wasn't thrilled to learn that Charles had been working with the matchmaking service for the last couple of months. He insisted on calling them together to discuss next steps because he felt she was a "flight risk." She was outraged at how accurate his assessment was.

Once her appointment was booked, he handed her a beautifully wrapped box. Inside was a turquoise designer tote—Eleanor's final secret gift, meant to help Aurelia carry these documents discreetly and in style.

As she walked to her car, the envious glances the bag received had her grinning from ear to ear. While starting her car, she burst into a brief fit of laughter over everything that happened in her meeting.

Charles's reference to her *future spouse*, someone she hadn't even met yet, was absurd, but the thick folder of "homework" in her new bag wasn't funny at all. Her first appointment with *Perfectly Paired Matchmaking* was officially scheduled for Thursday.

Thankfully, she still had her self-defense class that night. After her situation with Kyle, she joined almost a year ago. It was a lifeline, something to take back control, to release the fear that still clung to her. It also brought her one step closer to regaining her sense of self.

Will I ever stop looking over my shoulder?

Maybe not. But she could stop giving him space in her mind. Keeping busy helped. After Eleanor's diagnosis, she had stepped back from most activities, except this one.

Until recently, she had been volunteering with the Joia City School District, helping foster kids improve academically. Though not a court advocate, she mentored at-risk teens weekly.

As she merged onto the main road, Aurelia made a mental note to reconnect with them before the fall. She had never forgotten what it was like moving from home to home without help. Reading became her escape, her way of learning beyond the classroom.

When graduation came, she, like many foster youths, had no money for college. So, she lived in her car and worked every job she could: overnight caregiving, temporary jobs, waitressing...all while saving for a home of her own.

She did that for nearly a decade.

Then Eleanor hired her as a personal assistant and changed everything. Aurelia wished more kids could be given the same chance.

That was when the idea hit her: *I'll use the inheritance to create a program for kids aging out of foster care for shelter, support, and other opportunities.*

Suddenly, marrying a stranger didn't feel so terrible. It wasn't solely for her benefit; it could be the foundation for something bigger.

Her mood shifted into something bright and breezy. She turned up the radio and sang loudly and terribly along with the dance music, her hands tapping to the beat against her steering wheel.

When was the last time she truly let go?

Aurelia couldn't remember when she last allowed herself the freedom to do so. Perhaps it was time to start prioritizing herself more often.

Once class was over, she had to review the paperwork. And tomorrow? A salon trip. Maybe some shopping.

After all, she had a husband to impress.

CLASS CANCELLED – FAMILY EMERGENCY – SORRY FOR THE INCONVENIENCE!

Aurelia joined the crowd of classmates that gathered outside of *Francisco's Martial Arts* and read the sign on the door. She had been looking forward to her class tonight, but it must have been a serious emergency for the instructor to cancel class on such short notice. Normally, they would get an email and text message letting them know the class was cancelled.

Now she found herself in the heart of the bustling city, dressed for a workout in plain black athletic leggings and a sports bra with a hot pink long tank layered over it, and with no plans for the evening.

The thought of going home so early wasn't as appealing as it should've been. Kyle had never liked it when she became too friendly with others. Lord, she was tired of thinking about him and being alone.

She could be bold and muster up the courage to ask one of them to go grab dinner or do something else...to put herself out there and try to make a friend. Dig deep to find that fierce woman inside her that Eleanor claimed existed, and take a step towards rediscovering herself.

She gazed across the street at the park where young children ran around playing tag, their parents huddled on park benches chatting as they oversaw them. Further away, a group of guys were tossing a football back and forth. Aurelia scrunched her nose in concentration and pushed an errant lock of hair out of her eyes.

We're already here anyway....

Taking a deep breath, Aurelia turned around and faced the group of classmates, and with the most confident tone she could rally, she asked, "Does anyone want to do our class in the park?"

An hour later, a very sweaty but content Aurelia plopped herself down on the grass next to her classmate, Adelen Mazao, as she gulped down half of her water bottle. She tried to smooth down the wayward strands as she fastened her damp hair into a semblance of a bun atop her head.

When she asked her classmates about holding their own practice session in the park, she expected them to decline. Instead, they got excited and followed her across the street to the park to train together. Under a shady spot of trees, they paired up, reviewing the different maneuvers they had learned so far.

Aurelia partnered up with Adelen, who joined the class five weeks ago. She felt strangely comfortable around her, like they were kindred spirits. Selene always had the gift of easily making friends growing up, while Aurelia mainly kept to herself and the safety of her books.

It was a lonely way to live.

It was also why she was determined to change that, one small step at a time.

"I'm so glad everyone came to the park tonight. I really needed this." Aurelia glanced at Adelen, sitting next to her on the grass.

Adelen's legs were stretched out before her as she leaned back on her palms. She wore a similar black athletic outfit to Aurelia's, with a black tank top over it. Looking roughly the same age, her midnight hair was pulled back in a French braid, showing off her wide, expressive steel-colored eyes, fair skin, and cochlear implants. Her multiple ear piercings glittered in the sunlight.

She was gorgeous in a mysterious and dangerous sort of way.

And could probably kick Aurelia's ass if she wanted to. She almost laughed aloud, thinking about it.

"Do you want to go grab something to eat?" Aurelia blurted.

Well, that was unplanned.

She wanted to crawl under a rock and hide from her awkwardness. Feeling her cheeks warm from embarrassment, she thanked god for her post-workout flushed skin that masked it.

Adelen fiddled with the end of her braid, quietly contemplating her question for a moment before she said, "Yeah, why not? There's a burger place around the corner with amazing milkshakes."

"God, I could kill for a good milkshake right now," Aurelia groaned. She took a moment to enjoy the wave of relief that rocketed through her when Adelen agreed to go out.

Adelen snickered as they both stood and grabbed their water bottles. Aurelia's steps and soul were lighter as they walked to the diner.

As they approached the restaurant, Aurelia noticed Adelen's steps slow right before reaching the corner. Her head turned slightly, sharp eyes scanning the street and nearby doorways with a level of precision that made Aurelia pause. Adelen's shoulders tensed for the briefest moment before she took a slow, controlled breath and forced them down again. The movement was subtle and practiced...too practiced.

Aurelia was quite familiar with that routine herself, considering she had lived it for months after escaping Kyle. It left her always on edge, always checking exits, and running through worst-case scenarios. Hypervigilance became second nature when a person spent too much time waiting for the next blow to fall.

"You okay?" Aurelia asked gently, careful not to startle her.

Adelen's mouth twitched into a humorless half-smile, the kind that didn't quite reach her eyes. "Yeah...old habits," she murmured, her voice cool and even. She adjusted the strap of her bag across her chest like a shield and pushed open the door to the diner. "Come on. That milkshake isn't going to drink itself."

Aurelia let the moment pass, but something inside her stirred. There was more to Adelen than she let on, beneath layers of carefully placed walls and shadows she kept hidden beneath that mysterious exterior. Aurelia realized she wasn't the only one carrying invisible scars, unsure of whether to be comforted or concerned.

Aurelia followed Adelen into the diner; the warmth and chatter inside were a sharp contrast to the tension that clung to them moments ago. Sliding into the booth, Aurelia found herself studying the other woman across from her more closely, noticing her carefully controlled movements and the way she positioned herself with her back to the wall, always keeping the entrance in view.

She recognized that instinctive need to stay alert, to feel in control of her surroundings. It was a familiar kind of armor.

Strangely, Aurelia knew she didn't have to explain herself to this woman to be understood, and maybe Adelen didn't either.

A tentative smile tugged at her lips as she picked up the menu, a quiet sense of belonging settling between them.

One small step, she reminded herself. One small step that perhaps Adelen needed as much as she did.

CHAPTER 7

Levi

Tyler had been terrorizing Levi for months.

Part of it stemmed from his lack of understanding of Neuronix's technology.

The rest was because Tyler was a miserable asshole who believed he knew better than everyone else.

Levi stared across the table, waiting for the beady-eyed miniature demon possessing Tyler's body to speak. Tyler had been pushing for a premature release of Project DL from the beginning, ignoring repeated warnings that it wasn't ready.

The Board knew that Levi had been diagnosed with dyslexia as a child. It was why Neuronix existed: to level the playing field for people like him. And now, someone like Tyler was trying to weaponize that against him.

Levi was simply pissed off.

Pissed off at this disrespectful little troll across from him, who continued to undermine him in the very company he built.

Pissed off by how his struggles were being used against him at the place where his life's work was devoted to creating a space and environment for others to thrive. The one place he was supposed to feel safe.

And he was even more pissed off that no one on the Board had called Tyler out.

Finally, Tyler spoke.

"I've spent *months* offering valuable feedback and suggestions that would elevate the project and take it in a more lucrative direction, only to be ignored, *you prick*! I've asked *multiple* times when it will be ready to be released, and you have yet to dignify me with a response. I will *not* apologize for trying to make Project DL better because you are too pigheaded to listen to me," Tyler said hotly.

And there it was.

Levi stared, unmoved. Tyler believed repeating the same question over and over would wear him down.

He was about to learn how wrong he was.

"Pretty sure my answer is going to be the same as the dozen times you asked in the last two months alone. We are *not* rolling *anything* out when it is still in the early phases of development, especially if it hasn't even been evaluated yet. I don't even understand how you've made it this far in life without grasping this concept. Neuronix is *not* in the business of putting out crappy products when so many individuals rely on them to navigate everyday life. It's been an absolute *waste of my time* to continuously repeat myself, and I have better things to do than take part in your twisted games," Levi retorted.

Tyler leaned in, voice venomous. "Perhaps I'm starting to lose confidence in your ability to lead this company, particularly after the last media scandal we had to deal with. The level of judgment you've exercised in your personal life has been a joke and only shows that security concerns were a problem long before today. You can't even maintain a steady relationship, let alone lead this company."

Levi winced. His last girlfriend had stolen his badge and tried to break into the building. That was a PR nightmare...Owen was still pissed about it.

Before he could stop himself, he fired back, "While my love life is no one's business but my own, my fiancée and I are more than happy with our *private* relationship. But that has nothing to do with the fact that you exploited what we now know is a gaping hole in our security to satisfy some personal agenda of yours."

Isaac reacted visibly, catching the lie.

Tyler didn't miss it either.

A sinister smile spread across his face. "I, for one, look forward to meeting the *secret* woman who has *stolen* your heart. Let us hope this one doesn't try to break into the building like the last one—unless she doesn't exist."

Shit shit shit.

Levi regretted it the second the words left his mouth. He knew Tyler was waiting for a misstep, and Levi had now handed him ammunition.

With forced calm, Levi said, "I'm sorry, but is there a point you're trying to make?"

Pointing a stubby finger at Levi, he spat, "The point is that you aren't capable of exercising good judgment in your personal life, let alone in business."

Levi held his ground. "Yet it's been my ability to lead this company *that I built from scratch*, that's fattened your bank accounts, not my personal life. But no one's complaining about that. You're determined to sit in my seat without the qualifications."

Isaac cut in, irritated. "By all means, if you're so *desperate* to be involved in the development of this solution, then please send your resume to us both, and we'd be more than happy to review your credentials in consideration for a position on our development team."

Tyler smirked and said, "I'd be happy to send you my resume, but..." he paused dramatically to stare directly at Levi as he finished with, "...I wonder if you'd be able to read it efficiently without someone to help you. We all know how difficult it is for you to do something so simple."

Levi froze.

Air caught in his lungs.

The blood in his veins turned to ice.

He blinked slowly, rage building.

Turning to the meeting clerk, he said with measured calm, "I want a verbatim account of Chairman Faulkner's comments about my inability to read without assistance and my response captured in the meeting minutes." Tyler began to protest, but the clerk's glare shut him down.

Facing Tyler, Levi spoke, voice cold and cutting. "You seem to forget what Neuronix stands for—who we serve. Your comment proves how unfit you are to chair this Board. You're a liability and an embarrassment."

Levi shifted his attention to the other Board members. "Let me be clear. If anyone here mocks me or any Neuronix employee for their disability again, you'll be facing a very public discrimination suit. Imagine the headlines: *Board member at company supporting disabled users sued for mocking a disabled employee*."

Levi stood and swiftly gathered his things, then scrutinized everyone in the room. "*Your* silence enabled this monster. You've let his leash go slack, and now he's an uncontrollable menace."

As he angrily strode across the room with Isaac in tow, he continued, "Please consider this my formal notification: badge access for Board members has been restricted. You may now only access this floor's meeting area. Further entry will require an escort."

Stopping at the end of the conference table, Levi locked his eyes on Tyler and added, "I have a company to run. If you have any questions, email them to me and Ivy. You know...in case I need help reading the bullshit you keep spewing."

Without looking back at anyone's reactions, Levi walked out head held high, Isaac hot on his heels.

Levi stalked back to his office, radiating pure ire and still reeling from that debacle. No one had made him feel that inadequate since he was a teenager. To have it happen at Neuronix was enraging.

What Tyler said about his relationships wasn't appropriate...although it wasn't untrue either. The truth was that when he was in a relationship, he became blind to their flaws. He hated being alone and had anticipated being married with a family by now.

Instead, Lana was in jail after her foolish larceny attempt, while he was still very single. He was ashamed to admit he missed the extremely obvious red flags that were there. And that he didn't listen when his closest friends repeatedly told him that she was out of her mind.

Owen had yet to let him forget it.

He stopped mid-stride, realizing how awful his judgment of character had been when it came to his own love life. His spiraling thoughts were cut off as Isaac's massive body plowed into him from behind, sending them tumbling to the ground.

Isaac stood, picked up everything he dropped on the floor, pointed at Levi, and barked, "Your office. *Now*." He spun around and continued marching towards it, not looking back to see if Levi followed. Isaac was as dangerous as a live wire when he was angry.

Levi knew he was in deep shit.

Getting up as quickly as possible, he jogged down the hallway to catch up with Isaac, reaching him as they made it to his executive suite. Isaac greeted Ivy and curtly asked her to join them in Levi's office as he let himself in.

She looked at Levi with two raised and perfectly manicured eyebrows and said, "Well, this ought to be good." Levi rolled his eyes at her as he passed by.

Isaac's back was to him, hands in his pockets, as he stared out the glass panes of the high-rise. One of the biggest benefits of being CEO was having an office with uninterrupted panoramic views of Joia City. This advantage offered a view so breathtaking it seemed otherworldly, a city suspended between land, sea, and sky.

Beyond the windows, the city unfolded like a living mosaic, its rooftops and natural vegetation a dazzling array of colors that shimmered in the sunlight like scattered jewels. The city clung to the cliffs that rose sharply from the turquoise lagoons below, their calm waters cradling reflections of the colorful façades like a painter's palette. Narrow streets wound through the hillside like rivers of volcanic rock cobblestones, flanked by cascading terraces of vivid flowers.

The lagoons came in all shapes and sizes, tucked within the verdant embrace of volcanic craters, and glowed in an impossible array of colors—aquamarine, various shades of emerald, and one so deep a blue it looked as though the ocean itself had pooled within. From above, the mountains rose, cloaked in greenery so vibrant it almost felt unreal.

They both temporarily lost themselves in the view, not noticing when Ivy joined them. She soundlessly snuck up from behind and loudly said, "Which one of you stirred the pot time?"

They jumped, startled out of their thoughts.

Ivy chuckled and walked towards Levi's desk, her long sun-kissed almond hair swishing across her back from the slicked ponytail high on her head.

In her mid-thirties, like Levi and Isaac, she met both in college through Isaac's wife, Grace. She knew them as well as they knew themselves, if not better.

Levi stalked to his desk while Isaac took a seat in one of the cream overstuffed wingback chairs before it. The air was thick with tension and just as stifling.

Ivy gathered her notebook and pen before settling herself down in a round but plush oversized armchair that sat between the executive desk and the white oak conference table. It was a pea green monstrosity with sparkling lemon, orange, and lime slices embroidered into the velvet fabric, so much so that it stood out against the calming neutral tones throughout the rest of the suite.

Levi had begged her to replace it on multiple occasions, even going as far as offering to pay to reupholster it, but Ivy loved it exactly the way it was. She loved how much Levi hated it even more.

Ivy held two positions at Neuronix. She might have been listed on paper as Levi's Executive Assistant, but that title barely scratched the surface. She was his translator, his buffer, his fiercely loyal right hand—and the reason no one outside their inner circle ever questioned how seamlessly he managed the chaos of leading a global tech empire.

She understood exactly how his dyslexia affected his work, and without fanfare, quietly delegated the bulk of his administrative load to two trusted assistants she personally trained and managed. That gave her the space to do what she truly excelled at: running the show.

As Chief Operations Officer, Ivy kept the company humming behind the scenes with the accuracy only someone who knew how to anticipate Levi's every need could pull off. She protected him, not by hiding his struggles, but by building a system around him that let him lead without compromise.

Because of this, allowing such a ridiculous piece of furniture in his office that made her happy was a small sacrifice...one easily covered by a light blanket when she wasn't there.

Levi leaned on his desk with his head in his hands. Isaac sat back in his chair, his words clipped. "Where do we begin? Maybe with how Levi got into a pissing match with Tyler during the Board meeting...or the fact that he suddenly has this mystery *fiancée* that doesn't exist that Tyler's now extremely interested in meeting? You know, the one he rightfully suspects to be *fake*? Which stupid event do you want to address first?"

Ivy gasped in surprise as she snapped her attention to Levi, her bronze eyes shining equally with alarm and amusement.

She dramatically tapped a finger against her caramel-colored cheek and huffed out a mix between a deep breath and a laugh. "I'd *love* to hear about this fiancée and how you met, since all you do is work and work out." Her eyes sparkled with mischief as she added, "I can't wait to meet her. Tell me, how did you know she was *the one*?"

Drawing in a deep breath, Levi looked up at the ceiling in exasperation, his knee nervously bouncing beneath his desk. The five o'clock shadow was more pronounced now than it was this morning, adding to his haggard appearance.

He didn't know where to begin. Taking his silence as a cue, Isaac recounted what happened during the meeting.

Listening to Isaac, Levi's face heated again, the wound still fresh. He sank deeper and deeper into his seat until Isaac finished his story. A few beats of silence passed before Levi spoke. "I haven't felt this small since the last time I spoke to my old man," he said softly.

His relationship with his father growing up, or lack thereof, was a train wreck. Certain scars ran too deep to ever recover from.

This was one of them.

"That's because your father was a piece of shit," Isaac said gently, his voice laced with understanding. "He and Tyler were cut from the same cloth. Tyler did that to purposely get under your skin and, unfortunately, it worked—and now you have a different problem to deal with."

Isaac paused and looked at his friend intently before asking, "What in the world made you say you had a fiancée to begin with? Comments like that never bothered you before, even after the Lana incident."

Levi sat mutely for another minute, trying to find the right words to explain why he blurted that out—he didn't quite understand it himself.

That was a lie. He knew exactly why he said it.

He had no one to go home to at the end of the day. The thought of being alone in his large estate made him dread the drive back. On many nights, he didn't, opting to work late and on occasion sleep in his office overnight.

"You work too much—you've stretched yourself so thin. You need to ask yourself whether any of this is making you happy. Because, as an outsider looking in, I'd say no, and it hasn't for a long time now," Isaac said delicately while giving Levi's appearance a once-over.

Levi opened his mouth to respond when Ivy interrupted, "You need to start putting yourself first and not letting dickheads like Tyler get to you. We know firsthand what a psychopath Lana was and its effect on you."

Isaac hummed in agreement as Levi scowled at the memory.

"You don't laugh or smile as much as you used to, getting you to come out with us and have fun turns into a hostage negotiation, and your moods have become more volatile. You stopped playing baseball after work, your drum set hasn't been touched in over a year, and Owen has been whining about not going to concerts anymore. We've all noticed it, but when we try to bring it up, you brush it off," Ivy solemnly added. "I'm surprised you find time to hit the gym at this point."

Levi sighed. His friends always saw past his defenses even when he wasn't aware he had built them in the first place. It was annoying at times, but he was also grateful to have friends who cared this much.

He couldn't think of what else to say other than, "*We* built this company, and *we* are the heart and soul of it. It wouldn't exist if it weren't for us and Owen—so while I appreciate everything you just said, I need to remind you that we accomplished all that as a team. Thank god Owen isn't here to help bust my balls about it."

"Oh, I already texted him to amp him up to hear this tale later on," Isaac quipped.

Levi groaned and sat back in his chair. Of the entire group, Levi had known Owen the longest—they'd been friends since the fourth grade.

"Perhaps this is a blessing in disguise," Ivy said thoughtfully.

"I'm dying to hear in what possible way you think this ridiculous lie is a positive thing," Levi retorted dejectedly. This was undoubtedly the dumbest thing he had ever done.

The deadly glare she shot him instantly shut him up.

Then Ivy smugly said, "I know exactly where to find your fiancée."

Levi got exactly zero work done the rest of the day after Ivy's horrendous idea.

A goddamn matchmaker.

Her solution was to hire one of the best and most exclusive matchmaking services in the area. To his dismay, Isaac supported the idea. She didn't allow him to protest before running back to her desk to set it up.

Isaac smirked as he walked out of Levi's office, far too amused with the situation. There was no way he could get any work done now that his life had gone to shit in a matter of hours.

The realization that he may be getting married very soon was reason enough to skip out and find a bar to drink the day away.

He wasn't prepared to marry a stranger.

Hell, he wasn't prepared to get married at all.

Levi placed his head in his hands and groaned. He needed to get a hold of himself and his life.

When he thought it couldn't get any worse, Owen barged in. Making himself comfortable in a chair, Owen leaned back and put his feet up on Levi's desk. With a straight face, he asked, "When do I get to meet the future Mrs. Lockwood?"

"Owen, I swear to god I don't have the energy for your bullshit today," Levi growled in frustration.

That spurred Owen on more, his crystal blue eyes ringed with gold and green, crinkling with amusement. "Challenge accepted."

Owen was classically handsome with golden blond hair, tanned skin, and biceps that women regularly drooled over. Underneath that exterior hid a sharp wit and attention to detail...those eyes never missed a thing.

He was also a smart ass who never passed up an opportunity for drama. The twinkle in his eyes and the lopsided grin on his face confirmed that Owen spent all afternoon preparing for this interaction.

"No, no...there has been no challenge issued!"

"Incorrect. So, can I officiate the wedding? I can get a license online today."

"What? No!"

"Can I be the best man?"

"Absolutely not."

"Can I be the flower guy? I would be *amazing* at throwing flowers."

"Please don't do this to me right now; it's been a rough day already."

"If she's hot and has any hot sisters, will you set me up with one of them?"

"Owen, I will throw you down a flight of stairs if you don't stop it."

Owen rolled his eyes. "You couldn't even pick me up, princess. Fine, I'll settle for you naming your first child after me."

"If you have nothing useful to contribute, then please go away," Levi sighed.

"Can I investigate her?"

Levi was about to say no, but caught himself. "If this actually happens, then yes, you can investigate her."

Owen threw his hands in the air and let out a triumphant, "Aw yessssss!"

Levi leaned over his desk, head in his hands again, taking deep breaths. When he looked back up at Owen, all traces of amusement had faded from his face, replaced with contemplative concern.

"Do you want to hear my opinion, or are you committed to playing the part of the rich CEO who got into a dick-measuring contest and is upset about the consequences of the dumb shit he said?" Owen asked seriously.

"Not about my imaginary fiancée," he said defeatedly.

"Believe it or not, I understand that. I've been through enough with you to know that he pushed you to this." Levi looked up at him skeptically. "I also understand how badly you want to settle down." He slumped back into his chair.

"*But*," Owen continued, "I *do* think you need to step back and stop working so much—actually go out and do things and meet people. You've dealt with people like Tyler all your life—you know the second you get sloppy, it'll be used against you."

Levi knew he was right; nonetheless, it was a tough pill to swallow. "I haven't reacted like that in a long time," Levi admitted, "I truly hate that little goblin."

Owen cheekily offered, "If it makes you feel better, I'm confident you could throw *him* down a flight of stairs. But because I'm *such a good friend*, I'd even help you cover it up and make it look like an accident."

That earned a real smile from Levi, but it left as quickly as it appeared. "What do you think about the matchmaker idea? It screams desperate to me."

"You *are* desperate," Owen drawled. "I say do it and have an adventure? It can't possibly be worse than Lana, and if it is, then you have someone else to blame."

"Oh my god, can we *stop* bringing up Lana?" Levi exclaimed.

"Maybe we should go visit her—I bet she's lonely in jail," Owen quipped. Levi leveled a murderous glare at him. "Plus, Ivy sent me the matchmaker's information a couple of hours ago, and I already vetted them. Go get yourself a wife."

Levi threw a stapler at Owen, who had barely enough time to throw himself off the chair and out of the way. He rapidly picked it up and hummed it back at Levi, who caught it with one hand.

Owen stood up, fixing his clothes on the way out as he said, "I also went and applied for my license online, so I'm ready to officiate whenever this poor girl agrees to tie herself to you."

He quickly shut the door to Levi's office, just in time to avoid the stapler that came flying after him again.

CHAPTER 8

Levi

The next morning, Levi found Owen propped up in his bed, fully clothed, watching him sleep. It startled Levi so much that he instinctively yelped. Unknowingly tangled in his blankets, he fell back and off the bed, his pillow falling with him.

Owen howled with laughter. He peered over the edge of the bed where Levi was sprawled on the floor and drawled, "Rise and shine, sugar lips, we're fixin' to git you hitched."

Owen quickly rolled away as the pillow came flying towards his head. Levi untangled himself and managed to stand up.

"Thank the *gods* you're wearing underwear! I don't want to look at Little Levi," Owen chirped.

Levi was seriously contemplating where he could hide Owen's body after he murdered him when he said, "Ivy got blueberry muffins from that bakery you like, plus some other stuff."

Levi perked up a bit. Blueberry muffins were his favorite breakfast food. Owen sauntered towards him and took a strong sniff. Scrunching his nose in mild disgust, he said, "Definitely take a shower before you come down. There's a mustiness to you that could be considered an appetite ruiner. Everyone's already here," before he jogged out of the room and out of harm's way.

Levi sighed and looked at the clock. It was only 5:45 AM, and his blood pressure was already climbing.

This is a foreshadowing of things to come, he thought to himself as he entered the bathroom and started the shower.

After his shower, Levi joined everyone in his kitchen.

Yesterday, Ivy worked her magic and managed to get him a priority appointment with *Perfectly Paired Matchmaking*. He was officially a client. Everyone decided to take a couple of hours off from work this morning to help him rally for the assessments he would have to complete.

Ivy promised she would bring breakfast, and she followed through as promised. Levi's mouth watered as he eyed the massive spread of breakfast foods, juices, and coffee on the large island.

It was an early morning grazing board of breakfast foods; the rainbow-colored assortment stood out against the glittering black quartz countertops. There was nothing Levi loved more than a smorgasbord of food options.

"All this food *almost* makes up for me finding Owen in my bed," Levi said, placing one of the last blueberry muffins on his plate. He was lucky there were any muffins left at all.

Owen grinned at him widely, mouth full of raspberry danish as he leaned against the counter opposite the island, stuffing his face. Isaac was beside him, looking slightly more civilized, using a napkin instead of a plate.

"Having the keys to your house is the biggest perk of being your security guy," he garbled through the food in his mouth. "I'm probably the most attractive person you've woken up next to in months, and for your information, *good sir*, you wouldn't be the first to fall off the bed after waking up to me either."

Isaac gave Owen a long-suffering glance. "I think months is a bit of an exaggeration...and they probably fell off the bed in horror."

Owen gasped in mock outrage at Isaac's rebuttal while Levi scowled and threw a handful of grapes at them both. "I need new friends and new locks." Levi scooped up the remainder of his food before joining the ladies at the table.

The kitchen was the heart of the home and where his friends preferred to gather. His favorite place to lounge was at the large kitchen table within the eat-in breakfast nook, nestled against large windows with the best views of Joia City. He never used the formal dining room.

There was a concerning amount of paperwork spread on the dark wood-stained table. With empty plates set before them, Ivy and Grace—Isaac's wife—were chatting over half-finished coffee. They must've been here longer than he initially thought.

Ivy gave Levi a once-over, carefully examining his face, no doubt assessing the level of exhaustion that still lingered there. "You look a lot less like hell than you did yesterday," she said, eyes sparkling and promising nothing but trouble. "So, eat up, buttercup. You're going to need the energy for this."

Grace rolled her hazel eyes as she laughed, shaking her head at Ivy, her auburn curls bouncing as her shoulders shook.

Her tone took on a more serious note as she asked, "But seriously, Levi, how are you doing with all of this?" She reached over and squeezed Levi's hand in an extra show of support.

"I think I'm doing less okay than I initially thought," Levi said slowly, trying to focus on the warmth of her hand as a distraction. There was a jumble of feelings whirling around like a tornado in his mind, making it tough to pin them down.

He was acutely aware of Owen and Isaac's eyes on his back as they held their breath waiting for his reply. It was uncomfortable, like he was a bug inspected under a microscope. Their gaze prickled at his skin.

"I'm still upset and embarrassed about how I reacted in the Board meeting. I know I shouldn't have let Tyler get to me the way he did." He lowered his gaze and stared into his mug of coffee, as if the wisps of steam held the answers he needed.

"I'm tired," he said hoarsely. A sharp crack of pain settled in his chest. "I'm tired of having to spend so much extra time preparing for meetings just to be on par with everyone else. I'm tired of coming home alone to this uselessly large house that's creepy at night...and I'm simply tired of going through this life alone."

He looked up at both Ivy and Grace, both with eyes as glassy as his probably were. His knuckles were white from how hard he gripped his coffee mug. It was a miracle that the cup had not yet shattered.

"Don't get me wrong, you're the most amazing group of friends that anyone could ever ask for...but it's a different kind of support I'm missing." He looked longingly at Grace and Isaac when he sighed, "I want what you two have."

Taking a shuddering breath, he absently shrugged, peering back into his coffee. It had grown cold, much like the rest of his life, Levi realized.

"After what happened yesterday, it seems more like a sliver of hope that sliced through the fog I didn't realize I was trapped in. I'm actually kind of excited to go to a matchmaker. It's unconventional, but nothing else has worked either."

The silence that followed was thick and full of despair. No one uttered a single word, internalizing what Levi shared.

That is, until Levi heard what sounded like someone trying to conceal a soft sniffle behind him.

Confused, he glanced over his shoulder in time to catch Owen flipping his back to them, as if gazing out the kitchen window. He brushed a hand over the bridge of his nose as he growled, "There's nothing to see here, guys. I'm simply admiring the general splendor of the birds chirping in the overpriced backyard hydrangea bushes."

"I dream of the day you admire the general splendor of anything that isn't your reflection, you closet POLmArK TV Romance lover," Isaac said dryly, his eyes misty behind his glasses.

Owen's hackles rose as he twisted around, his voice growing marginally louder with indignation, "Who the hell do you think you are, sir? There is *nothing* wrong with a strong, virile man appreciating the comforting joy of a guaranteed happy ending—and in *no way* am I ashamed to admit that!"

"Is that a serious statement? I've caught you watching them so many times at our house after Gracie left the television on that channel—and *every single time*, you jumped like a baby deer in the woods who got spooked by a leaf blowing by," Isaac fired back, whatever emotion he had been experiencing replaced with exasperation.

Owen sneered. "For someone who loves data and making fact-based decisions, you sure are comfortable throwing out *wildly* unsubstantiated and incorrect accusations! I jump because you like to lurk in the shadows and leap out at me like a serial killer once I'm invested in the new love blossoming," he hotly countered.

Levi shook his head, internally questioning his judgment in friends for the umpteenth time that morning. He turned his attention back to Grace and Ivy. Continuing to bicker over the "mental health benefits" that Owen stated came from watching those movies, they were too engrossed in their argument to notice.

While Ivy's attention was on the spectacle unfolding behind them, Grace's face held a twinge of regret, seemingly blaming herself for not trying to help him sooner. She opened her mouth to speak, but Levi beat her to it. "There is nothing you could have done to help—even I hadn't come to terms with what I've been feeling. The only good thing Tyler's bullshit has done so far is make me realize it."

He finished off his coffee and went to refill it. He interrupted Owen and Isaac, their heated debate now focused on what Isaac referred to as "unrealistic occupations," by loudly saying, "While I agree that this is a very controversial topic that I too am personally invested in, could you two *maybe* put a pin in this for later?"

They abruptly stopped, remembering where they were and why. Sheepishly nodding their heads in agreement, they both began to relocate to the kitchen table where their two other friends were struggling to keep straight faces—but not before Owen pointed a finger in Isaac's face and said, "We are *not* done with this conversation."

They were there for a couple of hours, but that had been more than enough time for Levi to immensely regret involving his friends...or at least two of them. If they took a shot of liquor every time Owen wove in a TV romance movie reference, everyone would have alcohol poisoning.

Not one to be outdone, Isaac would instantly counter Owen's remark with what he felt was a logical rebuttal, and one that *everyone* needed to consider.

Levi wanted to punt them both off a cliff and into a lagoon.

Their incessant squabbling aside, it was more productive than he expected it to be, having obtained a solid understanding of the overall process and expectations. Levi was surprised to find himself a little excited about his consultation scheduled for tomorrow, especially since Ivy told him they already had a potential match in mind.

Levi tried his best not to get his hopes up, afraid of how far he would fall if it were too good to be true. But they had a 100% success rate, with dozens of successful matches behind them.

"They already agreed to take you on as a client, based on detailed information I provided about you—you're welcome, by the way," she said with sarcastic sweetness while Levi sorted through a bunch of sheets. "Tomorrow, you'll meet with the matchmaker for a detailed, confidential consultation. This is where they will focus on your goals, lifestyle, values, and expectations for the service."

Levi drew in a sharp intake of breath upon hearing the word "tomorrow," but didn't get a chance to reply before Owen interjected excitedly. "This is *exactly* how the movie *Spuds n' Love Buds* started—a professional potato cleaner was having a rough time on dating apps, so he agreed to go to someone who arranges marriages."

"Oh, I remember that one!" Grace exclaimed. "It was so cute!"

"I'm sorry, but what the hell kind of a job is a potato cleaner? This is the dumbest thing I've ever heard of," Isaac shouted, once again getting worked up over the topic.

"Whoa, take it down a notch there, son!" Owen turned to a bemused Grace and asked, "How did this robot who doesn't believe in the magic of love win your heart?"

"He has other...qualities that I find swoon-worthy," she giggled. Isaac cocked his head to the side and narrowed his eyes at his wife.

"It's astonishing that you clown shoes are in charge of running a multibillion-dollar company," Ivy cut in wryly, wrangling their attention back on track.

Levi fell back in his seat, tipped his head towards the ceiling, and exhaled forcefully. If there was ever a time for any kind of divine intervention, he prayed to whoever would listen for it to be now.

"*Anyway,*" Ivy continued, not keen on being interrupted, "there's a service agreement that outlines the scope of services, timelines, fees, confidentiality, and of course, your commitment to the process. They're already in contact with your attorney about some minor changes he wants to make. You should get a final draft later this afternoon."

The speed at which it was all happening had Levi breaking out into a sweat despite the cool temperature in the house. He swallowed hard.

This is really happening.

"The most important thing here is that you need to trust the matchmaker, or it isn't going to work out," Ivy stressed. "You also need to be honest with yourself. I suggest you spend the rest of the day thinking about exactly how much of yourself you're willing to put into the process. The whole point is to match you with someone who complements you—is your other half."

Blindly trusting a stranger to pick out a wife for him without his input? This part was doable. But agreeing to get married without even seeing her first? That was an extremely hard pill for Levi to swallow.

Figuring out whether he was ready to do this was harder.

Unfortunately, he didn't have a choice at this point. He dipped his head once in agreement, his expression bleak while trying to ignore the rising panic manifesting in his chest. He would deal with it once they all left.

Owen agreed with Ivy. "If you're not honest about what you want out of the relationship right from the beginning, it'll work against you both later on. That's what I learned from watching *Summoned for Love*, where a barrister in a foreign country fell in love with a tourist who was arrested for jaywalking. When they met, the tourist told the barrister that they were in the country for an extended visit, until she found out that the reason for the extension was because of the jaywalking charges...and she was assigned as his legal representation." Owen explained sagely.

Grace squealed, "Yes! She was upset because the tourist didn't tell her about the arrest, and she assumed he was moving there—or at least would be in the country long enough to pursue a relationship. The relocation issue almost broke them."

Hands on his hips, Isaac was incredulous. "Are you two serious right now? That doesn't even make any sense, nor is it an applicable parallel to draw against Levi's situation! These movies are *not* realistic."

Owen looked down his nose at Isaac and scoffed. "Au contraire, mon ami. You seem to be forgetting that we are actually in a situation where there is a fake fiancée, an arranged marriage about to happen, a groom who's a billionaire," he listed out, lifting a finger on one hand for each item checked, "but you don't think these movies are realistic enough to compare to?"

Owen glanced sidelong at Grace again, pure judgment in his eyes. "I really don't understand how he managed to woo you. Please tell me there was a secret grand gesture we don't know about because the lunacy I'm hearing from your husband's mouth is making me reconsider our friendship now."

"This entire day so far is making me reconsider my friendship with half of you," Levi mumbled to himself with a slow head shake.

Grace cut in before anyone else could offer any more commentary. "I think we've helped as much as we can today." Levi shot her a grateful look, internally thanking whoever was responsible for sending him the miracle that was Grace. "Levi, we're all going to head out so you can have time to yourself to think."

Owen was on the verge of objecting when she added, "Everyone is welcome to come to our place tomorrow night for dinner, though. Then Levi can give us an update on how his appointment went." She looked at Owen when she firmly added, "We can *all* interrogate him."

Temporarily placated, Owen kept his mouth shut and gave Grace a curt nod.

Everyone else agreed to dinner before they packed up and left, giving Levi time to think about Ivy's question.

"This is going to be a shit show," he muttered to himself.

CHAPTER 9

Aurelia

Maybe this wasn't the best idea, Aurelia thought to herself as she watched her hairstylist, Brandi, mix several different bowls of hair dye.

Her long chestnut hair was naturally wavy and had never been processed or chemically treated. Yet here she sat, with foils threaded throughout her head, actively lightening the strands in preparation for coloring.

Though her favorite color was turquoise, Aurelia loved all the bright colors of the rainbow. The beauty of colorful things like stained glass windows, freshly laid out produce at the grocery store, and the sunrise and sunset over the lagoon brought a quiet joy to her world.

It was fitting then that she boldly—and impulsively—decided to highlight her hair with quite literally a rainbow of colors. Each bowl of hair dye held a distinct color: red, hot pink, coral, teal, green, blue, and violet.

Initially taken aback by her request, Brandi's skepticism rapidly changed to excitement as she assessed Aurelia's appearance, no doubt picturing the outcome. Brandi clapped her hands together, assuring her that it would look amazing, and was thankful for the chance to try something so unique on a client.

Aurelia was excited too, but some habits were hard to break, and that familiar self-doubt crept in. But she didn't voice it aloud. There was no going back, and she needed to see it through. Worst case, if it were awful, she could dye it back to her natural color and pretend it never happened.

Brandi set a timer and moved her to one of the hair dryer stations to speed up the processing. Aurelia sat there for a while, fidgeting in the chair and continuously looking at the timer. The minutes seemed to drag on.

She didn't get much rest last night. After attempting to start the paperwork Charles gave her, she ultimately abandoned it until this morning. Avoiding it until the last minute wouldn't make anything easier, but she didn't have the energy to deal with her emotions. With foolish hopes of clearing her head and heart, she had gone to bed early.

Except she slept fitfully, afflicted by terrifying visions of the past and haunted by reminders of past pain.

After rolling out of bed and into the shower this morning, she finished the paperwork in preparation for her consultation tomorrow afternoon with *Perfectly Paired Matchmaking*.

But as she filled in the blanks in the documents about her personal history, a clear and very depressing pattern emerged—and it hurt more than any physical injuries she had experienced before.

No family.

Her mother had been more interested in her next high and whatever, or whoever, she had to do to achieve it. She was fairly sure her father was a one-night stand; potentially someone who had access to the substances her mother craved, and she let him use her body as payment.

Aurelia remembered a faint glimmer of a grandmother who cared about her for a little while before passing away, but she had been so young that the memory of her face was hazy. Her heart squeezed as the brief but very real memory of what it felt like to be loved by someone overtook her consciousness. Unfortunately, it wasn't long after that when they placed her in state care following her mother's deadly overdose.

She had not experienced that feeling of affection again until Eleanor. Her heart squeezed at the thought of her dear friend.

No friends.

Bouncing around from foster family to foster family made it impossible to make friends at school. The other kids in the homes treated one another as rivals, constantly competing for everything. Siblings stuck together, but otherwise, you were on your own.

Fighting for any scrap of love and attention you could get from a parental figure.

Territorial when it came to what little belongings you had to your name.

Alone, somehow, even though surrounded by other people. Selene had grown to be the exception; she was the only friend she had made during that time.

But those skills, or lack thereof, had ingrained themselves within her, making it difficult as an adult to truly connect with others. She actively volunteered in her community and participated in many local activities where she had met many wonderful people, yet she still failed to successfully take the next step towards building a friendship.

No lasting relationships.

She had dozens of past boyfriends, but every single one of them had a major character flaw that she overlooked, having been too naïve and inexperienced to see it until it was too late. If she were being honest with herself, there were a few where she had purposely overlooked warning signs in hopes of finally being loved.

She shuddered at the thought. Clearly, it had not worked out in her favor.

Reading what the matchmaking process needed from her was another punch to the gut. To her dismay, it required Aurelia to start unpacking the boxes of emotions and experiences that she had buried away in the back of her mind.

The nausea had slammed into her the moment she began to acknowledge them. She hadn't decided if she was angrier with herself for turning a blind eye to all the red flags that each of these partners had...or because she was so desperate for their love and affection that she lost her identity trying to get them to stay.

At that moment, Aurelia tried to block those feelings out and hurried through the rest of the paperwork, desperate to be done with it all. It was a heavy start to her day, and she hoped a little self-pampering at the salon would lighten her self-deprecating mood.

But as she sat baking under the hair dryer, an unwelcome image of Kyle Morris, her last boyfriend, and what he did to her flitted into her mind. Those memories always came with phantom aches and pains, a brutal reminder of what that love had cost her. An instant swell of a panic attack rose within her.

It had been about a year since she left him, but what he did—what she allowed him to do—still haunted her every day and every night. Though no longer in her life, his control over her still lingered like invisible strings in her subconscious, tethering her to him.

Aurelia hated it—hated herself for allowing it to happen and for not prioritizing herself more. She hated the version of herself it created.

She straightened in the chair and swore to herself that she would never again be in that position. Realizing that was easier said than done, especially considering she hadn't always been the best judge of character either, caused her to slump back into the chair.

Aurelia's mind circled back to her conversation with Charles and the instructions not to share details of the inheritance with anyone, not even Selene. She wondered if it would truly alter their friendship if Selene knew.

Then a question came to the forefront of her thoughts, like a whisper on a gentle wind: *What is it that I want?*

She reflected on the night she had met Adelen for milkshakes after their impromptu practice in the park. It had been such a small thing to share greasy fries with thick and too-sweet milkshakes at a corner diner, but to Aurelia it was a major milestone. For once, she wasn't treated like a complete outsider.

Aurelia knew there was more beneath that unruffled exterior, but she wasn't going to push for more information than Adelen was willing to give. Perhaps someday, Adelen would see her as someone trustworthy enough to hold her secrets.

Adelen hadn't felt compelled to drive the conversation or ask uncomfortable questions. She simply sat there, the picture of cool, quiet confidence, cracked a few jokes, and in her uniquely stoic way made space for Aurelia to simply...exist.

Smiling faintly at the memory, Aurelia could admit to herself that she had a mild girl-crush on her.

That moment stuck with her. The kind of simple, easy friendship she hadn't dared to hope for. Maybe there were people out there who wouldn't expect her to fight for their attention or earn their approval, people who might understand what it felt like to simply survive.

Because that's what she wanted, a real connection and a life that felt more than just endured—

The answer beginning to take shape was interrupted by the sound of loud buzzing.

Aurelia blinked, momentarily forgetting where she was.

She shifted uncomfortably in the chair as Brandi approached her and peeked inside a couple of foils to ensure they were ready.

Taking a deep, steady breath, Aurelia walked to the washing station as instructed, reclining in the chair towards the sink so Brandi could remove the foils.

The shampoo rinsed the chemicals down the drain, and she tried to let her fears wash away with it, taking an imaginary step across the line towards regaining her identity.

Aurelia stared at the woman reflected in the mirror.

It was her...and yet it wasn't.

She had the same large almond-shaped eyes, naturally thick eyebrows, straight nose, and full lips as Aurelia, but she looked more polished and confident. *Beautiful.*

Brandi begged to do her makeup once she finished blowing out Aurelia's hair, offering to do it free of charge because "it would be a crime to walk out without finishing the look." Aurelia eventually relented but made sure she paid for the extra service.

It was worth every penny.

And her hair...it was *amazing*—no, it was *sensational.*

The terrifyingly vivid colors in the bowls gave way to vibrant colored strands that blended in perfectly with her naturally dark hair. Instead of being too overpowering like she had feared, they peeked through in different shades and blended into the long, soft waves that cascaded past her shoulders, as if they had always been there.

"You obviously must practice some type of dark magic to have pulled off such a magnificent illusion," Aurelia whispered, leaning in closer to the mirror to get a better glimpse. Brandi stood tall behind her, arms crossed in satisfaction as she watched Aurelia's reflection.

"You were a knockout when you walked in the door. All I did was highlight what was already there." Authenticity shone brightly in Brandi's eyes as she gazed proudly at Aurelia.

"You have no idea how badly I want to ruin this moment with an awkward hug of thanks." She couldn't stop staring at her reflection, worried that if she dared to look away, it would stop being real. "Can you show me how you did my makeup?"

"I thought you'd never ask!" Brandi didn't waste any time as she pulled out her magical makeup set and began her tutorial.

By the time Aurelia made it home, she was exhausted but in the best way. It was remarkable how a small physical change could drastically impact one's self-esteem. While she knew it wouldn't fix all her problems, it was a step in the right direction.

Her eyes caught her reflection in the bathroom mirror as she was changing into pajamas, and she couldn't help but notice the lingering smile. A different and more assured version of herself emerged from the salon, one that was here to stay.

She fell asleep easily that night, excited for her consultation, and with a smile still gracing her lips.

CHAPTER 10

Levi

As much as he hated to admit it, Levi was impressed.

He walked in a silent skeptic, but that changed when Estrella Vale explained her approach to finding his match.

Estrella was in her mid-fifties, with lavender shoulder-length straight hair, and delicate features framed by a pair of smart black rimmed glasses. She was soft-spoken with a faint but enchanting accent that he couldn't quite place.

Nothing out of the ordinary except for her eyes. They appeared otherworldly, with different shades of blue swirling in their depths. There was something about them that unsettled him, but he couldn't pinpoint why.

The building—or rather the house—was small and nondescript, easily blending in with the other houses in the row. He might have missed it if he hadn't been looking for this exact address. The light blue craftsman front door had opened as he was poised to ring the doorbell, Estrella in the doorway, ready to greet him.

He was ushered into a light and airy room with white wainscoting, floral wallpaper in various shades of coral, gold, and green decorating the walls above. A single tan colored couch flanked by two cream plush armchairs faced a small historic brick fireplace, only separated by a light wood coffee table.

Levi had never seen a room so bright and yet so warm. While the colors weren't something he would have ever chosen for himself, he found it wonderfully comfortable and inviting.

"My research has proven that punctuality is a very attractive quality in a partner." Estrella extended her delicate hand in greeting, her mouth lifting in a playful half-smile. "It's a pleasure to meet you, Mr. Lockwood."

Levi smiled widely and eagerly shook her hand. "I'm at the mercy of your expertise and appreciate the expedited appointment."

That earned him a full smile from Estrella.

She turned and beckoned him to follow through the large opening in the direction of what looked like a kitchen. There was also a set of stairs, confirming that she lived in the house that lay on the other side of the entryway. "While appreciated, there is no need for such formalities here, Levi. I'm in the business of getting to know the real you, and that begins now."

Estrella continued into the kitchen, offering the option of a warm beverage. Hands in his pockets, Levi gratefully accepted a cup of coffee as he absentmindedly observed the space.

The same color scheme from the sitting room continued into this area. Natural wood tones were used throughout the counters and furniture, punctuated by a deep white farmhouse sink sitting atop coral colored cabinetry. Light wood open shelving displayed colorful dishes, cookware, and jars of dried ingredients and spices. The air held the scent of freshly baked apple pie that had his mouth watering.

This is what a home smells like, he thought, his eyes widening with the sudden realization. He had never lived anywhere that truly felt like a home, even as a child. The closest thing was when he was at Owen's house growing up, or at Grace and Isaac's house hanging out. Frowning, he made a mental note to visit Owen's mom. It wasn't only his friends he had been neglecting lately.

Yet deep down, he knew—this confirmed why he hated going home after work.

A low familiar ache in his chest decided to rear its ugly head again. Brushing it aside, he glanced at the farmhouse table nestled in front of a large wall of windows overlooking the colorful backyard.

The words came tumbling out of his mouth without warning. "I love your home."

He could hear her smile, rather than see it, from the other side of the kitchen. Estrella poured two steaming cups of coffee from a French press as promised. "I'm in the business of uniting two souls so they can build a home and life together. A stuffy office makes it so unnecessarily clinical." She carefully walked the two mugs over to the table. "I will give you the option of having our consultation here or in my office."

Levi didn't hesitate. "Let's stay in here. I honestly love this room." He was surprised that he liked the coral cabinets. They were bright and warm, which gave the space an added layer of calm…something he desperately needed at that moment.

"It's my favorite room too." She settled into a cushioned seat at the end of the table and motioned for Levi to do the same. As he sat down, he placed his notebook and documents on the table ensuring he was as prepared as possible.

Estrella turned her sharp gaze to his folder; her attention focused on the multiple colors of sticky notes layered within it, but she said nothing.

Levi followed her gaze, his cheeks heating a little. He wasn't sure what to expect from their meeting, so he did his best to be ready.

He went through the documents for today and marked pages with critical items to discuss. The color-coding system made sense to him, helping him to find a particular section quickly without spending too much time skimming through the text. "I like to be very prepared when going into unknown situations that could stress me out," he admitted with a nervous laugh, fingertips anxiously tapping on the table.

Those eyes—a whirlpool in the depths of a blue lagoon—bore into him again, rendering him still.

"I've been in contact with your attorney, Mitchell, so don't worry about paperwork during this appointment. The signed service agreement can wait until the end, so you have all the information to make an informed decision. No need to spend our time together reading when one can learn a great deal from talking and listening," she assured him with a secret smile.

He released the breath he had been holding. It was as if she knew what a struggle reading could be for him—though he supposed the heavily notated file probably was a clue. Regardless, he still appreciated this small mercy and let his shoulders relax a bit. "You may regret that once you find out how boring I can be," he teased.

She didn't so much as react to his joke aside from a slight head tilt. "What brings you to my doorstep? I spoke with your friend Ivy, and she shared quite a bit of detail about you and your situation, but I want to hear it directly from you." Her tone was serious, and her eyes continued to change hues. It was borderline distracting.

Levi felt like every pore on his body was being analyzed by a panel of overly judgmental church ladies. It was uncomfortable, exaggerated, and left him feeling like his flaws were the main attraction. This was exactly the kind of situation he actively avoided regularly.

"I'm not sure what Ivy told you specifically, but this whole thing came about because I was an idiot during a Board meeting and let one of our most abrasive members get under my skin." Levi could feel the anger bubbling up again, but clenched his teeth as he fought to tamp it down.

Once he had his emotions under control, he recounted the events of the meeting, including the derogatory comments Tyler had made. She didn't say a word, but her irises kept swirling as she listened.

If he was going to fully commit to this process, then he had to jump into the deep end of this pool—and try to ignore her unsettling eyes. Which meant opening up about himself, no matter how uncomfortable it was.

He took a calming breath.

"I'll start with why that Board member's comments bothered me so much. You've noticed how prepared I came today, and it's because I have dyslexia. Growing up with it was a nightmare, not because of how much I struggled in school, but because of how my peers and adults treated me."

This was going to be much harder than Levi thought. It was one thing to say the words aloud, but it was quite another to try to explain what dyslexia is and how it affects everyday life.

"The stereotypes—It's not just about letters being jumbled or backwards like many people think…it comes in so many different forms and affects every person differently. For me, the words are not static, meaning they don't stay still and seem to move around when I read, so following a linear sentence takes me significantly longer to get through than the average person."

This was why Tyler's words had cut Levi so deeply. He wasn't the first person in Levi's life to question or mock his ability to read. It reopened a deep wound that had never fully healed.

"It also makes writing harder—my penmanship was and still is a constant battle. It's mentally draining to try to decode something like that. People assumed I was lazy and unmotivated because I was tired all the time. I fell asleep at my desk on more than one occasion because I was trying so hard that it was physically taxing."

He swallowed audibly and turned to gaze out the window. He hated talking about these experiences. He hated feeling weak and vulnerable.

"Being mocked like that, at my own company, which was meant to be a safe place for people like me…I haven't felt that low in a long time. So, when he took another shot at me about my past and very public relationship failures, I was caught completely off guard. I don't know what came over me, but the next thing I knew, I had announced a fiancée I didn't have."

Despite his best efforts, Levi felt inadequate again, his voice beginning to waver. "I guess I snapped and didn't want to continue feeling like a failure."

Levi forced himself to face her. Estrella was still unmoving, still watching him with that unflinching and intense stare.

It was really starting to creep him out.

"In talking with my friends, they ultimately pushed me to finally stop and think about—an intervention of sorts. It made me realize what I've been ignoring for quite a long time now..." he trailed off softly.

He examined his trembling hands as they rested on the table. Clenching them into tight fists, he shifted them to his lap, while searching for the right words to explain.

He hated rambling—but he powered through.

"The reason I already love this kitchen is because it feels like a home—*that's* what I want. I have a large house, but it's not a *home*. It's cold, empty, and I hate being there. I hate it so much that I work almost all the time because I don't have time to think about how alone I am. But I was brutally reminded this week," he said bitterly, "that I *apparently* don't make good choices when it comes to selecting partners."

Levi looked Estrella directly in the eyes and with all the conviction he could summon, he revealed, "I want a home to share with someone who loves me, flaws and all, that I love just as acceptingly. I needed a kick in the ass to wake me up and, unfortunately, this Board member was the one who delivered it."

His deepest desire and his worst fear.

Every aspect of the silent battle he had waged within himself for the past few years was out in the open, no longer contained or repressed within him.

Levi held his breath and waited several moments for her to speak, acutely aware that patience was a test of sorts and one he desperately needed to pass. The longer the silence stretched, the more anxious he became, the air in the room suffocating with every second that ticked by.

The torrent of colors in her eyes began to subside, returning to a more static blue. Estrella then snapped out of whatever trance she had been in and took a slow, contemplative sip of her coffee.

"Fate sends us signs all the time. But it's up to us to decide if we are ready to see and understand them," she finally said. "I have to agree with you here—while it wasn't the most preferred method of delivery coming from your Board member, it was, in fact, a sign you needed." Her lips quirked up in mild amusement.

Just as quickly, her expression dimmed, and a hint of sadness crept into her tone. "I can sense how weary you are from the toll that the extra effort you expend fitting into this world has taken on your soul."

Something in Levi's chest eased at her words. She straightened as her face brightened.

"The good news is that I'm confident I can help you find a match...I may even have a prospect in mind who is currently being vetted. *But*," her tone sharpened, "you need to be committed to truly finding your other half, *not* a temporary placeholder. Otherwise, this will be a waste of everyone's time. So, be undeniably sure before moving forward—before you tell me what it is you want."

He didn't miss a beat, answering earnestly. "I want to find my match."

It was late evening, and Levi was still beside himself.

He had never revealed so much about himself in one sitting to anyone, let alone a stranger, the words yanked from him by some invisible force.

He didn't know what to make of it.

The rest of their time together continued well past lunchtime. Estrella was courteous enough to provide sandwiches and homemade lemonade as she laid out the next steps of the matchmaking process.

Levi's head swam as he recalled the detailed discussion about the psychological profiling, lifestyle analysis, and in-depth interviews he would have to do. If he took the time off from work and fully immersed himself, he could get it all done within two or three days.

Still...It was an intimidating level of information, and the blind nature of the match—which included no photos or names until the wedding—had him second-guessing this decision.

Estrella reinforced her perfect record of accomplishment and reminded him that he had a choice in the process...only to casually hint that she may already have someone in mind for him.

That caught Levi's attention, confirming what Ivy told him.

With time running out and leaving no room to wrestle with the vulnerability of marrying a stranger, Levi agreed to return the next day at 8:00 AM sharp, fully invested and fully committed.

It was all he could think about for the rest of the night. He drifted off to sleep, praying it was true: that he would have a match.

CHAPTER 11

Aurelia

With ten minutes to spare before her appointment, Aurelia rang the doorbell of an adorable house.

Shifting on her feet, she waited, trying to balance the weight of her tote bag and the box of macarons that she carried. With nervous energy to burn off, she impulsively decided to make them for today's consultation. It didn't feel right showing up empty-handed to something so personal.

Aurelia peered down at the solid light pink long-sleeved t-shirt with delicate lace detailing at the end of the sleeves and bottom, dark jeans, and flat brown sandals she wore, having opted for comfortable clothing. It was too late to hope she was dressed appropriately.

The door slowly opened, revealing a small-framed woman who looked old enough to be her mother, but still youthful enough to be mistaken for an older sister. But it was her shoulder-length hair that captured her attention, in a lovely shade of lilac.

Her blue eyes were an ethereal shade she had not seen before. They watched Aurelia through chic black framed glasses.

"You must be the Aurelia I've heard so much about. Please come in." She stepped aside with a wide smile, making room for Aurelia to enter.

Stepping through the door and into the sitting room, Aurelia's eyes roamed every square inch of the vibrant space. "I love everything about this room," she gushed, eyes wide as she spun around slowly. "This is exactly the vibe I've been trying to create in my own home."

She blushed, realizing she hadn't yet introduced herself. The woman sported an entertained grin as she leaned against the jamb of the opening that led to an equally stunning kitchen. "I'm so sorry, my manners went out the window when I crossed the threshold to this magical home. But yes, I'm Aurelia, and hopefully in the right place?"

"Indeed, you are, and thank you for the compliment." She moved towards Aurelia, hand extended. "I'm Estrella Vale. We will be working very closely together during your time with *Perfectly Paired Matchmaking*." Aurelia shook her small but firm hand and smiled, her nervousness ebbing.

She held up the box of dessert and offered it to Estrella. "I made an assortment of macarons for us to enjoy this afternoon, if that's okay?" It was strange how comfortable Aurelia felt with this woman, as if she had known Estrella her entire life somehow.

Those strangely beautiful blue eyes lit up behind her lenses.

"What a pleasant surprise! I *adore* macarons—and *you* have managed to surprise an old woman by making them yourself. Let's get ourselves settled, then. Would you like coffee or tea?" She waved Aurelia into the kitchen. "I already put the kettle on for some tea myself."

"Tea sounds amazing, thank you."

Aurelia placed the box on the gorgeous farmhouse table before sliding into one of the open seats. As she began removing files from her bag, Estrella joined her, bearing two steaming azulejo-style teacups and matching saucers. *Even her China set is beautiful*, Aurelia admired silently.

"I love your hair, by the way. It's a beautiful color."

Estrella beamed with surprised delight. "No one ever dares to comment on it—it's refreshing to hear. Though I must say," she said, eyeing Aurelia's hair again, "it doesn't compare to yours. The way it shimmers in the sunlight is simply marvelous. I can't believe Eleanor never mentioned it in all the times we met."

The mention of Eleanor caused Aurelia's smile to slip, dulling her good mood. Reflexively, her shoulders curled in a fraction, self-consciousness flooding her senses. She reached for the sugar and small carafe of milk and busied herself with her tea.

This wasn't the time to start crying.

"It's something I've always wanted to do, and yesterday felt like it was the right time to make it happen. After losing her…I needed a change for myself and decided to just go for it," she admitted.

"Her loss will be felt by every person whose life she touched. I've known her for a long time and can say there will never be someone quite like her. She was a star in her own right, called home to shine among them," Estrella said mournfully.

Aurelia's throat worked as she tried to hold back the flood of tears threatening to break through, the truth of Estrella's words hitting her hard. Forcing out a steadying breath, she agreed.

"That's a lovely way of framing it. Eleanor was definitely the center of attention wherever she went. If her life had been a reality show, it would have had the highest ratings every season—and she would have basked in the glory of it."

Thinking about all the antics Eleanor had pulled with the same air of nonchalance one had with something as mundane as tying their shoelaces brought a smile to her face. That woman had a knack for making simple activities over the top.

Estrella's mouth formed a small smile. "She never relied on signs from Fate to guide her in life; she simply barged right in and made those decisions for herself—which is exactly why you and I are here today." She looked at Aurelia intently as she reached across the table to the box of macarons.

Aurelia slid the box closer to her, not one to deny anyone a chance for a treat. Estrella gracefully selected two of each flavor of macarons and added them to her plate.

"I'll admit that this situation is quite an unorthodox one for me. Usually, clients approach me of their own volition. I don't advertise—every client is a referral from a prior one."

It was unorthodox because Eleanor was involved, Aurelia thought.

"Eleanor was candid about her wishes. She spoke so highly about the daughter she never had—how much she needed my help, that I couldn't say no. Quite honestly, I feel as if I already know you, considering how much Eleanor told me."

Aurelia let that sink in for a moment, wondering how often she had met with Estrella these last few months without her knowledge. Even in death, Eleanor was still a sneaky bitch...and it lifted her spirits a bit.

"I can only imagine the things she said about me," Aurelia said wryly, as Estrella bit into a strawberries and cream flavored macaron, humming in appreciation. "Eleanor's explanation delivered in her last video was as subtle as someone whispering secrets through a megaphone in a library."

The words slipped out of Aurelia's mouth before she could think them through. Estrella almost choked on the dessert with laughter, needing a long sip of her tea to wash it down. Once she regained her composure, the air in the room shifted as those mesmerizing eyes aligned with hers, an unnatural stillness befalling her.

It was a strange feeling that made her skin prickle.

"It's clear that despite the unusual circumstances, you've agreed to move forward with finding your match," Estrella stated.

Aurelia could have sworn her eyes were changing colors, but she pushed the thought from her mind as quickly as it arrived. *I'm imagining things.*

"Beyond the wealth at stake, what made you decide to come?"

The question stopped Aurelia in her tracks, and she thoughtfully considered her response. Ultimately, she decided to repeat exactly what she said to Charles in Eleanor's study only a couple of days prior.

"Because I've nothing left to lose. I'm sure Eleanor spilled all the gossip about my upbringing in foster care, how I came to be her personal assistant, and my past romantic entanglements."

It should have been harder to say the words aloud, but it was as if someone else was in control, her thoughts ill content to be silent any longer.

"I don't really have any friends; growing up, I was shuffled around so much that it became impossible to connect with other kids. Being thrown into the real world without any protections the day I turned eighteen forced me to put such trivialities on the back burner—surviving was more important."

Aurelia paused, that invisible tether drawing her story out, unable to stop it even if she tried. It was disconcerting; her instincts begged to erect a wall around her heart. She fought against it.

I'm fierce. I can do this.

"I was in my mid-twenties when I felt ready to go beyond basic survival...to try to live. Though I didn't know what that entailed. I started by volunteering for activities in my community; I took classes like beginner's crochet or line dancing to meet other people, but..." she bit her lower lip in hesitation.

I lied, maybe I can't do this.

She shook her head and that voice out of her mind. "I haven't been able to get past that first introduction and small talk. No one seems to be interested in pushing a friendship further than that."

Facing the windows leading to the backyard, Aurelia peered into the distance, reliving those memories and the accompanying feeling of embarrassment. Arms wrapped around herself protectively, she asked in a broken whisper, "Is there something wrong with me?"

Estrella said nothing. She dropped her arms and took a sip of tea to buy herself time to gather her thoughts and strength, hating how exposed she was—how vulnerable.

Hating how her voice progressively became more distraught as she continued.

"I have no issues getting attention from men. The problem is my inability to choose the right ones. Every relationship failed because I wasn't good enough for them to stay." Her inadequacy had become the only constant companion in her life.

Aurelia was so adrift in the memories of every failed past relationship, especially the most recent one, that she didn't feel the silent rivers streaming down her face, wrought with emotion.

"Losing Eleanor has affected me more than anything in my life so far; she was *literally* the only person who has ever cared deeply about me. Yes, she was my employer, but for me, our relationship went beyond that. She was the grandmother I never had—someone who let me be myself without pretense and fall apart without judgment. Eleanor made me feel *safe*."

She chanced a glance at Estrella, who, save for those swirling blue orbs, had not moved a muscle.

"I'm here because I have *nothing* left to lose by letting someone help me," Aurelia said, her voice steadier than she felt. "If it doesn't work out, fine—I'll be right back where I am now. The money itself doesn't mean anything to me, but it could help so many other people—kids like me who are aging out of foster care with nowhere to go, no support."

Confidence and determination began to replace her embarrassment.

"I *barely* made it on my own. This inheritance could create something real—a safety net that actually helps them, so they don't have to fight to survive like I did."

She took a shaky breath, surprised by the emotion rising in her chest. Emotion that didn't push her down for once; instead, it picked her up and pushed her forward.

"Ninety days before my eighteenth birthday, they gave me a transition plan...said it would help me find a safe place to live, a job. My foster parents even agreed to let me stay until I was settled. But all of that fell apart. I came home from work one night and found my bags already packed. They told me I had to leave—that another kid was coming and no room for me."

Aurelia's throat tightened at the memory. "So, I left. And with nowhere else to go...I ended up living in my car."

In a voice that sounded neither far away nor close—somehow everywhere at once, Estrella asked, "What is it that you want?"

That was just it.

No one had ever cared about what she wanted, so she never cared either.

Until now.

"I want to feel safe. I've *never* felt safe with a partner. I want someone who is my best friend...the first person I see and think about when I open my eyes in the morning and the last when I close them at night. I want to be able to break down knowing they'll help me back up. And—and I want to be strong enough to do the same for them."

That thing in her chest had cracked open—and it *hurt*.

Wiping her cheeks with the back of her hand, she whispered, "I want all of the things that I haven't been able to experience in life so far—love, a home, a family with someone who truly sees me."

How pathetic I must sound with my worst fears now laid out on the table like a weak hand of cards, she thought miserably to herself. Though there was a certain kind of finality in saying these words aloud, as if her needs and wants became a tangible thing.

Suddenly, Aurelia came to a sharp realization.

She knew she looked like a disaster right now in front of this woman she had met not an hour ago, but Aurelia found that she didn't care. She simply couldn't bring herself to care.

She didn't care if everything she said made her look weak.

She didn't care whether this woman pitied her or felt indifferent because Aurelia had already lived through much worse than someone else's judgment.

While it was true that no one had cared about her wants, she struck a silent bargain with herself to change that...because she *mattered*.

What she needed and wanted *mattered*.

Without warning, as if she were struck by an invisible electric current, Aurelia's very sense of self reset.

She stopped crying, and her eyes cleared.

She straightened her shoulders and sat up taller in her chair.

A strength she didn't know existed surged deep within her.

Staring Estrella in the eyes, Aurelia didn't falter when she said, "I want your help."

Those blue whirlpools stopped moving, returning to a homogenous hue as a satisfied smile formed on Estrella's face.

"There's the Aurelia Eleanor told me about. It's a pleasure to finally meet you."

CHAPTER 12

Aurelia

Hours after her emotional consultation, Aurelia lounged on her couch in pajamas, eating authentic ramen from her favorite restaurant by the fire. A muted POLmArK TV Romance played in the background.

She was still a wreck after baring her soul to Estrella and needed to talk to someone about it. She made several attempts to reach Selene via text and voicemail over the last two days, including her way home tonight. All had gone unanswered, and for the first time in the history of their friendship, it grated on her.

She aggressively stabbed at the noodles in her bowl with her chopsticks.

The amount of personal sharing she did today was unbelievably abnormal, and it would've been great to talk through some of her memories with the one person who would understand—someone who lived many of those traumatic moments with her.

Instead, she spent the last couple of hours replaying key conversations and moments with Selene over the years...and started to recognize a troubling pattern of one-sidedness in their friendship.

Like all the times Selene had invited Aurelia to go out, it was according to her availability, often cancelling at the last minute—sometimes when Aurelia was already on her way—with vague excuses and no offer to reschedule.

Or how most of their conversations revolved around Selene's problems. She would frequently call Aurelia in frustration or to vent, but rarely asked how Aurelia was doing or followed up on anything happening in her life.

Even on the rare occasion Aurelia shared good news, like a professional milestone or personal goal, Selene quickly changed the subject, downplayed it, or made it about herself.

But the worst was in moments like this, where Aurelia needed a friend, Selene would go radio silent. It was becoming clear that Selene wasn't equipped—or willing—to show up when Aurelia needed someone most.

The noodles slipped off the chopsticks and back into the bowl right as she was about to take a bite. Growling in frustration, she gave up on the damn noodles and tried to shift her focus to the assessments Estrella sent for the matchmaking process.

Her thoughts zeroed in on the potential mystery match Estrella alluded to...and how she had knocked over her teacup in shock. She about fell out of her chair when Estrella suggested they spend the next few days fully focused on "fast-tracking" the profile and assessment work.

She allowed herself to feel a flicker of hope at the thought of this...until it collided with panic at the thought of Kyle and the physical reminders she still bore of the last time she tried to open up to someone. Aurelia grabbed a nearby pillow and hugged it tightly, closing her eyes to squash the fear.

"I survived," Aurelia whispered in an attempt to ground herself. It was a mantra, a reminder of her resilience. She repeated it a few more times before cleaning up and extinguishing the fire.

She went to bed early, steeling herself for the next day's tasks and a surprise visit to Starhaven Manor.

Similar to Aurelia's mood, the playlist on the radio today was absolutely on fire. She sang along loudly, albeit terribly, as she drove to Starhaven Manor.

After getting up early, she completed her online assessments with laser focus over breakfast, feeling empowered by the insight they gave her. Her conflict resolution style hit hardest, a stark reflection of how her upbringing and past relationships shaped her avoidance of confrontation.

Marriage wouldn't allow her to run anymore. She needed to learn to stand her ground.

Visiting Selene today felt like a good first test.

As she turned into the grand drive leading to Starhaven, the manor's beauty struck her anew. Nestled on a cliff outside Joia City, the whitewashed villa with its red tiled roof and carved wooden accents was nothing short of magical. Her chest tightened as reality sank in.

This estate could soon be hers...if everything worked out.

She planned to speak with Charles about the upcoming Harvest Charity Ball, a Greaves family tradition. Despite its pretentiousness, Aurelia had loved planning it with Eleanor. The thought of doing it without her was less exciting, but also an opportunity for Aurelia to honor her friend.

Parking in the staff area, she composed herself and entered through the service door, winding her way to the expansive executive kitchen.

It had a large, curved window that allowed natural light to pour in, a number of spacious walk-in pantries, and a breakfast nook with a built-in banquette that could easily fit a large family.

Fitted with top-of-the-line gleaming stainless-steel appliances, high-gloss light wood cabinetry, and polished marble countertops wrapped around the space. The main attraction, however, was the massive center island housing a cooktop and sink, surrounded by multiple pendant lights suspended from the high ceiling...and where Selene stood with Chef Rodrigo, reviewing menus. She looked tired, and her smile briefly faltered when she saw Aurelia.

"Hey! I'm so glad you're here! We're working on the menu for the Harvest Charity Ball." Selene walked around the island toward Aurelia, dressed immaculately in an olive pantsuit.

"Before you say anything, I have a good reason for not calling you back yet," Selene began. They moved through the service wing toward Selene's office. "I have a few reasons, truth be told."

The modest and worn but elegant office was tucked in the back of the estate. It boasted the same lofty ceilings and cream walls found in the rest of the manor. Aurelia sat across from Selene's desk, the guest chair having seen better days.

"I was starting to get worried about you and figured I'd come and do a wellness check myself."

Selene handed her a water bottle from her mini refrigerator, then sank into her chair.

"It's been a hell of a week. I've been a bit disorganized and have spent more time than I'd care to admit putting out fires with the staff. It's put me behind on many things, so I've had to work later than usual."

She explained how she left her phone, purse, and coffee on the roof of her car and drove off the other day, only noticing when everything flew across her windshield.

"It hasn't worked right since then...I ordered a replacement that's arriving this weekend," Selene said apologetically, fiddling with a retractable pen.

"I'm so sorry that happened. I wanted to make sure you were alright and weren't mad at me for something. It's been a really strange few days," Aurelia said, guilt creeping over her for assuming the worst about her friend.

"No apology needed; it's definitely been a shit week," Selene sighed.

"Hopefully, I can help make things a little easier after I talk to Charles about the Harvest Charity Ball."

Selene perked up a bit at the mention of the event. "We've been pushing ahead with everything as if she were still here, so any help would be welcome." A flash of curiosity darted across her face. "Have you heard anything about who her heir is? None of us has heard a peep," Selene whispered conspiratorially.

Aurelia hedged, cautiously crafting a response. "I haven't been here in a few days, so I haven't heard anything...I'm sure it'll come out when it's time."

Falling dramatically back into her seat, Selene sighed again. "You're right...as usual. We have plenty to do around here in the meantime, like plan this Harvest Charity Ball."

Aurelia forced a smile, uncharacteristically annoyed with her friend. "I don't want to monopolize too much of your day. Give me a call when you're settled with your new phone so we can go grab drinks. My treat."

Selene grinned mischievously. "Absolutely."

Thankfully, Charles was in Eleanor's study when Aurelia peeked in. Her timing was perfect as he was currently between meetings. He smiled with relief as she sat.

"What a lovely surprise," he said warmly, then blinked. "Your hair!"

She grinned, running her fingers through it. "What do you think? It was a bit of an impulse, but I wanted something different."

"Definitely different! It's quite becoming on you. Had you asked my opinion before seeing it, I wouldn't have thought it a good idea. But even an old man can learn new things."

She blushed. Compliments still threw her off, but she was starting to enjoy receiving them.

"What brings you to see me? Hopefully, an update from your consultation?"

"A few things. First, I hadn't been able to get a hold of Selene for days, so I came here to track her down." She then noted Selene hadn't said a word about her hair and frowned.

Maybe that's why I was annoyed with her.

"Second, I wanted to talk about the Harvest Charity Ball and how I can help...and yes, also updates about the consultation."

"Let's start with the consultation." Charles pulled up a document. "I have a preliminary draft prenuptial agreement ready for your review. The most prominent section that I added states that any assets or inheritance, current or future, will remain separate."

Aurelia raised a brow.

"This protects you without requiring disclosure until you're ready. It's your choice whether or not to share with your husband. That conversation would fall under spousal privilege and not violate Eleanor's anonymity clause."

Relief washed over her, followed directly by unease.

"That makes sense." Her next sentence was slow and drawn out, a foolish attempt at evading the inevitable. "Estrella told me she had a potential match in mind," she said softly, toying with the strap of her bag.

Charles's brows shot up. "That quickly?"

"I met with her yesterday, and she had another client sign on at almost the same time...There could be a wedding in a week if everything works out."

"How do you feel about that? You're suspiciously calm."

Aurelia chuckled. "Scared. It hasn't completely hit me yet, so I'll probably panic the moment I have to make a real decision. That's how I felt driving in—realizing this estate might be mine too."

Understanding filled his gaze. "Take it one day at a time. Don't do anything you're not comfortable with and keep me updated."

"I did all the self-assessments this morning. Tomorrow is the full-day interview session. After that, it's up to her to match us. In the meantime, I figured I'd help with the Harvest Charity Ball." She needed something to distract her from the sharp U-turn her life had taken.

Charles exhaled loudly and hastily pushed a stack of folders toward her. "I can't express how excited I am to hear you say that! These are for you. I'm not a party planner and hereby officially delegate all of this to you. Selene has already requested to take this on and—"

"Wait, what do you mean she requested to take this over?"

The anger in her tone caught Charles—and herself—off guard. "I've helped Eleanor plan this event since I started working for her. I could do it in my sleep. Also, it's *not her job*."

Aurelia had concocted and selected the themes for the last three years. Eleanor valued her ideas, letting her make most of the decisions on her own. She wouldn't let Selene erase that.

Unsure of how to respond to her outburst, Charles hesitated before continuing. "She came in after you left on Tuesday. Since no heir had been named, she offered to take over, saying, 'that's what Eleanor would have wanted.'"

"That's what Eleanor would have wanted my ass," she muttered to herself. The smothered laugh that came from Charles caused her face to heat. Apparently, she wasn't as quiet as she thought.

Awkwardly clearing her throat, Aurelia replied, "That won't be necessary. I can take it from here. Send any future calls on the matter directly to my cell phone."

"Consider it done," Charles said. A hint of a smile still lingered on his lips; his eyes crinkled with amusement.

Aurelia gathered the documents as fast as reasonably possible and walked out, her resolve firm and purposeful.

Charles held back a smile as she left.

CHAPTER 13

Levi

Levi's eyes were so dry he feared they might fall out of his head.

He spent the entire afternoon completing the assessments Estrella had sent, not wanting to waste any time. The moment he got home, he locked himself in his office, booted up his laptop, and dove in. The tests measured everything from behavior and communication to conflict resolution.

Thankfully, Neuronix's *TNV Assist* app made the process three times faster. He often wished he'd had it in college, especially during those horrendous timed exams. Most professors were accepting, but a few weren't.

"The real world isn't going to accommodate you."

Levi remembered one particularly smug professor who had said that to him. Incensed, he had fired back with, *"You couldn't hack it as a developer in the real world, so now you're here tormenting students with this half-assed attempt at teaching."* That retort sent him straight to the Dean's office, threatening to go public if students didn't get the accommodations they deserved. After that, class was...different.

That experience fueled the birth of Neuronix. *TNV Assist* was the first tool he, Owen, and Isaac created, and it remained one of their most successful products. Today, it proved its worth again.

Rubbing his eyes, Levi tried to summon moisture. The results had been eye-opening. Unsurprisingly, his strengths lay in his directness and executive mindset, but the rest of the report challenged his self-image. He wasn't as spontaneous or adventurous as he thought. It became glaringly obvious as this pattern consistently emerged across multiple assessments.

At first, it mildly offended him until he tried to remember the last time he *was* spontaneous. The answer was a slap in the face when he realized it was when

Neuronix went public. To commemorate the success (and because Owen had a bet going with Isaac that Levi wouldn't do it), he had gotten a tattoo.

Spanning his upper back was a powerful tree rising from a mass of tangled, chaotic roots that twisted and coiled beneath the surface. They supported a strong, upright trunk with branches stretched wide across his shoulders. Each independent limb was etched into his skin with solid and purposeful scrolled lines.

His mouth dipped into a grim line as he finally understood what his friends had been telling him for months: he stopped enjoying life when Neuronix went public.

The tradeoff for fame and fortune was constant scrutiny. Spontaneity became a liability. The irony of his impulsive lie about a fiancée at the last Board meeting wasn't lost on him.

With a groan, Levi slumped in his seat, defeated. This level of self-reflection was draining. He just hoped it wasn't all for nothing.

"Why did you turn it off! I was in the middle of watching that!" Owen bellowed from inside Isaac and Grace's home.

Levi had arrived for dinner as promised and walked straight into chaos.

"Because it's nonsense and no one wants to watch it except for you!" Isaac shot back heatedly.

The Nolans lived in a sprawling ranch within a gated community set high on a cliff overlooking one of the largest lagoons. It had an open concept kitchen, dining, and living area adorned with modern minimalist décor. The high ceilings, huge floor-to-ceiling windows, and light wooden floors made the space feel fresh and inviting.

The dining table was set, the scent of lasagna filled the air, and Grace leaned against the kitchen island, wine in hand. Ivy sat on the other side of the island, eyes gleaming and trained on the other two in the living area.

Levi joined them, and Grace wordlessly passed him a cold beer.

"What's going—"

"Shhh!" Ivy whispered. "The main fight is about to start, and we want to see this play out."

"I purposely put on a POLmArK TV Romance to see what would happen," Grace added with a smirk.

"You didn't even give *Espressing Our Love* a chance!" Owen snapped, pointing an accusatory finger at Isaac.

"Because it's insanely idiotic, Owen! A coffee bean roaster? Fine. But what the hell is an espresso mustache barber?" Isaac roared as he threw his arms up in exasperation.

Grace and Ivy nearly spit out their wine. Levi settled on a stool at the island as well, already amused by their antics.

Owen scoffed. "It's exactly what it sounds like. There's a market for espresso foam mustaches. This barber satisfies that clientele and is very niche." He scrutinized Isaac, his voice dripping with disdain. "I think the real question is, why do you hate love?"

"I don't hate love…I hate these ridiculous movies with impossible jobs! They aren't even trying to be relatable!"

"You can't relate to people who spend money on niche services, which makes you biased against them. This is discrimination, and I, for one, am *appalled*."

Isaac looked at the ceiling, shaking his head in disbelief. "I wish I could say this is the stupidest argument we've ever had, but that would be a lie."

Owen grinned. "This wasn't an argument. I very clearly pointed out flaws in your logic."

Isaac prepared to retaliate, but the oven timer beeped.

As Grace turned to retrieve the lasagna, Owen leapt over the couch, yelling, "Food!" only to trip over the rug and crash to the floor like a felled redwood.

"I feel like I should feel bad for you…But I don't," Levi drawled. He took another swig of his beer as he stood from the stool.

"Go on without me," he groaned dramatically. "Have an extra piece of lasagna in my memory!"

Isaac stepped over him without pause. Grace set the dish on the table as everyone took their seats, ignoring Owen's theatrical display on the floor.

Levi had missed nights like this. He couldn't remember the last time he made space for friends. He had systematically allowed work and social obligations to take priority. That needed to change straightaway.

"Sounds like you had a hell of a day," Ivy said through a mouthful of lasagna after he finished recounting the consultation and assessments.

Owen eyeballed her with exaggerated disgust. "Excuse me, but Grace didn't pour her heart and soul into this decadent meal for you to let it slosh around your half-opened mouth while you talked."

Levi silently agreed with Owen. Grace was an incredible cook, and Levi appreciated that she had made his favorite dish without being asked.

Ivy glared at Owen, not bothering to hide the unbridled contempt in her eyes. He sipped his beer completely unbothered.

"As I was saying," Ivy repeated to Levi, eyes still locked on Owen, "sounds like you had a hell of a day."

Grace frowned. "Just so I'm clear...you're upset because you aren't as fun and spontaneous as you thought you were?"

"When you say it like that, it makes me sound whiny."

"Now you're upset because you found out you're whiny too," Owen added with a sad head shake. "We've been planning an intervention about it, but now seems like a good time to do it."

"You're not boring, Levi...under the right circumstances anyway," Isaac offered. "Remember that one summer in college, working for that landscaper, when we had to haul off that client's busted washing machine?"

"I remember Levi saying, 'let's push it off a cliff,' and me immediately agreeing," Owen laughed. "That was when I realized he was a natural leader."

"I'm not the one who set that poor landscaper's truck on fire," Levi countered, tossing a dinner roll at Owen's face.

"How did *that* happen?" Grace asked as Ivy's eyes widened.

"That moron was doing burnouts in the truck," Levi said, nodding at Owen. "He revved it in neutral, slammed it into drive, and the whole thing exploded. We barely made it out before it caught fire."

"I still have my half-melted driver's license from the wreckage," Owen wheezed, doubled over with laughter.

Levi cast a perturbed glance at Isaac. "And what do you mean by 'under the right circumstances'?"

Isaac shrugged. "You can be spontaneous and adventurous when you let yourself live a little."

Levi stiffened.

"That's why we keep saying you're working too much," Grace added quietly. "It's been months since we've all sat like this...together."

Silence fell. Levi nursed his beer, gaze fixed on the basket of dinner rolls. Ivy swirled her wine, staring at the wall. Owen kept eating, glancing at Grace's plate with interest.

Isaac gently rested a comforting hand on Levi's shoulder. "I'm saying it because we miss you, that's all. Now, tell us more about this potential match."

The tension eased a fraction.

"There isn't much to share. She said someone signed up at the same time I did, and she thinks we're a possible match. But she won't know until we've both finished the process."

Grace's forehead knitted in confusion. "Then how does she know if you're compatible?"

Levi didn't get the chance to answer.

"I think she's a witch, but a chaotic good one," Owen interjected matter-of-factly. "With the way you described those eyes? She without a doubt has a mystical gift. This is the plot of *404: Down for Love*—a witch café owner pairs a network admin and vintage bassoon restoration specialist together."

"Get out," Isaac barked, pointing to the door without looking up from his plate. Laughter erupted around the table.

"I will do no such thing," Owen huffed. "Also, as the officiant of Levi's future wedding, I need details to prepare for such an ostentatious event."

Levi groaned. "We don't need your services. She helps plan the wedding based on both our preferences. It can be as big or as small as we want. But we're getting ahead of ourselves."

"How? You're not going to let us help?" Ivy challenged.

Levi burst out laughing at the absurdity of the debate. "You're all forgetting one very important detail."

They waited.

"I'm going to have to ask my wife first."

CHAPTER 14

Levi

For the first time in ages, Levi had a restful night's sleep, thanks in large part to dinner with friends and finally taking Ivy's advice to take the rest of the week off. There was no way he could have focused on the matchmaking process and work at the same time.

Even so, nothing could have prepared him for how emotionally intense the in-depth interview with Estrella would be. At least her cozy home was a comforting contrast to the cold boardrooms he was used to.

When he arrived, she handed him a cup of hazelnut coffee. His favorite, of course. "Thank you," Levi muttered, sipping it as the warmth soothed his tension.

Estrella settled across from him in the sitting room, notebook on her lap. "Let's begin with something straightforward, Levi. What are your non-negotiables in a relationship?"

Startled by her directness, Levi almost spat out his coffee. Recovering quickly, he sputtered, "Loyalty. Honesty. I need to trust that the person I'm with values commitment. I've been burned before—more times than I'm comfortable confessing. I can't go through that again."

"That's understandable. Trust is foundational. What about building a family? Do you see that in your future?"

He hesitated. The idea felt distant but still stirred something in him. "I've always imagined having kids one day. But I need to trust that the person I'm with truly wants that—and will be a parent, not delegate it to others."

Estrella's gaze softened. "Relationships thrive when both partners are honest about their fears and hopes. Now, tell me something personal—something you find joy in."

Levi cracked a smile. "Cooking. I'm not great at it, but it's relaxing. It's methodical, but you can still experiment. I'd like to cook for someone—maybe a family, someday."

"Ah, yes. The journey is as important as the destination. How do you prefer to give and receive love?"

Levi frowned, unnerved by the line of questioning. He'd never said *I love you* to anyone besides his friends and maybe his parents as a kid. It was a humbling revelation.

"I like helping others—mainly showing love through actions. But I also like doing things, spending time together. I enjoy buying gifts too, but not when it's expected. That ruined every relationship I've had. They cared more about the gifts than me."

He failed to keep the bitterness from lacing his response. The pressure of being valued for his money alone had always weighed on him.

"As for receiving love...I don't really know. I've never really experienced it, I guess. Physical touch is great. But maybe someone who genuinely asks about my day and cares about the answer? This is a tough question."

Estrella laughed. "My dear Levi, this is only the beginning of the tough questions I've lined up for today. We are only getting deeper from this point forward."

She hadn't been kidding.

Hours passed as Levi confronted answers to questions he had long avoided. The soft afternoon light filtered through her curtains as he peeled back layers of himself he had not realized existed. Emotionally and physically drained but somehow lighter, he left her home a different man.

An ember of hope began to burn within him. Maybe even excitement for what came next.

CHAPTER 15

Aurelia

Aurelia sat in Estrella's softly lit kitchen, the scent of chamomile tea doing nothing to calm her down. She had buried herself in work since yesterday's meeting with Charles, hoping to focus on planning the Harvest Charity Ball, but Selene's attempt to take it over still gnawed at her.

Now, she found herself frowning at Estrella's farmhouse table, scattered with handouts and a list titled *Conversation Starters*. It had question topics like deal breakers, future children, values...each one feeling heavier than the paper they were printed on. Dreams she once considered impossible scribbled across wisps of paper.

Estrella's voice cut through the fog. "Take your time, Aurelia. There's no rush to answer."

But there *was* a rush.

The pressure in her chest grew with every suffocating question. Echoes of her past relationship surfaced with images of bruises, cruel words, and long sleeves in summer. How could she talk about what she wanted in a partner when she barely knew who she was anymore? How did she allow herself to be subjected to such abuse?

She rubbed her arms unconsciously, her mind spiraling. Would this man be kind? Patient? Capable of loving her? Even the question about physical attraction stumped her. She didn't know what she genuinely liked, only what didn't hurt and would get a positive reaction.

Sensing her struggle, Estrella offered gently, "Sometimes, the hardest part is permitting yourself to want things. Start small. What makes you feel safe? What brings you joy?"

Aurelia gave a small nod, throat tight.

All simple questions, and yet she had no answers.

Estrella shifted gears, sensitive to her inner turmoil. "How do you prefer to give and receive love?"

She paused, then answered honestly. "I have no issues with physical intimacy. It's the only time I feel like I have someone's full attention. When they initiate contact, it makes me feel desired. I've never been successful showing love in any other way...at least not enough to make it last."

Cringing at her own words, she added silently—*because I'm needy and desperate.*

Estrella leaned forward, voice calm but firm. "Don't let your past experiences control your future. They must not define you."

Aurelia blinked back tears and sank into her chair a bit further.

"Let's talk about your values. What matters to you in a partner?"

This question was easy to answer. "Kindness. Respect. Patience. I need to know that...that I'm safe. That disagreements won't turn into...something worse."

"Those are important values." Estrella had a knack for being reassuring when Aurelia needed her to be. "And you're brave for acknowledging them. Now, tell me something lighter. What's a small joy you'd want to share with someone?"

Aurelia laughed quietly. "I love to bake. When I'm stressed, I make things like macarons. I want someone who can laugh with me when the kitchen's a mess but will take a chance to try something new."

"Cooking and baking. It seems you're not the only one who enjoys the kitchen." Estrella murmured to herself.

Aurelia looked up, curious.

"The macarons were delicious," Estrella smiled. "I wouldn't be opposed to taking some off your hands next time."

"Duly noted," Aurelia grinned. Then, more softly, "Someone who wants children...who would be present for them, play with them..."

...and love them the way mine never loved me.

She didn't say it aloud, but Estrella seemed to understand.

"...and can laugh with me when our kids help turn the kitchen into a disaster. They *must* be there for those moments."

Estrella's eyes sparkled. "That's a beautiful image. A partner should share in those moments." She reached out and gently squeezed Aurelia's hand encouragingly. "You're doing great. Understanding yourself is the hardest and most important part of this process. You're not alone."

Aurelia exhaled slowly, comforted by her words, determined to push forward.

By the time she left, she owed Estrella at least two boxes of replacement tissues. The process had been excruciating as it pulled at wounds never given the chance to heal. Yet, Aurelia walked away with a clearer sense of herself: her strength, resilience, and even the unhealthy ways she bent to please others.

Later, as she sat on the dock with her feet swirling in the lagoon's warm waters, she found herself daydreaming about a future, a family, a partner who could see and accept her as she was...

Unaware that her match was closer than either of them realized.

CHAPTER 16

Aurelia

Aurelia stared at the thick envelope Estrella had couriered to her home that morning. She had glanced at it a dozen times throughout the day but couldn't bring herself to open it.

Until now.

Its contents were so much more than pieces of paper; it was her future. Once opened, there would be no going back. A stack of bricks would have weighed her down less than what was inside: the comprehensive profile of her match and a consent form to move forward with the wedding.

After one last moment of procrastination, she closed her eyes and tore it open. She peeked with one eye and pulled out the folder, her hands unsteady.

Baby steps.

She settled onto the couch in her living area and began to read. Estrella had also emailed a copy that she had actively avoided. Skimming through the profile, Aurelia noted striking similarities between them, like how they were both only children with no surviving family, both passionate about helping others and volunteering. It was hard not to be intrigued.

Then her eyes landed on one line: *Enjoys heavy and death metal music, often attends live concerts.*

Aurelia froze, nose wrinkling in disapproval. Death metal was unbearably loud, chaotic, and full of screeching that tried to pass as singing. The complete opposite of her upbeat playlists. "It's not a deal-breaker," she muttered unconvincingly.

As she continued reading, other details jumped out from the page that softened her skepticism. He was exceptionally loyal to friends, loved cooking, had a steady sense of responsibility, and was financially stable.

She smiled despite her worries. *She could work with this.*

With a deep breath and a prayer to all the gods in the universe for strength, she picked up her phone and sent a text message to Estrella.

Aurelia: *I've reviewed the file. Let's go ahead with this mystery man before I chicken out and change my mind.*

The next day, Aurelia sat in Eleanor's study, her signed copy of the prenuptial agreement resting on the desk. Charles had walked her through it thoroughly, addressing each clause and giving her time to ask questions. The names and final signatures would be added on the day of the wedding.

The inheritance clause brought relief, knowing she didn't have to explain everything yet. Though it could raise suspicions about her financial status from her future spouse, she may not be ready to answer either.

She only hoped this wasn't a huge mistake.

Later, as Aurelia drove home from work, Estrella called asking for wedding preferences. Her anxiety nearly drove her off the road.

"Aurelia, darling, I have several questions I need answered to narrow down your wedding preferences...starting with what kind of ceremony do you see for yourself?"

"Uh...what? I—I haven't really thought about it...*ever.*"

"Oh! Alright...No worries," Estrella said gently. "Let's start simple. Big or small?"

Am I seriously doing this right now?

"Small. Very small. Courthouse, even! Just...simple. Bare minimum. No big crowd." Her grip on the steering wheel could have cracked walnut shells. "Honestly, whatever you think is best for the other details is fine with me; I'm not very picky." Aurelia couldn't keep the panic from her voice.

Always in tune with her emotions, Estrella replied, "Understood. Leave the rest to me, darling. You focus on being ready to say *I do.*"

Aurelia shuddered in relief; glad she didn't have to think about marrying a stranger the rest of the drive home.

That relief lasted until she received a follow-up text that evening.

Estrella: *Your wedding is scheduled for Friday at 3:00 PM at the Joia City Courthouse. Please arrive by 2:30 PM. Further details will follow.*

Aurelia read it in stunned silence.

If she agreed, then in a few short days, she could be married.

Assuming she survived the tidal wave of panic crashing toward her.

CHAPTER 17

Levi

Levi leaned over his tablet, swiping the screen while studying the profile of his match. Everything about her was fascinating…her values, interests, and work history. He was searching for the little details; something useful to know if they chose to move forward.

Then he found one: her favorite color was turquoise.

A grin stretched across his lips.

He was thinking about rings, wanting them to be perfect and something she would cherish for hopefully forever. Levi's exes had all expected large diamonds and hadn't been shy about sharing their expectations, even early on in their relationship.

He wanted something non-traditional. Especially after reading how she didn't like fancy or over-the-top jewelry. His smile broadened as he pictured the design in his mind.

But then he paused, eyes catching a neon yellow piece of paper.

A small handwritten note stuck to the file which said: *History of past trauma; sensitive to conflict. Avoidant under pressure. Proceed gently.*

Levi's stomach lurched. The trauma must have been significant to warrant a private note like this.

What did that mean for their relationship? Worry crept in, making him wonder if he could handle someone carrying these kinds of invisible scars.

Levi rubbed his eyes, exhaustion settling in. He was no stranger to pain. Betrayal had left him guarded, too. But as he kept reading, her resilience stood out, and her quiet strength. Whatever happened to her, she had endured.

Levi's eyes flicked back to the note. An odd wave of protectiveness surged through him. He had never felt that before. And not this fiercely.

While unfamiliar, it told him everything he needed to know.

Leaning back in his chair, he grabbed his phone and typed a text to Estrella.
Levi: *I'm in. I want to marry her.*

When Estrella replied to confirm her agreement, relief overwhelmed him. He hadn't realized how afraid of rejection he was until that message came through.

Now, marriage was real. Imminent.

And possibly happening in less than a week.

His lawyer, Mitchell Davis, spoke with her legal team that morning, moving quickly to finalize the prenup. Levi appreciated the efficiency wealth afforded him, but a piece of him was on the verge of screaming to *slow down*.

The only notable change to the agreement was the clear addition of a clause regarding any current and future inheritances, requiring them to stay separate. It piqued Levi's curiosity, but he didn't ask them to elaborate.

Everyone had their secrets.

In Mitchell's office that afternoon, Levi finally reviewed and signed the document before handing it over. "The terms are fair enough...can't ask for more than that."

For the rest of the day, his mind continued to wander to the potential wedding and what his soon-to-be wife had in store for him, until Estrella's text arrived.

Estrella: *Your wedding is scheduled for Friday at 3:00 PM at the Joia City Courthouse. Please arrive by 2:30 PM. Further details will follow.*

Levi almost pissed in his pants.

There was no turning back now.

CHAPTER 18

Estrella

Estrella sat quietly in her office, with a tired yet satisfied smile playing at the corners of her lips.

Estrella was the type of person who couldn't rest until the job was done, willing to forego necessities like sleep if it meant bringing two souls in desperate need of finding one another.

And Levi and Aurelia *desperately* needed each other.

Now, after two long days, the in-depth interviews were complete, and the assessments were finished. She had worked late into the night to ensure their profiles were compiled. Before her lay two detailed files—one for Aurelia Douro and the other for Levi Lockwood.

They were a match.

But she had known they would be. She knew long before they signed their service agreements. Long before they completed any of the required work.

Because Estrella had a secret gift, one that allowed her to weave the threads of life itself and bind two souls together...like she did for Levi and Aurelia.

With a practiced hand, Estrella slipped each file into its respective envelope, sealing the carefully curated insights inside.

It was time for them to see the truth she already knew.

With those two special packages delivered earlier that morning, Estrella wasn't surprised when her phone buzzed with a new message on two separate occasions that evening. Though she recognized what they were for before she read them, she couldn't help but feel satisfied with the outcome anyway.

She didn't like to be overly arrogant, however, and still unlocked her phone to confirm what she already suspected.

Levi: *I'm in. I want to marry her.*

Aurelia: *I've reviewed the file. Let's go ahead with this mystery man before I chicken out and change my mind.*

Estrella smiled. *Perfect.*

Estrella's next task was to coordinate the wedding.

She contacted both Levi and Aurelia separately to discuss the details.

Levi's response was straightforward. "Whatever my future wife wants is fine with me. I prefer something small and as soon as possible. No need for a spectacle, but will happily do whatever she would like."

Aurelia, on the other hand, was equally decisive...or rather more frightened at the idea of deciding anything, opting for it to be as small and simple as possible. Estrella assured her that she would handle the rest.

She clasped her hands together, pleased. Simplicity and full control would make this wedding much easier...for everyone involved.

Within an hour, she sent out two identical, but separate messages.

Estrella: *Your wedding is scheduled for Friday at 3:00 PM at the Joia City Courthouse. Please arrive by 2:30 PM. Further details will follow.*

The date was set.

Their paths were sealed.

And so began the countdown to a marriage born of chance, timing, and a matchmaker's promise.

CHAPTER 19

Aurelia

Aurelia made her way up the black rock steps of the Joia City Judicial Complex, her heels clicking with purpose. She wasn't late yet, but cutting it close after spending most of the morning getting ready.

Her hair fell in soft waves over a long-sleeve lace ivory top paired with a form-fitting nude pencil skirt and matching stilettos. Her face was glowing from the makeup tutorial she mastered thanks to Brandi.

She *really* hoped she wasn't late.

Hurrying through the historic building, barely a glance was spared at the grand woodwork, tall ceilings, and sunlit windows as she navigated the halls. Finally, the large, ornately carved wooden doors of their assigned courtroom loomed imposingly before her.

The sound of a deep, silky voice drifting through the gap in the doors stopped her in her tracks. "I hope she gets here soon so we can get this over with. There's a situation unfolding that needs to be addressed immediately. I scheduled a meeting for this afternoon."

She blinked rapidly, paralyzed outside the doorway from what she heard.

Her pulse spiked as rage bubbled to the surface as the words registered.

It appeared their wedding was nothing more than an item to cross off on his—*her husband's*—to-do list.

She briefly considered turning on her heels and leaving.

No. I can stand up for myself.

After squaring her shoulders and assembling every ounce of defiance possible, she took a calming breath and shoved the doors open with determination.

She was ready for her first fight with her unsuspecting future husband.

CHAPTER 20

Levi

Levi was speechless.

The moment the courtroom doors swung open, and this firestorm of a woman blazed through, everything else faded. Thoughts? Gone. Breathing? Optional.

She was breathtaking.

Her flawless olive-toned skin radiated beneath thick, chestnut-brown waves threaded with iridescent rainbow streaks that shimmered as she moved.

But it was her eyes that held him hostage. Deep brown, almond-shaped, ringed in smoky gold and framed by bold brows. She was stunning, and intense, and her eyes…promised violence as she glared at him.

Her lips, full and glossed, curled in a deadly smile as she closed the distance between them, her cream lace top and nude pencil skirt hugging every curve. Her heels clacked with intent, each step a declaration: *I heard you, asshole.*

Levi didn't move. Couldn't move. His only instinct was to reach for her, but with the storm brewing in her eyes, he didn't dare.

She stopped before him, tilted her head almost imperceptibly, and delivered her opening shot.

"Let's get this show on the road so my betrothed can get to his extremely important meeting."

Shit.

Yeah. She definitely heard him. Or at least the worst possible part. Standing at a solid four inches shorter than him in those heels, and yet she was still a force to be reckoned with if the murderous intent in her eyes was any indication.

Fantastic first impression. He couldn't help but cringe a little.

Behind him, Owen coughed, trying to stifle a very obvious laugh. "Great! Everyone is here and accounted for!" Breaking the tension, he motioned to Estrella.

"You both have come quite a long way in a short amount of time, leading up to this moment. Aurelia Douro and Levi Lockwood, your journey begins now as you take this leap together into marriage."

Her name is Aurelia, Levi repeated in his head. *Aurelia Douro.* Beautiful. Fiery. Definitely kind of terrifying.

Estrella continued, "I will give you both a few minutes with your attorneys to sign the appropriate contracts as well as the marriage certificate before we begin the ceremony." Right on cue, Charles and Mitchell appeared from behind her, each holding a copy of the final prenuptial agreement, already tabbed with neon sticky notes.

"This is your last chance to back out of the wedding before it is too late," Estrella murmured.

Levi regarded Aurelia, silently pleading. "I have no intentions of backing out," he said firmly.

Aurelia scowled up at him. "I wouldn't be here if I was just going to walk away."

Not the heartfelt reply he hoped for, though she wasn't leaving after seeing him. That was enough...for now.

Estrella smiled faintly and laid the marriage certificate before them and next to the prenups. "You can sign this now, but it won't be valid until the ceremony takes place and two witnesses sign."

Charles explained, "These are the same documents you previously reviewed and signed. If you could each sign your spouse's copy, we'll be able to finalize everything."

Aurelia didn't speak, although her anger had yet to dissipate. She grabbed the pen Charles offered her and began signing each page with just a tad of aggression.

Levi followed suit, aware of the weight of every eye in the room. His shirt collar suddenly felt extremely tight and uncomfortable...much like this entire situation.

Once all necessary signatures were collected, the attorneys conferred, then nodded. "We're good," Charles said. "You'll each get a copy later today."

At that, Estrella beamed. "Time to get married."

Levi swallowed hard as he thought, *Please don't let me screw this up.*

CHAPTER 21

Aurelia

Aurelia scrutinized the courtroom as Estrella walked them through the final steps of the prenup and marriage certificate. For something so procedural, the room was surprisingly beautiful and intimate, precisely as she had requested.

Bouquets of ivory and white flowers were arranged in clusters throughout the room, softening the air with their delicate fragrance. It almost made her forget why she was so annoyed walking in.

Almost.

The guest list was sparse, with herself, Levi, both attorneys, Estrella, and she assumed, his friend officiating, and a court clerk. That's it. Just enough people to make it real. She couldn't tell anyone about the mandatory wedding clause or of the inheritance itself, but Aurelia still wished Selene could have been there with her anyway. Seeing someone she knew and trusted would have made it feel less stifling and clinical.

She snuck a glance at Levi and her scowl deepened.

Even she had to begrudgingly admit that he was gorgeous.

Dressed in a tailored navy suit and ivory shirt, his paisley tie in deep greens and blues brought everything together. A single white boutonniere sat on his lapel, right over the broad chest that filled his jacket far too well for her peace of mind.

He stood almost half a foot taller than her despite wearing heels. Wavy, expertly styled mahogany hair framed his striking face. But it was his eyes—vivid green and startlingly clear—that caught her attention the second she entered the room. They focused on her with such intensity, that she almost flinched, not used to someone seeing past her defenses.

His chiseled jawline, high cheekbones, and confident posture made him look both refined and rugged. *Damn it*, she thought. *At least Estrella got one thing right.*

Aurelia realized she was staring...and that Levi had noticed.

He rotated fully toward her then, catching her gaze with a small, unreadable smile. Embarrassment flared across her face as her cheeks warmed. She quickly looked away, searching for some kind of distraction...or maybe a hole to crawl into.

As if on cue, Estrella interrupted the moment by handing her a beautiful bridal bouquet.

Aurelia paused. Her arms had been crossed over her chest in defense for most of the ceremony prep. But slowly, she uncrossed them and took the bouquet, the weight of it bringing her back to reality.

Estrella quietly stepped aside and lifted her camera.

With nothing left to delay the ceremony, Aurelia looked up at Levi. The playfulness in his smile had faded. In its place, there was something quieter, uncertain, even. Vulnerable.

He was as nervous as she was.

The realization settled her. She inhaled deeply, closing her eyes as she slowly let it out. When she opened them again, her gaze found his.

Holding it, she said calmly, despite her racing heart, "Let's get this over with."

Owen's expression screamed, *You are so screwed*, when Levi finally glanced his way. He was enjoying this *way* too much.

And yes, Levi was absolutely screwed.

The ceremony was set before a simple wooden bench surrounded by extravagant white and cream floral arrangements. Through the windows behind it, the blue sky stretched above lush hills and a distant lagoon.

Owen stood tall and smug, waiting for them to step forward. When they did, he immediately turned his full attention to Aurelia and extended his hand with an infuriating feline smirk.

She hesitated before taking it.

Instead of shaking, he kissed the back of her hand and said, "It's a pleasure to finally meet you. I'm Owen Voss, Levi's favorite best friend, and, unfortunately for him, your officiant. I can't wait to tell you all his embarrassing secrets. We're going to be besties."

Aurelia huffed an unexpected laugh. Behind them, Levi glared at Owen.

"This is *exactly* why I said it was a bad idea for you to be here," Levi muttered.

"I'm creating core memories," Owen replied, deadpan, and gestured for them to face each other. With a flourish, he placed Aurelia's hand into Levi's, and Levi was momentarily startled by the warmth of her touch that rushed through him.

So much so that he didn't realize Estrella had snapped a photo before taking Aurelia's bouquet. He shook off the strange sense of awareness and tried to focus on the ceremony, only to be distracted by Aurelia's wide eyes as she stared at their joined hands.

Once they were ready, Owen began.

"We gather here today to witness the union of Levi Lockwood and Aurelia Douro. A marriage built on science, a million questionnaires, and..." he slid a side glance at Aurelia, "...hopefully, a very thorough background check."

Her brows shot up.

Levi considered smothering Owen with one of the floral arrangements then and there, witnesses be damned.

"May your foundation be friendship, trust, love, frequent laughter...and an abundance of babies."

Jaw clenched, Levi stared ahead, too stressed out by his friend to make eye contact with her.

"The promises you make today are not just ceremonial but a lasting and *very* legally binding agreement. Marriage is built on commitment, mutual support, and," Owen added with a wink, "the frequent and thorough ravishing of one another."

Aurelia choked on a breath.

Levi was another step closer to murdering him in broad daylight.

He didn't need to look at her to feel the heat of embarrassment radiating from her entire being. But when he finally risked a peek, her cheeks were crimson, and her wide eyes filled with stunned disbelief.

"Levi Lockwood," Owen pressed on, "do you take the stunning, vivacious Aurelia Douro to be your wife, to treat her with respect, worship the ground she walks on, deliver said ravishing promptly, and commit to building a life together?"

Owen looked expectantly at Levi with absolutely zero remorse, eyes dancing.

Despite it all, Levi couldn't help himself, and with a lopsided smile, said, "Yes, I do...particularly the ravishing."

Why the hell did I say that?

Aurelia's blush deepened. Her eyes narrowed...and not in a good way.

"And you, Aurelia Douro, do you take the brooding, virile Levi Lockwood to be your husband, to treat him with respect, keep him in check when he gets surly, demand the ravishing you are owed, and build a marriage that grows with time?"

Levi held his breath, praying she didn't change her mind.

"Yes, I do," she said softly, nervous but steady.

Relief crashed over him.

"Rings," Owen declared cheerfully.

Levi pulled the rings he commissioned from his pocket. In his extended palm lay a turquoise cabochon engagement ring encircled with fire diamond accents and wrapped in golden vines, paired with a wedding band echoing the design. While nontraditional, they were delicate, detailed, earthy, and in retrospect...exactly her.

Owen guided them through the vows. Levi slid the rings onto her finger, repeating, "I give you these rings as a symbol of my commitment and devotion, as we join our lives together today, tomorrow, and however many days Fate gives us beyond that."

Aurelia inhaled sharply, wordlessly staring at her hand.

Estrella passed her Levi's ring. His band was broader but shared the same organic, vine-like style with turquoise and diamond accents. A perfect match.

Aurelia's hands trembled as she unenthusiastically repeated her vows and slid the band onto his finger. He couldn't blame her; this entire experience was the opposite of how he expected to feel on the day of his wedding.

For a long moment, they stood in silence, looking at one another apprehensively.

Owen naturally broke the spell. "Marriage is more than legalities. It's a promise to show up for one another. On the best days, the worst days, and the utterly chaotic days. May you discover the missing pieces of yourselves in each other. And hopefully, populate the world with an entire brood of children."

Oh, for shit's sake...

Levi sighed loudly and shot him a pointed glare. Owen really couldn't stop and be normal for once. Judging by the cheeky grin he threw back at Levi, Owen didn't care either.

"By the power vested in me by the Joia City Clerk's Office, who graciously approved my online officiant application only this morning," he blew a kiss in the court clerk's direction, "I now pronounce you husband and wife. You may now share your first public kiss as a couple."

Owen gleefully pulled out his phone.

All the oxygen was sucked from his lungs. Of all the moments Levi had mentally rehearsed, this wasn't one of them.

He turned toward Aurelia...right when panic began to bloom across her face.

CHAPTER 22

Aurelia

The ceremony happened so fast, and she was still reeling from Owen's ridiculous antics, the bizarre vows, and the recording camera. She scarcely had time to process any of it before it was over.

And then, without warning, Levi's face was right in front of hers, closing the distance for a kiss. Panic flared.

This was a mistake.

She wasn't ready.

Unfortunately, her instincts kicked in.

Just as Levi's breath brushed her lips, she twisted her head to the side at the last second...and right into the path of Owen's phone.

He recorded the whole thing.

Owen let out a victorious cackle as he captured Levi's lips grazing her cheek, and the exact moment Levi realized what had happened.

Levi stepped back abruptly, his posture stiff, his gaze fixed somewhere, *anywhere*, that wasn't her. A red flush crept up his neck, spreading across his cheeks as his jaw ticked.

No one else seemed to notice his reaction. But she did.

And it was her fault.

Her breathing grew shallow, emotions beginning to overwhelm her senses. She took a slow step backward, trying to steady herself.

Owen had already moved in, pulling Levi into a celebratory bear hug, laughing loudly.

She took another step back.

The ceremony had become a spectacle—exactly what she had asked *not* to happen. Owen treated the vows like a colossal joke. And she...she had no idea how to respond, caught off guard and put on display.

Aurelia's chest tightened painfully. The room began to close in as the full force of humiliation pressed down on her.

Another step. The entryway loomed closer now.

Then Levi's voice echoed in her head, "*I hope she gets here soon so we can get this over with.*"

Not even enough time was cleared up on his calendar for their wedding.

Her gut twisted.

This wasn't a celebration.

She reached the doors as her vision blurred with unshed tears. No one noticed her retreat.

No one noticed her at all.

She cracked open one of the courtroom doors and slipped through, a silent sob breaking free from her lips. Another followed as she clutched her bouquet to her chest.

With trembling hands, she dropped her bouquet, slipped off her heels, one in each hand, and bolted down the corridor.

Sunlight exploded across her face as she burst through the main entrance, the summer heat searing the soles of her feet against the stone steps.

She didn't stop.

She wouldn't stop.

Her car was in sight. So close.

But just as she reached it, a pair of strong arms, clothed in navy, wrapped around her, halting her flight.

CHAPTER 23

Levi

Levi should have known she wouldn't be ready to kiss a stranger.

He was a fool who hadn't planned that far ahead. So, when she turned her head at the last second, it shouldn't have surprised him.

Shouldn't have bothered him.

But it did. More than he wanted to admit.

The sting of embarrassment hit instantly, the feeling so strong Levi couldn't even meet her eyes. Being the coward that he was, he looked away and instead made the mistake of looking at Owen. His anger immediately flared.

Owen, of course, was beaming. He had turned Levi's wedding day into a clown show. The intensity of Levi's fury could have incinerated the entire city.

"This was phenomenal! You're going to look back on this day when you're both old and wrinkly and laugh." Owen spat out, clapping him on the back. "I managed to get that amazing kiss on video, already sent it to the group chat. Instant classic!"

Levi just stared. Owen's grin faltered under the weight of Levi's silence.

"We'll talk about this later," Levi seethed through clenched teeth.

He spun around, expecting Aurelia to be right behind him.

Except she wasn't.

The pit in his stomach formed fast. He scanned the room, his anger shifting into worry when he didn't see her. The doors...one of them hung slightly open—wide enough for someone to slip through unnoticed.

"Shit," Owen muttered.

"You stay here," Levi barked, already moving. "You've done enough."

As the situation escalated between Levi and Owen, everyone else went silent.

He bolted through the door, skidding slightly on the tile. He nearly tripped over her abandoned bouquet before catching his balance and taking off down the corridor.

At the far end, he caught a glimpse of her crossing the threshold of the front entrance. Without delay, he chased after her, his long, powerful legs quickly making up for lost time.

Levi expertly dodged people loitering in the corridor as he sprinted, fueled by the adrenaline surging through him. When he surged through the courthouse doors, he spotted her—barefoot, heels in hand, hair flying in the wind—racing across the hot stone steps toward a white sedan.

Taking the stairs two at a time, he caught up to her as she reached her car. Acting on instinct, he reached out and wrapped his arms around her middle.

She yelped in terror, thrashing violently.

Levi cursed and let go, instantly backing off with his hands raised. "Aurelia—it's Levi," he said, voice thick with regret. "I'm sorry. I didn't mean to scare you."

But it was too late. Her breaths were shallow and fast, her body frozen in place. A panic attack. He recognized the signs straightaway.

He stayed a short distance away, crouching slightly to her eye level but not touching her. "You're safe. I swear, you're safe," he said softly. "I won't touch you again unless you ask me to."

For a few long moments, neither of them moved. Then, finally, her knees gave out and she sagged against the car.

Carefully, he stepped forward, slowly and deliberately. He didn't want to scare her any more than he already had. "Can I help you up?" he asked with uncertainty.

She didn't respond with words, but she didn't flinch when he reached out again, this time gently guiding her to a nearby alcove, out of view, in the shade.

He turned to face her but didn't touch her again. Instead, he stood still, silently opening his arms in an unspoken offer. She didn't move at first, the initial rejection cutting and surprisingly sharp.

Then, after a long breath, she stepped forward, hesitant but willing, allowing herself to fold into him.

Only then did he wrap his arms around her, gently pulling her in. He lowered his chin until it rested lightly atop her head, holding her without pressure, only presence.

"I'm sorry this wasn't the wedding you deserved," he murmured, voice low and steady. "But before we do or say anything else...can we at least *try* to talk to each other when we're upset instead of running? A runaway bride was not on my bingo card today."

At last, she went still, her arms gradually wrapping around his back. The hug she gave him was tentative, but it was still *something*.

Encouraged, he added, "I think we got off on the wrong foot. I'd like the chance to explain what I said earlier. I think you overheard something out of context."

He inhaled deeply, unintentionally catching the delicate blend of freesia, jasmine, and a hint of something sweet and juicy—her essence, draping around him like a memory.

"And Owen..." He let out a quiet growl. "He's one of my best friends. He's also a dumbass. A kind, loyal dumbass."

She snorted softly against his chest, relaxing against him by a degree.

They stood like that for a while. Two strangers who'd just gotten married, and are now trying to reset after the most chaotic hour of their lives.

Finally, Aurelia looked up. Her makeup was mostly intact, except where the tracks of her tears had stained her cheeks.

The sight of it tugged at something unknown within Levi.

"I don't think he meant to do that," she said, voice quiet. "I think he was trying to make things less awkward. He...didn't read the room well."

Levi bit back his disagreement but didn't argue. Instead, he kept gently rubbing small circles across her back, as she buried her face back in his chest.

"And yes," she continued haltingly, voice slightly muffled against him, "I'll try to talk things through next time. I can't promise I'll be great at it. But I *can* try."

Pulling her head back again, her gaze lingered on his chest, avoiding his face.

"Good enough for me." He smiled and hooked his finger gently under her chin, tilting her head up until her eyes met his.

"Temporary truce?" he offered sincerely. "Let's go grab an early dinner. I don't grovel well on an empty stomach."

Aurelia let out a soft laugh and stepped back, then quickly glanced down in mild horror.

"Where are my shoes?" she muttered, hastily spinning around.

Levi didn't waste any time joining her in the search. After a few minutes, they found both shoes surprisingly intact, flung halfway into the parking lot after he startled her. She slipped them on as he watched quietly, giving him the first real chance to take her in.

In the sunlight, her hair shimmered with wild, bright streaks of rainbow. His breath caught. He had never seen anything like it.

Then she looked up and smiled—really smiled—for the first time.
And that was it.
He was a goner.
Definitely, completely, utterly screwed.

CHAPTER 24

Aurelia

Aurelia sat in her car outside *Chez P'tit Chou-Fleur*, one of the most exclusive restaurants in Joia City, staring at her reflection in the visor mirror.

She winced. Puffy eyes stared back at her, the aftermath of her panic attack lingering on her skin. And Levi had seen it. Of course, he had.

So much for making a good first impression, she thought grimly.

As she reapplied mascara with the shaky grace of someone still recovering, her hand paused midair, mascara wand suspended.

She couldn't stop thinking about how amazing it felt when Levi held her in the parking lot.

Not awkward. Not forced. Just...safe.

It was a feeling so foreign she barely recognized it for what it was.

Still, it was too soon to make anything of it. She mentally folded the feeling up like a delicate blouse and tucked it into an imaginary suitcase to be unpacked later. She had been overwhelmed by emotions the entire day and didn't have the energy to address this. Not yet.

Satisfied with her appearance, she took a slow, steadying breath and stepped out of her car.

Levi parked behind her, now leaning against his silver sports car in wait, like a page out of a luxury magazine. Every detail about him, like his custom-tailored suit, the watch that likely cost more than her entire wardrobe, and the damn car, all oozed quiet wealth.

She glanced down at the ring on her left hand. Her newest accessory sparkled in the early evening sun. It was elegant and the design intentional.

Like everything about Levi.

That's when it struck her.

Estrella's file said he was "financially stable," a benign phrase that meant so much more. Between the rings, the car, and the restaurant where you needed a six-month waitlist or a surname with a crest to get a table...it was evident she hadn't even scratched the surface of who Levi Lockwood was.

And that realization twisted in her gut.

Because despite all the preparation, the disclosures, the vetting...she didn't *know* him. Not really.

This fact made her feel anything but safe.

Levi

Every ounce of Levi's willpower was channeled into keeping his hands to himself.

He didn't understand it...this relentless, inexplicable urge to touch her. To put an arm around her waist, to thread his fingers through hers...something. *Anything.*

Mid-stride, her eyes dropped to her hand, and a faint frown flickered across her face. That made his heart stutter.

He had put *so much* thought into those rings. Hours with his jeweler, reworking every detail. He wanted them to be perfect. To make her smile. And if they didn't, he would replace them in a heartbeat, over and over again, until he got it right. He didn't care about the price tag.

He wanted her to love them.

Levi hadn't expected to be *this* affected by a woman he just met. He never had to work this hard for attention. It was equally unnerving and exhilarating.

He focused on trying to appear relaxed by leaning casually against his sleek silver sports car. It was his first post-IPO indulgence, rarely used and plucked from storage just for today. Now, it felt...gauche. Arrogant, even.

Especially as he watched Aurelia's impassive gaze flick toward the car. He told Estrella from the beginning that he didn't want someone who gave a damn about his money. He wanted someone who saw *him.*

Nevertheless, he showed up today wrapped in symbols of wealth with the car, the suit, the rings, and the restaurant behind them.

The irony made him grimace and curse himself internally.

He had picked *Chez P'tit Chou-Fleur* because he knew the menu like the back of his hand. It was familiar, comforting. A selfish choice, in hindsight.

Levi's thoughts fell apart when she approached and stopped before him.

She was a *stunning* mix of elegance and edge, restraint and strength. And, by some cosmic twist of fate, she was now his wife.

My wife.

It struck him like a blow to the chest. Either the universe had gifted him something rare...or was teeing him up for a hell of a punchline to a cruel joke.

He sincerely hoped it was the former.

Straightening, Levi stepped away from the car and offered his arm with his best attempt at a flirtatious smile. "Our first meal together as Mr. and Mrs."

Aurelia quirked a brow, her face revealing nothing. "Hopefully, your friend Owen doesn't make an appearance."

He let out a low chuckle, grateful for the softness in her voice, and that she took his arm and didn't try to run away again.

CHAPTER 25

Aurelia

Aurelia had only heard stories about *Chez P'tit Chou-Fleur*, the kind of tabloid-glossy, invitation-only type of restaurant reserved for the rich and famous. Until today, she has never had a reason or the nerve to set foot inside.

Now, seated beside one of its expansive windows overlooking the lush emerald hills of Joia City, she had to admit the restaurant was beautiful. The rolling cliffs she loved so much framed the skyline, spilling elegance and grandeur into every corner of the veranda.

White and ivory flower arrangements, some with ornamental cabbage blooms, were tucked around the dining space. The warm light of chandeliers glittered off the fine China, polished silverware, and sparkling crystal, casting a golden hue over everything.

It was perfect.

And she hated it.

She hated how money whispered from every corner. How the atmosphere was engineered to feel airy and intimate yet somehow left her feeling stifled. It screamed, *You don't belong here*, if you didn't flaunt your financial portfolio like a designer label.

The way other diners assessed her as they walked through only confirmed it.

They hadn't even reached their table before she had clocked the subtle double-takes, the quiet once-overs, the polite nods sent Levi's way. Nods that stopped short of acknowledging her altogether. It was clear Levi was a frequent patron here.

Once seated, she allowed her gaze to settle on Levi, who looked downright devastating in the golden light.

She wasn't about to let him know that, though.

Some weaknesses were meant to stay hidden, especially when life had taught her how easily they could be weaponized.

After their server had taken their drink order and provided menus, they sat in awkward silence, unsure of what to say next. She didn't even glance at her menu.

"So," she said, not so subtly breaking the tension, "what exactly did I *misinterpret* earlier when I heard you say you hoped I got there soon so you could 'get this over with'?"

If Levi was surprised, he didn't show it. Calmly, he pulled out his phone, tapped through it, then turned the screen toward her.

The message from a contact labeled as "Ivy" read: *"I hope she gets here soon so we can get this over with. There is a situation unfolding that needs to be addressed immediately. I scheduled a meeting for this afternoon."*

Time stamp: 12:30 PM. Before she had even arrived.

Aurelia stared at the screen, feeling the first prickle of regret.

"Who's Ivy?" she squeaked, trying very hard not to let her voice betray her embarrassment.

No longer cool and collected, Levi hesitated before explaining. "My assistant and Chief Operations Officer. I'm the CEO of a large corporation. If you search my name online, it'll all come up. Along with some other stuff that probably deserves a separate conversation," he added with a sheepish wince.

He took a deliberate sip of water and continued. "There's an issue with a high-profile project at work. One of our employees crossed a line, and it required an escalation to HR. Ivy was updating me and scheduled a disciplinary meeting for this afternoon. The woman we were waiting on...wasn't you. It was the HR rep."

Aurelia blinked in confusion. "Then why read it out loud?"

Levi's expression sobered.

"Because Owen, aside from being an overgrown pain in my ass, is also our Chief Security Officer and arrived only minutes before you did. If someone in a significant leadership role needed to be escorted out or access revoked, he needed the heads-up. Unfortunately, this was a serious situation."

God, she felt foolish now. She may have overreacted a teensy bit over this.

"Oh...Sounds like I made some assumptions today...It was nerves and insecurity and, honestly, a little self-sabotage." She lifted her glass, attempting to lighten the mood with a half-smile. "Mark this moment down... you'll rarely catch me admitting I'm wrong."

Levi laughed, a deep, joyful sound that made her pulse skip. Her thighs instinctively squeezed together under the table.

Focus, Aurelia.

Trying to shift gears, she asked, "So...Owen. What exactly was *that*?"

Levi momentarily shut his eyes and groaned. "*That* was Owen on his best behavior, believe it or not. He insisted on being there. Said it was for my security, which is only partially true. He's extremely nosy and dramatic, as I'm sure you've learned."

She chuckled, then turned thoughtful and serious. "One day I'll look back and laugh about it, I suppose, but right now, it feels like our wedding was a joke." She shifted uncomfortably in her seat.

"He knows he's on my shit list," Levi muttered darkly.

Aurelia teased, "He's a dumbass, sure. But it's clear he's *your* dumbass. You love him anyway."

Before Levi could reply, her stomach gave a loud, traitorous grumble. He grinned, green eyes twinkling. "What kind of husband would I be if I stood between my wife and food?"

"A stupid one," she shot back. Instinct had an apology ready on the tip of her tongue, but she forced it down and opened her menu.

Conversation flowed more easily after that. She was perusing the menu when she noticed Levi hadn't bothered with his. His attention was solely focused on her.

"You must come here often if you've already memorized the menu."

"I do," he admitted. "Want recommendations?"

She nodded, and he rattled off several French classics like *Tartiflette, Blanquette de Veau,* and *Boeuf Bourguignon.*

But as she scanned the menu, her brow furrowed. "None of those are listed here."

He frowned. "They're standard items."

"They're not on *this* menu."

He paused, then opened his menu and fell silent. Several minutes later, he flagged their server over, a young redhead who looked barely out of college.

"Good evening!" the server chirped. "Ready to order, or perhaps begin with an aperitif?"

"Actually," Levi said smoothly, "has there been a recent menu change?"

"Absolutely! Chef Perreault recently overhauled the menu with fresh flavors, a new direction, and a very exclusive selection. Everything listed is brand new."

Levi's jaw ticked. "Could we have a few more minutes?"

"Of course," the server said, bowing out politely.

Levi sat there, staring down at the menu as if it had personally betrayed him.

"Sorry," he muttered. "I didn't expect them to change everything. This used to be one of my favorite places."

Aurelia noticed the tension in his shoulders, disappointment in his eyes, and a glimmer of something...else.

She didn't like it.

"How do you feel," she asked slowly, carefully laying her menu down, "about ditching this place and going somewhere less stuffy...with better food?"

Levi's head snapped up, surprised. Then the corners of his mouth lifted.

"I couldn't possibly say no to my brilliant wife."

CHAPTER 26

Levi

There was no argument from Levi when Aurelia suggested leaving *Chez P'tit Chou-Fleur*. He had hoped to make a strong first impression, ensuring their first meal together would be intimate and elegant. Her file had plainly stated she preferred more relaxed and low-key places, but he thought maybe, because this was a very special occasion, that she would enjoy it.

The menu change had derailed everything.

Dread had settled in the moment he opened it. He hadn't frozen like that in years, his brain shutting down at the thought of parsing an unfamiliar menu on the spot.

He could have used Neuronix's *PicText* app—snap a photo, enlarge the font, or have it read aloud to him—but he wasn't ready for the conversation that would ensue. Not with someone he just met.

Some truths took time.

When she miraculously proposed going somewhere else, he jumped at the opportunity. As it turned out, the food was *definitely* an improvement.

He paid for their untouched drinks and left a generous tip for the server, Dennis. It was only fair.

Following Aurelia across town, he parked behind her along a narrow side street. They walked side by side, the silence stretching between them. Not awkward, but companionable.

Levi found himself wanting to reach for her hand, to anchor himself in the ease of her presence. He unconsciously lifted his hand halfway before pulling it back.

Too soon.

They stopped in front of a slim building with unassuming glass doors. Levi's brows dipped in confusion. There was no signage. No bustling entrance. And in no way could an entire restaurant fit inside.

He glanced at her, skeptical.

She peered over her shoulder and gave him a small, secretive smile before opening the glass doors.

It wrecked him.

That smile alone could've convinced him to walk through the fires of hell for her. He let out a shaky breath and followed.

Inside, as he suspected, there was no restaurant, only a reception desk and an elevator. Aurelia, however, didn't pause as she bypassed the attendant with confidence and stepped into the elevator. Levi followed without hesitation.

What waited for them below was unexpected magic.

Moonlit Buns was a hidden gem beneath the city, elegant and warm in all the ways *Chez P'tit Chou-Fleur* wasn't. The ceilings were draped in ornate dark wooden latticework, casting shadows through hanging lanterns in deep amber and soft crimson. Private tables were separated by intricately carved screens that offered privacy without shutting the world out.

The ambiance was still romantic, but this time, relaxed. Unpretentious.

This was the kind of place she had meant. The kind of place *he* had wanted, too. He hadn't executed it well at all.

As they sat, Aurelia took the lead, scanning the menu with bright eyes and a playful gleam that made Levi smile before she even said a word. He could stare at her all night and never tire of it.

"Does my husband trust me to order for us, or do you want an equal say in this decision?" she teased, pen in hand, and oblivious to Levi's attention.

This version of Aurelia—loose, playful, teasing—was rapidly becoming his favorite.

He grinned. "The last two weeks have been full of risks. What's one more?"

"Good answer from a smart man. Happy wife, happy life," she chirped as she began checking off boxes on the order sheet. "We're getting Kurobuta pork soup dumplings, chicken dumplings, wonton soup, stir-fried bok choy, veggie fried rice...and for fun, two milk teas and chocolate mochi buns to finish."

Levi stared at her, amused and impressed.

"What?" she asked, suddenly self-conscious. "I'm hungry. And it's not *that* much. The portions are small!"

"I trust you," he said simply. The blush that crept up her cheeks was as delectable as her food selections.

After their order was placed, silence briefly returned. Then, in a move that surprised neither of them at this point, Aurelia cut straight to the chase.

"So...whose house are we living in?"

No warm-up before a direct hit.

He shrugged nonchalantly. "We can stay at mine. It's...larger than I need. More than enough space for your things."

She tilted her head, eyes glinting with mischief, as she smiled widely. "Define 'larger than I need.' Because based on the pompous car you drove, the ultra-fancy restaurant, the tailored designer suit, and the custom rings now weighing down my finger, I'm guessing that being understated is kind of your thing."

While her tone was teasing and playful, Levi's face hardened. "My *pompous* car?" he echoed. "I bought that car after my company went public. It was the first thing I let myself splurge on after years of sacrifice. I *earned* it."

Her grin faltered. "Levi, I was kidding—"

He didn't let her finish.

"So, what then?" he asked, irritation rising in his voice. "If my house *is* as big and lavish as you think, what does that say to you? That I'm some show-off? That I throw money around to prove my worth? That I'm just another flashy asshole in a suit?"

Confusion flickered across her face, quickly giving way to discomfort. She raised her hands between them, a gentle but firm barrier. "No—that's not what I meant. I wasn't—" Her voice wavered, the words tripping over rising alarm.

But he was already too far in.

"If I really cared about all that, Aurelia, I would have married one of the women who've been trying to crawl into my life for a cut of the profits. Trust me, there were plenty of options."

Around them, conversation at nearby tables quieted. Conversations stalled. The mood at their table had shifted incredibly fast.

He leaned forward, lowering his voice, but not the weight behind it.

"That's twice today. *Twice*, you've made assumptions about me without trying to understand who I actually am. And both times, you've made me feel like a walking stereotype."

The silence that followed was deafening.

And it was only then, when he *truly* looked at her, that he saw what he had done.

Aurelia wasn't snapping back. She wasn't rolling her eyes or calling him out. She sat frozen in place, hands clenched tightly in her lap, eyes fixed on the table. Her shoulders curled inward, her entire posture guarded and withdrawn.

She wasn't angry...she was scared.

Levi's gut twisted with shame.

His wealth and how women reacted to them was a sensitive topic for Levi, stemming from his insecurities. He had escalated it with his tone, bulldozing her with something sharp and defensive...and completely disproportionate to what had been a joke.

A nervous, lighthearted jab she had made while trying to find footing in unfamiliar territory...and he turned it into a minefield.

Remembering Estrella's handwritten note, Levi knew he had crossed a line.

Aurelia

Aurelia tried to slow her racing heart with concentrated, silent breaths, but it refused to listen, its beats wild and erratic.

This was all her fault.

Again.

Levi was right. It *was* the second time today she said something without thinking it through...he hadn't deserved it.

He made it too easy to talk to him—to let a sliver of her guard down. Too easy to forget that comfort could be a dangerous threat to her survival.

Her jab about his wealth had been meant as a joke—her awkward way of diffusing the tension, of softening the sharp edges around this whole ridiculous situation. She wasn't used to fancy restaurants or custom jewelry or the kind of polished confidence he wore so effortlessly. The teasing had been her armor.

The way he had responded, the snap in his voice, the heat behind it—it jabbed her like a sucker punch.

Because she knew that tone. That sudden shift. That cold defensiveness that came without warning made her body brace for impact.

It echoed far too clearly of the one who had come before. The one who had charmed her with smiles and sweet words, only to tear her down with carefully aimed barbs and strikes.

The way Levi looked at her—angry, wounded, disappointed—it hadn't been intentionally cruel. But even now, it made her flinch out of habit, unable to stop the instinct to protect herself. Not because of what he had said...but because of what it reminded her of.

Silence had been the safest response.

So that's what she gave him. Stillness. Quiet. The smallest version of herself she could muster.

Wishing desperately that she could rewind ten minutes and take it all back. Wishing she had never opened her mouth.

Of course, they'd live in his house. It was the practical choice, the obvious one. She should've just said that full stop. No sarcasm, no jokes. Because he was right—she had made assumptions, judged him based on surface details instead of giving him the benefit of the doubt.

She should have been grateful. He had done everything right.

And now...she owed him another apology.

She was unsure how long she sat like that. A statue locked in place, detached from everything. She didn't hear Levi if he had spoken at all. Didn't register the low murmur of the other tables or the quiet clink of utensils.

At least not until the first course arrived. The aroma of ginger, soy, and warm, spiced steam grounded her barely enough to breathe. Barely enough to remember where she was.

Not in the past. Not with *him*.

Her breathing evened out...not entirely, but enough.

She turned to face Levi, cautiously, and met his gaze. Her voice scarcely carried across the table.

"We can live in your house," she said, carefully measured. "Just let me know what works best for you."

She didn't explain.

She didn't ask for forgiveness or make excuses.

She simply gave in—quietly, completely.

CHAPTER 27

Levi

Fear and resignation.

That's what Levi saw in Aurelia's eyes when she finally looked up and said, "*We can live in your house. Just let me know what works best for you.*"

It wasn't the words that gutted him; it was the flat and hollow way she said them. Like someone flinching before the blow ever came, already giving up the fight.

It made him sick to his stomach.

She wasn't simply agreeing...she was surrendering.

He played the conversation back in his head during the long stretch of silence that followed. Her joke. His response. The shift in her posture. The way she had disappeared right in front of him.

And then it clicked.

He had misread her. *Spectacularly*. She hadn't been mocking him—she had been trying to keep things light. Trying to navigate unfamiliar ground with humor, he had responded like a man with something to prove.

Not because of her, but because of what he hadn't yet unpacked in himself.

He looked at her now, sitting still and small and silent, and all he could think was: *No. This wasn't how this night was supposed to go.*

God, he was such an ass.

"No," he said aloud, voice quiet but firm.

Aurelia blinked, the only indication that she heard him.

"No," he repeated, more strongly. "We'll stay at your house."

She frowned, like she didn't understand the words.

"It's not about convenience," he continued, calm and clear. "Your house matters to you. My place? It's a status symbol with walls. That's not home. Not to me. But if yours is...then that's where I want to be."

She didn't speak. Just watched him wearily, unsure if she should believe him.

And god, that did something to him. Made him feel like every carefully constructed part of himself was a sham.

He thought of Estrella's note again. *History of past trauma. Sensitive to conflict. Avoidant under pressure. Proceed gently.*

He hadn't proceeded gently at all.

So now, he would.

"This morning, we promised to be honest when we're upset," he said, his tone softer. He fiddled nervously with his chopsticks. "We blew that. Both of us. But maybe that's the point. We're not supposed to get it right on day one."

That earned a flash of something across her face—a ghost of a smile, uncertain but real.

"I know it wasn't about the house," he added apologetically. "You were joking. I see that now. But I've...been with people who only saw me for what I could give them. Not who I was. And it left some marks."

He didn't shy away from saying it. He wasn't hiding from it anymore.

When she finally looked up again, he saw the weight she was carrying, too.

Wordlessly, she reached across the table and held out her hand.

He grasped it.

It was firm. Stable. Grounding. Not an apology, but an understanding.

"I don't know how to deal with conflict," she said, so quietly he almost missed it. "When someone's upset, and I hear it in their voice, I...shut down."

He squeezed her hand gently. "Then we'll figure it out together."

Her shoulders loosened a fraction. When she let out the faintest breath of laughter, it was the only sound that mattered.

Levi didn't need a victory tonight.

He just needed her here.

Aurelia

Dinner had gone surprisingly well after *that* moment.

Aurelia had slowly begun to relax again, the storm inside her settling as Levi's words replayed in her mind. He hadn't excused himself. He hadn't tried to smooth things over with charm or pity.

He had seen her and acknowledged the amount of baggage she shouldered and offered something solid to stand on.

No one had ever done that before.

Not once.

Somehow, it had always been *her* fault.

Or maybe it was easier for them to blame her because she was so willing to accept it to keep the peace.

That part of her? The part that curled in on itself, silenced itself just to survive? That part needed to be buried six feet deep.

Levi wasn't like Kyle. She was starting to believe that.

But even Levi had said it, that *unlearning* didn't happen overnight. Reflexes don't ask permission before firing.

Now her focus shifted to the most daunting part of all—cohabitation.

Tonight. *In her house.*

Her heart was so out of control that she fleetingly debated getting it checked.

"So...are you okay with us staying at your place?" Levi asked carefully, as if reading her thoughts. "You can come check out mine after dinner. I need to grab clothes for the next couple of nights anyway."

She nodded, flushing with uncertainty...and to her surprise, desire.

This was stranger than a one-night stand. Because he wasn't leaving in the morning. Or the one after that.

The rest of dinner was a relaxed blur as they laughed and got to know one another. But now she recounted the events from dinner while following Levi's sleek, silver monument to indulgence through the winding streets of Joia City. They climbed steadily into the cliffs until the scenery gave way to silence, seclusion...and grandeur.

Not grandeur. *Excess.*

This was a neighborhood built entirely of *mansions*. Glass, metal, stone...the kind that screamed money and existed for no reason other than to announce it.

At the very end, they reached a cul-de-sac. Tall white stone walls wrapped around a massive estate, its entrance marked by an intricate set of wrought-iron gates. They swung open as Levi approached, his car gliding forward like it belonged there.

Aurelia followed hesitantly, eyeing the gleaming volcanic stone driveway, the curated garden beds, the towering modern structure waiting at the top of the slope.

Levi's car disappeared into a side garage. She parked where he directed, easing into a circular drive that wrapped around a ridiculous water feature.

Of course, there's a fountain, she thought. All these extravagant homes, like Starhaven, had a fountain.

She stepped out of her car, stunned into silence.

It was breathtaking. Sharp angles, expansive glass, soft lighting spilling from inside, marble staircases, and four garage bays. *Four.*

He met her gaze from the open garage bay, leaning casually against the outside wall like some fashion cover story come to life.

With a flick of his chin and a devilish smirk, he motioned for her to follow through the side garage. Which, as it turned out, was less a garage and more of a fleet warehouse. Each bay housed two different luxury vehicles. Nothing about it was practical.

It was a showroom.

This is insanity, she thought.

Not envy. Not awe. Only a complete and utter disconnect from everyday life.

Once inside, Levi stopped before her, hesitating, shyness suddenly taking hold. "Would you care for the grand tour?"

She forced a smile. "Lead the way, good sir."

He relaxed a bit at her tone and offered his arm. She kicked off her heels and looped her arm through his, preparing herself for what she was about to see.

The house was...as stunning as she expected it to be.

Every room on the lower level was an architectural marvel. Floor-to-ceiling windows, clean modern lines, custom lighting, luxury designer furniture arranged with perfect intention.

But not an ounce of life.

Even the kitchen was immaculate. Commercial-grade appliances. Black quartz counters that shimmered like obsidian. A breakfast nook tucked beside massive windows that opened onto a panoramic view of the hills and coastline. Beyond that, a glittering infinity pool hugged the backyard like a jewel.

It was *everything.* And yet...

Somehow, the bowl of fruit on the table, the stack of unopened mail, and the few dishes in the sink were the only signs that a human lived here.

Those small touches?

That was the real heart of the home.

And they were heartbreakingly rare.

The rest of the tour was a blur. There was a game room, theater, bowling alley, speakeasy, and an obscure metalsmith forge...all of which looked to be built for show, not for living.

She was surrounded by museum-grade perfection. All of it cold, curated with too much space and too little soul.

Finally, they ascended the grand staircase to the second floor, which had even more white walls. More shadowless lighting. More nothingness.

At this point, she didn't bother counting the bedrooms.

When Levi led her to the last one, the primary suite and his bedroom, her breath caught. It should have been the most personal space in the house. But it was like the others with cream bedding, flawless wood furniture, and stunning architecture. It was beautiful. And sterile...and so *empty*.

No clutter.

No warmth.

Not a photo.

Not a book.

Not even a forgotten sock.

And for some reason...it made her sad.

She tried not to—she *really* did—but she frowned deeply, and Levi caught it.

"What are you thinking?" he asked, gently. Not defensive, but curious.

She hesitated, trying to choose her words cautiously.

"Honest reaction, remember?" he coaxed, folding his arms and waiting with an amused smile that did *very* distracting things to her pulse.

She exhaled and met his eyes, heart pounding as she took the risk.

"This 'larger than what I needed' home of yours is stunning," she began carefully. "The views are incredible. The craftsmanship is...insane. But..."

She swallowed.

"I *hate* it."

Levi

Levi stood completely still, like a startled possum mid-death-feint.

For several seconds, he didn't move. No expression, no sound, only...shocked silence.

Then, something shifted.

First, his chest gave the slightest quiver.

Then his lips twitched.

And then *laughter* followed.

Big, booming, full-body laughter erupted from deep in his chest and echoed around the stark white walls of the mansion.

It was raw, unfiltered, and utterly unexpected.

Aurelia stared at him, caught somewhere between confusion and disbelief.

She had seemingly braced for a rebuttal or maybe some wounded pride. Possibly even a lecture.

Based on her expression, she hadn't expected him to laugh like she had delivered the best punchline in the world, and frankly, neither did he. But then again, in a twisted sort of irony...maybe she had.

He couldn't stop. And the more she stared at him like he had sprouted horns, the harder he laughed.

She crossed her arms, eyes narrowing. "Is that...amusement, or are you having a mental breakdown?"

Still chuckling, Levi finally composed himself enough to speak. "I promise I'm not laughing at you," he said, wiping the corner of his eye. "It's just...I *hate* this place, too."

"You what?" She said in disbelief.

"I hate it," he repeated, stepping toward her, a grin lingering on his lips. "I've never said that out loud before. Never admitted it. But hearing you say it, like you blurted out the truth I've been choking on for two years...God, it's a relief. It's invigorating."

She stared at him like he had told her he moonlighted as a fire-eating acrobat.

He softened a little, his gaze flicking briefly to her parted lips before meeting her eyes again. She was so unbelievably sexy, and his laughter was quickly replaced with a different unstoppable emotion. "Why do *you* hate it?" he asked, quieter now. He was sincerely curious.

He also wanted to see her lips move some more.

The laughter seemed to crack an inner wall, bringing them back to the honesty they'd promised each other with no pretending, no posturing.

Only them.

CHAPTER 28

Aurelia

Laughing wasn't at all how Aurelia expected Levi to react to her hating his house.

Yet there he stood, laughing his ass off anyway.

Having been more than a little nervous to admit it, she was relieved he wasn't angry with her. An unnatural reaction she knew would take a long time to correct.

The surprise she felt when he admitted his hatred of his house, and asked to hear her reasoning was a quiet reassurance she hadn't realized she needed.

It was only surpassed by that fleeting moment where his hunger-filled eyes flicked to her mouth and lingered. It was so brief that she was sure it was a figment of her imagination.

"It's so...*sterile*. It's white walls *everywhere*," she began hesitantly. She shifted on her feet, eyes darting around the space. But the more she thought about it, the more reasons came spilling out. Her voice grew steadier and braver as she ticked each one off on her slender fingers.

"It doesn't look like anyone even lives here."

She lifted her arms, animatedly gesturing to the furniture and walls. "There are no pictures of family, friends, or at a minimum of something you like. I can yell down the hallway, knowing the only thing I'll hear is the sound of my voice echoing back at me. So, unless you have a secret passion for yodeling—" she glanced at him suspiciously, praying he didn't harbor an undisclosed love for the singing style, "—then it's plain creepy."

Levi stood there, hands casually in his pockets, watching her with a broad smile as he listened. "I'll admit that the views and location are stunning," she conceded, gazing out the large windows that led to a small personal balcony. She glanced back at him, her eyes briefly catching on how his shirt clung like it had been tailored to his torso, which looked annoyingly sculpted beneath the fabric.

She didn't think it was possible, but Levi's smile seemed to stretch even wider. Her face went up in flames. *Focus Aurelia!*

"When was the last time you walked out here? I mean, sat on this balcony, and enjoyed a cup of coffee or unwound after a long day with a drink?"

His smile slipped, and her gut twisted. "It feels *empty.* I guess I don't see the point in having a place like this unless you have enough people constantly here to fill it with...*life.*"

Realizing the sheer volume of words she dumped on him, Aurelia winced and turned back towards the balcony window, hugging her arms around herself protectively.

Aurelia never talked this much, and she wished she hadn't, at least to save herself from feeling so self-conscious, replaying every word she said back in her head. The internal berating was interrupted by two large, strong hands, gently grasping her upper arms and caressing them.

Before she could stop it, her body instinctively leaned back into him, enveloping her in his scent and warmth. His hands paused on her arms briefly and then resumed as he whispered into her ear.

"That's why I hate it too."

Levi

Levi's heart pounded as he rushed to throw together a couple of days' worth of clothes and toiletries.

He hadn't imagined it, the way she leaned into him minutes ago. Levi had let himself savor the feel of her body pressed lightly against his for a heartbeat before she pulled away.

The absence of her touch was jarring, cold, and immediate, like walking into a room and forgetting why you were there. Though it was the strange sensation of persistent emptiness that followed that threw him off balance.

Now she stood outside on his balcony, silhouetted by fading light, her thoughts miles away as she rested against the iron railing. That wild, colorful hair was intensified by the sunset and electrified by the gentle breeze. Her gaze was fixed on the distant horizon, and her quiet stillness made something deep in his chest tighten.

He meant to tell her he finished packing five minutes ago. But instead, he remained rooted in place, captivated by the sight of her.

Estrella had bragged about her match success rate like it was gospel. She had been insulted when he even hinted at doubt. But Levi couldn't help but wonder...*Was it like this for every couple she matched?*

Because being with Aurelia already felt oddly natural...*alarmingly* natural. Like she had always existed in the background of his life, and only now he finally noticed.

And nothing in Estrella's meticulous dossier had prepared him for the woman on his balcony now. She was so real, so sharp-edged and soft-spoken all at once. Nor had it warned him how quickly he would feel the weight of the rings she wore...rings he had given her. His chest swelled with a sort of primitive male pride knowing she wore *his* rings.

His wife.

The word still felt foreign and impossible. But here they were.

Running a hand down his face, Levi exhaled slowly, grateful for one small mercy—it was Friday night. No work, no obligations. Just an open weekend ahead with a beautiful, sexy stranger who, against all odds, didn't feel like one.

He slung the bag over his shoulder.

It was time to leave this house behind. For now, maybe forever.

And for reasons he couldn't fully name, leaving had never felt more right.

CHAPTER 29

Aurelia

He's here. In my house. My husband.

Aurelia kept repeating the words in her head, hoping they would feel less surreal each time she said them. Levi Lockwood was no longer a hypothetical. He was *real*.

And currently standing in the middle of her kitchen.

Her husband.

She held her breath, gripping the edge of the island with white-knuckled fingers, watching as he took in her space. Part of her braced instinctively for criticism. Maybe he hated it. Maybe it was too small and too humble...like *her*.

He had arrived in a different vehicle, this time opting for a more low-key, sleek black SUV, though still undeniably high-end. Her white sedan was tucked neatly into one of the two garage bays. The second, currently a half-finished workshop, was scattered with tools and materials for the attic renovation, for an office she now realized she would need sooner than expected.

She had led the way into her home in silence, right up until a startled yelp escaped her lips. Her feet had left the ground without warning, and it took a breathless moment to realize Levi had swept her into his arms just before they crossed through the door.

"What kind of husband would I be if I didn't carry my wife over the threshold?" he murmured, his voice a rich, decadent rumble that skimmed across her skin. The heat from his hands felt like a brand wherever they touched.

Her mouth went dry at the sound of it. Embarrassment flushed hot across her face, but it did nothing to dull the ache blooming low in her belly.

Now, Levi stood silently in the center of the open space, hands in his pockets, slowly turning in place, his impassive gaze wandering over everything in quiet contemplation.

When his eyes finally landed on hers, they sparkled with what looked like delight.

"Could I entice the lady of the house," he said, his tone light and flirtatious, "to give her husband a proper tour?"

Cheeky bastard.

Aurelia playfully rolled her eyes, but the smile tugging at her lips gave her away. Without a word, she pushed off the counter and approached him, ready to show him her little slice of heaven.

Levi

Levi was *home.*

He hadn't known what to expect, but the overwhelming sense of belonging was undeniable. It settled into his bones like something long-missing had finally clicked into place. A soft, internal *snap* echoed inside him, a puzzle piece sliding into position.

He had made the right call not to stay in his own house.

Like his, Aurelia's property had a long, secluded driveway. Dense greenery masked it from the road until, all at once, her cottage came into view.

A charming white structure with a terracotta-tiled roof, an intricately carved turquoise door, and a two-car garage greeted him, perched above the lagoon like it had risen from the water itself. String lights glimmered across the back porch, casting reflections on the dark surface of the water. Flowers bloomed in planters and along the dock, their vibrant colors standing out against the twilight.

And he hadn't even gone inside yet.

He could already imagine mornings with her on that porch. Diving off the dock. Cooking together as they laughed and *lived.* He hadn't even stepped through the threshold, and he wanted all of it.

Aurelia gestured from her car window, directing him where to park. She slid into the garage bay closest to the house, while he pulled into the drive near the second bay, currently functioning as a workshop. Grabbing his overnight bag from the passenger seat, Levi followed her to the front entrance.

In a rare burst of spontaneity, Levi dropped his bag and, without a second thought, swept Aurelia into his arms like the treasure she was, fully intent on carrying her across the threshold. The surprised little squeak she made lit him up from the inside...and sent the heat rushing south in a way that was both inconvenient and completely worth it.

He didn't know what had possessed him to do it, but he had zero regrets. The moment passed, and after retrieving his bag from outside the entryway, his attention was now on her home.

Inside, the cottage unfolded around him like a living memory he didn't know existed. It was warm and inviting, a lived-in personal space. His gaze roamed in wonder as he dropped his overnight bag on the cushioned bench in the small foyer and stepped into the main room.

The living space unfolded into an open concept kitchen and family room anchored by a plush cream sectional, a natural stone fireplace, and two soaring built-in bookshelves. The entire back wall of the house was glass, framed with sheer white curtains, revealing the dock, porch, and dark shimmer of the water beyond.

Turquoise accents peeked out in the cabinetry, throws, dishware, like the stone in her wedding ring. He beamed, knowing that he had gotten that part exactly right.

The kitchen wasn't huge, but it didn't need to be. Everything had a purpose. Distressed gold hardware, warm wood finishes, and a four-seat island gave it a modern charm, elevated by soft lighting and thoughtful detail. It was stylish, but uniquely *hers*.

And hopefully now, *his*.

Aurelia stood quietly between the island and the sink, her fingers nervously twisting together. Levi turned to her, lifting a brow. "Could I entice the lady of the house to give her husband a proper tour?"

She rolled her eyes, but her smile gave her away. He offered his elbow again. She kicked off her shoes and linked her arm through his.

The hallway revealed more of the home's thoughtful layout, which included a half-bath tucked beneath the stairs, a compact laundry closet, and finally, her bedroom.

Her intoxicating scent hit him the second he stepped through the doorway.

The room was larger than he expected, wrapped in soft colors and natural light. Like the living area, floor-to-ceiling windows highlighted the lagoon.

Another set of sliding doors led to the back porch. A king-sized bed with creamy linens, vibrant throw pillows, and a soft rug beckoned.

There were books on the nightstand, a forgotten cardigan draped over a chair, and a faint mark on the floor from a moved piece of furniture.

Aurelia had made this place her own, and he wanted to be part of it.

But god, he couldn't stop the image that suddenly assaulted him of her sprawled out on that bed, tangled in the sheets, *tangled with him.*

Desperately needing a distraction and space between them, he peeked into the adjacent bathroom and found a dreamy, iridescent escape. Turquoise fish-scale tiles shimmered in the light. Gold fixtures adorned a shower built for two. The vanity matched the kitchen's natural aesthetic, with a built-in makeup station and tiny green plants softening the edges.

Every room was a reflection of her; undeniable proof that *someone lived here.*

His house, by comparison, was a showroom.

He turned back, finding her watching him in silence with those large brown eyes, her expression unreadable.

Levi slowly approached, gently hooked his finger under her chin, and tilted her face up toward him. Her expression melted into something dangerously alluring.

"I completely understand now," he said softly, eyes never leaving hers, "why my house sucked."

He smiled. "I love your home."

Aurelia

Aurelia was momentarily transfixed as Levi's fingers tilted her chin, drawing her gaze up to meet his. His green eyes burned into hers, as if peeling away every carefully constructed defense she had.

Maybe it was the way moonlight shimmered across the lagoon, its reflection dancing on the glass.

Or maybe it was the heady scent clinging to his skin—sun-warmed cedarwood and a hint of smoky vetiver, grounded by the subtle spice of black pepper. It was both comforting and strong, and undeniably *him.*

Whatever the reason, Aurelia stopped thinking.

She had learned to wield her body like a weapon, to chase the rush of being desired. At that moment, she needed to fulfill that desire. Nothing else mattered.

Closing the small space between them, she rose onto her toes and brushed the lightest, most deliberate kiss across his lips. A whisper of contact, soft and teasing, her hand flattening over his chest to feel the steady beat of his heart beneath her palm.

There would be no going back after this. She knew it. And she didn't care.

When she eased back, Levi remained perfectly still, his eyes glazed, his breath caught somewhere between restraint and wonder.

"That," she murmured, voice barely above a breath, "was the kiss you should have gotten during our wedding ceremony."

Her fingers began to move in slow, hypnotic circles across the firm planes of his chest. Her pulse hammered in her ears, but her voice was steady, commanding.

Levi swallowed hard, his jaw tightening as he took a shaky breath. "You don't have to do anything. Not tonight, not ever, not unless you *want* to. This is your call. Every step of the way. You're in charge here."

Aurelia's sultry laugh curled around them like smoke.

Of course, she was in charge. She had always known that, but hearing it from him made her feel unstoppable.

Dangerous, even.

She leaned in, lips brushing the stubble on his jaw as she whispered, "What if I said I wanted to consummate this marriage tonight?" Her fingers trailed lower, a slow descent that had Levi's muscles tightening beneath her touch.

"Would you deny your wife the ravishing she's entitled to?" she murmured, the words a gentle threat laced with longing.

His breath stuttered.

"We're both adults," she continued, her voice a velvet ribbon of temptation. "And I think it's safe to say we've each had...*less meaningful* nights with people we barely knew." Her meaning wasn't lost on him. His jaw clenched at the implication of another man's hands on her.

Good. She wanted that reaction. She wanted *him.*

Fully pressing her body to his, she left no room for doubt, no space for hesitation. She felt the full weight of his desire straining against her and leaned close, her lips grazing the shell of his ear.

"Would it be so wrong," she whispered, "if your wife wanted her husband to be hers, in every way, on her wedding night?" Her teeth grazed his earlobe. One hand curled around his length through his pants, slow and possessive.

"To feel you inside me?"

That was all it took for Levi's restraint to crack.

Levi

Levi's hands were immediately everywhere, urgent and reverent, as his mouth crashed against Aurelia's in a kiss that demanded and gave in equal measure.

This was reckless and probably too soon. It broke every rule of caution he set for himself going into this.

He didn't care. Not when she was pressed against him like this, all heat and hunger and wild permission. He had lived through enough calculated moments to recognize when life offered something precious. And Aurelia, *his wife*, was a miracle wrapped in flame.

He surrendered. He wanted to *burn*.

She broke the kiss, breathless, her chest rising and falling in heaving waves beneath her lace top. The sight nearly undid him.

Still, he paused, hands gentling against her waist, as his forehead rested against hers. "Are you sure?" he asked, voice low and rough with restraint. "I don't want you to feel rushed...or regret this later."

Aurelia answered with action. Her fingers slid his suit jacket off his shoulders, letting it fall to the floor in a whisper of fabric. She threaded her hands through his hair, tugging him down into a kiss that was no longer tender, but a fierce and possessive claiming.

Levi groaned against her mouth. She could have asked for anything in that moment, and he would have gladly scorched the earth to give it to her.

Her hands moved with intention, unbuttoning his shirt one agonizing button at a time. Each one loosened, revealed more golden skin, more muscle she was desperate to explore. He kissed her again, slower this time but no less consuming, his hands sliding over her hips, pulling her into the hard press of his body.

"I want my husband," she whispered, voice smoky and raw before sealing the vow with another punishing kiss.

His shirt joined the growing pile of clothing on the floor, her eyes catching the wisps of ink scrawled across the top of his shoulders as she ran her hands over his bare chest. Before she could follow the markings leading to his back, Levi spun her around.

His arm cinched around her waist, his arousal hard against the curve of her backside as he bent to her ear.

"Hold still."

With his free hand, he found the zipper of her lace top and drew it down in a slow, torturous path. Her skirt followed with the same deliberate ease, pooling around her feet. What remained was a delicate white lace set that left little to the imagination.

Levi's lips trailed kisses down her spine. His hands came up to cup the full weight of her breasts, thumbs teasing her nipples through the fabric, drawing breathy gasps from her as her body arched into his touch. He made quick work of releasing them from their fabric prison.

She was trembling now, the sensations unraveling her. When his fingers dipped beneath the waistband of her panties and found her slick and ready, Levi nearly lost his mind.

"God, you're perfect," he murmured against her skin, one hand working between her thighs, coaxing soft moans from her lips as she moved with him, riding the rhythm he set with practiced precision.

And then, just as suddenly, she turned. Her hands went to his waistband and undid him with a deftness that made his pulse jump. She pushed his pants and briefs down in one tug, and he hissed at the release. Her eyes flicked to him, dark with purpose.

Without a word, she backed him toward the bed and gave him a gentle shove. Levi fell onto the mattress, watching as she stalked toward him with predatory grace, each movement lighting him up from the inside out.

She stepped out of the remaining scrap of lace and straddled him slowly, teasingly, her bare skin brushing his. Her breasts hovered at eye level, begging for attention. He gave it willingly, his mouth finding one, then the other, lavishing each with hot, open-mouthed kisses and the scrape of his teeth.

Aurelia writhed in his lap, her hands tangled in his hair, her body pulsing with need. She leaned down, lips at his ear, her voice a silken promise, "I want to take my husband for a ride."

He came completely unraveled.

With a growl, Levi gripped her hips and, in one fluid motion, he thrust up as she sank onto him, the connection hitting them like lightning.

Aurelia cried out, overwhelmed by the sudden, perfect fullness of him. She stilled, breathing through the stretch, her hands braced on his chest.

Levi was trembling beneath her, eyes shut, jaw tight. "Tell me if it's too much," he rasped, fighting for control.

But she didn't stop. Her hips began to move, tentative at first, then demanding. Fast. Deep. Unrelenting. She rode him like she owned him, and Levi matched her pace, meeting every thrust with one of his own, their bodies locked in rhythm.

Her cries, her moans, her whispered curses...all of it filled the room like music.

When she shattered above him, Levi held on through the storm of her climax, his name breaking from her lips like a prayer. Only then did he let himself go, buried deep inside his wife, taking her in every way a man could.

They collapsed together in a tangle of limbs and sheets, hearts pounding and breaths uneven.

Wrapped in each other.

Silence eventually blanketed them, soft and sacred, until sleep took them under.

CHAPTER 30

Levi

Levi stirred as the morning sunlight filtered through sheer curtains, streaking gold across the bed and his bare skin. He blinked against the brightness, a low groan rumbling in his throat as he rolled over.

This wasn't his bed.

The realization hit fast, pulling him fully awake.

He sat up in a rush, eyes scanning the unfamiliar surroundings until they landed on the still, glassy waters of the lagoon beyond the window.

Aurelia's room...in her home.

His wife's home.

The word still sat oddly on his tongue, even inside his thoughts, and was equal parts thrilling and disorienting.

Flashes of last night rolled into his mind. Her mouth on his, her body wrapped around him, the way she had whispered that she wanted him. Every memory pulled tight across his chest like a cord wound with heat and vulnerability.

But the bed was empty and cold on her side.

Where was she?

He ran a hand across the sheets where she had been, fingers brushing over the faintest imprint left behind. The pang of disappointment was unexpected and sharp.

Leaning over the edge, he spotted his overnight bag perched neatly on the bench near the window. She must've brought it in after he passed out. He hadn't slept that deeply in years, effectively dead to the world, wrapped in the weight of exhaustion...and something comforting he hadn't been ready to name.

He muttered a quiet thanks into the stillness of the room, grabbed the bag, and pulled on a pair of sweats over his briefs. Modesty wasn't exactly the priority, but tracking down his wife while naked wasn't the kind of first morning impression he wanted to make.

On his way to the bathroom, he caught his reflection in the mirror.

It was a disaster.

His hair was sticking up at gravity-defying angles. A rough shadow of stubble dusted his jaw. But there was something else in the mirror that attracted his attention. His eyes looked rested.

Peaceful, even.

He couldn't remember the last time they looked like that.

He ran a hand through his wild hair with minimal success and shrugged. This was the real him. She might as well get used to the morning version of her husband.

Striding toward the hallway, Levi padded softly down the floorboards, listening for any sign of her.

He was a man on a mission to find his wife.

Aurelia

Aurelia slipped quietly out of bed before dawn, moving with practiced care as she pulled on soft pajamas, careful not to wake Levi. She paused at the foot of the bed, her gaze lingering on the sweeping tattoo across his back of a large, intricately scrolled tree that stretched across his shoulders and spine.

At first glance, he didn't seem like the type to have ink, let alone something that bold. But it suited him in a way that made her attention linger...and her thoughts stray somewhere far less innocent.

She needed to stop imagining crawling back under the covers and waking her new husband in ways that had nothing to do with sleep.

With a sigh, she slipped out of the room, only to return a minute later to quietly place his overnight bag by the door. Then, retreating to the kitchen, she focused her energy on something safer, though less satisfying...like breakfast.

Now, she stood at the stove, lost in a swirl of sizzling bacon and pancake batter, as she replayed last night's memories.

Her heart was still fluttering, though she tried to ignore it.

Everything about last night had been different.

She had shared her body, read the moment, and taken control before, but not like this. This wasn't the usual blur of desire and detachment. It was something quieter, deeper, and far more disarming, and she didn't know what to make of it.

They were strangers, yes, but they had also woken up legally married. That truth clung to her chest like a storm cloud refusing to break. She pushed those thoughts away, focusing her attention on the pancakes. But images from last night and of his back this morning kept infiltrating her thoughts.

There was something about him...something that whispered he would be the one to undo her, piece by piece.

On the other hand, she had slept through the night for once without any nightmares or tossing and turning. Waking up refreshed was a small miracle she credited only to exhaustion...and not to the man who had held her like she was something sacred.

As the bacon finished crisping in the pan, she absently picked up her phone. A casual curiosity became a black hole of discovery as she typed Levi Lockwood into her browser...and then promptly forgot how to breathe.

His face was everywhere, and his name was attached to article after article. The amount of information about him was never-ending.

Neuronix CEO.

Youngest founder to lead a multibillion-dollar company.

Tabloid mentions.

Financial reports.

Charitable endowments.

She had not realized the full weight of what he meant when he said he was a CEO. And now, the truth stared back at her from a glowing screen—her husband was Levi Lockwood, one of the most powerful men and eligible bachelor, in Joia City...possibly the continent.

And he was currently asleep bare-assed in her bed.

Aurelia didn't know how to interpret any of it, so she zeroed in on what she could control, which wasn't burning breakfast.

With food almost on the table, Aurelia was so deep in her thoughts, she didn't hear Levi's approach.

When she spun around, proudly holding a fresh stack of pancakes, she let out a startled cry...and the plate pitched, sending the pancakes soaring.

One hit Levi right in the face. The rest scattered on the floor. Time stood still.

Aurelia became a statue, afraid to move or even breath as she prayed for a hole to appear in her floor and swallow her whole.

Levi then slowly peeled the pancake off his eye, holding it between two fingers and examining it like a small, flour-based crime had been committed.

"I expected this morning to be somewhat awkward after last night," he deadpanned, "but not for this reason."

Aurelia was mortified. Why do these things happen to me?

She cleared her throat, mouth suddenly desert-dry, and managed to say, "In some cultures, it's tradition for a wife to slap her husband with breakfast foods after a perfectly adequate ravishing."

Levi threw his head back in a roar of laughter, and the sound was so warm, so real, that it made her heart ache in the best way. Her eyes widened in surprise.

She didn't make jokes, not like that at least.

She certainly didn't flirt either.

But something about Levi kept her mouth running, and for once, it didn't feel like something she needed to apologize for.

"I'm usually up early in the morning," she said quickly, the words tumbling out in a rush. "You looked exhausted, so I didn't want to wake you. I figured I'd start breakfast while you slept..."

Levi gave her a lazy smile and leaned back against the counter, shirtless, with his gray sweatpants hanging low enough to make it hard to think. The tendrils of ink peeking over his shoulders were more noticeable. She swallowed back the urge to better acquaint herself with each line with more than just her eyes.

Noticing her shift in mood, he pushed off the counter and closed the space between them. They were close enough for her to see the specks of gold in his eyes. He took her hand, lifting it to his mouth and pressing a soft kiss into her palm.

Did it just get hotter in here? Aurelia couldn't stop staring at his mouth.

"I appreciate the effort," he said, voice low, sincere, and laced with something more dangerous. "But please don't feel like you have to wait on me. I would have gotten my ass up to help you...even if it meant a much higher risk of a kitchen fire."

The idea of a kitchen fire snapped her out of the trance that had overtaken her. Aurelia grinned despite herself. Estrella might be chaotic, but she knew what she was doing. Levi in the morning, rumpled and shirtless, was dangerously charming.

"I prefer my kitchen as it is...not on fire." She pointed to a plate of surviving pancakes on the counter. A mound of crispy bacon waited beside them.

He stared at the pancakes, visibly distressed, and slowly picked one up. Levi took a bite, tried to chew and swallow it, and failed to hide a grimace as he forced it down.

She frowned. "Do they taste bad?" she asked, scanning the instructions on the box, worried she screwed them up.

"No, they came out perfectly fine," he said, valiantly forcing down another bite.

She narrowed her eyes. "Then why do you look like you're being subjected to cruel and unusual punishment?"

"...Because I don't like pancakes?" He answered with one cautious eye open, clearly expecting a fight.

She stared at him in disbelief. "Who doesn't like pancakes? Is it all breakfast sweets or just that?"

"I like waffles..." She opened her mouth to argue, but Levi cut her off. "...and no, they are not the same as pancakes." Levi crossed his arms defiantly with a petulant scowl.

"It's literally the same batter."

"Incorrect," he said flatly. "This batter is only appropriate for waffles."

"You can't be serious."

"Dead serious. We even ask during interviews at Neuronix what they prefer. If someone says 'pancakes,' they're bumped to the bottom of the list. Waffles are the only correct answer."

Her jaw dropped. "That's no way to conduct business!"

"The only exception would be if they say pancakes are acceptable only when used like bread in a breakfast sandwich. Then they're hired on the spot. Otherwise, pancakes are banned."

She gawked at him. "Do you at least like bacon? Please tell me you like bacon," she pleaded.

Levi gave a dramatic sigh. "Of course I like bacon, I'm a man, damn it. But..." his eyes danced as he popped a few crispy pieces in his mouth, "...crispy bacon is an atrocity. The sound of the crunch alone makes me cringe."

"An atrocity you don't seem to mind right now." Aurelia crossed her arms and glared at him.

"Because it's bacon. Only serial killers would say no to eating bacon." He winked. "Plus, my wife made it. I'm obligated to eat it even with the pancakes."

Aurelia eyed him skeptically. "I assume you drink your coffee black, too."

He playfully cocked his head. "Does my wife prefer her sugar and cream with a splash of coffee?"

She pointed a spatula at him. "Let me guess...you also think pasta shapes taste different."

He froze. "Each shape holds the sauce differently—of course they taste different!"

Aurelia raised both eyebrows high in a silent challenge.

Levi sighed ruefully. "My wife is a food tyrant."

CHAPTER 31

Levi

Levi had offered to clean up after breakfast and, much to his surprise, Aurelia agreed...though not without a begrudging look as she handed over the spatula. She disappeared into the bathroom to shower while he rolled up his sleeves and got to work wiping down counters and rinsing pans, the scent of bacon still lingering in the air.

He found himself smiling, lost in the memory of their earlier banter. The morning had gone smoothly than he expected. It was so light, easy, and natural. That debate over pancakes was somehow the perfect distraction from what could have been an unbearably awkward morning-after.

He still couldn't believe how good she looked fresh out of bed—sleep-ruffled, barefoot, in those clingy shorts and matching camisole. That had branded itself into his memory whether he wanted it to or not.

The pancake to the face was probably the only reason he snapped out of staring at her long enough to speak.

As the sink gurgled with suds, Levi reached for his phone to check his messages. He had ignored them since the ceremony yesterday.

Vaguely remembering Owen had tried calling him, he realized he had completely forgotten about it. Which meant there were likely a disturbing number of notifications waiting.

He steadied himself as he accessed his phone.

He definitely wasn't wrong.

The texts were endless...and mostly from Owen, who had entered a state of full-blown panic.

Levi ignored his email app entirely. He didn't need that kind of existential crisis today. He popped in an earbud and turned on the accessibility voice assist to help fly through the flood of messages while Aurelia was still in the shower. There was no way he could read this many in time but chose to focus on the congratulatory texts from Isaac and Ivy.

There was also one from Grace inviting them over for dinner the next night to celebrate. Levi knew it wasn't just about celebration; they were nosy, especially if they had seen Owen's video from the day before. He shifted to the voicemails, unease prickling at his skin.

The initial voicemails were brief and to the point: Estrella checking in on them both, Charles asking if Aurelia was alright, and Mitchell politely wondering if he needed an annulment.

The rest?

Mostly Owen.

Levi sighed and pressed play.

"It's Owen. I'm so sorry, man, I was trying to lighten the mood and put everyone at ease. I didn't mean to upset you or Aurelia. I'd also like to apologize for taking that video...and for sharing it with the gang before I realized what was happening. Call me back."

Levi's stomach dropped.

What video? He had been so fixated on their first kiss that he completely missed it.

He hesitated, but played the next message.

"Please call me—Owen, your best friend—so I can apologize...and make sure you're still alive. I haven't ruled out that she's an axe murderer yet. If I don't hear from you in the next ten minutes, I'm launching my own investigation. I love you. Bye."

Levi rubbed an anxious hand over his face.

Despite Owen being the best security expert around, there was something deeply unhinged about that voicemail.

The third came with a new level of uninvited escalation.

"Okay, seriously, call me, I feel really bad. I drove by your house, and you're obviously not there but that doesn't mean she didn't drown you in a lagoon yet. Don't worry though—I'll find you. Also, it's Owen, your extremely remorseful but easily forgivable best friend."

He was afraid to hit play on the fourth message. But he did it anyway.

And instantly regretted it.

"In case you weren't sure, it's Owen again." His heavy breathing suddenly made Levi unbelievably nervous. *"I took matters into my own hands and hunted down her address and decided to drive by. Now don't get mad—and remember,*

I did this because I'm your friend and I love you—but *once I saw your car in her driveway, and all the lights were off, it looked creepy and suspicious. So, I* might *have patrolled the perimeter of her house looking for you to make sure you were safe. And I* might *have looked in the windows to make sure you weren't lying in a pool of your own blood, taking your last breaths...and also, I* might *have seen you officially consummate your marriage.*

Levi felt his soul leave his body.

He was going to strangle Owen.

So, congratulations on that and not being murdered. But more importantly, I'm very *sorry I saw it. Rest assured, I'll be pouring bleach or some other strong disinfectant into my eyes. You're now forever unclean to me. Tell Aurelia I said hi and I'm sorry again."*

He let out an annoyed groan so loud it echoed off the kitchen walls right when Aurelia padded into the room. She was barefoot and glowing from her shower, dressed in tight maroon leggings and a soft cream-colored shirt that hugged her tantalizing curves. Her hair was damp and messy, twisted into a loose bun, that she was now pulling free with a stretch of her arms.

The voicemails temporarily forgotten, Levi nearly forgot how to breathe.

He still needed to shower, but with the way his gaze was locked onto her, he doubted he would make it to the bathroom without getting *distracted.*

Aurelia tilted her head, noting his expression. "What were you whining about?"

Levi snapped back to reality, exhaling a slow breath. "Well, I caught up on all my voicemails." He shrugged helplessly.

She waited, her expression expectant.

"Everyone from the ceremony called to make sure we survived yesterday," he said with a wry smile.

Aurelia flushed with color, clearly remembering the drama.

"Owen also left me four progressively questionable voicemails that I'll get to in a minute. The others—my nosy friends Isaac, Ivy, and Grace—sent their congratulations and invited us to dinner tomorrow night."

A sharp inhale from Aurelia made him stop, her unease evident. He softened his tone.

"If you're not comfortable going to dinner so soon, I'll tell them they've got better odds stacking marbles in a hurricane." The gang could be a handful on a good day; he wasn't entirely sure he was ready to unleash them either.

She tilted her head, thoughtfully considering the invitation. "They won't leave you alone until they meet me, will they?" There was no accusation in her voice. Just a quiet assessment of the facts.

"They will make my life hell, yes."

"Then let's do it. I wouldn't want my husband subjected to further torture after this morning's pancake incident," she said dryly.

He smiled, carefree for the first time in ages.

This was going to be fine. Possibly more than fine.

Until he remembered the other messages he received.

"So, about Owen's voicemails..."

CHAPTER 32

Aurelia

Aurelia sat in the passenger seat of Levi's SUV, pretending to be absorbed in the passing scenery as they drove toward the grocery store. It was necessary now that meals were no longer a solo endeavor, and snacks would mysteriously vanish twice as fast.

But grocery lists were the furthest thing from her mind.

She couldn't stop thinking about Owen.

Or more specifically *what* Owen saw through her bedroom window last night.

Her entire body burned remembering it. She had already died of mortification once that morning; she didn't know if she would survive dinner with him tomorrow night. Meeting Levi's closest friends had been daunting enough. Now she would be doing so knowing at least one of them had witnessed her most intimate moment like a live-action movie.

And she agreed to go before Levi told her what Owen said.

Such a rookie mistake.

Levi kept stealing sideways glances at her while he drove, like he expected her to unlatch the door mid-turn and execute a tuck-and-roll escape. Which honestly wasn't entirely off the table. The urge to disappear from this planet was currently ranked right up there with her desire to disappear into the leather seat.

Still, she tried to refocus on something safe, like dinner. Planning dinner didn't come with a side of emotional whiplash.

"Any thoughts on what you would like for dinner," she asked, forcing her voice to sound neutral. "I was thinking of one of my favorite dishes unless there is something else you prefer. It's this amazing, braised pea soup that has—" She stopped mid-sentence at the sheer horror etched across Levi's face.

Her brow furrowed. "What now? Is it soup that you have some deep-rooted issue with or is it peas..." Her voice trailed off as she watched him recoil like she had threatened his life.

"*Peas are Satan's food*," Levi declared. "If I died and went to hell right now, Satan would make me eat peas for all eternity. Peas and broccoli *together*." He shuddered like a man who had survived an unspeakable trauma.

Mouth tight, Aurelia exhaled through her nose, unsure if she wanted to laugh or attempt a leap from a moving vehicle.

Her husband was turning out to be a man-child. An absurdly charming, occasionally ridiculous man-child.

"You know, I feel like everything I learned so far today should have been disclosed in your file."

"You wound me, *my wife*." Levi pressed his hand dramatically to his chest. "Would you have passed on our match because of my strong waffle convictions and anti-pea mentality?"

He batted his lashes at her in mock innocence, momentarily taking his eyes away from the road—and nearly sideswiped a parked car.

"Shit!" he hissed, abruptly jerking the wheel as he glanced in the rearview mirror. "Okay, in my defense, that car came out of *nowhere*."

Aurelia rolled her eyes as he refocused on the road. Without another word, he reached across the console, slipping his hand into hers. He peppered small kisses along the back of her knuckles that had her cheeks heating for the hundredth time that day.

He didn't let go.

Not until they pulled into the grocery store parking lot.

Levi

The trip to the grocery store had gone off the rails.

Not because Aurelia reached for a box of plain *Cheerios* instead of *Honey Nut*, or because she placed a bag of regular *Doritos* in the cart while neglecting to add a bag of *Cool Ranch* flavor. No, the problem came when she started asking him for help finding ingredients on her list.

What should have been a simple errand turned into something else entirely.

At first, he tried. He tried so damn hard.

But as the labels blurred and the words refused to stay in place, the familiar knots of anxiety curled tightly within the very fibers of his being. He played it off, weakly joking that he was terrible at locating things in stores.

She hadn't said anything in response...but it was obvious she didn't buy it either.

Normally, Levi ordered his groceries online. The convenience was one part of it, but if he was being honest with himself, it was mostly to avoid this exact situation.

On the rare occasion he shopped alone, no one noticed how long he stared at a box. No one saw the way he sometimes had to read and reread the same label, hoping it would make sense the second or third time around.

He hadn't thought about any of that when he agreed to come along with Aurelia.

Now, the ride home was uncomfortably quiet. And Levi knew the silence was his fault.

Lips pressed together, he helped carry the bags in. Unpacked items onto the counter and shelves with the same soundless effort. Moved about the kitchen like a ghost, caught in his head, spiraling.

Aurelia stepped in front of him and gently took his hand.

She didn't say anything at first, the silence stretching taut between them. With quiet determination, she led him into the living room and guided him down onto the sectional. Before he could so much as object, she settled herself on his lap, her legs tucked on either side of him, anchoring him in place. An effective maneuver to prevent escape.

Levi blinked up at her, temporarily startled, only to shy away again. His jaw was tight, clenched in frustration, his eyes locked on something far beyond the back porch and the sparkling lagoon beyond it.

Aurelia gently cupped the side of his face, guiding his face to hers.

"Yesterday, someone made me promise to try and talk when something upset me. And now, that same frustrating person has gone completely silent on me *twice*."

Levi continued to brood. But he didn't pull away. He let her thumb gently stroke along his cheek, unable to break away, as if her touch steadied something in him.

Aurelia's voice dropped lower, more intimate.

"First, it was when you found out the menu had changed at *Chez P'tit Chou-Fleur*. You stared at it with this look of defeat on your face. The second time was today at the grocery store when I asked you to help me find some ingredients. You stared at the shelves with that same look."

She was undeterred, waiting for him to extend a sliver of trust.

He kept his eyes closed, soaking in the comfort of her hand like it was the only thing tethering him to the present moment.

"Levi," she whispered. "What is it that puts that look on your face?"

Slowly, he opened his eyes and found her patiently watching, unafraid, and unpitying. He stared into the brown depths of her eyes, temporarily mesmerized by the innocence and the raw honesty within them.

Covering her hand with his, he lowered them both to his lap. Drawing in a quiet breath, he gathered the strength to share one of the deepest pieces of himself.

"I'm dyslexic," he said. The words felt heavier than they should have, like they had been carried far too long.

He tensed, waiting for her reaction.

Aurelia

She wasn't sure what she expected to hear, but his admission wasn't one of them. It was a small extension of trust, and yet Levi looked up at her with something akin to worry and shame.

Aurelia frowned at that, confusion flitting across her features. That wasn't okay—not with her, and not about this.

Was he seriously ashamed to admit this? Ashamed of something he never chose; something that had shaped him into the brilliant, accomplished man sitting in front of her? The thought made her throat tighten.

No. Absolutely not.

She straightened her spine before looking him dead in the eyes.

Time to be fierce.

"So, you're moping over something you have no control over?"

Levi's head snapped toward her, his eyes flashing hot with sudden anger. "I'm not *moping*, I'm *embarrassed* that I couldn't do something basic in either of those situations. It makes me feel stupid when I can't even read a simple menu without it taking an extremely long time."

"*I* could barely read it and half of it was in French," she offered, trying to lighten the mood. Levi glared at her. She rolled her eyes in irritation. "Okay *fine*. Wrong time to joke."

She regarded him carefully, the firmness in her tone refusing to balk.

"So...are you suggesting that I married a dumbass?"

That, as expected, got a rise out of him.

"I'm *not* a dumbass," he snapped, insulted.

"Then why are you treating yourself like one?" she shot back, unable to hide her rising anger.

Levi opened his mouth to reply, but the words never quite made it past his lips. He had nothing to say.

She was on a roll and didn't let the silence stretch too long.

"While you were sleeping this morning, I searched your name online," she said, her tone calmer now, but no less resolute. "I have to admit, I'm extremely impressed that someone was able to take a disability and turn it into an empire. *Especially* one that is focused entirely on technology that helps others with disabilities navigate the world. That seems impossible for someone who supposedly can't keep up to achieve."

His green eyes fixed on her with rapt attention. He didn't interrupt this time, though he was still glowering.

"I guess I'm simply confused then. So please explain to me, *my darling husband*, how someone who founded a thriving company like Neuronix, that helps so many people *just like him*, is still ashamed of it—of being a customer."

His entire demeanor softened as her words sank in.

"The only stupid thing here is that it wasn't disclosed in your file," she continued, "because you were too afraid to tell your wife about it. So now I'm a little peeved because I could have learned more about it and avoided what happened today."

While Levi now felt a bit sheepish about not disclosing it sooner, he still believed his reasons for not doing so were valid.

"Congratulations on our first official fight as a married couple."

He couldn't help but notice how gorgeous Aurelia was even as she glared at him.

Levi gave a small nod, his gaze never leaving hers. "When you put it that way...I'm sorry for not telling you sooner," he murmured, voice tight. "But I won't apologize for not including it in my profile. This isn't something that's easily summed up in a couple lines of text, and considering the impact it has on my life, I deserve to decide how and when to disclose it."

Aurelia studied the man before her as she mulled over his logic. Realizing it wasn't all that different from her unwillingness to open up about her past, she relaxed in his lap.

"I understand why you didn't tell me—we're still very much strangers. But I don't ever want to see you pitying yourself like this or diminishing your contributions to the world. There's *nothing* to apologize for. It's as ridiculous as apologizing for your eyes being such a lovely shade of green."

She paused for a moment, watching him closely.

Levi knew she was right but still struggled to form a response. It was a welcome respite when her fingertips grazed his cheek again.

"It's up to you to decide if you want to treat it as a gift or a burden. All I see is how you've taken a piece of yourself and used it to create something bigger than all of us—something that helps others. Don't let anyone, including yourself, lessen that."

She barely finished speaking before Levi surged forward, devouring her mouth and overtaking her senses. It wasn't gentle; it was intense and full of everything he couldn't say aloud.

And she kissed him back with a ferocity that said more than words ever could.

When they finally parted for air, he rested his forehead to hers.

"Day two and I have to say that I'm *really* starting to enjoy how wise you are, dear wife," Levi murmured. He trailed featherlight kisses along her neck, and Aurelia laughed.

"Alright, Casanova, let's finish putting the groceries away before they begin to rot and have some lunch. Meanwhile, I want you to tell me everything about dyslexia."

She stood, despite his half-hearted protest, and tugged him up with her.

Together, they walked back to the kitchen, not only as husband and wife, but slowly, steadily, something stronger.

CHAPTER 33

Levi

The rest of the afternoon passed in a haze of sun and serenity.

They lounged on the back porch, tucked into matching coral Adirondack chairs, basking in the kind of quiet that only came with real comfort and presence. Levi couldn't remember the last time he had been able to just *be*. Not multitasking. Not thinking ten steps ahead.

He drank one of his favorite beers they had picked up earlier, while Aurelia enjoyed a tall glass of iced tea. When he asked her what she liked to drink, she surprised him.

"I never really saw a need nor acquired a taste for it," she had said. "I engage socially here and there with champagne or something mild like that, but it's simply not something that I use to unwind or have fun. So, I'll always be your designated driver," she added with a wink.

He hadn't verbalized it then, but Levi admired that kind of decision to resist the pressures or distractions that others so easily succumbed to.

With the breeze coming in from the lagoon and the warmth of the sun casting long shadows across the porch, Levi opened up about himself in a way he had not expected to do so early in their relationship.

"There are different types, and it varies from person to person. It's how the brain identifies speech, sounds, and how letters and words represent them. I have visual dyslexia, which feels like my brain isn't getting the entire picture of what my eyes are seeing. Text blurs or feels like it goes in and out of focus; kind of like it doubles. Following a line of text or keeping my place within it is hard."

Aurelia didn't interrupt, didn't try to fix or soften it. She *listened*, her attention wholly on him, and Levi felt it, like a tether grounding him.

Looking back, he didn't understand why he had been so afraid to tell her. Hindsight really *was* twenty-twenty.

"That's why the menu change at dinner was so stressful. Then all the different items and labels of the extremely specific ingredients you needed...it would have taken hours, and I'd end up with an epic migraine."

He took a sip of his beer, engrossed in the calming ripple of the water.

"Growing up was rough. I couldn't remember what I saw on a page, no matter how long I stared at it. Learning to spell and write was a nightmare. I fell asleep in class so many times because it was so fatiguing. My teachers thought I was lying about the constant headaches and dry eyes." He gripped his beer tightly. "That I was *lazy*. I excelled in everything else academically except reading and writing."

Aurelia carefully asked, "What about your parents?"

He gave a humorless laugh. "My drunk and useless father didn't give two shits about his 'stupid son' while my mother was too involved in herself to bother. The only person who cared was my grandfather—my dad's dad—but that lasted only so long, too. He passed away when I was thirteen. My mother soon followed a year later at the hands of my father..."

Aurelia gasped, almost knocking over her glass of iced tea, visibly stricken.

"...and thankfully, my father drank himself to death when I was nineteen. I've known Owen since we were kids. He took the role of kicking anyone's ass who made fun of me in school very seriously."

When Levi looked over at her, she was blinking hard, trying not to cry. The sight of it unraveled another piece of him.

"When you see him tomorrow, and only after you make him *grovel* for his transgressions, ask him how many times he was in detention or suspended for fighting because of me," he added with a faint grin.

"Will that make him upset?"

"Quite the opposite; he'll proudly share his war stories like a badge of honor. He's been threatening for years to get a tattoo tallying the numbers on his ass."

Aurelia snorted and shook her head gently. "I'm glad you had someone in your corner like that. But I'm sorry you had to experience any of this." She lit up with recognition. "Is that what the tattoo on your back is about?"

My wife is gorgeous and more intelligent than I am, he thought proudly.

"It sure is...meant to show how strong it has made me, although I obviously don't always feel that way. A phoenix seemed too cliché, and it was better than the options Isaac and Owen were pushing on me." He took a purposely long sip of his beer.

"Go on...you can't just stop there!"

Levi chuckled. "Isaac was insisting it be some kind of software code," Aurelia scrunched her nose in disapproval, "...and Owen was all in on it needing to be something manly and dominant like a bare-chested behemoth of a man riding on the back of a gigantic hawk as it flew over a sea of naked swooning people. After I promptly shut that idea down, I caught him trying to bribe the tattoo artist into hiding small penises in the branches of the tree."

The belly laugh that burst from his wife was the most beautiful sound he had ever heard—second only to how breathtaking she looked while cackling with unfiltered joy. It took her a moment to settle, wiping at her eyes as she eased back into the conversation where they'd left off.

"How does that affect you now?"

Levi sobered quickly and shrugged. "It's still part of my everyday life, but I've spent years building something that turns it into a strength, so no kid like me ever feels broken because their brain works differently."

Aurelia gave a small nod, the weight of it carrying silent understanding. "Good thing you now have an amazing wife on your side too," she said, her voice laced with warmth and certainty.

Levi studied her for a moment, the corners of his mouth lifting. The smile he gave her then was different than the others; not the cocky, practiced kind, but something gentler and authentic.

And for the first time in a very long time, he didn't feel alone.

Aurelia

Their earlier conversation echoed in Aurelia's mind as she worked beside Levi in the kitchen, hands dusted in flour, helping prepare the pizza dough.

She learned so much about her new husband and his harsh upbringing that it seemed no easier than hers. She admired how he turned his dyslexia into the basis for his success, instead of hindering it.

Despite wealth and privilege, he managed to raise himself in the ways that mattered most. She was unsure which was worse: growing up without any parents or growing up with parents who were physically present but emotionally void.

"So, what about you? What was it like growing up? Your profile didn't list too many details other than no other family and being a ward of the state," Levi asked, cutting through her thoughts with a question that was both direct and vulnerable.

Aurelia sucked in a breath. "Oh…um, there isn't much to say really," she hedged. "It wasn't the best situation—I think I grew up before I should have to be honest." Levi frowned but kept kneading the dough. She swallowed hard, fighting against the instinct to change the subject, never having warmed up to anyone enough to feel comfortable sharing. But that promise to be honest lingered in her mind.

Levi didn't push. He simply kept kneading, a frown tugging at his brow. If he could trust her with his truths…maybe she owed him the same.

She inhaled deeply, grounding herself.

I can do this, no big deal.

"My mother was an addict and I've never known who my father was. She never talked about him. I had to make dinner with whatever food we happened to have and figure out how to wash the minimal clothes I owned when I was really young through reading books at the library…sometimes I learned the hard way." She held out her forearm, displaying a patch of skin different from the rest. A burn-related scar. He blanched.

"One of our neighbors in the rundown complex we lived in could barely afford to take care of herself but still managed to give me food when she could. My mother liked to party hard and often wouldn't come home for days, so my neighbor kept an eye on me."

Levi stilled, dough forgotten as he gaped at her, horrified, but Aurelia didn't notice. She was no longer present, mind locked on the past.

"One night she came home, worse than I'd ever seen her, but I helped her undress and get into bed. I made sure she was lying on her side so she wouldn't choke if she threw up, like I usually did. The next morning, I looked in her room, and she was sleeping—which was normal—so I got myself ready and off to school."

"When I got home, she wasn't out of her room yet, which was unusual. I went to check on her again, only to find that she was—she hadn't moved at all, still in the exact same spot and position as the night before. I didn't feel anything other than fear of what would happen to me. I knocked on my neighbor's door and told her what happened. The next thing I knew, the police were there trying to explain what 'overdose' meant, and I was taken to a stranger's house."

Aurelia's voice was flat now, devoid of emotion. She focused on slicing the bell peppers for the pizza toppings with unnecessary force. "Then I was hopping from home to home, hoping some family would adopt me, fighting to keep whatever possessions I had safe, trying to make it through school. Cycle repeated until the last home where I stayed until I turned eighteen and aged out."

She finally looked at Levi when he let out a low whistle.

"How old were you when your mother died?"

"Eight."

He paled. "No other family that could take you in?"

"None that they could find."

Levi shook his head, rattled. "What was school like?"

She shrugged. "Lonely but otherwise fine. Making friends was tough because of the constant moving, especially in middle school and high school. I kept mostly to myself—wasn't bullied except for a brief period when I was twelve."

He raised an eyebrow and leaned rigidly against the island, arms crossed. Aurelia handed him the rolling pin, an unspoken command to start rolling the dough.

"That's how I met my best friend, Selene. We didn't hit it off right away when I got placed into the same home. She tormented me at first. Tried to take my clothes and personal items, which led to several brawls. She and her friends made fun of me in school. It almost got her moved to a new foster home. After that, she left me alone and started trying to get to know me. We've been good friends ever since."

"I'll have to meet her at some point so I can get the real dirt on what teenage Aurelia was like," Levi teased. "You at least managed to graduate high school. What happened then?"

"I did well in school academically. I always loved reading and can learn virtually anything from a book. It wasn't enough to get scholarships or aid for college though. I couldn't afford to do the extracurriculars that admissions wanted to see or afford the cost of tuition, so I started working right away."

As they layered sauce and toppings on the dough, Aurelia recounted how she worked part-time jobs from the moment she was old enough, saving every dollar. How she eventually bought a car and lived out of it for years. How a YMCA membership gave her a warm place and a hot shower.

How every single decision had been about survival...until Eleanor.

That one unexpected opportunity, being hired as Eleanor's personal assistant, had changed her entire life.

Levi said nothing the whole time and simply listened, eyes never straying, until the oven timer chimed. He carefully pulled out the hot, bubbling pizza.

They ate at the small table in quiet companionship, and for a while, it was enough. Up until Aurelia finally asked what had been lingering in the back of her mind.

"What made you decide to seek out a matchmaker?"

Levi nearly choked on a bite of pizza. "Well...that's an interesting story," he said after coughing out a nervous laugh. "You're *really* going to judge me, but...the short version is I got mad and accidentally told my company's Board of Directors I had a fiancée—which, as I'm sure you are aware, I certainly didn't have. I understandably needed to find one. With limited options, my friend Ivy suggested a matchmaker."

Try as she might, there was no way Aurelia could have hidden her shock in that moment.

He took a long swallow of beer and ran a hand through his hair. "Then it became an intervention with my friends about how I work too much, and this would be a good thing for me. I could break up with my fake fiancée and be done, but the truth is, I wanted more than that. I wanted something real and figured this was a blessing in disguise...and here we are."

It was a strange set of circumstances, but somehow, it made her feel a little better about how she had ended up in this mess. Weirdly, they were perfectly matched.

"You're right, I'm *totally* judging you on this," Aurelia joked. Levi cracked a reluctant smile. "Now I want to hear how this unfolded."

And so, grumbling playfully, Levi began from the beginning and told her everything.

"This Tyler person sounds like a complete ass," Aurelia said humorlessly as Levi wrapped up his matchmaking story.

Levi snorted. "That's because he *is* an ass. Thinking about him makes me want to set his car on fire."

She smirked. "And I thought I was the impulsive one."

"What about you?" he asked, his tone shifting with genuine curiosity. "What made you go the matchmaking route?"

"Oh, mine's a tale that might rival yours."

"Impossible. Mine was peak sketchiness."

"The jury is still out on that one."

Levi laughed harder than he had in months as Aurelia recounted the events of Eleanor's farewell party. The absolute chaos of backhanded eulogies, the surprise inheritance with marriage requirements, and the video message that caused a minor senior citizen uprising, had him in stitches.

But his laughter lessened when she reached the part about the personalized video message Eleanor had left her, the one with instructions, hopes, and consequences. Authenticity laced her words as she admitted how little she had left to lose when she agreed to this matchmaker plan, stirring something deeply possessive within him.

She sat back, her fingers nervously tapping the armrest. "That part of it, the inheritance, needs to stay between us, okay? I understand why making an effort is a requirement, so I figured...why not? After all my disastrous relationships, it felt like the least risky option left."

Levi gave a thoughtful nod, then raised his beer in salute. "I stand corrected. Your story wins. It's insane."

Relieved, Aurelia laughed, clinking her glass of iced tea against his. "Here's to creating even more insane stories together."

As the last golden rays of sun dipped beneath the horizon, Levi leaned forward on the kitchen island, his eyes on the rippling lagoon outside. They had opened the back doors, letting the warm breeze drift in. The soft hush of water and the scent of salt and jasmine mingled in the air. It was peaceful, grounding—and utterly exhilarating.

Then he felt her.

Aurelia's hands slid up his back, slow and deliberate, her touch mapping the contours of his muscles. Her body pressed against his from behind, her curves fitting perfectly into the lines of his frame.

Levi froze, not out of discomfort, but anticipation. He had been thinking about tasting her again all day, remembering the wild beauty of last night...and now, as her arms wrapped around his waist, it was like she had read his mind.

He set his beer down, turned to face her, and slid his hands to her waist. She looked up at him with what was becoming a familiar fire in her eyes as her hand trailed from his jaw down his chest, pausing at the waistband of his jeans. With a wicked glint in her eye, she gave him a slow, purposeful stroke.

"I think it's time for dessert," Aurelia purred, her voice silk over heat.

His thoughts vanished as instinct roared to life.

Levi pressed his mouth to hers in a kiss so deep and dominating, it left them both breathless. His hands gripped her hips, pulling her flush against him, grinding into the soft give of her body. She moaned, pressing harder against him, lips grazing his neck.

"There's always room for dessert," she whispered, her hand now stroking him through the denim with maddening slowness.

Levi growled low in his throat. "My hungry wife," he murmured, nipping her earlobe as he angled her soft curves up against the kitchen island.

With one deft movement, he slipped a hand beneath her waistband, bypassing her leggings entirely, fingers finding her hot and soaked.

"Sweet hell, Aurelia," he groaned. "So ready for me already...Tell me what you want, sweetheart."

"I want you inside me," she gasped, rubbing against his fingers. "*Now.*"

Levi needed no further invitation.

Their mouths collided again as he unhooked her leggings and panties, dragging them down with a sense of urgency. She reached for his jeans, freeing him in seconds. Her hand wrapped around him was electrifying, her thumb teasing the sensitive head, sending a jolt straight through him, and he nearly lost it.

In one swift motion, he turned her around, bending her over the counter with practiced ease. He guided her hands to the cool stone surface, his hard body engulfing her. Seeing her flushed skin and knowing he was the reason for it was the final blow that shattered his restraint. He thrust into her in a single powerful stroke unable to hold back any longer.

Aurelia cried out, throwing her head back as she stretched to accommodate his size. She was unbelievably warm, soaked, and tight—her walls clenched around him, pulling him deeper. Nothing else existed outside of them and this moment.

Levi's hand slid between her thighs again, finding that aching spot and pulling a desperate sound from her lips as he drove into her with a brutal, demanding rhythm. Her moans tangled with his ragged breaths, filling the kitchen and spilling out into the night like a secret too wild to keep.

"Levi," she whimpered, trembling beneath him against the cool countertop.

"I've got you, baby," he whispered hoarsely, slamming into her harder, angling until she shattered with a strangled cry. Her orgasm ripped through her, and he felt her pulse around him as he let go, losing himself in her.

They collapsed against the counter, breathless and tangled in the quiet aftermath.

Levi didn't care that the back doors were wide open.

Didn't care that the night air carried their sounds into the dark.

All that mattered was the way she fit against him, like they were beginning to head down a path that led to something that felt like home.

As the stars began to twinkle outside, Levi ran a slow, reverent hand down her spine, smiling against her neck.

"You were right," he murmured. "The view from this angle really is breathtaking."

CHAPTER 34

Levi

Levi stared down at the sleeping form curled against him, wishing for the second time that morning that today could be another lazy day.

He had been awake long enough to watch the first blush of dawn creep across the horizon, the soft light unfurling over the lagoon like a whispered promise. There was something humbling about the quiet way the sun announced its arrival, slipping into the sky while the world still slept, unaware that a new day had already begun.

A miracle wrapped in silence.

Just like his wife.

Aurelia was tucked into his side, one arm flung possessively across his chest, her breathing slow and even. The rise and fall of her body against his seemed to settle a part of himself he had long stopped acknowledging. It had only been a couple of days, but already, he couldn't imagine his life without her. And though logic told him it was impossible to feel this way so soon, every instinct he had—the same instincts that built an empire—told him this was exactly where he was supposed to be.

She had awakened something in him he thought long dead.

God, how he wished they had one more day like this. No obligations. No looming reality. Only the chance to get lost in each other again before life demanded its due.

He shifted slightly, careful not to disturb her, and stared out at the early morning sky. Brilliant streaks of gold and pink stretched across the water, a perfect reflection of the chaotic beauty this weekend had become.

They hadn't talked nearly as much as he had expected. Not in the ways that mattered, at least. Their time together had been intense and intoxicating, but also a little too good at distracting them from the important questions. Like how they were going to navigate this marriage...or each other.

And then, of course, there was the conversation he had avoided entirely—the dark, ugly truth about his parents. His jaw tensed at the thought, his vision darkening at the edges. The memory was a poison he didn't dare spill into this fragile peace, not yet. Maybe not ever.

With a heavy sigh, he forced his thoughts elsewhere, toward what came next.

This morning, he would have to return to that cavernous, empty mansion and pack a proper bag. The overnight one he brought wasn't going to cut it, especially with work starting again tomorrow. He needed business attire, the everyday essentials, and whatever creature comforts would help him settle into this new life under Aurelia's roof. The idea of fully moving into her home made him break out in a nervous sweat...and yet, it also felt oddly right.

And tonight, God help him, they were having dinner at Grace and Isaac's house. He winced thinking about it. He loved his friends, but this was going to be a social ambush, disguised as a friendly dinner. And after Owen's antics at the courthouse, there was no telling what fresh hell awaited them.

At least Owen had the decency to be mortified, even if his apologies came wrapped in ridiculousness. Levi told Aurelia about what Owen had seen outside her window, and despite her bravery, he knew she was dreading this dinner as much as he was.

He sighed again, long and slow before leaning his head back against the pillows. No sense worrying about it now.

For this one quiet moment, he allowed himself to simply exist wrapped in the warmth of her body, the softness of her breath, and the fragile, perfect peace of a new day breaking beyond the window.

Tomorrow would come soon enough.

But right now...he held the sunrise in his arms.

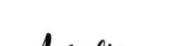

Aurelia

After lingering in bed longer than they should have, Aurelia and Levi eventually faced the truth that the day wasn't going to wait for them.

Aurelia watched with mild disgust as Levi sipped his revolting hazelnut coffee...black, no cream, no sugar. Every time he caught her watching, he shot her a mischievous grin before taking another exaggerated sip, as if daring her to comment. She didn't, having learned a lesson the hard way about challenging him in the kitchen and wasn't about to repeat the great breakfast debacle of yesterday.

After their simple breakfast, Levi planned to head back to his house to pack up his clothes and essentials, officially beginning the process of moving in. She had opted to stay behind, saying she needed time to make room in the closet and drawers for his things. That wasn't a lie...but it also wasn't the whole truth. She needed space—time to sort through the quiet panic brewing beneath the surface.

The honeymoon haze of the weekend was lifting, and the return to daily life loomed closer with every passing hour. The version of herself she had let him see these past two days—the flirty, confident, adventurous woman—felt like a mask she would have to remove soon. What happened when he saw the everyday Aurelia? The quiet, self-contained, occasionally awkward woman who worked too much and lived too cautiously?

What if he realized she wasn't enough?

Sensing her mood dampening, Levi filled the silence with a casual, "So, what's up on the second floor? I can tell there's more to this place, but you haven't shown me yet."

The haze lifted, and she was grateful for the change in topic. "That's because it's unfinished. But if you're curious..."

"I'm very curious." He drained the last of his coffee and sprang up from his chair with the enthusiasm of a man about to uncover a hidden treasure. "Lead the way, milady."

Aurelia shook her head, a reluctant smile tugging at her lips as she set her mug down. She led him to the door tucked beside the half-bath and flipped on the light, revealing a narrow staircase. Levi followed close behind as they climbed to the top.

When they reached the attic, she stood back and let him explore.

"This is...way bigger than I expected," he murmured, his voice full of wonder as he moved from one end of the open space to the other. "Deceptively large. I could actually fit my drum set in here," he murmured to himself.

The exposed A-frame roof cut into the space, but otherwise, the attic stretched the entire length of the house—from above her bedroom all the way over the garage bays. It was unfinished and brimming with possibility.

"I always planned to finish it," she admitted. "Turn part of it into an office, maybe a reading nook...or apparently a music room for a drum set."

Levi cast her a wickedly handsome smile. Her breath caught.

"But the house needed so much work when I bought it that this space became the 'someday' project. I did what I could—hired contractors for the major stuff—but a lot of this?" She gestured toward the walls and the rough flooring. "I learned how to do it myself. Spent years watching tutorials and reading everything I could get my hands on."

Levi turned to her; eyes filled with something that made her stomach flip. It looked suspiciously like genuine admiration. "You did all that on your own?"

She crossed her arms, feeling defensive even though his tone wasn't judgmental. "Not everyone has the luxury of throwing money at a problem, Levi. I had to figure it out, one step at a time." Her voice softened as she added, "Though...I'm starting to think Eleanor might've pulled a few strings without telling me. The contractors suddenly had open schedules with prices that didn't match the market at the time..."

Levi stepped closer, his expression warm and sincere. "I didn't mean it as anything but a compliment. I'm really impressed. And, if I'm being honest, a tad emasculated. You built this place into a home with your own two hands, and I'm not even sure I can hold a hammer properly." He spun slowly in a circle, arms outstretched. "And now look at you. You've got unlimited potential up here for a few small bedrooms...definitely an office. Hell, you could put in a small bowling alley."

She snorted. "I don't want a bowling alley, small or otherwise."

"Agree to disagree. But seriously, this is incredible, Auri. You should be proud of what you've done here."

Auri. No one had ever called her anything other than her full name before.

"Sorry...Is it okay if I call you Auri?" Levi's tentative question melted any hesitation she had.

She allowed the warmth of his words, and the intimacy of the name settle under her skin as she nodded. She didn't want it to matter. She barely knew him...but it did.

Pulling herself together, she turned toward the stairs. "Alright, let's get this day started. I'm going to need every available second to mentally prepare for meeting your friends tonight."

Levi let out a long, dramatic sigh. "I'm not sure even divine intervention could prepare you for this performance," he muttered.

And despite herself, she laughed.

Levi

Levi finished packing in far less time than he expected. He wasn't sure if that was a good thing or a quiet reflection of how empty his life was. Either way, it meant he would be home before lunch, with time to spare—enough time to brace Aurelia for the impending circus of meeting his friends.

They meant well, but that didn't mean they weren't a collective disaster when put in the same room.

As he loaded his overnight bags into the car, his mind kept circling back to Aurelia's story, specifically about sleeping in her car, alone, night after night. The thought of her curled up in the backseat, parking in questionable areas simply to get a few hours of restless sleep, made his chest ache. That kind of survival wasn't only difficult—it was dangerous. And yet, despite all of it, she hadn't just survived; she had built something beautiful from nothing.

She deserved the world, and Levi had every intention of learning how to give it to her. If she let him.

The matchmaking profiles had only scratched the surface, neat little summaries that left out the cracks and scars that told the real stories. If he wanted to understand his wife, he would have to earn that knowledge the hard way, through time and trust.

But first...they had to survive dinner with his friends.

Aurelia insisted on bringing dessert despite his assurances that it wasn't necessary.

"I'm not showing up empty-handed. That's bad manners," she said, giving him the kind of glare that made it clear this wasn't a topic open for debate.

Levi had wisely decided this wasn't the hill to die on.

When he returned to the house with the first load of bags, he found Aurelia at the stove, stirring something thick and suspiciously lumpy. A faintly sweet, lemony aroma filled the air, but the texture...he couldn't hide the skepticism on his face even if he tried.

Aurelia turned, immediately spotting the look. One hand perched firmly on her hip while the other brandished a wooden spoon at him like a weapon.

"What's that look for?" she demanded, arching a brow in challenge.

Levi lifted his hands in mock surrender. "Nothing! I'm merely wondering what sort of weird, lumpy concoction you're brewing over there. I thought you said this was *dessert*?"

Her eyes narrowed into dangerous slits. "This *is* the dessert," she hissed.

"Oh. Right." He cleared his throat, trying, and failing profoundly, to sound convincing. "Looks...delicious?"

She scoffed, leveling the spoon at him with deadly precision. "You've obviously never had rice pudding. And it shows."

So many things he could have said, yet he had chosen *that*. Fantastic.

Levi tried to backpedal. "Well, by all means, educate me on this prestigious rice pudding. I'm a willing student."

"Absolutely not." She turned back to the stove, her tone smug. "You lost the privilege of an advance tasting. You can try it later—*with your friends*."

He held up his hands again in surrender, grinning despite himself. "Message received, ma'am."

"Good. Now hurry up and finish bringing your stuff in so you can start preparing me for whatever shenanigans I'm about to walk into tonight."

With one last wary glance at the mysterious pot, Levi turned and dutifully headed back out to the car. Some battles weren't worth fighting, although he had a sneaking suspicion rice pudding might become one of them.

Levi was starving by the time he finished unpacking and headed back into the kitchen. He was about to start rummaging for lunch when Aurelia, still standing at the stove stirring her mysterious pot of rice pudding, spoke without turning around.

"There's a sandwich in the fridge for you, along with some fruit salad," she said casually, as if she hadn't just rescued him from the brink of death by starvation.

His stomach growled in gratitude, but experience made him pause. With this woman, food had already proven to be dangerous territory. "What kind of sandwich?" he asked warily.

Aurelia let out a dramatic sigh and gave a little shake of her head. Levi watched her shoulders rise and fall with exaggerated patience before she finally answered.

"It's roast beef with mayonnaise."

Levi's eyes widened in shock. "That's my favorite sandwich. How did you know that?" He *knew* he hadn't put that anywhere in his matchmaking profile, and it definitely hadn't come up in conversation.

She cast him a haughty look over her shoulder, her eyes glinting with mischief. "Easy. I asked myself what my least favorite cold cut was, and the answer was roast beef. Since you enjoy the worst possible foods, it felt like a safe bet. And you look like the kind of man with unresolved childhood trauma involving mustard. So...mayonnaise."

Levi could only gape at her, completely speechless.

That victorious little smirk tugged at her lips as she turned back to her pudding. "Glad to see I nailed it," she tossed over her shoulder like a parting shot.

*Of all the shit to say...*And the worst part? She *had* nailed it. He wasn't sure if he was more offended by the accuracy or the fact that it made the sandwich taste slightly less special now.

Over the next couple of hours, they settled into an easy rhythm. Levi walked her through detailed introductions to each of his friends, complete with colorful anecdotes and background stories that probably should have come with warning labels.

Aurelia listened attentively, asking sharp, thoughtful questions between finishing the rice pudding. He had to admit...now that it was nestled in a glass casserole dish, topped with a delicate sprinkle of cinnamon, it looked divine. The entire house smelled of warm vanilla and fresh lemon.

He might have...*faintly* regretted his earlier skepticism.

Unable to resist, Levi tried to sneak a taste straight from the dish.

Without even turning around, Aurelia smacked his hand with the wooden spoon like some kind of domestic ninja.

He was beginning to believe she had eyes in the back of her head.

When he finally finished his rundown of the gang, Aurelia wiped her hands on a dish towel and leaned against the counter.

"Let me make sure I've got this straight," she began, counting off on her fingers. "Isaac is the stoic, brooding one. His wife, Grace, is the sweet and probably terrifying one who runs everything behind the scenes. Ivy is a lovable, sarcastic bitch, and Owen...Owen is basically a stray puppy you brought home from school one day and never got rid of."

Levi blinked. "I mean...when you put it like that..." He scrubbed a hand over his face, trying not to laugh. "Yeah. That about sums it up."

"Fantastic." She gave him a dazzling, utterly unapologetic smile. "We should probably get ready to go. You shower first while I clean up."

For a long moment, Levi stood there and stared at her, wondering how he ended up with someone so effortlessly perfect for him.

And then he laughed, shaking his head.

She was going to be fine tonight.

Possibly a little too fine. And that thought made him both excited and very, very afraid.

Aurelia

Aurelia sat at her bathroom vanity, applying her makeup, dressed only in a sheer lace bra, matching panties, and a loosely wrapped silk robe. The robe barely clung to her shoulders, its delicate fabric a poor guardian against the tension humming through her body. She had told herself she needed time to choose what to wear, but really, she was stalling, trying to slow the frantic beat of her heart.

Tonight, she would meet Levi's friends. *His real life, his people.*

Through the mirror, she caught her own reflection—the flush high on her cheeks, the uncertain flicker in her eyes. Her pulse fluttered beneath her skin, right when the bathroom door creaked open behind her.

She startled in her chair, spinning slightly toward the sound.

Levi stood in the doorway, tall and utterly still, his eyes locked on hers through the mirror.

"I'm sorry," he said, his voice low and slightly rough. "I should have knocked, but I can't find..." His words completely trailed off as his gaze shifted—slowly, deliberately—downward.

Aurelia's brows drew together. "Can't find what?" she asked, her voice a faint whisper.

But Levi didn't answer.

He took a slow, predatory step forward. The air around them thickened, humming with electricity as his eyes tracked lower—watching her robe slide farther off one shoulder, revealing the delicate emerald lace of her bra.

Her breath hitched.

It was a bra so sheer it might as well not have existed. Her hardened nipples pressed visibly through the thin fabric, and when she caught Levi's darkened expression in the mirror, something bold and incredibly reckless ignited inside her.

Without breaking his gaze, she reached up and pushed the robe off her other shoulder, baring herself completely to him.

Levi's hands found her shoulders in the next breath, his palms broad and warm against her flushed skin. His thumbs moved in slow, teasing circles, his voice a low growl against her ear.

"You're tense about meeting my friends," he murmured, eyes locked with hers in the mirror. "I think I know how to fix that."

Aurelia gasped softly and gave a tiny nod, unable to form words as his hands began their sinful work.

What started as a firm massage quickly became something far more dangerous. His fingers drifted under her bra straps, brushing against sensitive skin, then lower as they trailed along the curves of her breasts, teasing her already aching nipples.

Up and down, he moved with maddening patience. Grazing. Rolling. Tugging.

She pressed her thighs together, desperate for relief, but the mirror...oh god, the mirror made everything worse.

She couldn't look away.

Couldn't tear her eyes from the sight of Levi's strong, capable hands as they pushed her bra cups down, freeing her breasts completely to his touch.

Her breathing turned ragged. Every stroke of his fingers felt like it was tied directly to the pulsing ache between her legs, pulling her tighter, winding her up unbearably.

Levi never looked away from her face. Every gasp, every tremble studied with intense, ravenous focus.

"They won't mind if we're...a little late, will they?" she whispered, her voice breathless and breaking.

She stood abruptly, turning into him, her fists clutching the front of his shirt as she dragged his mouth down to hers in a fierce, consuming kiss.

That was all Levi needed.

With a low growl, Levi scooped her up and seated her on the vanity counter, his hands already working at his belt with practiced urgency. His jeans hit the floor in a blink, and then he was there, his hand sliding between her thighs, pushing aside the last barrier of lace.

He drove into her hard, his movements primal and desperate.

There was nothing soft about this—nothing sweet. Nothing other than raw, relentless need.

Aurelia moved with him, her hips rising to meet every thrust, their bodies locked in a frantic, consuming rhythm. They didn't care about the time. Didn't care about dinner or obligations or appearances.

They only cared about the edge looming before them, the inevitable descent—

And the blissful freefall they took together, lost and utterly undone.

Levi

Levi was still reeling as he pulled himself together for the second time that afternoon, trying to look presentable after what could only be described as the most sinfully delicious delay of his life.

He hadn't been prepared for how utterly insatiable his wife was...nor how little self-control he seemed to possess around her. Every plan, every ounce of logic, scattered the second she touched him.

Yes, they were clearly *in lust*...and that wasn't a bad thing. It proved they had chemistry, that undeniable pull between them. But it also left Levi feeling a thread of unease. He experienced enough to know that no relationship could survive on passion alone. Lust burned like a double-ended candle—and burned out fast if there wasn't something real beneath it.

And yet...they had barely known each other for forty-eight hours. It was absurd to worry about how fast things were moving when their entire marriage had begun in a rush. Jumping in headfirst was the whole point of this arrangement.

Still, as he adjusted his shirt and glanced at himself in the mirror, Levi made a silent vow:

This won't be driven by desire. I'm going to do this right. I'm going to learn every single thing about the woman I married.

The drive to Grace and Isaac's home passed in a companionable silence. Levi held Aurelia's hand the entire way, his thumb brushing over her skin absentmindedly. She seemed lost in thought, her expression unreadable as she stared out the window.

Levi used the quiet to map out his next steps.

Real dates. Real conversations. Real time together, he decided.

He would take her out the way he would have if they had met under normal circumstances—late-night dinners, museum strolls, lazy Sunday coffee runs. Anything and everything to discover who she truly was beyond the bedroom.

It also meant something far more challenging: he would have to restructure his life. Starting with his unforgiving work schedule.

The thought of the disaster waiting for him in his inbox tomorrow morning made his stomach tighten. The issue from his wedding day still loomed over his head like a dark cloud, and he had purposefully ignored it all weekend. He never ignored work. Come morning, the full weight of it would hit him like a freight train.

But staring at Aurelia now, her fingers loosely entwined with his, her lips pressed together in that soft contemplative pout...Levi knew there were more important things to fight for.

I'm going to woo the pants off my wife...literally and figuratively, he thought with a half-smile as he pulled into the driveway of Grace and Isaac's home.

Time to deal with the shenanigans. And this time, he wasn't walking in alone.

CHAPTER 35

Aurelia

"We're the last ones to arrive," Levi noted as he pulled into the long driveway, parking next to Owen's car.

Aurelia unbuckled her seatbelt, cheeks blazing as she *definitely* remembered why they were the last ones there. She tried not to meet Levi's eyes, knowing full well that self-satisfied smirk was spreading across his face. Willing her nerves into submission, she grabbed the rice pudding and her purse before following him to the door.

What she didn't expect was for Levi to simply walk in without knocking.

The gesture spoke volumes about the comfort and trust between him and his friends. It struck her, a little painfully, that even after all these years, she never had that kind of easy familiarity with Selene, let alone anyone else.

Before she could dwell on it, voices drifted in from somewhere beyond the foyer.

"Grace, I forbid you from ever making flan again," came an indignant, unmistakable voice. Owen.

"Don't listen to him. Just because he's being a baby doesn't mean the rest of us don't appreciate it," responded a second voice—deeper, calm. Isaac, she assumed.

"I'm *not* being a baby! I'm rational. Flan is an abomination and shouldn't be classified as dessert—or even as food."

Aurelia glanced at Levi, who had stopped dead in his tracks, pinching the bridge of his nose with a weary shake of his head.

She cast an inquisitive glance, silently asking: *Seriously?*

He sighed. *I warned you,* that sigh seemed to say, before motioning for her to keep walking.

"What exactly is your issue with it?" a teasing female voice chimed in— undoubtedly Ivy, tossing more fuel on the fire.

"It can't be both pudding *and* Jell-O! That level of culinary arrogance is offensive. The texture is wrong, the taste is bizarre, and you don't toss eggs into a pudding and call it a day! The taste and how it feels in my mouth is weird," Owen declared with dramatic flair.

"Pretty sure that's not the first time you've ever said that," Ivy shot back dryly, laughter immediately following.

Despite her nerves, Aurelia smiled as they entered the living room.

As soon as they stepped inside, all eyes turned toward them.

Without thinking, she blurted out, "If you think flan's an abomination, I can't wait to hear your thoughts on the rice pudding I brought."

Silence.

Panic set in. *Why can't I stop making awkward jokes?*

And then laughter erupted.

Owen looked vaguely horrified, clearly remembering their...shared history, while the others practically howled. Levi laughed too, his eyes warm as he shot her a look of pure admiration.

The laughter barely subsided before she was swept into a flurry of hugs and congratulations. It was overwhelming and entirely too much physical affection for someone who had carefully built walls for most of her life.

Sensing her discomfort, Levi cut through the crowd, creating space with a commanding but kind, "Alright, alright. Let her breathe."

Aurelia threw him a grateful glance as a beautiful auburn-haired woman stepped forward, her hazel eyes warm and welcoming.

"I'm Grace," she said brightly, taking the rice pudding from Aurelia's hands without hesitation. "And this troublemaker over here—" she gestured toward a caramel-skinned woman perched at the kitchen island, fingers wiggling in greeting, "—is Ivy. That handsome man in red is my husband, Isaac, and I'm sure you remember Owen."

Isaac offered a warm smile from the couch, his deep blue eyes crinkling against his mocha skin and neatly trimmed beard.

"Oh, I'm sure Aurelia remembers me," Owen chirped with far too much confidence.

"No matter how hard we try to forget," Levi muttered.

Unfazed, Owen turned back to Aurelia. "Now, the real question—where do you stand on the hotly debated topic of flan? Choose your words carefully. This is a defining moment."

"Except it's not," Isaac interjected with a roll of his eyes.

"I caught some of the debate on the way in," Aurelia said, feeling bolder now. "And while flan is technically a custard, I wouldn't call it a personal favorite. I *did* bring rice pudding, so that probably answers your question."

Owen's face twisted in horror. "Why—why would you *do* that?"

She shrugged, eyes twinkling with mischief. "I don't know...maybe next time you can sneak over and watch through my kitchen window to find out."

The color drained from Owen's face as everyone burst into another round of laughter. He clapped a hand over his heart. "Touché, Aurelia. Touché."

Before anyone could recover, Owen stood dramatically. "I, uh...need to find that champagne bottle I bought. Probably rolled under the car seat. Be right back!"

As Owen disappeared, Levi shot her a proud, knowing smile.

Ivy patted the stool beside her, an open invitation. "Come sit. And tell us everything about your hair. It's *amazing*. I could never pull that off," she gushed.

Aurelia found herself sliding into the seat, feeling more relaxed by the second.

"Would you like some wine?" Ivy asked, lifting an empty bottle with a playful grin.

Aurelia winced apologetically. "Not really a drinker. I've never developed a taste for it."

"Oh, me neither," Grace chimed in. "Unless it's something sweet that barely tastes like alcohol, I'm out. Although, dealing with Owen may drive you to it."

Relief flooded through her. Maybe this wouldn't be as intimidating as she thought.

"Your home is gorgeous," Aurelia added sincerely. "Thank you for having us. Can I help with anything before dinner?"

Grace smiled, her warmth palpable. "Everything's handled. Shepherd's pie is in the oven, salad's in the fridge, and you brought dessert. All that's left is relaxing—and trying not to kill Owen when he starts in again."

"It's inevitable," Ivy sighed.

Before Aurelia could respond, Owen returned triumphantly holding up a bottle of champagne.

"Found it! Also found someone's phone out there between our cars. Either of you missing one?"

Aurelia patted her purse with a sinking feeling and realized it was hers.

"Mine! Thank you," she called, accepting the phone with an embarrassed smile. It must have fallen from her purse as she exited the car.

"Is it *finally* time to eat?" Owen groaned as he collapsed dramatically onto the couch.

And right on cue, the oven timer chimed.

Grace shot a knowing look at Ivy and Aurelia. "Showtime," she whispered, before heading toward the kitchen.

Levi

Levi sat back on the couch, his attention fully captured by the sight of Aurelia laughing with Grace and Ivy. She belonged there, seamlessly folding into their little circle like she had always been part of it. The sight stirred something deep inside him, a comforting warmth that felt a lot like hope.

He took a slow sip of his beer, letting the hum of conversation swirl around him.

Then Owen's voice shattered the moment.

"So, are you *still* mad at me for the ceremony and my investigation? Aurelia sure hasn't forgotten." Owen dropped onto the couch beside him, clearly aiming for lighthearted...but the guilt in his eyes betrayed him.

Levi gave him a long, pointed look, his brow arching in disbelief. "Would you expect either of us to be over it already? The ceremony was already nerve-wracking, and you somehow found a way to make it weirder—and as if that weren't enough chaos, you had to add your special brand of insanity afterward."

He turned toward Isaac, leveling him with a look. "Did he tell you what he did?"

Isaac held his hands up in mock surrender, barely suppressing a knowing smirk.

Before Owen could defend himself, Levi cut in. "He filmed the whole disaster and sent the video to all of you—which, by the way, I'm still trying to wrap my head around—and then, when I didn't answer his calls, he took it upon himself to *investigate* by driving to Aurelia's house, sneaking onto her property, and *peeking through the windows* like some deranged stalker. And that's how he got a front-row seat to…well, you know."

Levi's ears burned as the memory flashed through his mind, and Isaac let out a low whistle, grinning widely.

Before anyone could respond, the unmistakable sound of shattering glass cut through the air.

Levi shot to his feet, his heart in his throat as he turned toward the kitchen.

Aurelia was crouched on the floor, frantically gathering the shards of a broken glass, her long hair veiling her face. Her hands trembled as she tried to sweep the pieces into her palm. Her phone had fallen too, lying a short distance away like a silent witness to whatever had unraveled her.

Grace and Ivy were immediately at her side, murmuring soft reassurances as they carefully helped her clean up. But when Ivy lifted her gaze toward the living room, her eyes were sharp, her mouth set in a tight, grim line.

"You might want to check the tabloids, Levi," she said coldly. "Looks like you're tonight's headliner."

Levi's stomach dropped.

He and Owen fumbled for their phones, while Isaac grabbed the TV remote and flipped to the local news station.

The headline blazed across the screen like a slap to the face: LOCKWOOD LOCKED DOWN: Trouble in Paradise Already?

Levi's chest tightened painfully as the photos flashed across the screen…crystal clear shots taken with a long-range lens.

Of Aurelia turning her cheek at the courthouse, refusing his kiss.

Another of her running for her car.

And the worst—him gripping her waist in the parking lot, his face a mix of desperation and regret.

Every humiliating second of that day was now immortalized for public consumption.

His mind raced. *Who tipped them off?*

Aside from the court clerk, no one should have known about the ceremony. And now…now it was everywhere.

He raked trembling hands through his hair, his thoughts moving at a thousand miles an hour. Even through the swirl of panic, one realization cut through all the noise.

He turned back to the kitchen. Aurelia was gone.

And Levi had no idea where she would run this time.

Aurelia

To be alone from prying eyes.

That's all Aurelia wanted—*needed*—as she burst through the sliding doors and into the quiet of Grace and Isaac's backyard, her vision blurring with unshed tears.

Everything had been going fine. Better than fine. Conversation had flowed so easily with Grace and Ivy that, for the first time in what felt like forever, she believed she could belong somewhere. Maybe she had a shot at this life she stumbled into.

And then her phone chimed.

One message. From Selene.

Wow, glad to find out my best friend got married a few days ago from the NEWS...Nothing screams desperate gold digger like an arranged marriage!!! Super rich though, huh? That's probably why you picked him. SO PISSED AT YOU RIGHT NOW!!!

The text was a punch to the gut, but it wasn't the worst of it. The link Selene had included was though.

It was all right there.

Her shame, her humiliation, her *entire life*, wide open for the world to mock.

Someone—God, *who?*—had leaked their marriage details. And someone else had waited, hidden outside the courthouse like a vulture, a camera ready to capture every raw, unguarded moment.

The photos. They were *everywhere*.

Her refusing Levi's kiss.

Her running to her car.

Him holding her back, his arms wrapped around her waist as she thrashed against him.

Each image was a perfectly framed disaster. The headlines were unequivocally brutal. But the comments were unforgivable.

Mail-order bride.

Gold digger.

Desperate nobody.

The words blurred together as her phone wobbled. The glass of water slipped from her grip, shattering on the tile. She didn't even feel it. Couldn't think. Couldn't breathe.

Body failing, her senses completely *shut down*.

Her mind spiraled, shame pulling her under like a rip tide she couldn't escape. Selene was angry—furious that she had kept this secret. And she couldn't blame her only friend for such betrayal. Eleanor…what would she have thought if she were still alive to see this spectacle? Would she be ashamed too?

Unbidden, the worst thought of all pushed forward, taking center stage—*what will Levi think of me now?*

She hadn't considered that marrying him would entail a public profile. One she was woefully unprepared for.

The backyard spun around her as anxiety took hold. Her airways constricted, forcing her to gulp down air with deep swallows. Her heart pounded against her ribs like it was trying to escape the same way she just escaped the interior of the house, the urge overpowering.

She needed *out* and away from their knowing looks, away from the pity, away from the judgment that was crawling across her skin.

Before she could act, strong, familiar arms wrapped around her from behind. Levi.

His touch was warm, steady, and without a single ounce of hesitation. Gently, he came around to face her, his worried green eyes scanning every inch of tear-streaked skin.

And then he did the one thing she didn't know she needed…he held her.

Simply held her.

Without demands. Without questions.

He stood there, unmoving, becoming her anchor in the middle of the storm she couldn't fight off. He held her while she trembled against him, her sobs breaking free, silent, and desperate.

And he didn't let go.

Not when her tears soaked his shirt.

Not when her knees nearly gave out.

Not even when his own heart broke for her right there in his arms.

Levi simply became her strength when she had none left of her own.

CHAPTER 36

Aurelia

Aurelia shook the nervousness out of her hands and arms before stepping out of her car and walking toward the imposing face of Starhaven Manor.

The heaviness of last night's events was a persistent burden that pushed down on her heart. Facing Selene was one thing—after her angry texts and unanswered calls Aurelia received—but facing Charles...that was something else entirely.

She wasn't sure which encounter she dreaded more.

This morning, Levi gently reminded her that even *he* hadn't been prepared for the scrutiny that came with his life—how long it took to build the impenetrable walls that protected him, and how unfair it was to expect her to be ready after a few days. He promised to find out who had leaked their wedding details, and—perhaps more surprisingly—so did his friends.

For the first time in her life, she had a group of people willing to support her.

But that didn't make today any easier.

Selene had ignored every text, every call since the scandal broke. And now, with the Harvest Charity Ball looming on the horizon and the headlines still circling, Aurelia was preparing for whatever tongue-lashing Charles had in store for her.

The honeymoon is over. Time to face reality, she thought grimly as she slipped through the back entrance, trying to avoid drawing too much attention.

Her posture radiated cool detachment, the way she had seen Eleanor do countless times before; as if the world hadn't just labeled her a gold-digging, mail-order wife. But every step felt heavier than the last. Her heart pounded painfully against her ribs.

She had to fake it to make...even when all she wanted was to disappear.

To not hear the whispers trailing behind her.

To not see the curious glances or, worse, the pitying ones.

To not feel like a living headline every time she entered a room.

Her pace quickened as she headed toward Eleanor's study, her sanctuary, praying Selene might appear and get this inevitable confrontation over with. But she found only empty corridors, the silence somehow louder than the imagined voices in her head.

It allowed the latest recurring thought to creep in...*Eleanor would be so disappointed in me.*

The sharp burn of tears threatened to rise again, but she swallowed them down. *Not here. Not now.*

Reaching the sitting room attached to the study, she snuck inside and closed the door behind her. Leaning backwards against it, she pressed the back of her head to the cool wood and inhaled deeply, trying to steady her breathing.

It took a full minute before she realized...she wasn't alone.

Selene stood by the window, arms crossed, eyes full of fire.

And in that moment, every self-preservation instinct Aurelia had honed over years of survival kicked in. She started to shrink inward, to get ready for the storm, to apologize and beg forgiveness. *Anything to stop Selene from being mad at her.*

But Selene beat her to it.

"Save it," Selene snapped, her tone frosty and eyes ice-cold. "You've had *plenty* of chances to tell me about your sugar daddy—sorry, *fiancé*—whatever he is. But you didn't. I had to find out like everyone else. From the goddamn news, Aurelia. You're such a shitty friend."

The words sliced through the air like a blade, and for a moment, Aurelia's mind went completely blank.

Shitty friend. The phrase echoed in her consciousness.

The old Aurelia—the one who would grovel, take the blame, and make herself small—wanted to agree and apologize, anything to keep the peace.

But she didn't.

Something fundamental inside her snapped.

Instead of cowering, Aurelia stood straighter as she studied her friend, her words still reverberating through her mind. Calm washed over her like a quiet resolve. The rush of fear dulled, replaced by something sharper, clearer. Her voice didn't tremble. Her silence carried weight.

"You've had plenty of chances to spend time with me," she shot back, her voice solid but tight. "I kept asking, and you kept blowing me off. Last time, I had to track you down at work because you ghosted me—you said your phone was broken, but somehow, you still managed to read my messages. So don't stand there and act like I've been keeping secrets when you couldn't even be bothered to answer a text!"

Selene blinked, her anger faltering under the weight of Aurelia's words.

"And you know what?" Aurelia pressed on, her voice rising as she took a measured step closer. "You expected me to spill the most personal details of my life—of *someone else's* life, someone you've never even met—at work, of all places? For what? So the whole office could gossip about me, too?"

The raw emotion poured out of her, unstoppable now.

"The real shitty friend is standing in front of me—too busy to call, too busy to care, but not too busy to pass judgment the second she reads a headline!"

Selene stood rooted to the floor, stunned, her mouth opening and closing as if the words wouldn't form.

For the first time in their friendship, Aurelia had put herself first. And it felt *good.*

With a deep, calming breath, the fragile pieces of her composure slid back into place. "The ball's in your court, Selene. If you want to talk—*really* talk—you know where to find me. But it'll be outside business hours. I'm done being an afterthought on your schedule."

She twisted toward the door...and froze.

Charles was leaning against the doorframe, his expression unreadable, but his eyes held a flicker of unmistakable amusement.

He had seen everything.

"Well, that's one way to start the day," Charles said with a bemused grin, closing the door behind him and settling into his chair like a witness to the opening act of a spectacular drama.

Aurelia sank into the nearest seat, her earlier burst of confidence collapsing beneath the weight of shame. She rubbed her temples, the fight gone from her posture. "I—I'm so sorry about that," she stammered. "I don't know what came over me. That was...so incredibly unprofessional." Her words were muffled; her gaze locked on the floor.

Charles studied her with quiet patience. "Is that really how you'd describe what just happened?"

"Yes," she answered immediately, eyes flashing up to meet his. "I take this job seriously. Letting personal matters bleed into my work life is a distraction, and it's inappropriate."

He tilted his head, considering her with a look that made her feel like she had missed something obvious. "We'll have to agree to disagree, then," he said calmly. "Because what I saw wasn't unprofessional, it was necessary. An employee tried to drag you into a personal confrontation at work. You stood your ground. You set a boundary. That's leadership, Aurelia, a show of strength, not weakness."

She wanted to believe him. But the immense stress of everything else—the headlines, the photos, Selene's betrayal, her insecurities in the relationship she was building with Levi—made it almost impossible to breathe, let alone feel proud of herself.

She swallowed thickly. "I think that's the least of my worries right now," she admitted quietly. "I'm assuming you've seen the news."

The amusement faded from Charles's features, his mouth a grim thin line.

"Unfortunately, I have," he said. "And I'm more than a little concerned about how the media even found out about the ceremony in the first place." He leaned back, steepling his fingers in consternation. "I've already contacted the Clerk's office. While the marriage certificate is technically a public record, they claim no one from their office leaked any information. So, if it didn't come from us— and we know it didn't—then the next logical place to look is your new husband."

The accusation, even implied, hit her like a slap.

Charles sighed. "I'm not saying it was him, but you both signed confidentiality agreements. And there's also Estrella's contract to consider. She's...not pleased with the media scrutiny either."

Aurelia closed her eyes, pinching the bridge of her nose as the beginnings of a headache started to thrum behind her temples.

"And that's only one of the issues," Charles continued, his voice more subdued but no less firm. "The more pressing concern is that I've received calls from three of the charities originally slated to participate in the Harvest Charity Ball. All of them have pulled out."

Her eyes snapped open. "All three?" she choked out, unable to believe it.

Charles nodded gravely. "They rescinded their agreements as of this morning. Each one insisted they wouldn't be involved unless you were removed from overseeing the event." Displeasure etched in the lines of his face. "I made it very clear that we have zero plans to do any such thing. If they can't separate tabloids from your professional track record, then frankly, they don't belong at the ball at all."

Aurelia sat frozen while her mind struggled to catch up with what she had just heard. The Clowns for Climate Change Awareness. Penguins on Parade Coalition. Underwater Basket Weavers United. These organizations had been part of the event for over a decade. And now, because of a scandal she couldn't even control, they were gone.

"What...what exactly did they say?" she asked timidly.

Charles hesitated, then answered with deliberate precision. "They said your 'reckless behavior' at the wedding, combined with the optics of an arranged and financially advantageous marriage, would tarnish Eleanor's legacy and damage their brand by association. They feel you've compromised the integrity of the event...and want you fired immediately to preserve its reputation."

Her mouth parted, but no words came out.

"This isn't only about you, Aurelia," he added gently. "Your husband's name doesn't help. He's had his share of very public...incidents. And the fact that no one knows you're Eleanor's heir yet? That only fuels their assumptions. Right now, to these organizations, you're merely a headline."

Aurelia deflated entirely, the fight bleeding out of her like a slow leak from a punctured tire. She pressed her fists into her eyes to hold back the tears.

"Eleanor would be so disappointed in me," she whispered, finally voicing the constant fear aloud.

Charles's brow creased with something close to sympathy. Or perhaps it was frustration. "Do you truly believe that?" he asked carefully. "Because I can tell you, without a shadow of a doubt, if Eleanor were here, she'd be throwing a fit. Not at you, Aurelia. *At them.* She'd ban those charities for life and declare the ball a roaring success out of spite alone."

He leaned forward, his voice low but purposeful. "The real question is...what are you going to do now?"

Aurelia swallowed the lump in her throat, as Eleanor's voice seemed to echo through her memory: *Never let small-minded people decide your worth or tell you what to do.*

She drew herself up, folding tension into every line of her body. "Sounds like I've got three new charities to find."

Charles smiled faintly, his eyes gleaming with a familiar spark of mischief. "Now that's what the Eleanor I remember would do."

CHAPTER 37

Levi

It had been weeks since the wedding, the tabloid headlines...and the HR nightmare that sparked Levi's first real misunderstanding with Aurelia.

Since then, he had been consumed by the fallout, spending late nights with Isaac and the development team dissecting every line of code tied to Project DL. His days blurred into endless hours of crisis management; his nights were no better, fractured by Aurelia's restless sleep and the sharp cries of her nightmares. The exhaustion was becoming bone-deep.

But nothing haunted him more than the meeting he had on his first day back in the office—a conversation that played on an endless, anxiety-fueled loop in his mind.

"I'm extremely concerned about the changes made to Project DL's underlying code," Isaac said grimly, sitting across from Levi's desk.

Ivy stood nearby, arms crossed, nodding in agreement. "We didn't tell you last week because we knew you'd postpone the wedding and throw yourself into this," she admitted. "It's contained for now, but...barely."

Levi's knuckles turned white as he gripped the armrests of his chair. His voice was tight. "Start from the beginning."

Isaac shifted in his seat, angling his body closer. "There was a scheduled release to QA for data collection and security evaluation. Everything was stable...until it wasn't. The test PII dataset behaved erratically—data was being stored improperly, violating every documented security policy. None of it matched our approved code. That's when we discovered the changes."

"Unauthorized changes," Ivy added, her jaw clenched. "Made by Harris Wilkerson. He wasn't even assigned to that part of the project."

Levi exhaled slowly through his nose, temper on a razor's edge.

"And that's not the worst part," Ivy continued. "Harris was the same employee Tyler cornered outside the elevator the day of the security breach. Last Friday, we pulled him into a meeting. He's been terminated."

Isaac recounted every agonizing second of that meeting.

"Thank you for joining us, Harris," Diana began, her tone calm but unyielding as she folded her hands neatly on the table. "Let's get straight to the point. After a thorough review, we've determined your recent changes to Project DL's code were unauthorized, well outside the scope of your role, and a direct violation of company policy."

Harris leaned back in his chair, arms crossed tight against his chest. "Are we seriously making a federal case out of this? The changes were meant to improve performance and data collection. They worked, didn't they?" His voice rose defensively, his arms dropping to grip the chair's armrests.

Isaac sat forward, his voice low and sharp. "This isn't about whether they worked—which, incidentally, they didn't. QA flagged them immediately. The only reason we even found out about this is because your changes caused catastrophic failures in the test environment. You bypassed every review process, ignored CI/CD safeguards, and pushed code straight to QA. Do you even understand the kind of risk you created for this company?"

Harris's jaw tightened. "I understand the risks, but I also have a vision for what this product should be. I took initiative. The project's behind schedule, and while everyone else sat on their hands, I did something about it. Frankly, no one else around here—including you, Isaac—seems to have the guts or imagination to see what's possible."

Isaac's eyes narrowed, his voice sharply carving through the tension. "It's not your job to make those calls, Harris. There's a structured process for a reason: to protect this company from exactly this kind of reckless behavior. And let's not pretend this is your first offense. You've already been warned after you violated security protocols and let a Board member into a restricted development area without clearance." His eyes locked with Harris's, hard and uncompromising. "The real question is whether this vision you're so proud of is yours...or Tyler Faulkner's."

Diana stepped in smoothly before Harris could lash out again. "This wasn't a decision we made lightly," she said, her voice cool and even. "But your actions have undermined trust, created operational and legal risks, and compromised the integrity of this team. Senior leadership has agreed...your employment is terminated, effective immediately."

For a moment, Harris stared at them, his face a mask of disbelief. "You're...firing me? Just like that? After everything I've done for this company?" His voice cracked on the last word, hands gripping the arms of the chair like he might snap them off.

Isaac's response was blunt. "We value innovation, Harris, but only within the boundaries of authority and accountability. Your actions did more than put the project at risk—it put this entire company in jeopardy. This isn't about your talent. It's about the trust you destroyed."

Diana slid a folder across the table toward him. "This outlines your severance package, the return of company property, and next steps for transitioning out. We've also included resources to support your job search. Do you have any questions about the logistics?"

Harris stared at the folder like it might catch fire. His voice dropped to a low, bitter rasp. "I guess I don't have a choice, do I? You already had this all worked out before you dragged me in here."

Isaac's expression didn't waver. "You made your choices, Harris. Actions have consequences. I sincerely hope you learn something from this because the next company won't be as forgiving."

Diana stood, signaling the meeting's end. "You're free to take a moment before you leave. Security is waiting to escort you out."

For a long moment, Harris didn't move. Then, slowly, he stood, scooping up the folder with shaking hands. But right as he turned to leave, he paused, casting one final look at Isaac.

A bitter, almost crazed smile stretched across his face. "You're going to regret this," he promised in a low, venomous growl. "Firing me. Dismissing my vision. Just wait...you'll see."

With that, he stalked out of the room, his shoulders squared against the humiliation waiting beyond the door.

There was nothing Levi wanted to do more in that moment than punch a hole in the wall—or desk—anything really.

Levi's anger churned like a storm behind a cracking dam. And when he thought he had heard the worst of it, the door to his office slammed open.

Like a demon summoned by pure rage, Tyler Faulkner crossed the threshold, eyes wild and filled with fury.

"You," he snarled, jabbing a finger in Levi's face. "You're costing me money with your incompetence! The scandal with your wife—if that's what we're calling the pretty little whore—is tanking our stock, and you're doing nothing about it!"

Levi moved faster than anyone could stop him. One second, he was seated; the next, he was inches from Tyler, gripping his collar and lifting him off the floor like a sack of feathers. His voice was a low, dangerous growl.

"Call her that again," Levi warned in a menacing whisper, "and you'll be leaving this building in a body bag."

He dropped Tyler unceremoniously to the floor, hardly containing the violent tremor coursing through him. Isaac was swiftly at his side, a silent wall of support.

Tyler scrambled to his feet, straightened his jacket, and sneered. "Mark my words, Lockwood. The consequences of your actions are coming. I'm counting down the days."

"Get the hell out of my office," Levi ground out through clenched teeth.

And with a final, lingering glance—one that promised trouble—Tyler was gone.

Three weeks later, Levi couldn't shake those words.

I'm counting down the days.

He could feel a storm gathering on the horizon and the invisible sands of time slipping away toward some inevitable disaster.

And no matter how hard he tried to prepare, he knew deep down nothing could prime him for what was coming.

CHAPTER 38

Aurelia

The honeymoon phase was over. Completely, undeniably over.

The whirlwind of their wedding and the languid, blissful weekend that followed felt like a fading dream. Reality had crept back in on quiet feet, settling between them like a silent barrier neither had the time nor energy to dismantle.

It had only been three weeks.

Aurelia sighed, her fingers tightening around the steering wheel as she navigated through the crowded streets of Joia City. She was headed home after a short day at Starhaven Manor, having spent a couple of hours that morning finalizing some outstanding details. Even with the reduced workload, her thoughts were a mess.

Securing new charities after the wedding scandal had been a logistical nightmare. Her public bridal photoshoot made more of an impact than she originally thought, scandalizing the city and closing doors she had counted on for years. The gossip surrounding it had yet to die down.

But somehow...she pulled it off.

Tapping into her old contacts at District Child Welfare Services, she managed to secure their involvement. Inspired by Levi, she had secured a commitment from the National Dyslexia Foundation. And in a final, almost laughable twist of fate, she stumbled across Glow Sticks for the Elderly, an organization dedicated to bringing rave culture into retirement homes. It was obscure and delightfully offbeat, and she had no doubt Eleanor would have adored the chaotic brilliance of it.

Of course, their participation came with a hidden cost: a full-fledged "mini-rave" during the reception. She had agreed without hesitation. Now, she had to figure out how to turn glow sticks into something elegant enough for the Harvest

Charity Ball. Wrapping them in gauzy, jeweled fabric to refract the light into dazzling prisms seemed like a fitting compromise.

Against all odds, the rest of the planning had fallen into place.

The final menu tasting was scheduled. The décor was locked in and featured bold fall colors intertwined with metallics and diamond accents. Bronze, copper, deep reds and purples, all softened by enchanted forest elements: faux trees, cascading vines, and whimsical lighting. Guests had been encouraged to embrace the theme and attend in formal wear with a "hint of magic." It was the closest thing to a fairytale she could conjure...and she needed a little magic right now.

The one person who remained conspicuously absent from her preparations was Selene. She was always just out of reach—leaving rooms as Aurelia entered them, conveniently "in meetings" every time she called. The sting of that cold shoulder hurt more than she wanted to admit, but she meant what she had said the last time they spoke.

The ball was in Selene's court now.

Her thoughts drifted to Levi, and the familiar ache settled in her chest. She needed to talk to him about the event, about everything, but they hadn't found a spare minute to discuss the details. She wanted to extend the invitation to his friends, too, but every time she planned to bring it up, the moment passed unspoken.

Outside of work, the honeymoon was...over.

She began to understand why Levi's friends had been so concerned about him. Levi was married to his job, and she felt like a distant second. They'd barely seen each other lately.

Monday, he missed dinner entirely, caught up in some crisis at work. Tuesday was her self-defense class—a much-needed distraction—but by the time she came home, he was still at the office. Wednesday and Thursday followed the same pattern.

She had even tried to surprise him with lunch earlier in the week, bringing takeout to his office. It turned into something far more heated, and while he had been grateful, his exhaustion had been written all over his face.

Tonight, when he texted again to say he wouldn't be home for dinner, she refused to let the loneliness sink its claws into her. Instead, she took a risk and asked Adelen, the new student she had met in her self-defense class, to grab a quick bite afterward. To her surprise, the woman had agreed.

Maybe I should text her again...see if she's free this weekend. It seems like I'll have plenty of time to myself again.

The thought was meant to be dismissive, but it stung anyway.

Her mind spun in circles. Was Levi already tired of her and planning to leave? Had he realized, like every other man before him, that she was boring once the shine wore off?

Except for Kyle. I had to run from him.

The car felt stifling as old doubts crept in, uninvited and unwelcome.

This time was supposed to be different.

Levi was different.

And yet, every night this week, and so many others before, he came home long after dinner, looking worn down to his soul. A quick kiss on the cheek, a plate of reheated food, and then a long shower that seemed more about washing off his stress than relaxing.

She flushed, her face heating at the memory of that one night when she couldn't stand the distance anymore and slipped into the shower with him. For a short while, it felt like they'd found their way back to each other.

But even that moment felt like a lifetime ago.

Aurelia slipped quietly into the bathroom, her bare feet silent against the cool tiles. She paused for a moment, drinking in the sight of those long, athletic legs braced apart, and toned muscles taut beneath golden skin.

His back was to her, broad shoulders hunched as his strong arms pressed against the shower wall. The image permanently emblazoned on his back was stark and dangerous...and as tempting as forbidden fruit. His head bowed under the warm cascade of water; his eyes shut like the weight of the world rested on his shoulders.

He hadn't noticed her yet.

With a slow, deliberate movement, she undressed, letting her clothes fall silently to the floor. The shower door creaked faintly as she opened it, a whisper of cool air rushing inside. That's when he felt her.

Levi stiffened for a heartbeat before the powerful lines of his back flexed with tension as he shifted his body to face her. His forest eyes, dark and unreadable, glided over her exposed skin with an intensity that made her pulse trip. Every inch of her was devoured by that heated gaze, his silence louder than any words.

Then she crossed the distance between them, rising to press her mouth against his in a slow, torturous kiss.

Whatever shadows had haunted his mind were obliterated in that instant.

Without hesitation, his hands found her thighs, gripping them with a strength that made her gasp as he lifted her effortlessly. Her back met the cool tile with a soft thud, her legs instinctively wrapping around his waist. There was no preamble, no gentle exploration—no time wasted.

With a low, guttural sound, Levi drove into her, his hips snapping forward with a punishing rhythm. She cried out, the sound swallowed by the roar of the water and his hungry mouth covering hers again.

There was nothing soft about this. Nothing careful.

It was primal.

Every thrust was deep, relentless, hitting that perfect spot again and again until the pressure inside her wound impossibly tight. Her fingers dug into his slick shoulders, her head falling back against the shimmering tiled wall as the pleasure overwhelmed her, shattering her apart in his arms.

He followed her over the edge moments later, his groan vibrating against her throat, his entire body tensing before he collapsed against her, breathless.

For a long moment, they simply stayed there, their chests heaving, the water cascading over their tangled bodies.

And then, with a tenderness that stole her breath all over again, Levi gently set her down.

In silence, his hands moved over her, washing her with such care it felt like worship. His fingers lingered over every curve, every sensitive spot, tracing along her skin as if to memorize her by touch alone.

He didn't speak. He didn't need to.

In that quiet act, she heard everything he couldn't bring himself to say.

Everything she needed to know.

Swallowing hard, Aurelia forced herself to shake off the doubt and unease, to focus on the road ahead. Whatever it was Levi had been battling this week, she didn't know, though it wasn't for lack of trying.

Every time she had asked, he had brushed her off with a quiet, tired smile and the same maddening reply: *I don't want to burden you with my problems.*

That answer gnawed at her.

But what gnawed at her more was the slow, creeping understanding that learning to live with a stranger—even one who could kiss her into oblivion and touch her like she was something precious—was far harder than she anticipated.

The not-so-cute nuances were piling up.

The perpetually sticky toothpaste tube they now shared, no matter how many times she wiped it clean. Like clockwork, she would find it smeared again after he used it, the faintest reminder that even in their most mundane routines, they moved out of sync.

Or how he turned the neatly made bed into a mangled mess every night, sheets and blankets untucked and tangled because *it's too restrictive*, as he put it.

And she didn't want to think about the dishwasher again.

He would run it half-full, and yet somehow still leave a pile of dishes in the sink that clearly could have fit. It was like a strategic puzzle he refused to play.

It's an adjustment period; she told herself for the hundredth time. *Every couple goes through this.*

And yet...

That old, familiar fear—the one that lived directly beneath her skin—whispered louder with each passing day. *He's already bored with me, like everyone else was.*

She banished the negative thoughts away as she turned into the driveway, exhaling a long breath of relief. It was finally Friday.

A spark of determination lit inside her.

If Levi wasn't going to make time to escape work for her, she would give him every reason to want to, using the only thing that he couldn't say no to.

A slow, devilish grin curved her lips as she exited the car and went inside.

It was time to lure her husband home.

CHAPTER 39

Levi

It had been a brutal week, and Levi could feel every bit of it in the tight coil of his shoulders and the pounding tension headache threatening to settle behind his eyes.

Back-to-back meetings consumed his entire morning, leaving him no time to actually get any meaningful work done. The hour after lunch had been spent hunched over his desk, poring through a relentless flood of emails and grim updates about Project DL. His calendar mocked him with one final meeting scheduled late in the day. The perfect end to a thoroughly miserable week.

And then it hit him.

It was Friday.

A cold dread settled in his gut as he leaned back in his chair, running a tired hand down his face. He worked late every single night this week. He had barely seen Aurelia, let alone spent any real time with her. The sex was phenomenal, but that was all they had time for.

It wasn't enough.

Isaac's words echoed in his mind. *I think you're working too much.*

He hadn't wanted to believe it. But what had he been doing? Avoiding home? Avoiding the complicated emotions that surfaced every time he walked through the door and saw a wife he barely knew waiting for him? Or worse…disappointing her before they'd even had a chance to build their relationship?

He kept his troubles to himself under the guise of protecting her, not wanting to burden her with his stress. But maybe that wasn't as noble as he told himself. Maybe that was cowardice dressed up as chivalry.

Whatever it was, it had to stop.

He wasn't spending another Friday night buried in work. No, tonight he was going to take his wife out, look her in the eyes, and finally start building something real between them. He pushed away from his desk, already strategizing how to pull together a proper date, when his phone lit up.

Aurelia's name flashed across the screen.

The tension in his chest loosened a fraction as a smile tugged at his lips. He answered immediately.

"Good afternoon, my wife," he drawled.

"Good afternoon, dear husband," she purred in response, her voice rich and teasing. "How's your day going?"

Levi chuckled, leaning forward, elbows on his desk. "It was horrendous until about thirty seconds ago. Now it's looking up."

He heard the warmth in her laugh, and it curled deliciously through his blood.

"Such an astonishing turn of events," she mused. "Tell me, how's the rest of your afternoon looking?"

Levi sighed. "Back-to-back meetings until four-thirty. The first one starts in about twenty minutes."

A low, sympathetic sound hummed through the line. "That sounds dreadful..." Her voice dropped to a sultry whisper. "Unfortunately, I'm about to make it even harder for you. Well...*make you a bit harder.*"

Levi sat up so fast he cracked his knee against the underside of his desk. He bit back a curse.

She continued before he could recover.

"I've been alone in this house all afternoon," she murmured, her voice a dark, sensual caress, "wearing nothing but thin purple lace that doesn't cover much of anything..."

His pulse slammed in his throat.

"And it's definitely not enough to keep me warm."

He felt the air in his office thicken, heat spiking as her words wrapped around him.

"I haven't been able to stop thinking about my husband," she went on, slow and decadent, "thinking about the ravishing he promised me...and how desperately I need it. Right. Now. But apparently, I'm going to have to wait."

He gripped the edge of his desk, his knuckles bone-white.

"I'm not a very patient woman, Levi. If you're not home and *inside me* by five o'clock..." Her breath hitched. "Then I'll have to start without you."

He was already on his feet, stalking toward his private bathroom like a man possessed.

Voice low and dangerous, he growled, "If I get home and find you've started without me, I won't be gentle, Auri."

Her breathless laugh curled through the phone. "Whether you come on time is completely up to you. I'll be taken care of either way. Have a productive afternoon."

The line went dead.

Levi stared at his phone in stunned disbelief before a new message came through.

With shaking hands, he opened it.

And there she was—laid out on their bed in nothing but the sheerest purple lace, her wild rainbow hair a halo around her flushed face, full breasts peaked and straining against the delicate fabric. One hand was planted above her head snapping the photo...while the other was slipping lower.

Locked in his private bathroom, he swore viciously under his breath.

And then he lost the battle entirely, unfastening his pants. Groaning, he took himself in his hand, desperate to take the edge off. His eyes never left the screen as his mind filled in every torturous detail of what waited for him at home.

Five o'clock couldn't come fast enough.

The next three and a half hours were pure torture.

Levi had tried desperately to cancel at least his last meeting of the day, but no amount of pleading or rescheduling magic could get him out of it. Another endless Board meeting, the same recycled agenda, and the same power struggles.

The only thing Levi could focus on was the ticking clock and the unbearable ache building beneath his belt.

He was barely holding it together when the room went quiet, every head swiveling toward him. Levi snapped his gaze up from the table to find a sea of expectant faces...and Tyler Faulkner glaring at him like he wanted to commit murder.

"You haven't heard a single word that's been said, Lockwood," Tyler snapped, his face an alarming shade of red. "Do you have more pressing matters than running this company? Or are you too busy playing house?"

If only he knew.

Levi swallowed the smirk threatening to break across his face. His mind flashed to the image of Aurelia sprawled across their bed, that sheer purple lace clinging to her curves. There was absolutely something he would rather be doing right now. Over and over again.

Tyler must have caught the tell—something Levi couldn't quite keep out of his expression.

"You've completely lost your focus ever since you acquired that mail-order bride of yours," Tyler sneered, his voice oily with contempt. "Maybe it's time you stopped thinking with the head between your legs and—"

Levi cut him off smoothly, his tone edged with lethal calm. "You've taken a really strange interest in my sex life lately, Tyler. It's becoming...obsessive. Should I be concerned?"

The room went still. Someone stifled a laugh.

"And while we're on the subject," Levi continued, standing and gathering his things with practiced efficiency, "you've managed to drone on about the same topics for forty-five minutes without a single new idea. If you're here to listen to yourself talk, kindly schedule these meetings for a time when I'm less inclined to gouge out my own eyes."

Tyler's face turned a dangerous shade of crimson, which he didn't think was possible, as Levi checked the time.

4:33 PM.

Shit.

Snapping his briefcase shut, Levi looked Tyler dead in the eye. "You scheduled this meeting to end at 4:30. I don't appreciate your inability to run a competent agenda, interfering with my other commitments." He paused, his smile sharp enough to cut glass. "But don't end on my account. I'd hate to deprive everyone of the sound of your voice."

With that, Levi turned on his heel and walked out calm, collected, and in complete control.

At least until he cleared the boardroom doors.

The second he hit the hallway, he sprinted like hell was on his heels. His office was a blur. Papers were shoved into his bag. Backpack slung over his shoulder. He barely tossed a wave toward Ivy as he tore past her desk.

"Don't ask!" he called over his shoulder as the elevator took a full two agonizing minutes to arrive. He spent every second of it staring at his phone, thumbing over the photo Aurelia had sent him earlier, his version of paradise wrapped in purple lace.

The image was seared into his brain, and no matter how hard he tried, his body refused to calm down.

By the time he slid behind the wheel and tore out of the parking garage, it was 4:49 PM. The house was a solid fifteen minutes away—without traffic. Levi had zero intention of obeying speed limits today.

He cut through the streets like a bat out of hell, one eye on the road, the other on the ticking clock. If a cop pulled him over, he would hand over his license, show them the picture, and beg for mercy.

At exactly 5:00 PM, while taking the last turn home, his phone chimed.

An audio message. From his wife.

He pressed play over the Bluetooth...and almost lost control of the car.

Aurelia's voice filled the cabin, low, husky, dripping with promise.

"Time's up, husband."

Levi floored it.

Aurelia

Aurelia had set out to drive Levi insane today...She just hadn't expected to take herself right along for the ride.

The moment she arrived home, she slipped into that sheer scrap of purple lace, fully intending to snap a single teasing photo and be done with it. But something deeper, something darker and more primal took hold of her.

She never took it off.

Not even as the hours stretched by.

Not even as the ache between her thighs grew into a desperate, throbbing need.

With nothing beneath it, the silky fabric became a constant, agonizing reminder of the game she started. And she refused to end it early. Her body begged for relief, but she denied herself the satisfaction. Not until 5:00 PM.

She watched the clock like a crazed woman.

By 4:45 PM, she was in bed, draped across the sheets, her colorful hair fanned out around her, the low light of the room painting her skin in soft, golden hues.

At exactly 5:00 PM, she hit record on her phone and sent the message that would light her husband's world on fire.

Time's up, husband.

But the moment she pressed send, her carefully maintained control splintered.

Her hand slipped lower, fingers trembling as they found their mark. She let out a strangled moan, her touch instantly igniting the need she held at bay all afternoon.

There was no finesse, no slow buildup, only determination and precision as her fingers moved faster, her body climbing toward that blinding peak she had denied for hours.

So close. Need one more second—

The bedroom door slammed open.

Levi appeared like a storm rolling through her sanctuary, eyes blazing, chest heaving, his shirt gone, and his pants barely clinging to his hips before they joined the trail of discarded clothes.

He was over her in an instant, pinning her to the bed with his body, and then—with a single, brutal thrust—he buried himself deep.

Aurelia cried out, her head falling back, her hips arching to take him even deeper as her orgasm detonated through her.

Levi was relentless, his pace savage as he took over the rhythm her fingers had started. His hand shot out, catching her wrist and dragging her slick fingers to his mouth. He groaned low and dangerously as he tasted her, his tongue swirling over her knuckles before he bit gently down.

Wild-eyed, he watched her writhe beneath him, her legs locked tight around his waist, her body soft and trembling beneath his brutal onslaught.

His focus dropped to her breasts, the lace doing nothing to hide the hard peaks begging for attention. With a feral growl, he bent down and captured one between his lips, his tongue flicking before his teeth lightly tugged the sensitive tip.

Aurelia cried out, her nails raking down his back as her hips bucked against his with frantic urgency. She was undone, completely lost in pleasure, panting his name like a prayer and a curse all in one breath.

Levi drove into her harder, faster, his control hanging by a fraying thread as he felt her body tighten around him, her second climax crashing into her as violently as the first.

With a raw, primal roar, he thrust once...twice...and spilled into her with a force that left them both shaking.

He sank onto her, his face pressed into the crook of her neck, mouths parted from breathless gasps. Their bodies remained entwined, slick, and trembling from the storm they'd unleashed.

In that moment, nothing else mattered.

Only this. Just them.

Levi

"I'm impressed you made it home so early."

Levi smiled against the soft tangle of hair beneath his chin. Neither of them had moved, content to stay wrapped in each other's arms, their bodies still humming from what they'd shared moments ago.

"Considering the ultimatum you gave me, I was hard-pressed to stay any longer," he murmured, his voice still rough with the aftermath of pleasure.

Aurelia tilted her head, her lips curving into a mischievous grin. "If I recall correctly, that's not the only thing you were hard-pressed with."

A low, rich laugh rumbled from his chest, vibrating against her bare skin.

"Well," he drawled, his fingers tracing lazy circles along her spine, "I've been working late all week. I figured by now you were either desperately pining for me or had completely forgotten what I look like."

She snorted against his skin, but he caught the way her arms tightened around him.

"Since I couldn't bear the idea of my beautiful wife wasting away from longing, or worse, mistaking me for some handsome intruder, I had every intention of surprising you with a real date tonight." His lips brushed her temple as he added, "That was the plan...until I received the most provocative phone call."

Levi felt the blush rise along her neck before he saw it, and it lit him up from the inside out. That gorgeous flush painted across her skin because of him.

He smoothed his palm along her back, savoring the moment.

"A date actually sounds perfect," she admitted softly, her breath warm against his chest. "It's been a long week..."

"Good, because I'm starving, and not just for you this time." His mouth curled into a grin as he glanced at the clock. "I made reservations for seven at Fondue Rendezvous. We've got about fifteen minutes before we need to head out."

She pushed up on her elbows, her eyes widening with delight. "You got us into that place? I've been trying for months!" Her expression shifted into playful suspicion as she narrowed her eyes. "Did you shamelessly abuse your billionaire powers for this?"

Levi feigned a dramatic look of offense. "That cut me deep, Auri. What's the point of being rich and powerful if I can't use it to spoil my wife with melted chocolate and inappropriate things to dip into it?"

She rolled her eyes, but the smile on her face was impossible to hide. "Let me freshen up, and then you can continue your salacious attempts at wooing me over dinner."

As she stood and padded toward the bathroom, Levi's gaze lingered on the sway of her hips, a warmth spreading through him that had nothing to do with desire.

Yeah, he could definitely get used to that.

CHAPTER 40

Aurelia

Though it was late summer, the night air had a surprising chill, coaxing them both into long sleeves.

Aurelia reveled in the cool breeze as they walked hand-in-hand toward the restaurant, stealing glances at Levi beside her. Every line of his strong jaw, every flicker of his eyes beneath those dark lashes, was committed to memory like a woman desperate to bottle a perfect moment.

Then it struck her...she was falling for him fast. Too fast.

She had no time to think beyond that realization before a host, dressed in flowing jewel-toned silks, led them to their table. Distracted, Aurelia couldn't help but marvel at the Moroccan-inspired splendor around her.

Settling into a plush amethyst-colored chair, she ran her fingers over the intricately carved wooden table between them. Overhead, delicate metal lanterns spilled out soft golden light, creating playful shadows across the rich tapestries and patterned tiles that adorned the walls and floors. Jewel-toned drapes in green, sapphire, and deep crimson swayed gently from the ceiling.

It was spectacular—for a place where you have to cook your food.

"Not as spectacular as my view," Levi said, his voice a low rumble that rolled across the table and curled around her like a caress.

It took Aurelia a stunned moment to realize she had spoken her last thought aloud. Heat rose to her cheeks in a flood of mortification.

Recovering quickly, she lifted her chin and shot back, "I guess one could say you're...easy on the eyes."

Levi threw his head back and laughed, the sound warm and full, scattering the last of her embarrassment.

Their server chose that moment to arrive and take their drink orders, explaining the fondue process with practiced enthusiasm. Before he could even finish, Levi leaned back in his chair with a dramatic groan.

"I'm so hungry I could eat the ass hole of a dead horse right now," he declared with absolute seriousness.

The poor server stood frozen, eyes wide, as if he weren't sure whether to laugh or bolt for the kitchen. He opted for a quick nod before scurrying away.

Aurelia gaped at Levi. "I can't believe you said that! That poor man looked traumatized."

Levi shrugged unapologetically. "What? I'm that hungry. If it were on the menu, I'd consider it."

She shuddered. "That's disgusting! Subject change, please."

She seized the moment to launch into details about the upcoming Harvest Charity Ball, but as she spoke, her nerves tangled her words together into one breathless, rambling run-on sentence.

Frustrated with herself, she abandoned the speech entirely and asked directly, "Are you still planning to come with me?"

Before he could respond, she rushed to add, "You don't have to if you don't want to. But it'd be great if you did. And, of course, your friends are welcome too..."

She shifted in her seat uncomfortably.

Levi's intense green gaze locked on her, his mouth curving into a slow, knowing smile. "On two conditions."

She narrowed her eyes. "What do you mean, two conditions?"

That mischievous glint she was learning to both love and fear sparked in his eyes. "First, I get to pick out your dress for the event."

That didn't sound so bad. "Fine. What's the second?"

His expression sobered, the teasing fading into something more serious and far more dangerous. "I get to choose the next topic of conversation. And whatever it is, you have to answer me truthfully."

Aurelia's heart gave a painful thud. She knew—*knew*—this wasn't going to go in her favor.

Everything in her screamed to redirect the conversation, to make an awkward joke, and escape whatever he was about to ask. But the open and vulnerable look on Levi's face held her fast.

She let out a long, resigned sigh. "Deal."

Levi leaned back in his chair, a satisfied but unreadable smile on his face.

God help her...what had she agreed to?

Levi

There was a reason Levi was a force in business.

He knew how to negotiate, how to recognize opportunity, and most importantly, when to strike. But no amount of boardroom finesse prepared him for the guilt that curled low in his stomach as he watched the color drain from Aurelia's face.

Still, some conversations couldn't wait. And this one...this was too important to leave unspoken.

He didn't ease into it or offer false comfort. He ripped the bandage off in one clean, brutal pull.

"Tell me about your past relationships," he asked quietly. "Your exes. Why didn't they work out?"

She stilled, her body rigid, and for one terrifying moment, Levi wondered if she had stopped breathing altogether. Her eyes were wide, haunted, and there was something else there...something that made his pulse roar in his ears. Fear.

His hands clenched into fists under the table, knuckles turning white. He forced himself to stay silent, to give her the time she needed to wrestle her thoughts free from whatever dark place she had been dragged back to.

Finally, with a shuddering breath, she slumped in her chair, the fight visibly bleeding out of her.

"I've...dated a few guys," she began in a voice barely above a whisper, her eyes locked on the small candle flickering between them. "But most of them didn't last more than a few months before they grew bored and left."

Her throat bobbed with the effort to keep speaking, her fingers trembling as she reached for her water glass. Levi could see the way she braced herself for his judgment, for rejection.

"I was too quiet...didn't have enough friends, not enough education. Too poor. Too boring." Her bitter smile cut him deeper than any sharp word could have. "Take your pick. The reasons were endless."

Levi's jaw flexed painfully. Rage burned under his skin, but he kept his expression carefully blank. The moment he opened his mouth and let that fury loose, she would retreat...and he wasn't letting her close that door tonight.

"Many didn't even have the decency to say it to my face," she continued, her voice brittle. "Some...disappeared. Ghosted me like I didn't exist. And then, like clockwork, there'd be a new picture posted online of them with someone else. Someone better."

She finally lifted her eyes, and Levi's heart broke at the acceptance he saw in them. Like she truly believed she wasn't worth staying for.

"I'm a placeholder," she whispered. "Until someone better comes along."

God. He couldn't breathe past the iron band tightening around his ribs.

But Levi wasn't finished. Not yet. He had to understand all of it—all of her—if he was ever going to show her how wrong she was.

"You said most of them didn't last long..." His voice was low, gentle, even though everything in him wanted to roar. "What about the ones who did?"

Another jolt of tension snapped through her, locking every muscle in place. Her wide, pleading eyes silently begged him not to make her answer.

He held her gaze, his fingers reaching out slowly, giving her the choice to take his hand or pull away.

"You don't have to say much," he promised softly. "Just...help me understand."

Before she could respond, their server reappeared with their first course, oblivious to the razor's edge they both balanced on. Plates were placed before them, and explanations about the process were offered. Steam curled from the fondue pots as the scents of melted cheese and seasoned broth filled the air.

As soon as they were alone again, Levi forced himself to move, to do something other than hunt down every single one of these exes that contributed to her agony. He speared a few vegetables and chunks of meat, dropping them into the simmering broth. When he looked up again, she hadn't touched a thing.

And then, in a voice so quiet he almost didn't hear her, she spoke.

"The only one who stayed longer..." She swallowed hard, her gaze fixed somewhere far away. "...gave me more attention than anyone ever had before."

She dragged her hands into her lap, her fingers knotting together as she forced the words out.

"But his attention was...different." Her lips trembled. "It depended on his mood, or if something set him off that day. Sometimes it came from his fists. Other days, his legs would kick me down. And if he was really feeling lazy..." she closed her eyes, the words barely a breath, "...he let the stairs handle it for him."

Levi's vision went red. His mind blanked out in a wash of blinding rage, and for one horrifying second, he saw exactly how easy it would be to kill a man with his bare hands.

But Aurelia wasn't done.

"It took me a long time to get out. It took longer to feel safe enough to file for a restraining order. And I..." Her voice cracked. "I can't talk about it more than that. Not yet."

A heavy, suffocating silence settled over the table.

Levi couldn't think, couldn't breathe past the sheer violence pounding through his veins. But he forced his voice to steady and reached for her trembling hand.

"Thank you...for trusting me with that." He swallowed down the fury burning his throat and offered her the faintest, most reassuring smile he could muster. "Now it's my turn to show you some of my scars."

Because if there was anything she deserved, it was knowing that he wasn't going anywhere.

Aurelia

It took every ounce of willpower for Aurelia to slow her racing heart, to breathe past the tightness in her chest threatening to steal her composure. But somehow—somehow, Levi's hand, warm and steady over hers, anchored her. His touch wasn't demanding or expectant. It was simply there...again offering quiet strength when she had none left.

And when he finally began to speak, his voice was low and unhurried; it felt like the tension in the air shifted.

He began to tell her about his relationships, which were more like a series of betrayals and disappointments that seemed so at odds with the confident, charming man sitting across from her. So far, it had been a couple of stories about women who'd fallen for his lifestyle but never truly seen him, who had chased the fantasy of his wealth while offering nothing real in return.

As he talked, he reached over to the fondue pot, pulling out several pieces of pork.

Aurelia's eyes immediately widened in horror. "Those haven't been in there long enough to cook! You're going to get sick!"

Levi shot her a roguish grin, entirely unconcerned. "They're small," he said with ridiculous certainty, popping one into his mouth like it was candy. "They don't need that long to cook."

"Oh my god!" she gasped, in half horror and half disgust.

He swallowed with a dramatic groan of satisfaction and reached for more. "I'm starving, Auri. At this point, I'm perfectly willing to take my chances."

Aurelia shook her head incredulously, but the corner of her mouth tugged upward despite herself. Only this man could follow up the heaviest conversation of her life by attempting to win a Darwin Award at the dinner table.

"If you end up in the ER with food poisoning, I'm going to say 'I told you so' while you're hooked up to an IV, Porky," she warned, crossing her arms.

His fork froze midair as he gawked. "Did you just call me, Porky?"

"Yes, because you deserve a terrible nickname after making such a terrible decision!"

Levi grinned widely and winked. "If that happens, I'll deserve it. But hey...every hero's journey needs a little danger, right?"

Her laughter came before she could stop it, light and genuine, and for the first time that night, it didn't feel blighted by the past.

And that, she thought, watching the ridiculously pleased look on his face, was the real danger here.

He was slowly, completely, and undeniably becoming her peace.

It wasn't fine.

In fact, it was astonishingly and epically not fine.

The evening following dinner had been perfect...almost too perfect. A romantic stroll through the glowing streets of downtown, his hand warm against hers, their laughter mingling with the vibrant hum of the city.

They talked about everything and nothing, that sweet anticipation of what might happen once the front door closed behind them, simmering beneath the surface.

And then...disaster struck.

One moment, Levi was tugging her closer, his eyes dark with promise. The next, they filled with horror, a hand clamping over his stomach as he paled.

"Levi?" she asked, alarmed.

Without a word, he bolted.

Gone was the charming husband ready to ravish her senseless. In his place was a man sprinting for the bathroom like his very soul depended on it.

And that was exactly where he stayed.

For the rest of the night and the better part of the next morning.

Because, as it turned out, even billionaires couldn't negotiate their way out of food poisoning...from undercooked pork.

And the worst part?

He still had the nerve to grumble dramatically from the bathroom floor and say, between bouts of misery, "*Worth it.*"

CHAPTER 41

Levi

It had never taken Levi so long to recover from such a spectacularly reckless mistake.

Food poisoning now sat at the top of his growing list titled "Things I Will Never, Ever Do Again."

Aurelia hadn't complained once—hadn't even said more than a single, perfectly timed, and absolutely deserved, "I told you so." Instead, she had quietly spent the weekend caring for him, coaxing him to sip water and electrolyte drinks, brushing damp hair back from his clammy forehead, and staying close whenever he felt the worst of it coming on.

She did, however, continue to call him Porky. Forever cementing his decision as a term of endearment. He couldn't even be mad about it.

Levi, on the other hand, had spent most of the weekend camping out in the bathroom like it was his new permanent address. At one point, he had even dragged in a pillow and blankets, turning the cold tile floor into his sad little fortress of misery. Either he was kneeling before the toilet or praying for death on it...sometimes with barely a moment's warning.

To make matters worse, Aurelia had texted Ivy to let her know he wouldn't be coming in on Monday. Naturally, Ivy found this hilarious—and she had zero intention of keeping that information to herself.

Which meant one thing: Owen.

The man was a menace, a one-man torment machine who lived for this kind of humiliation. Sure enough, Owen showed up completely uninvited on Sunday, grinning ear-to-ear under the flimsy guise of "checking in on his best buddy, Porky."

Levi—still pale, weak, and barely able to stand—had managed to throw him out by sheer force of will. His wife barely stifled a laugh at Owen's use of his new nickname.

Of course, that wasn't the end of it.

For the next several days, as Levi slowly recovered, his phone exploded with jokes, GIFs, and memes about his condition and about pork. Owen had found every bathroom-related meme in existence and sent them at regular intervals...because why suffer in silence when you can suffer publicly?

Levi vowed that, once fully recovered, he would throttle him.

Still, somewhere between surviving the ordeal and enduring Owen's torment, he managed to pull himself together enough to arrange the surprise he had been planning for Aurelia. With Ivy's help, of course.

He had given her a very clear vision of the dress he wanted for his wife—something that would leave the entire ballroom breathless. Ivy's delighted squeal over the phone had told him he was onto something good. She had immediately taken charge, assuring him she would handle every last detail.

Now, after another long week spent helping his team unravel the lingering mess Harris Wilkerson left behind, while still recovering from his ill-fated fondue dinner, the night of the Harvest Charity Ball had finally arrived.

Aurelia had been up since dawn, fretting over final details, too busy to remember she hadn't even seen her dress yet.

Ivy and Grace were scheduled to come over later that evening to help her get ready with an entire pre-ball ritual that Levi found secretly endearing. Of all his friends, only Owen would be attending tonight. Isaac was still pulling late nights at the office, and Grace didn't want to go without him. And if Grace wasn't going, then Ivy wouldn't go.

Levi, for his part, decided not to go into the office today. He wanted to be close if Aurelia needed him...and, if he was being honest, he needed to see the look on her face when she saw the dress for the first time.

So, he cleared his calendar and was now en route to pick it up himself.

He couldn't stop smiling as he parked on a side street, stepped out of his car, and made his way toward the most exclusive designer boutique in Joia City.

Tonight, his wife was going to own that ballroom, and Levi couldn't wait to see her in the dress that would start it all.

Aurelia

The Harvest Charity Ball was tonight, and Aurelia was freaking out.

Sleep had been impossible. She had tossed and turned half the night, plagued by another nightmare that had her waking in a panicked sweat, heart racing, the phantom grip of terror still curling its icy fingers around her throat.

Will these nightmares ever stop?

By dawn, she had given up entirely, the sheets tangled hopelessly around her legs. There was no point trying to rest when her mind refused to quiet. Instead, she threw herself into motion, channeling every shred of that anxious energy into something—*anything*—productive.

She made herself eat a toasted English muffin and forced down a cup of coffee, though it felt like her nerves had already consumed her from the inside out. Right as she grabbed her bag and tried to dart out the door, Levi caught her around the waist and pulled her back against his chest.

For a moment, everything stilled.

Wrapped safely in his arms, her body instinctively relaxed, soaking in his warmth, his steady presence. He held her tight, one large hand tracing slow, reassuring circles along her back.

With his chin resting against the top of her head, his deep voice rumbled softly, "You've done an incredible job, Auri. I haven't even seen the final result yet, but I'm already impressed. I know you're nervous...but you have absolutely nothing to be nervous about."

Then he tipped her chin up, his lips brushing against hers in a kiss so slow and devastatingly tender it left her breathless and a little dazed. She stood there, staring at his mouth even after he pulled back, her mind blank except for the lingering warmth of his kiss.

Grinning, he pressed one more kiss to her forehead and murmured, "Now go show everyone who's really in charge."

It was exactly what she needed to hear.

While it still felt foreign to have someone so supportive in her life—someone who believed in her without question—it also made her painfully aware of everything she had been missing. Of how low she had set the bar before this.

The smile Levi put on her face didn't fade once, even after she stepped into Starhaven Manor and slipped seamlessly back into her professional role.

By the time she crossed the grand threshold, the nerves were buried under her measured calmness. She lived and breathed by the precise event checklist she had crafted to keep everything running smoothly.

The ballroom was nearly finished with the tables arranged in perfect symmetry, the temporary stage set, and all audio-visual equipment tested the day before.

Outside, the transformation had already begun earlier in the week. Guests attending tonight would be greeted by a wonderland of twinkling string lights woven through faux vines and branches arching over the driveway, immersing them in the enchanting forest theme from the moment they arrive.

That same magic continued throughout the estate. Lavish arrangements of rich autumnal flowers accented every space. The final touches were being applied even now to the ballroom, as the catering company busied itself in the kitchen, having taken over preparations for tonight's menu days ago.

There was only one thing she hadn't micromanaged.

Her dress.

Levi had insisted on handling that himself, with Ivy's help. It had been a relief at first...but now she was terrified. What if it didn't fit? What if she hated it? How would she possibly tell Levi without hurting his feelings?

At least Ivy had seen it firsthand, and that gave her some comfort. But still, her stomach churned with uncertainty.

Grace and Ivy were coming over later to help her get ready. From what she had gathered, they had a magical talent for hair and makeup. Neither of them ever needed a professional for big events, and tonight, they were bestowing that gift on her.

Aurelia had been added to a separate group chat with them immediately after they had all met. It had been filled with raunchy memes, courtesy of Ivy, book recommendations from Grace, girls' night invitations, and anything else that popped into their minds. It was another safe space where she could be herself.

While their friendships were still growing, for the first time in a very long time, Aurelia felt...accepted. Like she was part of something bigger. Like she belonged.

She wasn't sure she had the words to describe how much that meant.

And while she had spent the last few weeks building new friendships, she had also finally sat down with Selene.

They'd met after work earlier this week while Levi was still recovering. The conversation had been strange—tentative and careful, but friendly.

And, in many ways, long overdue.

Aurelia stepped into the cozy, familiar atmosphere of Coffee Beans 'n' Things, the warm smell of roasted espresso and vanilla chai curling through the air. Her gaze immediately found Selene already seated at a corner table, hands wrapped tightly around a ceramic mug. She was staring into it like it held the answers to all of life's hardest questions.

A second mug sat on the table, steam curling delicately above it. It was Aurelia's favorite, a vanilla chai latte.

The small gesture softened something tight in Aurelia's chest as she made her way over.

Selene looked up the moment Aurelia sat down, offering a tentative, rueful smile. "Thanks for meeting me," she murmured, her voice quieter than usual.

Aurelia's expression gentled. "Of course, I would meet you. We can't throw away years of friendship over one fight. I...I think we owe it to each other to talk this through. It's been stressful for both of us."

Selene's lips tugged into a faint, watery smile that didn't quite reach her eyes. "I've never been good at apologies," she admitted, staring down at her mug. Her voice cracked just a little. "But I need you to know that I'm really, truly sorry. I never should have said those things. You're not just a friend; you're the best friend I've ever had, and I know I hurt you." She paused, her fingers tightening around the mug. "The truth is, I was angry. Not at you, but at myself. I felt shut out, and it scared me. We've always shared everything, and it felt like...you didn't trust me enough to tell me. I know that wasn't fair to you. I was selfish. And I'm so sorry, Aurelia."

The rawness in her voice twisted Aurelia's heart.

She swallowed, choosing her words carefully—thoughtfully. She had spent the entire afternoon preparing for this conversation, but now that she was here, the only thing that mattered was mending what had cracked between them.

"You had every right to feel that way," she said softly. "I would have been upset too. However, it all happened so fast, and we hadn't had the chance to see each other or even talk much lately. I didn't want to just throw something like that at you over a text message. And honestly..." she hesitated, "I had to think about his

privacy too. You know how the gossip mills at Starhaven spin. The last thing I wanted was for something this personal to become office entertainment."

Selene sat in contemplative silence for a long moment before she sighed and leaned back in her chair, her shoulders finally relaxing. "God, thank you for understanding. This has been eating away at me for a week." She gave a weak laugh. "I suck at this whole heartfelt apology thing."

Aurelia snorted, the tension between them breaking a little.

Selene leaned forward again, curiosity now dancing in her eyes. "Okay, so...I have to ask. How did you meet him? Because, girl, from the photos and everything online...he is fine," she teased, waggling her eyebrows.

Aurelia laughed, grateful for the return of their usual rhythm. "He is definitely a catch," she admitted. "It was...a whirlwind. A mutual acquaintance introduced us, and we hit it off. One thing led to another, and the next thing I knew, we eloped." She lifted her mug and took a sip, adding carefully, "It was a risky decision, but I figured...why not take a chance for once?"

It wasn't the whole story—but it was enough. And it was the truth.

Selene let out a low, impressed whistle. "Wow. Risky, but clearly working out for you." She tilted her head. "So...will I finally get to meet the mysterious Mr. Tall, Dark, and Gorgeous at the Harvest Charity Ball?"

Aurelia smiled. "Yes, he'll be there. And he's looking forward to meeting you, too."

Selene's eyes sparkled with excitement as she lifted her coffee mug. "Well then, here's to what's shaping up to be the most unforgettable Harvest Charity Ball ever."

Aurelia clinked her mug against hers, a genuine, wide smile breaking across her face for the first time in days.

"Unforgettable," she agreed.

Everything was falling perfectly into place...but that gnawing sense of unease refused to let go.

Aurelia couldn't explain it, couldn't pin down a reason, but it clung to her like a shadow, growing heavier the closer she got home. She had triple-checked every last detail, every task on her list completed with the kind of meticulous precision that left no room for error. And still...the feeling persisted.

Selene had been incredible all week, diving headfirst into helping her tie up loose ends. Aurelia hadn't realized how much she missed the effortless rhythm they shared until the week flew by in a whirlwind of teamwork. Before she knew it, the ball had crept up on her, and so had her arrival home.

Snapping out of her trance, Aurelia realized she was already in the driveway, her car idling beside Levi's SUV. Her earlier nerves shifted, replaced with hesitant excitement at the thought of seeing the dress Levi had picked out.

Please don't be taffeta...please, anything but taffeta, she silently chanted while climbing out of the car and making her way inside.

She found Levi exactly where she expected, lounging on the couch with his laptop perched beside him, a glass of whiskey in hand like he hadn't a care in the world. When his eyes landed on her, a lazy, predatory smile curved his lips.

"You're home early," he drawled, voice rich and velvety with mischief.

Aurelia rolled her eyes, ignoring the way her stomach flipped at the sight of him. "Finished everything earlier than expected," she answered, her words coming out more breathless than she liked. For a moment, she hesitated, then blurted, "Can I see my dress?"

Levi laughed, deep and indulgent, pushing to his feet with slow, deliberate grace. He tipped his head toward her bedroom. "Who am I to deny my wife anything?"

He had barely finished the sentence before Aurelia was gone, barreling toward her room like a woman on a mission.

Levi followed at a much more leisurely pace, his grin only growing as he leaned against the doorframe and watched her approach the long garment bag hanging on the dressing rack.

Her hands trembled slightly as she reached for the zipper. Drawing in a bracing breath, she pulled it down...and the world held its breath with her.

The fabric glimmered under the soft lighting, a masterpiece of elegance and enchantment. Words completely abandoned her. She took a slow, awed step back, overwhelmed by the sheer beauty of the dress.

Tears stung her eyes before she could stop them. No one—*no one*—had ever done something like this for her.

When she turned to face Levi, the emotion on her face caused him to immediately tense. He stepped forward, his expression clouded with worry.

But then, through trembling lips, she whispered, "Thank you."

The tension bled from his shoulders.

"Thank you," she repeated, this time stronger, the emotion behind it cracking something wide open between them.

Levi didn't have a chance to respond before she threw herself into his arms. He caught her easily, holding her tightly, desperately wishing to never let her go.

When she looked up at him, her eyes searching his face, her gaze fell to his mouth...and that was it.

Their lips met in a kiss that held every word she couldn't say aloud, every wall crumbling around her heart. Levi scooped her up and carried her to bed, laying her down with the kind of veneration that made her chest ache.

This time was different; slow and exploratory with something...more.

Every piece of clothing removed was a new act of devotion, every touch unhurried and filled with intent. Levi pulled back, sitting on his heels to simply look at her, his eyes drinking her in like she was a living, breathing miracle.

"You are perfect," he whispered, his voice thick with something more than desire.

Aurelia had never been seen like this before—never mattered like this before. And in that quiet, soul-baring moment, the wall around her heart collapsed completely.

She reached for him, trailing her fingers over her skin in a way that made his control snap.

Without a word, he settled between her thighs, the tension in his body shaking as he held himself back, his eyes locked on hers in silent question.

Aurelia answered with a real, radiant smile and wrapped her legs around his waist, pulling him into her completely.

The moan that tore from Levi's throat was nothing short of euphoric as he sank into her, slow and deep.

They moved together with the kind of perfect rhythm that felt ancient, inevitable. Every thrust drew them closer to that precipice, every soft sigh and low cry a symphony of connection and release.

When it came, it hit them both like a tidal wave, crashing and wild and breathtaking.

And when it was over, neither moved.

Wrapped around each other, tangled in sheets and sunlight, the world outside their door ceased to exist.

Levi held her tighter, pressing a soft kiss to her temple.

"We should probably move this party to the shower before Ivy and Grace show up," she murmured against his skin. "Although, for the record, I'm not even a little bit ashamed if they catch us like this."

Levi's laughter vibrated against her chest, and she knew, without a single doubt, that she could spend the rest of her life listening to that sound.

And she really hoped to.

Turns out the banging on the door wasn't some metaphorical knock of impending doom. It was very real...and very loud.

Ivy's voice rang out dramatically from the front steps. "Open up, woman! We're here to save your life!"

Levi moved faster than she had seen him all week, towel drying his hair as he threw on a pair of gym shorts and padded barefoot to the door. Aurelia took the opportunity to finish her shower alone, silently praying she wouldn't regret inviting these two into her home today.

By the time she emerged—hair wrapped in a towel and her favorite lavender silk robe tied hastily around her body—Ivy and Grace were already in full battle formation at the foot of her bed.

Gone were the playful friends she had come to know. In their place stood two formidable forces of feminine power, assessing her from head to toe like a mission-critical project.

Aurelia gulped.

Mistake. This was a huge mistake.

Her panicked gaze darted toward Levi, who stood in the bedroom doorway looking thoroughly amused, his arms crossed over his bare, glistening chest. His tousled hair dripped faintly onto his skin, and the roguish grin tugging at his lips made it clear he was in no rush to help.

"I'll make a noble sacrifice to the gods," he said with mock solemnity. "And pray you survive whatever unholy rituals they're about to perform."

Then—with the worst timing known to man—he abandoned her. Just...vanished down the hall, leaving her to the mercy of two cosmetic commandos.

They moved fast. Unbelievably fast. Before she knew it, the bathroom counters and vanity were overrun with makeup palettes, curling irons, bottles of mysterious potions, and hair tools that looked more like medieval torture devices.

"Sit," Ivy ordered, patting the chair in front of the mirror.

Aurelia sat. She wasn't sure if it was free will or fear that got her there faster.

With military precision, Ivy whipped the towel from her head and attacked her damp hair with a comb and a series of expertly applied products. Meanwhile, Grace stood before her, gently cupping Aurelia's chin, tilting her face this way and that as she murmured to herself about bone structure and undertones.

It should have been unsettling, but instead...it felt like something else entirely.

They were doing this because they cared. Because they wanted her to feel beautiful and confident. Like she mattered.

And that recognition hit her so hard she almost choked on it.

Tears welled before she could stop them, slipping silently down her cheeks. Lost in the whirlwind of emotion, she didn't even notice the way Ivy and Grace had paused until she glanced up to find them staring at her with shared concern.

"Do you want to talk about it?" Grace asked softly, her voice as gentle as the hand she laid on Aurelia's shoulder.

Aurelia swallowed hard. She was tired of running from this. From all of it.

Blowing out a shaky breath, she confessed, "I'm feeling...everything all at once. And I don't know what to do with it. I've spent a long time burying my feelings. Ignoring them. Now they're all right here, and I don't know how to handle it." She gave a watery, self-deprecating laugh. "I don't even know *how* to be this person."

Her voice cracked, but the truth made her feel lighter.

With a trembling but genuine smile, she looked between them and added, "But I do know this—I think you're the first real friends who've ever made me feel like I matter. And that means more than I can even explain. Thank you. Both of you. So much."

Ivy let out a choked squeak and turned her back to them, furiously dabbing at her eyes.

Grace gasped in dramatic fashion, pointing. "Oh my God. You broke Ivy! She's crying! Ivy never cries. Quick, where's my phone! I need pics or it didn't happen!"

Ivy spun around, eyes blazing, her long ponytail nearly taking Aurelia's head off. "Try it, Grace. Try it, and Isaac will be scraping your remains off the driveway by midnight."

The three of them held each other's gazes for a tense heartbeat—and then the tension shattered into wild, helpless laughter.

They laughed until they cried for an entirely different reason, the heavy weight of emotion transforming into something bright and full of life.

This.

This was what she had been missing. Another priceless gift that had quietly found its way into her life because of Levi.

Once the laughter faded, the mood shifted again, and the cosmetic commandos re-emerged, their playful banter giving way to fierce determination.

With a knowing glance between them, they got to work—their magic tangible in every brush stroke and curl of her hair. And for the first time in a long time, Aurelia sat perfectly still, no longer resisting the transformation...but embracing it.

Tonight, she wouldn't just attend the ball.

She would own it.

Levi

Levi hadn't been allowed near their bathroom since Ivy and Grace commandeered it. He felt a brief pang of sympathy for Aurelia, trapped in their clutches with no escape. He knew firsthand how relentless his friends could be when it came to getting someone ready for an event.

Already dressed, Levi adjusted the cuffs of his tailored black tuxedo. He had foregone the usual bow tie in favor of a formal paisley print tie threaded with rich fall tones—deep golds, coppers, and burgundy—woven seamlessly into the fabric. His dark hair was styled back in precise waves, giving him a sharp, regal edge.

The outfit was perfect, but it was nothing compared to what he knew was coming next.

With one last glance in the mirror, he joined Owen on the couch. His best friend had shown up a while ago and was now flipping through the channels, looking entirely too comfortable in his own sleek tuxedo and classic black bow tie.

Levi's knee bounced restlessly as he kept glancing at the closed bedroom door.

Owen shot him an amused glance. "Your anxiety is nauseating. The whole couch is shaking. If you wanted me bouncing like this, Lockwood, you should have bought me dinner first."

Levi stilled his knee but didn't bother replying. The second the door cracked open, he flew to his feet.

Ivy and Grace exited first, appearing far too pleased with themselves. Then...Aurelia stepped into view.

Levi forgot how to breathe.

She was nothing short of divine, a vision that seemed to step straight out of his most impossible dreams.

Her long chestnut hair flowed in soft, cascading waves, the vibrant rainbow strands threaded through like stolen light from a prism. Her skin glowed beneath the warm lighting, every soft curve of her face touched by it, her full lips parted slightly as her deep brown eyes, lit from within, locked onto his.

And then there was the dress.

The sheer, nude-toned fabric clung to her curves like a second skin, dusted with thousands of iridescent crystals that sparkled in every imaginable color, casting light across the room as she moved.

The bodice was a masterpiece, clusters of crystals blooming into intricate vines and floral patterns, winding their way delicately along her torso. Whisper-light tulle sleeves floated over her arms, each dotted with crystals that seemed to hover weightlessly on her skin.

The skirt deepened into rich ombré shades of eggplant and crimson, as if she carried the sunset itself in her gown. She looked like she belonged to another world—half goddess, half queen—and all his.

Levi's throat tightened painfully.

"I could search every language and still never find the words to describe how beautiful you are," he rasped, his voice hoarse with emotion.

Aurelia's cheeks flushed pink, her soft smile dazzling. She then twirled in the dress, a beam of pure joy lighting up her face.

"It even has pockets!" she squealed.

Levi let out a relieved laugh, pride swelling in his chest. That tiny design detail, one he had requested personally, was the crowning jewel in her eyes.

Joy surged through him, but it collided with the unmistakable punch of dread settling low and hard. If she looked this stunning to him, the rest of the men at the ball were going to lose their minds.

He would have to keep his jealousy in check, or he was going to lose his shit every time another man glanced her way. Tonight wasn't about him. Before he could think any further, a heavy hand clapped his shoulder.

Owen leaned in, a devilish grin curling his mouth. "This is going to be *so* entertaining to watch," he murmured.

Levi groaned internally. *I'm completely and utterly screwed.*

CHAPTER 42

Aurelia

Ivy and Grace left soon after the grand reveal, leaving Levi, Aurelia, and Owen to head to Starhaven Manor together. Aurelia took the back seat, carefully spreading out her gown and trying to ignore the lingering unease clinging to her.

She glanced down at the sandals Levi had bought her. They were Greek goddess-inspired flats adorned with the same crystals as her gown, delicate vines wrapping past her ankles. Even she felt like she had become the embodiment of the Harvest Charity Ball.

As they pulled into the long, winding driveway, the view took her breath away. By day, it had been beautiful, but at night...it was like stepping through a portal to a hidden realm. Twinkling lights wove through autumnal vines and lush greenery, casting a soft, enchanted glow.

Even Owen was struck silent for a moment. Then, with a theatrical bow, he declared, "Damn...even I'll bow before you, oh woodland goddess. This is incredible!"

An attendant directed them to the designated parking area. Once parked, Levi circled to open Aurelia's door. She took his hand, stepping carefully down, her dress shimmering under the lights. When she tucked herself against his side, Levi leaned in and nipped her ear.

"I haven't even seen the inside yet, and I'm already amazed," he murmured. "But mostly, I'm amazed by you, Auri."

Heat flooded her cheeks, but before she could reply, Owen clapped his hands dramatically. "Let's find the snacks before I start chewing on the decorations!"

They made their way up the grand stone steps, passing under an arch of glittering lights and vines that turned the entryway into a living fairytale.

At the entrance, guests were handed the upscale glow sticks Aurelia had commissioned. When she explained their purpose, Owen chuckled. "Someone's definitely breaking a hip tonight."

Levi tried—and failed—not to laugh.

Inside the ballroom, the transformation was beyond anything Aurelia could have imagined. The space had become a magical forest under starlit skies. Nymphs and woodland creatures served hors d'oeuvres. A waterfall of sorbet punch flowed from a sculpted tree trunk, surrounded by lavish displays of fruits, vegetables, and charcuterie.

Canopies of flowers and vines hung from the ceiling, glittering crystals and warm lights peeking through like stars. The dance floor, bar, silent auction table, and stage blended seamlessly into the enchanted setting.

Levi's sharp inhale and soft, awed, "Wow," made her heart soar.

"What do you think?" she asked nervously.

He turned to her, his eyes shining. "I think you're in charge of every event we ever host from now on." And before she could react, he pulled her close and kissed her like they were the only two people in the room.

She was still dazed when Charles approached, dressed in a classic black tuxedo, a glass of bourbon in hand.

"You've outdone yourself, Aurelia," he praised warmly. "I'd say this might even surpass Eleanor's finest events."

Blushing, Aurelia smiled shyly.

Charles studied her for a moment longer, his voice humming with approval. "You also look stunning, as though you were born to rule this magical kingdom tonight."

Levi instinctively reached for her hand, grounding himself as he fought off a possessive growl.

Charles gave Levi a knowing smile, then leaned in close to whisper something in Aurelia's ear. Levi stiffened until Charles stepped back with a tender smile, gazing at Aurelia the way a grandfather would his granddaughter. Levi's chest loosened a bit. Aurelia's expression melted into stunned disbelief before she threw her arms around Charles.

"Thank you," she whispered, her voice thick with emotion.

"You deserve it," Charles replied, his eyes misting.

Aurelia twirled back to Levi, pressing against him in a fierce embrace, her lips brushing his ear.

"Charles submitted the paperwork. It's official—He feels that I've met the terms of Eleanor's inheritance!"

Levi held her tighter, his lips brushing her hair in a quiet confession of everything he couldn't say aloud. He marveled at the quiet satisfaction on Charles's face—a satisfaction that told him Aurelia had gone above and beyond to make this marriage work, that she had earned every penny of that inheritance with real effort and commitment.

His heart skipped a beat as he internalized what that meant.

Before he could add his thoughts, Owen ruined the moment by waggling his eyebrows suggestively, and Levi sighed. He really couldn't take him anywhere.

Charles cleared his throat. "I have to steal Aurelia for a bit to go over final details with the charity reps."

Before Aurelia could respond, a high, sugary voice cut through the air.

"There you are! I've been looking all over for you!"

Aurelia turned as Selene approached, her pale blue eyes assessing every detail of Aurelia's gown. She wore a simple bronze taffeta dress and smiled tightly. Charles's jaw visibly tightened.

"We just arrived," Aurelia explained.

"The representatives have been asking when we'll start," Selene said, before turning to the men. "Oh! I didn't see you there."

Owen, ever the opportunist, stepped forward with a dazzling smile. "And who might you be?"

"This is Selene," Aurelia introduced quickly. "Chief of Staff...and my best friend."

Selene's eyes barely flicked over Levi and Owen, her polite smile not quite reaching her eyes.

"It's so nice to finally meet you both," she said sweetly before turning her attention back to Aurelia and Charles. "We need to begin now if we're going to stay on schedule."

Levi pressed his lips to Aurelia's temple. "Go show them what the Greaves heir is made of," he whispered.

She smiled at him, gave him one last kiss, and turned to follow Charles and Selene, gliding through the ballroom like she had owned it her whole life.

It had only been an hour, and already Aurelia was exhausted. She wasn't accustomed to this much small talk or being the center of attention for so long.

With a smile plastered on her face, she managed to work her way through the charity representatives, the last of whom was Martin Strasburg, chair of The National Dyslexia Foundation.

Martin was a tall, heavyset man with curly copper hair and pale blue eyes magnified behind silver frames. His thick beard held streaks of gray, and a scattering of freckles crossed the bridge of his nose. Despite his imposing appearance, his easy laugh was loud and infectious, putting her instantly at ease.

"Thank you so much for including us," Martin said warmly. "I've lived here all my life, and I know what a big deal it is to be part of this event."

Aurelia beamed. "The pleasure's mine. It's a cause very close to my heart, and frankly, we should have included you sooner."

"I'd also like to offer my congratulations on your marriage," he added with a knowing smile. "Levi's one of the finest men I've ever worked for."

That caught her off guard, her surprise unmistakable. "You work for Levi?"

Martin chuckled. "I'm a Senior Director at Neuronix. Levi personally hired me when the company was starting to take off. I was hoping to catch him tonight."

Aurelia couldn't resist a teasing smile. "So...exactly how bossy is he as a boss? Asking for a friend."

Martin let out a hearty laugh but quickly sobered. "Honestly? Levi built something remarkable. As someone who also has dyslexia, I can say there's no better place to work. He made sure those of us with disabilities have the tools we need to succeed without stigma. He even let us keep partial rights to the technologies we helped create. That kind of leadership is rare. If Levi ever left Neuronix, I think half the company would walk out the door with him."

Aurelia's pride swelled at the sincerity of his words, a fresh wave of emotion building in her chest. She had fallen for Levi before she really understood how deeply his kindness and integrity ran.

"You and Levi are changing lives," she whispered, blinking fast to fight back the tears threatening again.

Martin smiled kindly before excusing himself to find Levi.

Aurelia barely had a chance to gather her composure before she spotted Darcy Newman, her old case worker from District Child Welfare Services. It felt surreal seeing her again under these circumstances—so much better than the difficult meetings of her youth.

Darcy's eyes brimmed with unshed tears as she pulled Aurelia into a motherly hug. "I'm so proud of you, sweetheart. You beat the odds and turned it into something beautiful. I always knew you would."

Aurelia held her tightly, grateful beyond words for the woman who had once tried to give her a better future.

When they finally parted, Aurelia moved on to meet the representatives from Glow Sticks for the Elderly, who were thrilled about the upcoming rave. Their excitement was contagious, but the second the conversation ended, her stomach reminded her loudly that she hadn't eaten since her rushed breakfast.

She turned to find a passing server, but instead, she found herself face-to-face with Bertrand Dallingford.

Despite his worsening limp and deepening hunch, his beady yellow eyes remained sharp as ever—sharper, unfortunately, when it came to roving over her body with far too much interest. She tried not to cringe.

"This is a lovely event, Miss Aurelia," he said, his voice low and oily, his gaze unapologetically fixed on her chest. "I'm particularly looking forward to this rave everyone keeps whispering about."

Then, in a conspiratorial tone, he leaned closer. "I hear there are special...pills that make those experiences far more pleasurable. I managed to get my hands on a few. Care to join me?"

Aurelia's stomach flipped for entirely different reasons. "Oh, no. No—no, thank you. I have a job to do," she said quickly, already stepping out of reach and before he could offer anything further.

What in the world had Eleanor gotten herself involved with to know people like him?

With her appetite gone, she headed for the stage where Charles was waiting, every step helping her push aside the unease Bertrand's comment stirred in her.

She rose into herself—shoulders back, chin steady—calling on every thread of strength woven into her bones. It was time to open the Harvest Charity Ball—and she would do it like she owned the entire damn night.

CHAPTER 43

Unknown

A cool breeze drifted through the open glass doors, offering the crowded ballroom a brief, natural respite from the stifling heat of packed bodies and too much motion.

At the open bar, the line never seemed to shorten, guests endlessly returning for more, their thirst insatiable. But no drink could ease the dryness they felt tonight.

This wasn't a thirst of the ordinary kind.

It was something deeper. Hungrier.

No substance on earth could cool the fury in their veins—the parched, unforgiving ache of being robbed of what they had earned.

It clawed at their mind, a maddening, festering frustration that blurred the line between anger and insanity. And maybe...there was no line left at all.

Their gaze never strayed far from Aurelia, tracking her every graceful step as she moved toward the stage. The sight of her in that shimmering gown—*a gown she didn't deserve*—made their fingers clench tightly around their drink like a vice.

She had taken *everything*.

Every secret she kept, every lie she lived...she took what belonged to them.

They drew in a slow, deliberate breath, masking the storm that churned just beneath the surface.

From the shadowed edge of the ballroom, they nursed their drink and watched as Aurelia made her way toward the DJ booth, ready to take the stage, oblivious to the eyes tracking her every step.

A predator stalking its prey.

Soon. Very soon.

CHAPTER 44

Levi

Levi was genuinely impressed...and a bit horrified by how much food Owen could inhale in one sitting.

Three fully loaded plates from the grazing station had already disappeared, each one stacked higher than the last. It earned him more than a few scandalized looks from Joia City's high society. But all it took was Owen flashing that Hollywood smile, and their disapproval melted into charmed amusement.

The highlight of the evening—aside from watching Owen systematically destroy the buffet—had been running into Martin Strasburg, one of his senior directors from Neuronix. Catching up outside of the office was a rare treat...though the moment was somewhat dampened by Owen's insatiable appetite. He flagged down a wood nymph server and charmed her into handing over an entire platter of bacon-wrapped scallops, mini arancini, and beef wellingtons...for himself.

Martin watched the spectacle with morbid fascination. "I can't decide if I'm impressed or mildly concerned," he muttered.

Owen, his mouth full of flaky pastry, shrugged. "I'm a young, strapping man who requires constant nourishment. This is survival." He eyed the platter as if debating whether to share it with Levi and Martin. Deciding against it, he popped another scallop into his mouth and pulled the plate closer. "Besides, I'm doing you both a favor. Wouldn't want either of you throwing your backs out trying to lift me off the floor if I faint from low blood sugar. You're welcome."

Levi shook his head. "You've somehow turned gluttony into performance art," he deadpanned. He flicked his chin toward a nearby table. "And you've developed a fan club. Those retirees over there haven't stopped watching you devour food like it's an Olympic sport."

Owen glanced over and smirked. "They're probably hoping I'll ram something else down their gullets. Saucy little minxes." He snorted, nearly choking on a beef wellington.

Serves him right, Levi thought.

Martin covered his mouth to hide his laughter and turned back to Levi, extending his hand. "Congratulations on landing yourself one hell of a beautiful wife," he said warmly. "She told me you're the reason our foundation is even here tonight. That means the world to me."

Levi shook his hand, his eyes instinctively searching the crowd. His heart stuttered when he found Aurelia near the stage, deep in conversation with Charles and the DJ. In that gown, under the lights, she looked every bit the goddess he already knew she was.

Martin's voice pulled him back. "I don't know her well," he said, his tone thoughtful, "but I think she's good for you."

Owen grunted in agreement around the stockpile of food in his mouth.

Levi blinked in shock.

"You've always carried the world like it's yours alone to bear. But this version of you? The one who knows how to share the load...I like this Levi better."

Martin's words hit harder than expected.

He wasn't done. "My wife, Amy, couldn't make it tonight because of the chaos of our kids, but I'll tell you something. I don't know how I'd make it through life without her. When the weight's too much, she carries it with me. That's love, Levi. The real kind. And from where I'm standing...it looks like you've found it."

Love.

The word echoed through Levi's mind, resounding long after Martin drifted back into the crowd.

Even as Charles stepped onto the stage to open the event, Levi was still standing there, staring at the woman who'd somehow become his entire world, not knowing when it happened.

Aurelia

"Time to get this show on the road," Charles said quietly, nodding toward the stage.

Aurelia's stomach twisted into knots as she nodded absentmindedly. The mere thought of public speaking had her seriously contemplating whether she could slip out unnoticed. After years spent blending into the background, this moment felt almost unbearable.

Change was hitting her from all directions, and she wasn't ready for any of it.

She hadn't eaten, hadn't had a sip of water all day, and now her stomach growled in protest as nerves and the ever-present sense of unease gnawed at her.

A sudden shiver ran down her spine, the hairs at the back of her neck prickling. That eerie feeling of being watched settled over her like a heavy blanket. She scanned the room, heart pounding...then chastised herself.

Of course, she was being watched. Charles had already taken the stage, and every eye in the room would be there next.

"Welcome, guests, friends, and honored participants to the eighty-fifth annual Harvest Charity Ball!" Charles's voice boomed over the sound system.

While the crowd applauded, Aurelia searched for Levi. Her breath hitched when she finally spotted him, those deep green eyes locked on her with nothing but pride and encouragement.

And then Owen caught her attention—grinning shamelessly through a mouthful of food, wiggling his fingers at her before returning to a large platter stacked to scandalous proportions. She narrowed her eyes. That was an excessive number of appetizers for one man.

Mental note: Investigate Owen's hoarding habits later.

Charles continued. "This event has long been a treasured tradition within the Greaves family. Sadly, the last member of this prestigious family left us a few months ago. Let's honor her memory with a moment of silence."

The hush that fell was profound, but for Aurelia, the silence echoed with her unprocessed grief. She had kept so busy planning this event that she hadn't left room for mourning. And now it threatened to crash over her.

Selene appeared at her side just in time, pressing a cold diet soda into her hand.

"The Harvest Charity Ball has always been about supporting those who make the world a better place," Charles continued. "And this year, we expanded that reach, allowing even those who couldn't attend tonight to contribute online."

"You haven't stopped moving all day," Selene whispered. "Have you had anything to drink or to eat?"

Aurelia shook her head and took a long sip, not realizing until now how parched she was. "You're a lifesaver," she whispered back.

"That's what friends are for. And you're going to crush this, so stop doubting yourself," Selene said, nudging her shoulder playfully.

Aurelia smiled weakly and drained the rest of the contents as Charles wrapped up his introduction. Selene took her glass and gave her a final thumbs-up before shooing her toward the stage.

With one last deep breath, Aurelia stepped into the stage lights, the microphone trembling slightly in her hands. She found Levi in the crowd again and anchored herself to the unwavering pride in his eyes.

"Thank you all for coming and supporting our headlining charities," she began, her voice shaky at first but growing steadier. "We took a slightly different direction this year, but your incredible generosity has already made this night one for the record books—one that Eleanor would have been proud of. We raised over three million dollars online before the night even began!"

Thunderous applause filled the room and her head. She pressed on despite the growing warmth under the lights and the wave of nausea beginning to crest.

"We selected three organizations for tonight's event. First, District Child Welfare Services, which is a cause close to my heart, as I was once a child in their care. Your support gives children the chance to find safety, security, and a real future."

More applause. The room spun slightly as another unwelcome wave of nausea rolled over her. She needed to get through this.

"The National Dyslexia Foundation also holds special meaning for me. I've met so many incredible people whose invisible disabilities never held them back. People who, with the right resources, thrive beyond imagination."

The floor swayed beneath her feet. She needed to get outside for some fresh air.

"And lastly..." she pushed the words out through gritted teeth, her vision tunneling, "in honor of Eleanor Greaves—who would have loved every minute of this night—we welcome Glow Sticks for the Elderly, a grassroots organization focused on encouraging and promoting vitality among our senior population. They do this by bringing rave culture to retirement homes across the nation. Time to take out your glow sticks, get on that dance floor, and kick off the rave!"

The crowd roared as the lights dimmed, and the floor lit up. Aurelia barely registered it as she staggered off the stage, nearly tripping over her dress in the process.

Selene was there in an instant, her arm looping under Aurelia's. Charles cast her a concerned glance.

"Hey, are you okay?"

"I...I'm not sure. I think...I need some air." Her words sounded distant to her ears, her tongue thick and slow.

Selene looked at Charles and said, "I'll take care of her." He nodded hesitantly.

Aurelia knew without a doubt that whatever was happening was the source of the unease she had felt throughout the day. She tried to tell Selene this as they walked towards the patio, but her vocal cords were paralyzed.

Selene sat her down on a nearby vacant bench before rushing off to find Levi. Something was wrong with her.

The moment Selene crossed the threshold back into the ballroom, a shadow loomed over her. A firm hand gripped her arm and mercilessly yanked her back onto her feet.

Aurelia turned with the last of her strength...and then the darkness encircled her.

CHAPTER 45

Levi

Levi's attention was fixed on Aurelia the entire time she was on stage. The moment her gaze found him, it was as if no one else existed. He knew she was speaking only to him. He had become the rock she needed to steady herself.

Despite her nerves, she did an incredible job, and he couldn't have been prouder to call her his wife.

By then, Martin had excused himself to rejoin his group. While they tried not to talk too much about work, Martin had discreetly shared his growing concerns about Project DL, confirming Levi's worst fears about the mess Harris had left behind. There was something critical buried in that code, something they were all missing. Owen agreed, based on the limited information he had. They promised to revisit it on Monday, and with final congratulations, Martin headed off.

As soon as the lights dimmed and the dance floor lit up, Levi was on his feet, ready to find Aurelia. She had disappeared backstage, looking distraught. She was possibly overwhelmed by nerves.

Owen stood beside him, mouth dipped down in concern.

"She didn't look good toward the end there," he murmured.

Levi nodded grimly. "She's introverted and has been dreading this speech for weeks. The pressure must've gotten to her." His voice relaxed. "But I'm still amazed by what she's pulled off."

"Yes, but..." Owen trailed off, his eyes scanning the room, his brow tight with worry.

It wasn't often Owen dropped his carefree act. Few people knew about his real gift—his calculating, analytical mind. It's what made him invaluable in both corporate and personal security.

Levi tensed. "But what?"

Owen gave a slow shake of his head. "I'm still digging into her history like I promised, but something isn't adding up. It's premature to say anything concrete, and part of it really should come from her. I just...I can't shake the feeling I'm missing something. And that it's right in front of me."

Levi's anxiety spiked. He scanned the crowd but couldn't spot Aurelia's shimmering silhouette. The crystals on her dress were supposed to make her easy to find. A beacon in the dark.

"Let's find her," Levi said.

But before they could take a step, six elderly women materialized out of nowhere, blocking their path.

"Mr. Lockwood! I've been *dying* to meet Aurelia's new husband," cackled the woman directly in front of him. "Gladys Heringsworth, longtime friend of Eleanor's. Aurelia did a superb job tonight."

She radiated luxury and entitlement, her sharp dark eyes glittering beneath arched brows. Though her frame was slight, Levi instinctively knew not to underestimate her.

"Allow me to introduce my friends," she said grandly, gesturing to the imposing women flanking her. "Margaret Carrington, Nancy Fitzwalter, Judith Vanderlyn, Gertrude Pavendish, and Ophelia Draycott."

Each was a formidable, perfectly groomed relic of Joia City's social elite—and Levi had a very bad feeling about this as they quickly encircled them. He glanced at Owen, who looked equally alarmed.

"This is our first rave experience!" Gladys announced with glee. Her friends murmured excitedly. "Would you and your friend..." she looked expectantly at Owen.

Levi supplied dryly, "Owen."

Owen shot him a glare promising payback.

"Ah, yes! Would you and *Owen* do us the honor of sharing our very first rave dance?"

This was not at all what Levi wanted to do. He racked his brain in a desperate attempt to form an excuse, but none came.

They were trapped.

Outnumbered six to two by a gaggle of determined senior citizens who undoubtedly had planned this ambush. His heart rate spiked off the charts with the overwhelming need to find Aurelia.

Levi exchanged a helpless glance with Owen. The look on his friend's face said everything: *We can take these silver birds out.*

Levi shook his head slightly. *No, there's no way out of this.*

Owen's jaw clenched, his expression murderous, but Levi turned to Gladys and forced a tight smile.

"It would be our pleasure."

The moment the words left his mouth, the silver-haired horde descended.

They were dragged onto the dance floor when the DJ dropped the first bass-heavy track. Glow sticks lit the room as the ancient women threw themselves into chaotic, wild flailing that barely qualified as dancing.

Before Levi knew what hit him, Gladys, Ophelia, and Judith were practically draped over him, their hands wandering far too freely.

"Ladies, please—" Levi protested.

"Hey!" Owen shouted nearby. "No means no, Margaret! I didn't consent to this!"

Gertrude waved a glow stick at them. "Stop being such fuddy-duddies! Let the music take you!"

They needed to get out of there *immediately.*

Nancy purred from Levi's other side. "You boys need to *relax*...and I have *just* the thing to help with that."

Levi stared in horror as she produced a small pill from her clutch.

"What the hell is that?" he barked.

"Bertrand called it 'molly.' Said it makes these things more fun."

No no no no no.

Levi looked at her incredulously. "Did you take one of these?"

Ophelia, still swaying wildly, chimed in. "Of course! Bertrand assured us that based on his research, it's what all young people do. I've never felt so *free!*"

Levi's brain nearly short-circuited. *Impossible...How is this my life?*

Owen elbowed his way to Levi's side, his face pale with disbelief. "Look at me *right now*. We need to go. I'm being sexually assaulted by old ladies who are tripping balls, and I didn't sign up for this," he hissed.

Levi couldn't agree more. "Let's get the hell out of here."

As they wrestled free, a disheveled figure, with feral unfocused eyes staggered toward them. It was Bertrand Dallingford. He somehow lost his tuxedo jacket, his shirt was partially untucked, and his tie was now knotted around his head. His toupee slid awkwardly to the side as he waved his cane like a weapon.

"Everyone, take cover! The chopper's too low!" he bellowed.

Gladys scowled. "What nonsense is your face hole spouting this time, Bertrand?"

Bertrand's eyes darted around wildly. "I can hear them in the tree line! Take cover!"

To Levi's horror, and with a speed a man his age should not have, Bertrand tossed his cane aside and flipped over the nearest table with a mighty grunt—plates and glasses crashed to the floor.

"This can't be happening," Levi muttered.

"Oh, it's happening," Owen replied grimly.

"Heaven's pearls! Have you lost your mind?" Gladys shrieked.

Several people had stopped dancing at this point, disturbed by the commotion. Even the DJ had paused the music.

Having dropped to one knee, Bertrand popped up like a deranged gopher from behind the table. "We have to take cover in this trench! I can hear Oscar calling for help out there...*We need backup*!

"Who's Oscar, and is he single?" asked Gertrude, a dreamy, faraway look on her face. Sweat had begun to bead on her upper lip.

Judith angrily turned on Gertrude. "Why do *you* get to meet Oscar first? You *always* try to snap up any eligible bachelor the second you can, parading your expired clam to anyone and everyone—"

"Hand me the ammo!" Bertrand hollered. His breathing labored as he gestured towards scattered food and dinnerware. "We've got to hold them off until reinforcements arrive!"

Owen tried to approach the old man to calm him down and stand him up, only to quickly jump back, narrowly avoiding the butter knife Bertrand swiped across his midsection. "This is war, son—if you're not on our side, then you're the enemy. Get any closer, boy, and I will gut you like a fish! They trained us soldiers well, traitor!"

For once, Owen was at a loss. He didn't know how to handle this situation. Retreating cautiously, he held his hands and his phone in the air where Bertrand could see them. "Look, I'm only trying to help you, sir. Your commander sent me ahead of reinforcements to let you know backup is coming."

WHAT?

Levi was going to strangle him for feeding into this hallucination...*and* for taking out his phone and filming it.

A seething Gladys marched over to Bertrand. "You have *never* left this country at any point during your ninety-five miserable years of existence, let alone served in the military, you sack of wet grains!"

Levi turned to the other situation unfolding on the dance floor. Gertrude, face beet red, was dangerously close to Judith.

"Who do you think you are, hussy? Just because your dusty bread box isn't bringing anyone into your bakery doesn't mean I have to live a life of chastity. Maybe if you had something tastier to offer, you wouldn't be so jealous of me!"

Something soft but deliberate struck Levi's shoulder. A dinner roll, which came from the direction of—

"You shut your whore mouth, Gladys!" Bertrand roared as he continued rifling through the scattered items, eyes savage as he seized a handful of grapes like they were grenades. "I've only got a few left," he muttered to no one but himself.

The old man's aim was so poor that Levi was again pelted with food instead of Gladys, the intended target. Levi and Owen both watched as Bertrand's toupee slithered down and over his face, blocking his vision. A moment later, the man panicked. "I'll never surrender!" Bertrand cried, wrestling with his sliding toupee.

That was the precise moment everything descended into absolute chaos, the tipping point that would become forever emblazoned in Levi's mind.

With a strangled shout, Bertrand collapsed onto his wig, thrashing like he was fighting a wild animal, shouting, "You will never capture me alive!"

At the same time, Judith shoved Gertrude, who fell backward into Ophelia. Ophelia slipped on a grape and went down hard with a loud crack right as Gertrude flung herself at Judith, tackling her to the ground.

"My hip! My hip!" Ophelia wailed.

The lights flickered on, illuminating the carnage.

It was so much worse with the lights on.

Levi pressed a hand to his forehead. *I'm officially in hell.*

Selene stormed in with security and police in tow, her expression thunderous.

An intimidating police officer approached them both. "Gentlemen, I take it you witnessed...whatever *this* is?"

Levi sighed. "Unfortunately...I don't think you are going to believe us, though."

Owen nodded solemnly. "And if you don't believe us, I've got the whole thing on video. I give it ten out of ten stars—easily the wildest thing I've seen in my entire life."

The officer's mouth twitched, but he waved them toward a nearby table.

As they sat down to give their statements, Levi glanced toward the crowd, searching again for the only person who mattered in all this anarchy. The situation only amplified the anxiety he already felt.

Levi prayed she would find him first.

It took three hours to interview witnesses and clear the area.

Levi's exhaustion was bone-deep.

The police hadn't allowed anyone to leave until they were satisfied they'd spoken to every guest. They prioritized those who needed medical attention first—especially anyone who'd taken illegal substances or managed to injure themselves in the melee.

Rubbing his temples, Levi tried to drown out Owen's voice as he mused, "I'm honestly impressed Bertrand found the strength to flip a table. I expected this event to be filled with stiff socialites in overpriced suits, but this? Senior citizens high on ecstasy, brawling at a rave? Never saw that one coming."

Owen let out a victorious laugh. "Told you someone was going to break a hip! And Bertrand? Worst case of fake survivor's guilt I've ever seen."

Levi grunted. He had forgotten about the infamous farewell party Eleanor hosted—the one Aurelia had told him about. Turns out, several of tonight's guests had prior records from that fiasco. Now they were officially repeat offenders, and several had been arrested...again.

His headache pounded harder.

This night needed to end.

He had tried calling Aurelia multiple times. Either her phone was set to silent, or—worse—she was ignoring his calls.

No. Don't think like that. There's a logical explanation.

Right on cue, Charles approached, bearing the same level of exhaustion Levi felt.

"Even in death, Eleanor's drama still haunts us all," Charles muttered.

Levi didn't waste time. "Have you seen Aurelia?" His voice was tight, his nerves fraying. "I haven't seen her since she left the stage hours ago."

Charles's brows knit together. "No...I haven't either."

Levi's stomach dropped. He cast a quick, worried glance at Owen, who was also frowning.

"She mentioned needing some air after she stepped off stage," Charles said after a moment, brow still furrowed. "Selene offered to take her out to the patio. Then I was instantly pulled aside by a guest, and by the time the bedlam started, I hadn't seen either of them again."

Charles scanned the crowd and pointed. "There's Selene now. She must know where Aurelia went."

"Thanks, Charles," Owen said, already moving. Levi was right behind him.

They covered the distance fast, their long, determined strides cutting through the mass of people remaining.

Selene didn't see them approach, too busy barking orders at the staff to begin breaking down the ballroom. Owen cleared his throat loudly, making her jump.

For a brief second—a quick flash—Levi swore he saw something dark in her expression. Contempt? But it was gone before he could be sure, the same weariness and fatigue they all felt replacing it.

Selene pressed her hand to her chest, her eyes wide. "You startled me!"

"Apologies," Owen said smoothly, flashing his trademark disarming smile.

Selene gave a tight, polite smile in return.

"Have you seen Aurelia?" Owen asked directly.

There was a flicker in Selene's eyes—one Levi missed...but Owen didn't.

"Charles told us she wasn't feeling well," Owen added. "Said you escorted her outside for some air."

Selene nodded, her expression carefully neutral. "She was nervous about the speech. Had a few drinks for courage but no food, and she started feeling woozy. I helped her outside to get some fresh air, and she nearly tripped again. Luckily, a young man caught her before she fell and helped her into a chair."

Levi's blood pressure soared.

"They started...talking, and then I came back in here to get her some water. I got pulled into an issue in the kitchen, and the next thing I knew, everything here had...escalated."

Her casual shrug made Levi's gut twist.

"Do you know who the man was?" Owen pressed.

Selene shook her head. "No, but I assumed he was a guest she already knew...Although it wouldn't be the first time she's had a few drinks and left a party with someone—"

She abruptly stopped, her eyes going wide when she realized what she had implied.

"I-I didn't mean that," she stammered, her voice rising. "I'm sure she's still here. Maybe she's in the study, waiting for the alcohol to wear off."

Levi stood frozen, his mind racing.

Would she do something like that?

The harsh reality hit him like a sack of bricks—he didn't know. It felt like he had gotten to know her pretty well, but the truth was, they'd barely scratched the surface of each other's lives.

Doubt crept in. That old, familiar fear of betrayal resurfaced, fueled by memories of past relationships gone wrong.

But if anyone knows the truth...it'd be her best friend, right?

And her best friend didn't make it seem like everything was fine.

Owen

Owen took one look at Levi and instantaneously recognized the signs of where his mind was headed.

"Shit," he muttered under his breath, his gaze snapping back to Selene. The coolness in his eyes made her flinch.

"Thank you for your help," Owen said, his voice clipped and cold. "If you see her before we do, please tell her we're looking for her."

He didn't wait for a response. Grabbing Levi by the arm, he pulled him toward a less crowded part of the room. With his free hand, he fired off a quick text to Isaac: *Need you at the manor. Now.*

Seconds later, Isaac responded: *On my way.*

Owen's sharp eyes scanned the ballroom, locking on Charles across the room. Without missing a step, he changed course, pulling Levi toward him. Charles took one look at Levi's pale, panicked face and instantly knew something was very wrong.

"Selene says she walked her out for air, and then Aurelia started chatting with some guy. She left her there and hasn't seen her since," Owen explained in a low, urgent voice.

Charles inhaled sharply, his concern written plainly across his features.

Owen turned back to Levi, his voice quieter but no less firm. "I know what you're thinking...but she wouldn't do that to you."

Levi only managed a robotic nod, his eyes distant. That worried Owen more than anything else.

"I'm sure she's still here somewhere," Charles offered, though his tone betrayed his doubt. "Why don't we start searching the grounds?"

Levi straightened slightly, a glimmer of hope returning. "That would be great."

As Levi and Charles started toward the ballroom entrance, Owen held back.

"I'm going to stay here in case she shows up," he called after them. "Charles, I need a favor before you go."

Charles paused. Levi kept walking, too far gone in his thoughts to notice.

Owen pointed to a tall, broad-shouldered man stationed at the ballroom entrance. "Can you tell that security officer over there to follow any instructions I give him? Something isn't right, and I've got a hunch I need to follow up on."

Charles studied Owen for a long moment, searching his expression for something unspoken. Then, with a single nod, he agreed.

"I'll let him know. Good luck."

Charles jogged after Levi, pausing briefly to speak with the security officer and point toward Owen.

Owen approached the guard and introduced himself. "Owen Voss. I'm a close friend of Aurelia's and head of security at her husband's company."

The officer extended his hand. "Edwin McFale. How can I help?"

"We can't locate Aurelia, and we don't know when—or with whom—she was last seen," Owen explained, his voice tight. "Charles and Levi are combing the property, but I need your team ready in case this escalates. Also, a man named Isaac Nolan should be arriving any minute. Let him through when he gets here. He'll help me support Levi if things...don't go well."

Edwin nodded, immediately radioing his team to coordinate.

"In the meantime, I want all surveillance footage from noon today through tomorrow morning pulled and prepared for review. Charles will need it. And if my instincts are right, the police may too."

"Understood." Edwin took Owen's contact information and disappeared into the crowd.

Finally alone, Owen moved to a quiet corner of the ballroom and let the gravity of the situation settle on him.

Something was off—deeply, obviously wrong. And Selene...

That nagging thought wouldn't leave him alone.

Then clarity slammed into him.

Aurelia's dress. Levi had requested it to be tailored with hidden pockets. Big enough to hold small essentials...like a phone.

Fingers moving fast, Owen pulled out his phone and opened a secure tracking app. He rarely used it, but had installed it for situations like this.

That night at Isaac's house when they all first met, Owen hadn't left to grab the champagne. He had swiped Aurelia's phone from her purse and slipped a physical tracking device inside it before returning. He knew it was wrong, but was glad he had the foresight to do it anyway.

He prayed to whatever powers were listening that it would pay off now.

The app loaded. Blips marked everyone's locations exactly where they should be—except for one.

Aurelia.

Her tracker showed her far from the manor...at a hotel downtown. And she hadn't moved from that spot for a while.

Dread surged through him as he dialed the hotel's front desk.

"Thank you for calling Terra Nova Hotel. How may I assist you?"

"Hi, I'm looking for a friend who's missing. Has anyone come through recently wearing a nude-colored ball gown covered in crystals? Long dark hair with rainbow streaks? You'd definitely remember her."

The receptionist paused. "Actually, yes. I remember that couple."

Couple?

"They arrived earlier but didn't stop at the desk to check in. The gentleman already had a key to their room."

Shit.

At that moment, Isaac burst into the ballroom, looking disheveled and worried. His eyes found Owen immediately, his pace quickening as he crossed the room.

Owen swore under his breath, still clutching the phone, and Isaac's worry deepened.

Before Owen could hang up, Levi stormed back into the ballroom with Charles trailing behind him. His face was dark with rage.

Isaac stepped into his path, intercepting him before the man could spiral further.

They needed to get to Aurelia. *Fast.*

CHAPTER 46

Levi

Levi was struggling to rein in his temper, knowing he was seconds from reaching his breaking point. No matter how hard he tried to stay calm, his worst fear kept replaying in his head, the scratchy echo of a broken record grinding away at the last shred of his defenses.

She left with another man...She left with another man...

He was about to detonate.

Owen's sharp curse snapped everyone's attention his way. With his back still turned to them, he shoved his phone into his pocket and straightened, his shoulders squared and his face a mask of pure determination.

"Give me your car keys," Owen ordered, his hand outstretched toward Levi.

Levi opened his mouth to argue, his fists clenched and ready for a fight, but Owen cut him off with a hard glare. "*Now.* I'll explain in the car."

He cast Charles a cutting look. "I left my contact info with Edwin and gave clear instructions. Check in with him and keep me updated. Be ready for my call."

Something inside Levi coiled tight, making each breath feel like a task. Owen's hand remained outstretched, his silent demand dominating his senses.

At last, Levi yanked the keys from his pocket and slapped them into Owen's palm.

Gripping them tightly, Owen met both Levi's and Isaac's eyes. "Let's get our girl."

The car tore through the city at a reckless pace, the screech of tires and roar of the engine doing little to distract Levi from the storm raging in his mind.

Owen had already explained an abridged version of what he knew. The tracking device he planted in Aurelia's phone a month ago. His growing suspicions about Selene. His unease over the entire situation.

Isaac, pale and visibly rattled, sat in the back seat, his face etched with worry.

"I have to ask," Isaac leaned forward between the seats. "Is she the only one, or do all of us have trackers in our phones?"

Owen lifted a single eyebrow at him through the rearview mirror.

Isaac slumped back against the leather seat, muttering under his breath, "Wow."

"We're almost there," Owen began, his voice tight. "Here's the plan—"

Levi didn't hear a single word of it.

His world had stopped the moment Owen confirmed Aurelia's phone was at the Terra Nova Hotel...and she hadn't arrived there alone.

He didn't hear the part about Owen still digging through Aurelia's background. Or the concern about prior police reports of domestic violence from her past relationship with a man named Kyle Morris.

He didn't hear that there had been a temporary restraining order, forgetting when Aurelia had shared bits and pieces of this part of her life over dinner.

Or that hotel security had confirmed through surveillance footage that she had entered room 415, heavily leaning against the man who took her there.

All Levi could see were flashes of every betrayal he had ever suffered. Every woman who had left him. Every compromising position he had been subjected to viewing. He tried to stop it and focus on the present, but he couldn't prevent the onslaught of memories.

Because this time was worse.

Because this time, he had fallen in love with his wife.

And tonight, she inherited millions of dollars and left with another man.

What does she need me for now?

The looming silhouette of the Terra Nova Hotel rose before them like a cruel mirage. A beacon promising answers Levi wasn't sure he could survive.

Isaac and Owen exchanged tense looks, reading Levi's stiff posture and barely controlled fury as he climbed out of the car and strode toward the hotel.

He didn't wait for them.

Didn't even remember his friends were there.

He powered toward the entrance alone and ready to face whatever truth waited for him on the other side.

CHAPTER 47

Aurelia

Aurelia had been awake for a while, though she was unsure exactly how long.

She hadn't dared move a muscle, feigning sleep and just listening. Her survival depended on it.

That voice—the one from her nightmares—was here. In the room.

She lay on her stomach in an unfamiliar bed, her head turned to the side, tangled hair spilling across her face. Completely naked under the covers. But it was the pain—the blinding, all-consuming pain—that held her attention.

It took every shred of willpower not to cry out. Even breathing was excruciating.

"Shouldn't she have woken up by now? It's been hours," the voice muttered, presumably into a phone.

Kyle Morris.

His name sent her body into fight-or-flight mode, raw terror crawling up her spine. Flashbacks of bruised ribs, broken bones, and endless pain blasted into her.

She bit down on a whimper as cold understanding dawned. She knew exactly why she hurt. No one ever forgot what fractured ribs felt like. Her left ankle was aflame, her wrist throbbed painfully.

Kyle hadn't even waited for her to be conscious before lashing out at her.

How did I get here?

A question she had been silently asking herself for the last hour.

The last thing she remembered was the Harvest Charity Ball...talking to Selene. She didn't consume anything but water and diet soda. Yet, she felt hungover and groggy.

Before that...Martin Strasburg, chair of The National Dyslexia Foundation. Levi had been mingling while she checked on the event staff. Owen had been plowing through a platter of appetizers.

Everything after that was a black hole.

"We're running out of time," Kyle sneered. "And you promised me one last round with her. Teach her a lesson about leaving me."

No, no...please no—not again...

Aurelia fought to stay calm against the rising terror, forcing herself to focus. She needed to escape. She used her other senses to gauge where Kyle was in the room—somewhere in front of her.

Cracking one eye open a sliver, she instantly regretted it. Her head pounded, the light too bright.

Kyle's back was turned, phone pressed to his ear, wearing nothing but red boxer briefs. The sight of him made her stomach lurch. She bit back the urge to physically gag.

Gritting her teeth, she scanned the room. A hotel room. She was close to the edge of the bed, within reach of the nightstand that held a brass lamp...and an alarm clock.

2:37 AM

If that was correct, then she had been unconscious for hours...and awake for at least another one.

And if she stayed here, she was dead.

Her self-defense training wouldn't save her now—not like this. Her eyes locked onto the lamp again, as a plan began to formulate.

One chance. One shot. Make it count.

Kyle ended his call with a sharp curse and turned around.

She opened her eyes fully, knowing he would see.

He didn't disappoint.

"Well, now...ask and you shall receive," he purred, his voice thick with menace. "I've been waiting a long time for this. Too long. You really shouldn't have left me, Aurelia. You need to be reminded of what happens when you run."

She didn't move. She couldn't—not yet.

He stalked toward her, the bed dipping as he knelt behind her.

This is it. Now or never.

She reached for the nightstand as he simultaneously grabbed her waist and flipped her onto her back.

Kyle didn't even see the lamp until it connected with his temple.

With every ounce of strength she had left, she slammed it into his head.

Kyle dropped onto her like dead weight, knocking the air from her lungs. Pain shot through her chest as the pressure crushed her injured ribs.

Gritting her teeth against the agony, she shoved him off and slid free, gasping for air. He was out cold, face down on the bed.

Darkness crept at the edges of her vision, but she forced herself to stay conscious, to move. She was naked, bruised, and broken, but she was alive.

Adrenaline surged. She searched for her dress, her phone—anything.

A loud pounding on the door made her jump, her heart leaping into her throat.

"Open the door, Aurelia!"

Levi.

With a sob of relief, she grabbed a bedsheet crumpled on the floor, wrapping it tightly around herself, and stumbled to the door.

When she opened it, she barely registered Owen and Isaac standing behind Levi. All she could focus on was Levi…and his expression frozen in horror as his gaze shot past her to the bed.

To Kyle. Half-naked. And then back to her, barefoot, wrapped only in a sheet.

For the rest of her life, she would never forget the way his eyes turned to ice.

Rage. Disgust.

And then he turned his back on her. On them. On everything they'd worked for.

In a matter of seconds, her entire world imploded.

Levi

Levi was *so* tired.

Tired of the lies. Tired of being toyed with.

He hadn't wanted to believe Selene when she told him Aurelia left with another man. He wanted to believe his friends and that something about this entire night didn't add up. That Aurelia was different.

She was *supposed* to be different.

But what he saw in that hotel room couldn't be denied.

The ache hit him like a physical blow, a crushing weight tightening around his chest. He could *feel* his heartbeat slowing, could *feel* something fracturing deep inside as he turned and stepped back into the hallway.

She had opened that door looking terrified—terrified that *he* was the one who found her. Draped in nothing but a goddamn bedsheet, like decency was too much to ask.

That was the moment Levi broke.

The anger hit him fast and hard, a wildfire that burned through every piece of him. He whipped back around towards the hotel room door.

"How could you do this?" His voice cracked under the weight of his grief. "You *knew* what everyone before you did to me—how they used me. And the first chance you got, you walked away with someone else?"

He barked out a humorless, bitter laugh. The memory of the inheritance news from earlier sliced through his mind again, bruising and sharp.

"You finally got what you wanted, didn't you?" His voice rose to a shout. "The inheritance you were waiting for, but at what cost?"

"Levi—" Owen's warning growl cut through the air, but Levi didn't hear him.

Couldn't hear him. Right now, there was nothing and no one but him and Aurelia.

"Was I not enough?" His voice dropped to a pleading whisper, broken and raw.

"Levi, *please*—please let me explain," Aurelia choked out, shivering on unsteady legs, tears streaming down her face.

But it was too late.

"I *can't*." His voice was barely a rasp, and yet it carried the weight of finality.

He took a stumbling step back, retreating like her very presence burned him. "*I can't do this.*"

Isaac's hand landed on his shoulder, but Levi shrugged it off in agitation. He was vaguely aware of Isac speaking, but his words sounded distant, muffled, like they were coming from underwater.

None of it mattered anymore. His voice was hollow and devoid of emotion when he spoke again.

"I'll just...let you get back to whatever you've been doing." His devastated gaze flicked back to the room, his chest tightening painfully. "He can have you."

He grabbed the car keys still dangling from Owen's hand. Without another word, Levi disappeared down the corridor—his pace quick, desperate to outrun the destruction behind him.

He had to get out of there. He had to get away from *her*.

Isaac called after him, his voice growing fainter with every step.

Levi didn't hear him. He didn't hear anything anymore except for the deafening sound of his hope shattering into pieces.

Aurelia

Levi broke his promise...and with it, he broke *her*.

He didn't even try to listen.

Didn't give her the chance to explain, to fight for what little hope still existed between them.

The moment he turned his back and walked away, he wasn't simply leaving a hotel room—he was leaving *her*, destroying the fragile trust she had so carefully begun to build.

Aurelia had wanted to believe she could trust Levi so badly. She couldn't believe how blind and stupid she was to think things would be different this time. That Levi was different.

Isaac chased after him, but Owen stayed behind.

He stood in the doorway like a silent sentinel, his sharp eyes scanning the room, cataloging every horrifying detail.

Cold rage took hold of his features as he pieced together what Kyle unconscious on the bed, the twisted sheets, and the bruises already darkening her exposed skin signified.

When his gaze finally found hers, something inside her broke completely.

The tears she had fought so hard to hold back spilled free, mingling with the raw tremble of her lips. She sagged under the unbearable stress of it all, unable to hold herself together any longer as despair overwhelmed her.

"I...I hit Kyle with the lamp," she choked out between sobs, her voice barely a whisper, brittle and frayed at the edges.

Owen's eyes widened, comprehension smashing into him like a freight train.

"Please..." Her voice cracked on that one desperate word, her body trembling violently. "I think...I need an ambulance, I—"

But she couldn't finish.

The darkness closed in, stealing her away just as the last word spoken left her lips. Her knees buckled, and Owen rushed forward.

She collapsed into his arms, like a broken, bloodied angel wrapped in nothing but a sheet and sorrow.

Owen

Owen caught Aurelia as she fell unconscious, cradling her limp body against his chest. He knew with gut-wrenching certainty that this night had irrevocably destroyed her. And if Levi didn't come to his senses soon...It would destroy him, too.

Owen rarely got angry. It took a hell of a lot to rattle him, and even then, he was always the first to crack a joke, smooth things over, and let it roll off his back.

But not tonight. Not with Aurelia unconscious and broken in his arms.

As he gently lowered her to the floor, careful not to jostle her battered body, a slow, boiling rage unfurled inside him, cold and deadly in its precision.

First, it was the pathetic excuse for a man sprawled unconscious on the bed.

The second she whispered the name *Kyle*, it all clicked into place. Kyle Morris. The abusive bastard from the police reports, the one whose history Owen had uncovered and quietly kept an eye on. He was nothing more than a violent parasite who should have rotted behind bars years ago. And now?

Owen wasn't leaving this hotel until Kyle was hauled out of here in handcuffs—or a body bag.

But the anger didn't stop there.

No, the worst of it—the blackest, ugliest part of his fury—was reserved for his so-called best friend.

Levi.

The man who should have been here. The man who promised to protect her.

Instead, Levi took one look before he tucked his tail and ran. Didn't even stop to think, didn't let her speak, didn't listen to him when Owen spelled it all out in the car.

He had left her bleeding, in pieces, barely conscious, and standing alone in her worst nightmare.

And that? That was something Owen wasn't sure he could forgive.

His hands shook as he pulled out his phone and dialed for an ambulance, his voice tight but controlled as he rattled off the details. When the police arrived, he was all business, laying out exactly what had happened, his eyes burning holes in Kyle's unconscious body as the officers cuffed him.

He stayed with Aurelia every second, his broad shoulders a silent shield as the paramedics worked, his jaw clenched so hard it ached.

When they lifted her onto the stretcher, her fragile body engulfed by the hospital blankets, Owen climbed into the ambulance without any qualms.

"She's been drugged," he told the paramedics grimly. "I'm absolutely confident you'll find something in her system. Run the tox screen."

He didn't leave her side, not once, until the ER doors swung open for her and a nurse gently guided him to a quiet waiting room far from the chaos.

He sat there for god knows how long, unmoving, his fists clenched so severely his knuckles could have split open from how tightly his skin was stretched, his mind a whirlwind of fury and betrayal.

The phone in his pocket wouldn't stop buzzing—Levi, over and over again.

Owen let it ring.

Let it burn.

For the first time in his life, Owen Voss didn't have a single goddamn thing left to say to his best friend.

Isaac

Isaac stayed close behind Levi, following him down every flight of stairs from the eighth floor, all the way into the parking lot. Levi had stormed out without a word, avoiding the elevator like it offended him. But when Isaac stepped in front of the driver's side door, blocking his path, that finally forced a stop.

"Get out of my way, Isaac," Levi growled, his voice raw with fury.

"You're in no condition to drive," Isaac said evenly, extending his hand. "If you're going to run, then hand over the keys and get in the passenger seat."

Levi's glare dropped to Isaac's outstretched palm. For a brief, dangerous second, Isaac saw the flicker of violence in his friend's eyes—like Levi might shove him aside and take the wheel anyway. But after a tense, silent moment, he ripped the keys from his pocket and slammed them into Isaac's hand before stalking around to the passenger side and slamming the door shut.

Isaac exhaled the breath he hadn't realized he was holding and slid behind the wheel. He pulled out of the lot and drove without a destination, circling the city while waiting for Levi to break the silence, willing him to say something, anything.

But Levi sat motionless, forehead pressed to the window, fingers tangled in his hair, his reflection in the glass as lost as he felt.

Isaac's thoughts returned to that hotel room and what he saw when the door finally swung open. At first glance, it looked bad...very bad. But the longer he stood there, the more wrong it felt in a way he couldn't explain. When he caught Owen's eye, the same doubt was written all over his face.

The man passed out on the bed hadn't so much as flinched when Levi battered down the door and shouted loud enough to wake the dead. And Aurelia...

It wasn't relief on her face when they found her. Not at first. No, there'd been raw, bone-deep fear in her eyes. Relief had only flickered through for a heartbeat—right before Levi lost control.

And lord, did he lose control. He hadn't seen her fear. He didn't notice her uncontrollable shaking or the unadulterated fear in her wide eyes. Owen had tried to snap him out of it, but Levi was too far gone, his emotions drowning out every rational thought.

Isaac winced, recalling the awful things Levi had said. Words so harsh they might never be forgiven. He couldn't imagine ever saying something like that to Grace.

He kept circling back to the part that didn't fit. He had come to learn that Aurelia wasn't the type to do something this reckless. She had been so anxious about this event and had worked herself to exhaustion over every detail. To leave it early—and in that state? It didn't add up.

Owen said she hadn't touched a drink all night. Isaac couldn't remember a single time she ever had. She had told their tight circle of friends once that she didn't really drink. Looking back, he couldn't recall a time she had proved that wrong.

If anything, it all felt like—

Levi's voice cracked the silence, raw and broken. "Now what do I do?" His voice trembled. "What is it about me that's never enough? That makes every single one of them do this?"

Isaac gripped the wheel tighter. "I can't tell you why this keeps happening, Levi," he said carefully. "But I think you made a mistake tonight in running before you heard her side."

Levi snapped his head toward him, eyes blazing. "Did you not see what I saw?" His fists clenched, his whole body straining to hold himself together.

"I did. But I'm not the one drowning in it. I'm the one still thinking clearly. And Levi...a lot of things don't add up. Owen saw it too."

Levi's expression twisted with mistrust. "Like what?" he spat.

Isaac calmly walked him through every detail—Aurelia's fear, the unnatural stillness of the man on the bed, the timeline that didn't make sense. As he spoke, Levi seemed to unravel piece by piece, his fury slowly caving under the weight of his guilt.

By the end of it, Levi sat slumped in the seat, his face pale and wrecked.

"You think I should have listened to her?" he asked, his voice barely above a whisper.

Isaac gave a solemn nod. "What if it's not what you think it is?"

Levi didn't answer. He didn't need to.

Without another word, Isaac turned the car around and headed back to the hotel. This time, Levi didn't object, mired in his thoughts.

But when they pulled into the lot, a wall of flashing lights greeted them. Police cruisers. Two ambulances. And chaos spilling out of the hotel entrance.

They arrived in time to see paramedics rolling a stretcher toward one of the ambulances. A small, motionless figure lay beneath the blanket, colorful dark hair tangled wildly around her pale face.

Owen trailed behind the stretcher, his expression a severe mask of grim fury. When he spotted their car, his eyes locked on Levi with a glare that could have torn him apart.

Then Owen climbed into the ambulance, the doors slammed shut, and the sirens wailed into the night.

CHAPTER 48

Owen

It wasn't long before a nurse came looking for Owen.

"She's awake," the nurse said quietly. "And she's asking for you."

Owen shot to his feet, his heart pounding as he followed the nurse down a long, sterile corridor. They stopped outside a curtained-off space, with the temporary walls meant to give the illusion of privacy in a place where nothing felt safe.

Inside, Aurelia lay motionless in the hospital bed, the backrest slightly elevated. She wore a thin patient gown, a blanket drawn over her like a fragile shield against the world.

Pain clung to her, visible in every shallow breath and every tiny wince, but her pain went beyond body aches.

It was something much more profound.

When she finally noticed him standing there, his carefully guarded expression collapsed under the strain of seeing her like this. But it wasn't the bruises or the IV line that crushed him.

It was her eyes.

They were empty and devoid of life. The light he had always seen in her, no matter how dim the day was, now extinguished.

"Hey, bestie," Owen said softly, his voice catching despite the teasing nickname.

At the sound of it, her eyes shuttered further. He watched helplessly as she pulled away behind invisible walls, brick by agonizing brick. A piece of him broke watching those walls go up.

In a matter of weeks, she had become family to him, like the little sister he had always wanted but never had. And now she was slipping away.

"Please...don't shut me out," he whispered, his voice raw. His arms hung limply at his sides, unconsciously clenching and unclenching his fists.

Her face crumpled. "I would never shut you out," she rasped, the words barely audible before the unstoppable silent tears broke free. They slid down her cheeks as she gasped for air between sobs, each breath a fresh wound, her ribs protesting with every shudder.

"You stayed," she choked out. "When everything fell apart, you were there." Her voice fractured as she struggled to keep up with her breath. "Thank you...for staying."

Owen swallowed hard, his throat thick. "There are always three sides to a story," he said gently. "And I've gotten to know you. You could never do what he thinks you did. You don't have to say a word—I see it. Anyone would. Even I can tell how much you love him."

Her broken laugh sounded more like a sob. "*Loved* him," she whispered bitterly. "I *loved* a man who made promises he never intended to keep. Who didn't even stop to listen before leaving—leaving me alone with *him*." Her voice broke entirely. "That *monster*..."

She collapsed into sobs, each one wracking her chest so violently it made her fractured ribs scream in protest, the bed rattling beneath her. Owen felt powerless, unsure how to help her.

"I don't want him here!" she cried, her voice rising in undiluted agony. "I don't want to see him. I don't want to hear his voice. I want him out of my life—I want his things *gone*! I can't...I *can't*..." Her words dissolved into gut-wrenching howls, each one a dagger to Owen's heart.

Without hesitation, Owen pulled the chair as close as it would go and took her trembling hand in his, holding on through every painful breath, every ragged sob, until the storm quieted into faint, exhausted whimpers.

Time passed in silence, broken only by the distant beeping of monitors and an unnatural chill that settled over him.

The facility itself seemed to thrum with detachment, its coldness deepening the weight of an already somber moment.

He thought she had drifted off to sleep when she stirred again, her hands trembling as she slid her wedding band and engagement ring from her finger.

She held them out to him, her palm open, her voice barely a whisper.

"I want a divorce."

Aurelia

Aurelia was finally moved to a private room. It was an unspoken acknowledgment that her situation had shifted from personal tragedy to an active police investigation.

The hotel room became an active crime scene. Statements were required from both her and Owen.

At her quiet request, Owen contacted Charles, her attorney, to be present before the police arrived. Charles wasted no time arriving minutes before the on-call physician returned, this time flanked by two uniformed officers.

The news hit everyone with brutal intensity.

Kyle had been taken to the hospital in a separate ambulance. He remained unconscious and unresponsive since the moment Aurelia struck him with the heavy, solid metal lamp. The blow had fractured his skull. He hadn't woken up, but the moment he did and was lucid enough, police custody would be waiting.

In the sterile light of the hospital room, surrounded by law enforcement and her attorney, the physician reviewed the test results.

The toxicology report was damning. Traces of flunitrazepam—Rohypnol—were found in her bloodstream. A drug infamous for dissolving easily into drinks, stripping away willpower, inducing drowsiness, and wiping memories. The kind of drug that made it easy for someone to lead her away without a scene.

Aurelia's mind couldn't process it. She stared at the floor, her hands clenched into fists beneath the thin blanket as she disassociated.

The physician continued, his voice clinical and detached as if he wasn't tearing open fresh wounds with every word.

She had several fractured ribs and deep tissue bruising. Miraculously, there were no major internal injuries, but six to eight weeks of recovery lay ahead. Her left ankle was twisted, most likely from stumbling in her heels, and her right wrist was mildly sprained, a textbook injury from bracing herself in a fall.

At the mention of falling, her breath hitched, her gaze locking on a distant memory she couldn't escape. How many times had she fallen before at Kyle's hands? Too many to count.

It was the ribs that were the worst of it. Six to eight weeks to heal…if she rested. If she let herself recover.

Aurelia didn't allow herself to believe in the illusion of recovery. Not anymore.

The doctor said she could go home in a few hours once the paperwork was done and the police had their interviews.

Home.

The word was foreign and out of place. Did she even know what it meant?

Beside her, Owen was strategizing how to rally the rest of their friends to help with her recovery—minus one glaring exception.

Then came the part she dreaded most. The officers began their questions, their pens poised to capture every tarnished piece of her story.

Aurelia answered numbly, her voice flat, as if these events had drained every last trace of feeling from her that not even an injury could summon a reaction.

She told them about the drinks, how she had only had soda and water. She explained Kyle's history of violence, how their relationship had ended, and how she had spent the final hour in that hotel room waiting him out while he took a mysterious phone call with someone she couldn't identify.

Owen stiffened so abruptly in his seat that it was almost comical. When it was his turn, Owen gave his account, explaining how he found her and what he saw when he arrived.

Aurelia shot him a sharp glare when he casually mentioned the tracker he had slipped into her phone—something she didn't know about...or consented to.

Owen met her glare with a flat, unapologetic stare and kept talking. A complete invasion of privacy that saved her life. He was finishing up when the sound of raised voices echoed through the corridor.

Aurelia paled, her turbulent brown eyes locking onto him with a silent, desperate plea. She didn't need to say a word; his curt nod relaying his understanding.

Owen rose immediately, his chair scraping harshly against the floor. Without hesitation, he strode for the door, a police officer falling in step behind him.

He was more than ready to handle whoever dared disturb her peace.

CHAPTER 49

Isaac

Isaac's stomach turned as he watched the ambulance disappear down the street. Only two people were in that hotel room. And only one with that hair could have been on that stretcher.

He didn't need to hear the strangled sound from the passenger seat to know the moment Levi figured it out, too. That sound was raw and soul-crushing...and one Isaac knew he would never forget.

He trailed the ambulance to the hospital on autopilot, hands clenched on the wheel, Levi frantically working his phone beside him.

Call after call went straight to Owen's voicemail.

The car echoed with each unanswered ring, Levi's curses growing louder, more desperate with every failed attempt. He kept trying, again and again, the entire ride there—every rejection hitting like a fresh blow.

At the hospital, they were forced to park farther away in a separate lot, nowhere near the emergency entrance. Once they made it inside, Levi called, searching frantically for Owen, prompting the approach of two police officers. They were questioned about the incident, which only separated Levi from Aurelia further.

Isaac answered numbly. Levi paced like a caged animal, his agitation barely contained. When the officers vanished behind the double doors to the patient's wing, Levi snapped.

He stormed the reception desk, demanding answers, his voice thundering through the waiting room.

"I need to see my wife!" he roared, slamming his hands against the counter.

The staff couldn't tell him anything. She had no assigned room yet, was only allowed one visitor...and someone was already with her.

Levi wasn't listening to reason anymore. He raised his voice, his desperation boiling over into a full-blown scene. Isaac tried to intervene, but Levi shoved him to the side, where he now stood helplessly, wondering if someone could sedate his friend before security had to be called.

Then, like a lightning bolt breaking through storm clouds, Owen burst through the doors, his expression nothing short of homicidal. One of the earlier police officers trailed close behind him, though Isaac doubted even he would have been able to come between his two friends if the situation escalated.

"You," Owen snarled, jabbing a finger in Levi's chest, "need to shut it down. Right now." His voice was a deadly growl. "She can hear you back there—every pathetic word—and you're sending her into another goddamn panic attack."

Levi froze, his eyes wide with guilt and panic, his fury instantly abating.

"H-how is she?" he begged. "Please...Can I see her? I just—I need to—"

"Absolutely not," Owen cut him off, eyes blazing. The force of that refusal nearly knocked Levi back. Isaac held his breath.

"Physically?" Owen's words dripped with barely leashed fury. "She'll heal. Her sprained wrist and twisted ankle will be fine in a few weeks. But her ribs?" He shot Levi a pointed glare. "Cracked. It'll take eight weeks before she can even breathe easy again. And that's nothing compared to the bruises she's wearing right now like a second damn skin."

Isaac paled, his stomach rolling. "Holy shit..." he muttered under his breath.

Owen wasn't close to being done.

"Emotionally?" His tone dropped to something far more dangerous. "She might never come back from this. She was drugged, Levi, at her own event. Kyle Morris—her abusive ex—escorted her out like it was nothing. Took her to that hotel and assaulted her while she was unconscious."

Isaac turned a shade greener hearing Owen confirm the truth they suspected. Levi stood frozen, his expression blank, as if the shock hadn't fully reached him yet.

"He was waiting for her to wake up," Owen snarled. "Waiting to do even worse. She pretended to be unconscious for an hour, Levi. And when she saw her only chance, she fought back. Cracked his damn skull with a lamp. That woman—you left her. You walked away and left her with a monster!"

Levi crumbled, sinking into a nearby chair, his head buried in his hands.

"I don't deserve her forgiveness," he rasped, his voice hollow. "But god, I'm so sorry. I need to see her. To tell her..." His eyes brimmed with tears, his voice breaking apart.

For an instant, Owen stared at him, torn between fury and the painful tug of loyalty and friendship. Levi looked so demolished, so lost, it dulled the sharp edges of his anger.

But some truths couldn't be softened or easily forgiven.

Owen's voice dropped, deadly calm. "She doesn't want to see you, Levi. She doesn't even want to hear your name right now."

Levi's head snapped up, distraught. "What?"

"She asked for your things to be cleared out of her house," Owen continued quietly, delivering the final blow. "She said you broke your promise when you turned your back on her without listening to or talking to her. And right now...she's in there with Charles, discussing how to file for divorce."

With a grim finality, Owen opened his palm. Isaac swore.

In his hand lay two gold and turquoise rings—Aurelia's engagement ring and wedding band.

Levi stared at them as if they caused him pain just by existing. His hands trembled as he reached out, his fingers closing over the cold metal.

It was over.

It was really over.

And Levi had no one to blame but himself.

He sat motionless, tears slipping unabashedly down his cheeks, every breath a glaring reminder of everything he couldn't fix.

"She didn't deserve this," he choked out after several long minutes, defeated. "And I—I didn't deserve her. If divorce is what she needs to heal, I'll give it to her. I'll give her anything she asks, even if it means losing her forever."

His fingers curled around the rings like lifelines; his frame wracked with silent sobs as the hours bled into nothing.

At some point, Isaac and Owen sat down beside him, one on each side. No words were exchanged. They simply sat with him in silence, sharing the unbearable weight of everything he had lost.

And in that long, agonizing quiet, Levi mourned.

Mourned his marriage.

Mourned the love of his life.

Mourned the part of himself he knew he would never get back.

CHAPTER 50

Aurelia

"Are you sure you want to do this?" Charles asked gently, his eyes searching hers for any flicker of indecision. He occupied the guest chair by her hospital bed, a notebook balanced on his knee, his brow furrowed in concern.

Aurelia's fingers twisted in the blanket; her gaze fixed on the sterile sheets.

The truth was, she wasn't sure about anything anymore. Her body ached, her heart felt fragmented beyond repair, and her mind replayed every horrible moment of the past twenty-four hours on an endless loop.

But one memory stood out in sharp, unforgiving clarity—Levi's face when he saw her in that hotel room.

That *look*. The raw accusation. The disgust. *At her.*

She would never forget how she had begged him to listen, pleading for one moment to explain, and how quickly it was denied when he walked away. After the hateful things he had said—things meant to cut deep and leave a scar—he *left*.

He had made promises, held her to them when it was convenient for him. But the first time their marriage was tested, he proved what he really thought of her.

He didn't trust her.

She had given as much of herself as possible. Had laid herself bare, shared her deepest fears and vulnerabilities...and still, he believed the worst.

A marriage without trust wasn't a marriage at all. It was a prison sentence.

Eleanor's inheritance was thrown in her face like a weapon, as if every hardship she had survived, like living out of her car and fighting for every scrap of stability, meant nothing. She didn't flinch, but the words left a ringing silence in their wake, like a slap that never quite landed but hurt all the same.

In a matter of seconds, Levi had become everything she hated—no better than Kyle. Abuse didn't always leave bruises. Sometimes it left invisible wounds that never quite healed.

She wouldn't let anyone treat her like that again. *Not ever.*

While the doctors ran their endless tests, while the police asked their endless questions, she had had plenty of time to think. To feel. And to realize that no one could save her from this pain but herself.

Her thoughts circled back to Eleanor and her final message—how love wasn't the goal. Living life on her terms was. Becoming the fierce woman Eleanor always believed she could be.

Levi had cracked her open, forced her to face the world again...but he was also the reason she was closing herself off now.

No.

She pushed that thought away. That was the old Aurelia talking. She wasn't that timid woman anymore and was in control of who she became. And she refused to let the Kyles—or the Levis—of this world have that power over her again.

She was enough.

She always had been.

"Yes," she said, her voice low but unshakably steady. "I'm sure. File it. Serve it. I don't care about the cost. I don't want anything from him. I just want it over."

Charles faltered, his concern deepening. Then he nodded slowly. "Understood. I can have the paperwork ready tomorrow."

Aurelia stared down at her hands, her throat tightening. In a whisper, she confessed, "I went into this heart and mind wide open. I thought...I really thought it could work. I tried *so* hard." Her voice trembled. "I'm sorry I failed. If you want to rescind your decision from last night, I'd understand. No hard feelings. But even after all of this, I know one thing for sure..." She swallowed hard, fighting back fresh tears. "I'm enough. Even if I'm alone, I'm *enough.*"

The words weren't a mantra. They were a promise to herself.

Charles exhaled a long, weary breath and shook his head, his expression morphing into something more paternal. He looked at her the way Eleanor used to...right before delivering one of her trademark, soul-rattling lectures.

But instead, Charles surprised her.

"You know," he began, his voice distant with memory, "Eleanor went through something a lot like this once. Head over heels in love. Engaged, even."

Aurelia's head snapped up, frowning. "She never told me that."

"She wouldn't," Charles said with a sad smile. "It was one of the most painful chapters of her life. And...it's how we became friends."

He leaned back in his chair, eyes faraway.

"I was working in the kitchen part-time back then while I was in college. I stumbled into one of the old pantries during her engagement party...only to find her fiancé and one of the housekeepers together."

Aurelia gasped, her hands flying to her mouth.

Charles chuckled humorlessly. "Before I could even process what I saw, I realized Eleanor had followed me. She was practically breathing down my neck. And when she saw them..." He shook his head with a faint smile that didn't reach his eyes. "She let out a scream so loud I couldn't hear properly for six days."

Aurelia's eyes brimmed with fresh tears, not from sadness of her troubles this time, but from the heartbreak of knowing even Eleanor had once fallen so low.

"She locked herself away for weeks after that," Charles continued softly. "Didn't eat. Didn't speak. I volunteered to bring her meals to help keep the gossip away. Over time, she started to talk. And little by little...she started to heal."

Aurelia's voice was a mere breath. "How did she come back from that?"

"I'm not sure she ever fully did. But one morning, she got out of bed, walked into the dining room like a woman reborn, and declared she was done living by anyone else's rules. She refused to marry. Took lovers when she wanted and lived life however she saw fit. And when children never came, that's when the search for you began."

Aurelia's chest clenched. "She chose me...because I reminded her of herself?"

Charles gave her a knowing look. "She said you'd figure that out eventually."

Aurelia laughed through her tears, the sound uncomfortable but real.

Letting her process this revelation, Charles stood and gathered his things, preparing to leave. At the door, he turned back one final time.

"You've fulfilled the terms of her will," he said quietly. "You opened your heart. You learned that you are enough, as you are. That's all she ever wanted for you. My decision stands."

Aurelia could barely speak past the lump in her throat. "Thank you," she managed weakly.

Charles nodded, but before he left, he offered one last truth and the hardest one of all.

"I was married nearly fifty years to the love of my life. And even we had moments where we almost didn't make it. Pain and fear...they'll convince you to run before you even know what you're running from."

He paused, his eyes sharp despite the kindness in them.

"Everyone comes with baggage, Aurelia. But sometimes...it's the way we carry it that makes all the difference. Don't let fear choose for you. And don't shut the door before he's even had the chance to apologize and fight like hell for you."

With that, he was gone, the door clicking softly shut behind him.

Though she knew, deep down, Charles was right...she wasn't ready to believe it. *Not yet.*

Hours later, she was discharged.

Owen walked silently at her side, his presence steady as he escorted her through the hospital's sliding doors and into the cool morning air. She slid into his car without a word, the familiar weight of exhaustion and heartbreak pressing down on her.

Home, she told herself. *I'm home now.*

But it rang hollow. The moment she stepped through her front door, the lie unraveled. What had once been her refuge, a sanctuary at the end of every long, weary day, now felt empty. Lifeless.

Precisely as she had asked, Owen had seen to it that every trace of Levi was gone before she returned. His things were gone. His scent. His presence.

Her house was exactly as it had been before him: perfectly in order, everything in its rightful place.

And yet...It felt wrong.

Too quiet. Too still. Too lonely.

She walked through the house in a daze, each empty room echoing with memories she didn't want but couldn't stop reliving. Though she had never spoken it aloud, she knew what her heart had been screaming for weeks.

She loved him. It's why every cruel word Levi hurled at her, every moment he refused to listen, every hateful look he gave her hurt so much. She was splintering apart from the inside out.

Owen offered no details about what happened after he left her hospital room, only that Levi had been there—worried, desperate to see her—and that he had "taken care of it." His voice was distant, painfully formal, when he confirmed that Levi had received her message...and was moving out.

She didn't ask how long Owen had been gone before returning to her hospital room. She didn't ask why his eyes were red or why his jaw had been clenched tight enough to crack bone. Owen was Levi's friend before he was hers. Whatever happened in that waiting room...It appeared to have destroyed *him*, too.

Now, sitting on a stool at her kitchen island, Aurelia stared at the single object left behind.

A key.

Levi had left it there, right where she had asked him to.

It gleamed faintly under the soft overhead lights, a tiny, shining symbol of everything she had lost, and everything she had chosen to let go.

But Charles's words circled endlessly through her mind, each one cutting deeper than the last.

Everyone comes with baggage, Aurelia. But sometimes...it's the way we carry it that makes all the difference. Don't let fear choose for you. And don't shut the door before he's even had the chance to fight for you.

Her fingers curled into fists on the cold marble counter. And still...she couldn't bring herself to move that key.

Not yet. Maybe not ever.

The weekend crawled by in a haze of sleepless nights and endless tears. Time lost all meaning.

Morning, afternoon, night...it all blurred together as Aurelia drifted through the motions of existing, hollowed out and numb.

The home she had poured her heart into and what once was a refuge she built for herself was as comforting as a mausoleum now. Filled with cold silence and haunted by the ghost of memories she couldn't escape. Everywhere she turned, she found him, even though he was gone.

Physically, her body ached, every breath a painful reminder of the bruises and fractures left behind on Friday night. But worse than that was the ache in her chest. It had festered into a deep, consuming sorrow that no medication could touch.

The bedroom felt foreign, the air heavier without him in it. She wasn't content to simply lie there alone anymore. It didn't feel right, like a part of her had been severed and left bleeding.

She hated herself for it, but when she attempted to go in there every night, she clung to his pillow, pressing her face into the fading traces of his warm and earthy scent, desperate to hold onto what little of him remained.

Levi had flooded her phone with text after text, voicemail after voicemail all weekend, each one a reminder of the tangled mess she found herself in. She hadn't dared open a single one—too afraid they'd be filled with more venom and anger, confirming every horrible thing she feared about herself.

Self-doubt had crept into her mind and grown like an invasive weed, causing Aurelia to question her decision. After all, she had been the one to ask for the divorce, even though she missed him more than she could ever imagine. Maybe he hated her now, and maybe he was right to.

So, she cried in the bathroom, staring at the empty counter where his toothbrush used to rest, the shower now devoid of his things.

She wept in the closet, half of it glaringly empty.

She sobbed in the kitchen, staring at a refrigerator stocked with groceries she bought specifically for him—foods she would never eat.

Everywhere she looked, she cried.

Because everywhere she looked, he was gone.

Saturday night, when she couldn't take the crushing silence anymore, Ivy and Grace showed up unannounced. Grace brought a pot of homemade chicken soup. Ivy carried a tub of black raspberry ice cream, Aurelia's favorite.

The moment she saw them standing there, she fell apart all over again. They didn't try to talk her out of it or tell her to be strong. They simply came in, held her, and sat with her in the heavy quiet.

And as much as she loved them for it, their presence only reminded her more of what she had lost. Of *whom* she had lost. She fought it for as long as she could, but eventually the words slipped free, bleak, and vulnerable.

"How...how is he?" she whispered, her voice wobbly.

Grace and Ivy exchanged loaded glances before Grace finally answered.

"You want the truth?"

Aurelia nodded quickly. Lies had no place in her life anymore.

Grace drew in a deep breath. "He's...not doing well. He knows he made the biggest mistake of his life—one he'll regret forever. And he's realizing he has demons of his own to deal with...things he's never faced or acknowledged. Things that broke him before this even happened. He says he needs to fix himself, so this...so something like this never happens again."

The admission cut her open all over again. Charles's words echoed through her mind like a cruel reminder.

Everyone comes with baggage, Aurelia. But sometimes...it's the way we carry it that makes all the difference. Don't let fear choose for you. And don't shut the door before he's even had the chance to fight for you.

"I don't care what issues he's working through," Ivy snapped, her arms crossed tightly over her chest. "He should have listened to you first. End of story."

Grace sighed heavily, shaking her head. "I'm not excusing what he did, Ivy. But I understand why he reacted the way he did. That doesn't make it right...but at least he's not pretending it's okay. He knows how badly he screwed up. And he's trying to figure out why—so he never does it again to anyone else."

To anyone else.

The words hit Aurelia like a gut punch.

Anyone else.

She couldn't explain why, but the thought of Levi simply accepting the divorce...walking away from her without a fight...It carved out another delicate piece of her soul.

Aurelia had demanded this ending, but now, staring into that dark abyss of finality, she wasn't sure she was strong enough to handle it. The tears came in a violent rush, wracking sobs tearing from her throat and stealing the breath from her lungs. Each one sent fire lancing through her ribs, the bruised bone flaring with pain no medication could fully numb.

Ivy and Grace sat on either side of her, rubbing her back in comfort as she cried it all out.

When the storm of grief finally passed, and her breathing evened out into shallow, shaky breaths, she lifted her tear-swollen eyes to them.

"Do you...Do you think I should talk to him?" she asked, her voice barely audible. "Hear him out?"

Another glance of an unspoken conversation passed between them.

This time, it was Ivy who answered, her tone gentler than before.

"Even though I'm mad as hell at him...I think you owe it to yourself to listen. Give yourself the closure he couldn't give you that night. Then...you decide what you want. No one else."

Grace nodded slowly, her expression muted and understanding.

Aurelia inhaled a long, unsteady breath, her mind and heart caught in a war she didn't know how to end.

For the first time all weekend, she wondered if she was truly ready to let him go.

The next day, it was Owen who showed up at her door, completely unexpected, uninvited, and...exactly what she needed.

He stayed the entire day and long into the night, camped out on her couch with takeout containers piled high and a marathon of POLmArK TV romances playing back-to-back.

Of all Levi's friends, she felt safest with Owen. She couldn't quite explain why, especially considering how their friendship had started, but in that moment, she was secretly grateful beyond words that he refused to leave her alone.

Between the inevitable waves of tears, Owen managed to coax out reluctant smiles...and even a few real laughs. At one point, he turned to her, utterly serious, and declared, "Mark my words, Aurelia. One day, I'm going to be in a POLmArK movie."

She blinked at him, caught off guard. "You? In these?" She gestured at the screen where a rugged small-town lumberjack was dramatically confessing his love to a woman in the middle of a banana tree farm.

"I don't care if it's as an extra walking through a background farmer's market scene," he said solemnly. "It counts. And it's going to happen."

Aurelia let out a weak laugh, her ribs protesting even that small movement. "Why do you love these ridiculous movies so much?"

She meant it with genuine curiosity. It wasn't every day you met a towering, broad-shouldered man who openly admitted to binging cheesy romance films.

Owen's expression turned thoughtful, his voice wistful.

"Because no matter how bad things get, no matter how messy it all looks halfway through...you know it's going to end happily," he said quietly. "I can put one on at any point—doesn't matter if it's the beginning or halfway through—and I'll still know they'll figure it out. There's always some big, dramatic fight or impossible obstacle, but they don't let it stop them. They find a way."

Aurelia stared at him in awe. She had never thought of it that way before.

And the earnest, unguarded look in Owen's eyes made her realize he was letting her see a side of him most people never got close enough to witness.

"It's like...a reset button," he added, rubbing the back of his neck. "When life completely falls apart, these movies remind me that things can work out. They give me hope, even if it's temporary."

Aurelia swallowed against the sudden lump in her throat, turning his words over in her mind, astutely aware of how perfectly they applied to her own life.

"Have you ever told Isaac all this?" she asked carefully.

Owen snorted, his humor snapping back into place like a reflex. "Are you kidding me? He already makes fun of me for the unrealistic professions like the cupcake tycoon, snowplow mogul, and espresso mustache barber. If he ever found out how much I actually love these movies, I'd never hear the end of it."

He paused, eyes narrowing as his own words sank in. "And if you tell him, I swear on my future POLmArK career, I'll toss your body into a lagoon myself. No one will ever find you."

The laugh that broke free from Aurelia startled them both. A deep, genuine laugh that echoed through the house, sharp and sweet and painful all at once. She pressed a hand to her ribs, groaning through the sting but unwilling to regret it. She hadn't laughed like that in so long.

When the moment passed, she turned to Owen, her smile fading into something reflective, her eyes damp but grateful.

"Thank you," she whispered. "For being here. For being...you."

The hard lines of Owen's face relaxed, a rare warmth filling his expression. "Anytime, bestie."

Aurelia exhaled a long, shaky breath.

"Believe it or not," she said quietly, eyes distant as her thoughts swirled, "you've given me a lot to think about."

Owen offered her a knowing smile. "Good. Just don't take too long thinking about it. Even POLmArK movies only have a two-hour runtime before somebody makes a move."

Aurelia's lips twitched despite herself. For the first time since that awful night, she felt a sliver of something beyond heartbreak.

CHAPTER 51

Levi

The bright, cloudless sky over Joia City shimmered against glittering rooftops and the still, mirror-like waters of the lagoons. The world moved on, oblivious to the fact that, for Levi, everything had come to a full stop.

He stood motionless at the floor-to-ceiling windows of his office, his gaze fixed somewhere beyond the skyline, unblinking. As if the world outside might offer answers he couldn't find within. It was all muted now, bland and tinged with gray.

Coming in today was a mistake.

Saturday morning, before Aurelia was discharged, he had done exactly as she asked and moved everything out of her house. He cleaned, organized, and virtually restored the place to how it was before he ever stepped inside her world.

It was the very least he could do after the way he had destroyed her trust.

He had tried to reach her again and again. He left messages and voicemails, but was met with silence. Levi would have gotten down on his knees and begged if she would let him. He didn't care about pride. He only wanted the chance to apologize...and to see with his own eyes that she was okay.

But the silence spoke volumes.

As of an hour ago, his real estate agent had listed his mansion for sale. He couldn't set foot in that house again. Not after knowing what a real home felt like.

He had crashed at Isaac's place last night, but the luxurious guest suite was just a plush holding cell. Grace tried to be kind, her empathy tempered by loyalty to Aurelia. She had offered a few soft words and a disappointed look that hit harder than a fist to the jaw would have.

Ivy, on the other hand, had made her stance crystal clear. She hadn't spoken to him unless it was work-related. He had never experienced the short, frigid, and calculated side of her directly. Not that he could blame her either...it just hurt more than he expected.

Today wasn't going to be productive. He had known it the moment he walked through the door. He was about to call it a day when the office doors burst open with the force of a battering ram.

Ivy barreled in, breathless and wild-eyed. The look on her face sent him instantly on alert, every muscle tensed.

"What's wrong?" he barked, his body already moving before his mind caught up. "Are you hurt?"

"No," she gasped, still catching her breath. "The Board called an emergency meeting. They're gathering in the conference room right now—and Levi—it's really bad. You need to see the news reports now."

A hole of dread opened in his gut.

She hesitated through her panting. "Photos of Aurelia...from that hotel room...someone leaked them. The media's all over it. They're—"

Before she could finish, Isaac and Owen came skidding into the office, Owen nearly tripping over his own feet in the rush.

Isaac looked like he hadn't slept. His hair was a disaster, his shirt wrinkled, and his expression was one of total devastation. Owen was seething, practically vibrating with rage.

Isaac was the first to speak, his voice heavy with alarm. "It's everywhere, even on national news. A massive customer data breach was leaked by an anonymous tip. Grace is trying to put out the fire, but it's chaos."

"It was Martin Strasburg who found it," Owen added, his jaw tight. "Came straight to me. Said Wilkerson built a backdoor into the system before we terminated him. The bastard's been inside our network this whole time."

"Months," Isaac said, horrified. "It was buried, layered so deep no one saw it. But now the leak's public and—"

"And Aurelia's private trauma has been blasted across the internet," Owen finished bitterly.

Levi sank into his chair. His head spun with everything they lobbed at him.

Wilkerson's code. The public breach.

Sexually explicit photos of Aurelia were plastered on newsfeeds and social media.

It wasn't a coincidence. It was a full-scale ambush.

A coup.

And he had been too broken, too distracted, too blind to see it coming.

He lifted his eyes to his team—his family—every one of them waiting for direction. Waiting for their leader.

He knew what the emergency Board meeting was for.

Taking him down.

He swallowed hard, bracing himself. Then, with slow precision, he rose to his full height in his chair, the calm, calculating mask of a CEO slipping into place like armor.

"Go to your offices," he said firmly. "Start packing up your things."

The silence was instant and complete. Isaac blinked. Owen stared. Ivy's mouth dropped open.

"What?" Isaac finally whispered.

"Tell Grace to do the same," Levi said, his voice stronger now. "This was Tyler's endgame all along—take control of the company. And I think..." He paused, a breath hitching in his chest. "I think he succeeded."

They didn't move. Couldn't. The weight of his words paralyzed them.

"When I walk into that meeting," Levi said, tone flat, "it'll likely be for the last time."

He stood then, unhurried and steady, straightening his blazer in anticipation of the battle looming on the horizon.

"But we're not going to give them the satisfaction of watching us fall apart. No panic. No scrambling. We walk out of here calmly. Cool. Lethal." His voice hardened, each word sharpened to a blade's edge.

"They want a spectacle? Give them swagger. Channel your inner asshole. Make it a goddamn performance. Pack like you knew this was coming—because deep down, we always did."

Something shifted in the air. They drew themselves upright, eyes blazing with the promise of a fight.

And then Ivy smirked, her eyes blazing fiercely. It wasn't a nice smile. It was feral, sharp, vicious, and promised to draw blood. "Let's go raise some hell," she said.

Levi's grin mirrored hers as they lined up ready to march into the storm...unbroken, unbowed, and ready for battle.

Levi moved through his office with swift, efficient accuracy, methodically packing every personal item that mattered into his backpack. Anything that wasn't essential was left behind.

He cast one ultimate, lingering glance around the office space. This was the place where he had built his empire, made impossible decisions, and dreamed bigger than anyone thought possible.

And then, like a man documenting the last moments before a battle was lost, he pulled out his phone and started snapping photos from every angle. One final memory preserved as evidence and proof of what remained. A testament before the end.

Across the hall, Ivy sat at her desk like she had all the time in the world, legs casually propped up, her tote bag already packed at her feet. She lounged in her chair, perfectly at ease, snapping selfies like this was another normal day at the office.

Levi couldn't help but let out a low laugh. Even in the face of disaster, Ivy could make defiance look effortless. Then an idea struck him.

"Hey, Ivy," he called. "Take a picture of us. Right now."

Her eyebrows shot up. "You want a *selfie* with me while your company burns down?"

"Not just a selfie," he clarified, a glint of mischief returning to his eyes. "I want a shot of me standing in the doorway to my office and one as you are with your feet up, looking completely unbothered. Then send it to me. *Immediately.*"

Her grin was wicked as she grabbed her phone and snapped some photos.

The moment his phone buzzed with the incoming message, Levi pulled it up and began tapping furiously, thumbs flying across the screen. Then, without missing a beat, he lifted the phone and started speaking rapid text commands into it.

When he was done, he turned the screen toward Ivy, that dangerous, familiar spark back in his eyes.

She read it once—twice—and then threw her head back with a sharp, barking laugh. The first real laugh from her after the weekend's traumatic events.

"You're insane," she wheezed. "And I love it."

Levi slung his backpack over his shoulder and shot her a devil-may-care smile as he headed for the door.

"Spread the word," he called back. "I'll see you on the other side."

With the confidence he was known for, he strolled out, every step oozing the smug calm of a man who knew the storm was his to unleash.

The fall might be inevitable. But he sure as hell wasn't going quietly.

It took every ounce of Levi's restraint not to march across the conference room and wipe that smug grin right off that self-serving demon Tyler's face with his fist. He was kicking himself for missing the obvious signs of what Tyler had been working towards these past months.

But that wasn't the weapon he had chosen today.

No, he was going to bury Tyler with his own arrogance.

Levi sauntered into the room like he owned it, even as his empire crumbled beneath his feet. Exactly as expected, Tyler had staged the scene perfectly with two reporters stationed near the end of the table, their pens already poised like vultures ready to tear apart the carcass of his career.

Right on cue.

He flashed them a brilliant, easy smile as he strolled by, catching the not-so-subtle exchange of knowing glances between them.

Good. Let them watch.

Two large, unfamiliar men stood near the walls. He snorted at the fact that Tyler hired private security for this. Levi offered them a pleasant nod as he ambled to the far end of the table, to the seat that was still, technically, his...for now.

He settled in easily, setting his backpack on the floor, his body loose and unbothered. Out of the corner of his eye, he saw it—that glorious moment when Tyler's smug confidence flickered with disappointment.

And right beneath that...fear.

Levi smirked. *You wanted outrage and humiliation, Tyler? Sorry. Not today.*

Tyler opened his mouth to speak, but Levi casually lifted a finger, cutting him off with the simplest, most dismissive gesture imaginable.

Wait your turn.

He casually took out his phone, swiped open the camera app, and adjusted the angle until every single person in the room was in view.

"Gentlemen," he addressed the security guards smoothly, "Would you mind stepping a little to the left? I want to make sure we get everyone on camera before I start recording."

The guards exchanged wary looks but shifted obligingly. The Board members squirmed. Tyler's eyes darted to the journalists, his confidence starting to fracture.

With a satisfied smile, Levi hit record.

The screech of Tyler's chair echoed through the room as he shot to his feet. "Turn that *off*!" he barked, pointing furiously across the table. "You don't have my consent—or anyone else's—to record this meeting!"

Levi reclined back in his chair like he had all the time in the world, a smug smile that was pure provocation played on his lips. His voice was taunting and dripping with careless confidence.

"Actually," he said, angling the phone to zoom in on the surveillance signs posted clearly on the walls, "you all waived that right the second you walked into this building. As you can see, this entire space is under constant video surveillance."

He turned the camera back on Tyler, his smile sharpening into something dangerous. "And since you haven't voted to fire me yet, I'm still an employee, and fully entitled to my legal workplace accommodations under the Citizens with Disabilities Act."

He let that hang for a moment before dropping the bomb.

"And since we're talking about accommodations," Levi kicked the sarcasm up a degree, his voice cool and razor-sharp, "let's not forget that I'm dyslexic. Officially diagnosed. Permanently protected. And I am fully entitled to record meetings for my personal reference. It's in my file, Tyler. Would you like me to read it aloud for you, or would that be too ironic?"

Tyler's face flushed an ugly shade of red. His mouth opened, but nothing came out.

Levi leaned forward, the humor vanishing like a switch had been flipped. His gaze turned lethal, and when he spoke, his voice was razor-sharp and impossible to ignore, slicing through the room like a drawn knife.

"And I'll *never* forget that Board meeting two months ago," he said, his glare pinning Tyler like a bug under glass. "When I reminded you that your job didn't give you the license to interfere in our operations. How you lost your badge access after tailgating an employee into a restricted area, or how you tried to coerce my developers into altering the code to collect personal data."

He turned the phone deliberately toward the reporters.

"I have the official meeting minutes if you're interested. Would you like to know what this man said to me that day?" Both journalists fidgeted, eyes bright with anticipation. Levi savored the moment, then delivered the fatal strike.

"I told him if he was that desperate to be a developer, he should apply for the job. His response?" Levi paused for effect, his voice dropping to a low, dangerous purr.

"I'd be happy to send you my resume, but...I wonder if you'd be able to read it efficiently without someone to help you. We all know how difficult it is for you to do something so simple."

Gasps rippled through the room. The reporters' pens flew across their notepads. Even the security guards exchanged a disgusted look.

Levi sat back slowly, eyes glittering with cold satisfaction. "And since we're laying all our cards on the table..." Levi ticked his fingers off one by one.

"One—You've harassed and discriminated against me for my disability."

Tick.

"Two—You conspired with a now-former employee to deliberately orchestrate a data breach that miraculously hit the media before I even learned of it."

Tick.

"Three, and perhaps most damning of all, someone leaked explicit photos of my wife in the middle of a vicious assault that *just so happened* to break at the exact same time as this data breach. And wouldn't you know...it all conveniently coincides with this little coup d'état you've been planning for months."

Tick.

The room was deathly silent, the faint hum of cool air passing through the vents echoing loudly through the room.

"Now," he said, his voice low and lethal, "we all know you've been choreographing this moment since the day you thought you could run this company better than me. So, if you'll kindly proceed with this pitiful attempt at humiliation by firing me publicly...I have better things to do with my time."

Levi relaxed in his seat, pulling his backpack onto his lap.

"Oh...and the other founders of Neuronix? Our COO, CTO, CSO, and CMO?" His eyes danced in amusement as he patted his bag dramatically. "They're packed and ready to go."

His smile faded, his final words carrying the weight of a storm on the horizon.

"Whatever consequences you think you've prepared for, Tyler..." His voice dropped into a promise. "...you're not ready for *me*."

After delivering that final promise, Levi sat in the wreckage of the empire they'd stolen, quietly waiting for Tyler to deliver the final blow.

A blow Levi didn't think would even affect him...after what happened with Aurelia, he had already lost everything.

Everyone gathered at Isaac and Grace's house after the Board meeting.

Levi had called it perfectly: every calculated move, every smug expression, every humiliating blow. Tyler executed his hostile takeover like a poorly written script he had been rehearsing for years. Despite knowing it was coming, nothing prepared them for the final, brutal reality of watching the company they built from nothing slip through their fingers.

One financial outlet called it *"the most dramatic executive shake-up in recent history."*

Financially, they'd all be fine. That was never the worry.

Thanks to their annually renewed 10b5-1 trading plans, the moment their termination status hit the HR system, all their Neuronix stock automatically sold at top dollar. The market didn't even have time to react before the transactions cleared.

Levi strode out of that boardroom richer than ever before. But what did it matter? They lost the only thing that meant something to them: their control in the company they bled for. No amount of wealth could buy that back.

Outside, the media frenzy exploded. Footage of the firings dominated every major network. But Levi had his own narrative to share.

He delivered the video of the Board meeting directly to the two reporters that followed him outside—and posted the now-infamous photo of him and Ivy to his public social media feed with a caption that was pure Levi:

Me and my Executive Assistant packed up and about to get fired in an "emergency board meeting." #hostiletakeover #newsknewbeforeus #neuronix #freetime #tylerfaulknersucks #foundersfired

His friends followed suit with similar pointed posts:

Ivy, lounging with her feet up, smirking like a queen. Owen sprawled across his desk, chin resting on his fists like a bored model. Isaac dramatically tossing files into a recycling bin. Grace doodling across her reports with neon markers like she was back in kindergarten.

And when it was over, they all walked out together, finding strength in each other, smiling for the cameras as if it were another sunny day and not the collapse of their careers.

But the smiles faded the moment they stepped out of the spotlight. Now, behind closed doors, the finality of what happened was inescapable.

Levi didn't think the day could possibly get any worse. But the universe, never one to be outdone, decided otherwise.

The sheriff's cruiser pulled up behind him once he parked outside Isaac's house. Before he could even open his mouth, the envelope was pressed into his hands. He was terrified to pull out the contents, but he forced himself to face it, stomach dropping as he read the cover page, the paper as heavy as a brick.

Divorce papers.

The warmth in the air evaporated, the temperature dropped, and everything turned to ice.

In an instant, the thin thread of hope he had been clinging to snapped, unraveling everything inside him. Losing the company was survivable.

But this? This...he wouldn't recover from.

It felt like something had carved him out from the inside, scooping out every last piece until there was nothing left but an empty husk. That sudden coldness began to seep into that fresh gaping hole.

Somewhere along the way, he had fallen hopelessly in love with his wife.

The first inklings hit Levi in the early hours of the Harvest Charity Ball, but he wasn't ready to admit it. Not until she went missing and his world stopped spinning.

And then, when she opened that hotel room door...when he saw her standing there and his heart was ripped straight from his chest, he reacted the only way his damaged soul knew how. He destroyed the one thing he couldn't bear to lose.

Now it was too late.

The moment that scalding envelope burned his hands, every dream of fixing things—of fighting for her—turned to ash.

Levi didn't remember walking inside. Didn't remember sitting on the couch. Someone spoke to him, but the words didn't land.

A hand rested gently on his shoulder, trying to pull him back from wherever he had fallen...he couldn't feel it.

Someone knelt in front of him, their voice breaking with urgency, but it barely registered. He stared through them, eyes dull and unfocused, as if sound, light, and meaning had all drained from the world.

He was just...

Gone.

CHAPTER 52

Owen

Levi was destroyed. He hadn't spoken in hours and hadn't moved from his spot on the couch since the moment they walked through the door.

He sat there like a man carved from stone, eyes dull and unfocused, staring into nothing. His expression was bleak and devoid of life.

Hopeless.

Owen stood nearby, helpless and pacing with no idea what to do. He had seen Levi down before, but never like this. He made his feelings about how Levi handled the entire situation perfectly clear, but it didn't mean he wanted to see his oldest friend in such a state.

This wasn't the fallout from a difficult day or a rough breakup. This was a complete internal collapse. Owen was genuinely starting to wonder if Levi would ever come back from it.

Being served divorce papers right after losing the company—his life's work? That wasn't merely a low blow; it was a death sentence to whatever hope Levi had been desperately clinging to.

Owen's phone buzzed, slicing through the suffocating silence. He glanced down and immediately answered the incoming call from Charles Pierce, the tension in Owen's chest loosening a bit at the familiar name.

"Mr. Voss," Charles greeted, his voice calm but laced with sorrow. "I apologize for the timing of this call. I saw the news...and what happened today. I'm truly sorry for the injustice you and the others are enduring."

"Thank you, sir," Owen said somberly, glancing again at Levi, still unmoving and unblinking. "It's out of our hands now. One step at a time, right?"

He tried to sound hopeful but failed miserably.

Charles exhaled heavily on the other end. "I'll be brief. First, I was hoping you might have time to come to the manor tonight. Our security team has gathered all the footage for the police, but I'd like your eyes on it before we turn it over. I haven't reviewed it yet, but I trust your instincts."

Owen was already grabbing his keys, motioning to Isaac that he was heading out. Isaac frowned but gave a reluctant nod when Owen mimed a texting gesture.

"I'm on my way now," Owen confirmed.

"Good." Charles paused. His next words came quieter, more hesitant. "The only other reason I called...How's Levi?"

Owen briefly paused in the doorway, his heart heavy as he turned back for one last look at his friend. Levi sat exactly where he had left him—lost and unreachable.

"Not good," Owen admitted roughly, as he slid into the driver's seat of his car. "He's...checked out, Charles. Completely. He hasn't moved in hours. Hasn't spoken or acknowledged anyone. It's like..." His throat tightened painfully. "It's like he died inside, and his body's now waiting to catch up."

For a long stretch, Charles said nothing. Owen put his car in gear, the call connecting to the stereo system as he slipped his phone into his pocket and headed to the manor. Finally, the older man spoke again, his voice softer but weighted with unspoken meaning.

"It's not my place to interfere," Charles began carefully, "but I would encourage you, and the others, to spend time with Aurelia. Convince her to at least talk to him. I've advised her, as gently as I could, that no matter how this ends, some things should be said before the silence becomes permanent."

Another pause.

"My unofficial legal advice?" Charles continued. "Tell Levi not to sign those papers. Not yet. Hold out as long as he can. Sometimes people don't realize what they're truly ready for...until it's too late. I'll see you shortly."

The call disconnected before Owen could respond.

He gripped the steering wheel tighter as the city lights blurred past him. All he could think about the entire drive was how dangerously close "too late" was becoming.

Owen had spent hours glued to the security footage, eyes red and gritty, his vision blurring from the relentless strain. His stomach growled, an increasingly loud reminder that he hadn't eaten since—god, when? Owen *never* missed dinner.

He should have walked away, called it a night, let fresh eyes take over in the morning.

But something kept him locked in place. It was that gnawing instinct he had learned over the years never to ignore. The answer was here. Right in front of him.

Yet, he kept missing it. It was really pissing him off.

He had already found Kyle, slipping in through the back patio, dressed like a guest. That alone had him grinding his teeth, but it was the nagging certainty that a second unknown player was involved that kept him rooted to the spot. Aurelia had mentioned in her statement that this piece of shit was on the phone with someone else when she regained consciousness.

Charles was equally frustrated, pacing behind him, relaying everything he had seen that night.

"How he got in through the back...I'm not sure," Charles muttered, starting over again. "Selene helped Aurelia off the stage and then—"

Wait.

Owen's eyes snapped back to the screen. His mind replayed that moment like a film suddenly running in reverse.

Selene helped Aurelia off the stage...

He scrubbed back through the footage, zeroing in on the moment Kyle entered from the gardens. The estate's security was top-notch, so how did Kyle know exactly where to go and how to avoid them?

He was so focused on Kyle's movements that he completely overlooked everyone else in the frame. Owen slowed the footage, homing in on Selene's location.

She was near the bar by the double glass doors—the very doors Kyle slipped through. And when he did, she was *right there*, in Kyle's direct line of sight. They made eye contact. Just for a second. But it was there.

Owen's heart hammered as he kept watching.

Selene picked up a tall glass filled with a dark liquid, her hand brushing over the rim almost too quickly to catch. Kyle melted back into the shadows, eyes never leaving her. Then Selene crossed the room directly to Aurelia...and handed her the drink.

The rest was a memory Owen could never unsee, as Aurelia drank the entire glass, smiling politely, and getting up on stage completely unaware of what was going to happen next. She stepped off the stage, almost tripping over her dress, and Selene had been there waiting to catch her...before guiding her gently toward the gardens.

Owen's fists clenched so tight his knuckles cracked. "Son of a bitch," he growled under his breath.

"What is it?" Charles asked, voice tight with urgency.

Owen barely heard him.

"Where's Selene?" he demanded, as his fingers flew over his phone, already calling Isaac. "Did she come in today?"

Charles's brow furrowed before his face drained of color. "No—she wasn't here. I heard someone mention in passing she didn't show up, but I didn't think anything of it."

Owen was already moving, shoving his chair back, and sprinting for the door. Charles launched into motion, pulling out his phone to alert the police.

But Owen wasn't listening.

He was already outside and running to his car, barking into the phone as Isaac answered.

"Get to Aurelia's house. *Now*. I'm on my way."

There was no time to explain. They had to get there.

Before Selene did.

Levi

Levi felt like he was drowning, and mentally, he welcomed it.

He had begged for the darkness to pull him under, to keep him there. Because resurfacing meant facing a world without her...a reality he didn't know how to survive.

Barely breaking the surface, his friends' voices crashed into him all at once, cutting through the fog.

They were saying her name. Over and over again. Aurelia.

Hearing it made his chest seize. For a brief, fragile moment, he stayed still, listening. The moment he let the world back in, the raw emotions he buried came roaring to life, unstoppable.

His mind went utterly blank again when he heard Isaac curse and disconnect a call, his movements frantic as he searched for his keys.

"That was Owen," Isaac said, his voice sharp with panic. "Selene is the one who drugged her, and she didn't show up to work today. He thinks she's in danger!"

Grace and Ivy exchanged wide-eyed, terrified looks.

"Owen's already on the way to Aurelia's house," Isaac added quickly. "And Charles...he's got the police involved."

The room tilted under Levi's feet. Before anyone could say another word, he shot up from the couch.

"I'm coming with you," he snapped, already moving toward the door.

Isaac didn't argue. He didn't have time to; he was too busy charging ahead, the front door slamming open as they bolted to the car. The second they hit the road, Isaac filled him in on the rest—what Owen had found in the security footage, the truth they'd missed staring them in the face all along.

Selene...Auri's best friend. The woman who had stood by her side since childhood. How could she do something so vile?

Levi's stomach twisted violently. Owen had known and felt that night that something wasn't right, but they'd dismissed it because she was her friend. Now, all Levi could think about was getting to Aurelia before something irreversible happened.

The full weight of his failures barreled into him, threatening to pull him under again. He forced himself to be calm and rational this time because if anything happened to her...he would never forgive himself.

This time, there wouldn't be a second chance.

CHAPTER 53

Aurelia

Aurelia spent the morning curled up on her couch, propped up by pillows, doing everything she could to avoid thinking about Levi.

After lunch, she tried to lose herself in the newest release from her favorite author, a book she had been dying to read for months. But no matter how many times she forced her eyes across the page, nothing stuck.

Her focus fractured and drifted, the words blurring until she realized it wasn't just her mind, as tears had started falling again, clouding her vision. With a shaky breath, she gave up and set the book aside when her phone buzzed with an incoming call from Selene.

Not in the mood to be personable, Aurelia hesitated before answering, but guilt won out.

Selene's voice came through the line, breathless and concerned. She was mortified, apologizing profusely for Kyle somehow slipping past security. She swore she was already investigating it with the security team, promising to hold whoever was responsible accountable.

"I'm so sorry, Aurelia. I let you down," Selene said, her voice thick with remorse. "This never should have happened."

Aurelia tried to soothe her. "Stop blaming yourself," she said softly. "Kyle has always been above the rules, above the law. You couldn't have known he'd be there."

It wasn't only Kyle's arrogance—it was his patience. His terrifying ability to wait, to bide his time until his next cruel move. That was the most terrifying part.

Selene knew that better than anyone. She knew what Kyle had done to her. Knew all the dark corners of her trauma. Aurelia had to believe that if she had seen him there that night, he would've been escorted out by security.

The conversation was almost enough to settle her nerves—until Selene mentioned the photos.

Her hands began to tremble the moment Selene mentioned them.

"They're everywhere," Selene whispered. "The news...social media...I didn't want you to find out through a media outlet, but photos of you are plastered everywhere, and it's...it's not good."

Aurelia's heart dropped to her stomach as she fumbled for the remote, her fingers numb with dread.

They were on every channel...every headline. The photos—*those photos*—plastered across the screen. Images of her unconscious, posed like a sick and twisted prize beside Kyle. The news stations had blurred the worst of it, but it wasn't enough. Not nearly enough.

She sat there, frozen in horror, as Selene's voice buzzed in her ear, offering soft words of comfort that Aurelia couldn't process. Her mind was screaming, her body locked in place, and the edges of her vision had begun to go white.

Selene's voice cut through the fog. "I'll come over tonight after work," she offered gently. "I'll bring your favorite takeout, and we'll have that long-overdue girls' night. You shouldn't be alone right now."

Aurelia almost declined. After two nights of company, she had been looking forward to the silence.

However, if she was being honest...the idea of being alone tonight, in this house that felt too big and too empty without Levi...it scared her.

So, with a heavy sigh and a gloomy heart, Aurelia agreed. As soon as the call disconnected, she burst into fresh tears.

Aurelia was horrified to realize she wasn't the only one having a newsworthy Monday. After her call with Selene, she spent most of the afternoon glued to the television, her book a distant memory.

She watched as her story became one part of the media storm surrounding Neuronix. Not only were they dealing with her personal scandal, but also a massive data breach. And then came the worst news: that Levi had been fired as CEO, along with Owen, Isaac, Grace, and Ivy.

Everyone she cared about, everyone who worked so hard to build that company, had been thrown out in one humiliating sweep. Her heart broke all over again.

Charles had called earlier to confirm that Levi was served with the divorce papers, right after they all walked away from the company for the last time.

Guilt gnawed at her. Maybe she had been too quick to file them. She was still angry with Levi, but the timing...this could have waited. Especially after seeing the video of his final meeting, which was leaked to the press.

In it, Levi accused Tyler Faulkner of playing a role in her being drugged, kidnapped, and assaulted...and of orchestrating the release of those photos alongside the data breach scandal.

She hadn't stopped thinking about it since. The timing wasn't a coincidence. She remembered Kyle on the phone with someone that night. She just didn't know who.

Before she could spiral further, the doorbell rang.

Selene must be here with dinner, having texted Aurelia twenty minutes earlier to let her know she was on her way. After the day she'd had, Aurelia was starving.

"Come on in!" she called, carefully rising from the couch despite the pain. The front door opened, and Selene stepped inside.

She managed to hobble a few steps towards her friend before noticing Selene wasn't carrying anything. Aurelia glanced past her, expecting to see a takeout bag left by the door. But there was nothing.

Confused, she turned back and saw Selene's expression shift.

Gone was the concerned friend. In her place stood a stranger, face twisted with pure hatred.

And then Aurelia saw it—the glint of metal in Selene's hand as it caught the light. A knife. Long, curved, and deadly.

The color drained from Aurelia's face.

"I've waited a long time for this," Selene hissed, stepping closer.

Aurelia instinctively backed away, keeping the kitchen island between them, ignoring the burning pain in her ribs.

"Kyle was supposed to keep you busy until I got there," Selene sneered. "But things didn't go as planned, did they?"

Aurelia tried to stay calm, tried to think. One wrong move and...she couldn't let herself finish that thought. But the disbelief tumbled out before she could stop it.

"You...you're the one who drugged me?"

Selene mocked her, her voice a cruel imitation. *"You're the one who drugged me?"*

The memory slammed into her—the diet soda Selene handed her that night. How could she have forgotten?

Except she hadn't. This was how their friendship always worked. Aurelia had spent years overlooking the small betrayals, desperate to hold onto the one friend she had.

That blind loyalty nearly cost her everything. *Her life.*

Selene took another step forward, the knife glinting ominously. "I'm so tired of you getting everything I worked for," she spat. "Since the day you showed up at the Hayder house, you've taken everything from me."

Aurelia's mind flashed back to those early days in foster care, remembering Selene's bullying, the stolen possessions, the endless fights. Until one day, Selene had simply...changed. She apologized. Pretended to be her friend. And Aurelia, desperate and lonely, had accepted it.

But that version of her was *gone.* The old Aurelia would have cowered and apologized, doing anything to avoid conflict. But that woman died the night she smashed a lamp over Kyle's head.

The woman standing here now had walked through fire. And she wasn't about to break.

Looking at Selene—at the stranger holding a knife in her own home—Aurelia felt something she hadn't expected.

Undiluted rage.

She stood tall, refusing to cower, and met Selene's glare with a cold, steady gaze.

"You and I have very different memories of how things went back then," Aurelia said coolly. "From what I recall, you were a nasty little brat who couldn't keep her hands off things that didn't belong to her. And when I asked nicely, you didn't listen. You always had to learn the hard way."

Selene's entire body vibrated with rage.

"*No!*" she screamed. "I came to visit Eleanor's *heir*! I worked for that old witch for years, and she gave it all to you! You're nothing without me!"

"You're the one who introduced me to her!" Aurelia snapped back. "You told me to apply for the job!"

Selene laughed, bitter and sharp. "I did it as a joke! I wanted to see you fail, but of course, you got the job and the matchmaker." Her face darkened further. "You got *my* life. Even your husband should have been mine!"

The mention of Levi made something inside Aurelia rupture.

"The highlight of my life," Selene went on, her voice sickeningly sweet, "was when you were dating Kyle. Seeing his bruises all over you? That was a masterpiece. And knowing he'd get to do it again? That was the cherry on top."

Aurelia's stomach turned, bile rising in her throat.

Selene smirked, enjoying her cruelty. "You thought you were free of him when you got that no-contact order, didn't you?" she sneered. "But guess what? I stayed in touch with Kyle the whole time, just waiting for the perfect moment for us to both get our revenge."

She took another step, her smirk deepening. "It was so easy to get him to share those photos—saved me the trouble of leaking them myself. And it turns out, I'm not the only one you've pissed off."

Something cold and deadly settled over Aurelia's heart.

This wasn't her friend. This was a threat.

Selene rolled her shoulders back, bracing herself. "I'm done talking," she said coldly, her voice like steel. "Consider this a mercy...putting you out of *my* misery."

Aurelia's patience cracked. Her vision burned red as pure, blinding rage took over.

She'd had enough.

Enough of the lies. Enough of being used. Enough of being someone else's punching bag.

Enough of this bitch standing in her house.

The lingering pain from her injuries faded under the surge of adrenaline. Her body moved on instinct as Selene lunged, knife aimed low.

Foster care had made her scrappy. But the self-defense training she had forced herself through over the last few years took that scrappiness to the next level.

Aurelia deflected Selene's knife with her forearm and grabbed her wrist in one smooth motion. Selene let out a startled yelp as Aurelia twisted her arm hard, forcing the knife free.

The blade clattered across the floor as Aurelia swept Selene's legs out from under her and shoved her back.

Caught completely off guard—exactly as Aurelia intended—Selene crashed to the floor, her head bouncing off the hardwood with a sickening bang.

Before she could react, Aurelia was on her, straddling her chest, pinning her down.

Selene thrashed, wild and desperate, but she couldn't break free. Couldn't block the blows that followed.

Aurelia swung hard. Again. And again.

"I was your *friend!*"

Selene's nose crunched under her fist.

"I didn't *deserve* this!"

Blood poured from Selene's split lip as Aurelia kept hitting her, years of pain and betrayal fueling every strike.

"I didn't deserve this!" she cried out again, pounding her fists into the woman who pretended to be her friend.

She barely noticed the strong arms that wrapped around her from behind, pulling her back. She fought against them, kept swinging, lost in the storm.

It wasn't until she was lifted off Selene, yanked back into a solid chest, that she felt herself starting to break. They fell to the ground together, her body cradled against hard muscles and warm, familiar arms.

She didn't fight anymore. She simply sobbed. Her whole body shook as the weight of it all poured out of her.

The arms holding her rocked gently, keeping her upright when she didn't have the strength. Soft kisses rained down from above before a chin rested on her head.

"You didn't deserve this," Levi's broken voice whispered against her ear. His cheek pressed against hers, his tears mingling with her own.

Safe. She was safe.

Somehow, Levi had come for her, exactly when she needed him most. Through the haze, through the regret, she realized how close she had come to never seeing him again.

Her cries quieted. Her body sagged against his, her mind finally allowing her to take in her surroundings. The pain from her fresh injuries returned, sharper now. But it didn't matter.

Levi came for me. He's here.

His arms held her tight as the darkness took her. And for the first time in a long time, she let it.

Levi

Until the day he died, Levi would never forget the fear that gripped him during the entire drive to Aurelia's house.

But nothing could have prepared him for the sheer terror that slammed into him when he walked through her door and saw Selene lunging, knife in hand, straight at the woman he loved.

For a split second, he and Isaac stood frozen, horrified by the scene unfolding before them. By the time they remembered to move their bodies, Aurelia had already acted. A fast and fierce blur that disarmed Selene, took her down, and pinned her to the floor in a matter of moments.

Those few heart-stopping seconds would haunt Levi forever. He was terrified he was too late.

Now, with the police on scene and the chaos behind them, his chest filled with pride and awe. He couldn't stop shaking every time that lunge replayed in his mind, but his brave, unstoppable wife had defended herself. She had faced a monster and forced it to submit.

That was the woman he had always known lived beneath her soft exterior.

But it was the raw, blinding rage that had overtaken her after—the fury that had truly gutted him.

If he hadn't reached her when he did, he had no doubt she would have beaten Selene to death. There was no way in hell he would let her go to prison for taking the justice she rightfully deserved.

He tried to be careful when he pulled her off, mindful of her injured ribs, but he knew he couldn't avoid hurting her a little. There was no other way. He prayed he hadn't made things worse.

Isaac had rushed to Selene to make sure she was still alive and no longer a threat, while they waited for the police. They arrived about ten minutes later, with Owen right behind them.

Everything after that became a haze.

All Levi could focus on was the unconscious woman in his arms and getting her the help she needed. This was her second ambulance ride in as many days. But this time, he was going with her.

He wasn't leaving her side. Not now. Not ever.

And when he got the chance, he would tear up those divorce papers himself. This marriage wasn't over.

After what felt like the longest ambulance ride of his life, they arrived at the hospital. Staff immediately rushed her into testing, assessing the damage. She didn't wake up through any of it.

Much like Kyle, Selene had also been unconscious when the paramedics arrived, her bloodied face unrecognizable. As soon as she recovered enough, she would be taken into custody.

Levi silently thanked every higher power that the doctors ruled out any head trauma. Her unconsciousness was due to shock and exhaustion, something she was becoming too acquainted with lately.

He refused to leave and stayed at her bedside for hours, keeping everyone updated after every test and conversation with the medical staff. He didn't care about sleep. He didn't care about food. He only cared about her and being there when she finally opened her eyes.

While he sat with her, the police finished their investigation. No longer considered a crime scene, Ivy and Grace headed to her house to clean up what was left of the nightmare, while Owen and Isaac gathered Levi's things.

They were moving him back into that house—their house—where he belonged. Even if he had to sleep on the couch, he didn't care. He was going home, and he was taking care of his wife.

CHAPTER 54

Aurelia

A blinding white light pierced through the pounding in Aurelia's head as she cracked her eyes open.

It took a moment to register where she was...a hospital bed. Again. Stark white walls slowly came into focus with the soft, rhythmic beep of monitors filling the background.

How did I end up back here?

Muffled voices drifted from directly outside her door, but she couldn't make out what they were saying. She tried to sit up, craning her neck toward the sound, only for blinding pain to tear through her ribs. A sharp cry escaped her lips before she could stop it.

The voices outside her room went silent. The door swung open a second later, and Levi rushed in with a doctor close behind.

He was at her side in an instant, his emerald eyes scanning every inch of her as if he needed to make sure she was still whole—and still *there*. When his gaze met hers, she saw everything he was feeling written plainly across his face: worry, relief, guilt, and fear.

He didn't say a word. He didn't have to. It was all there in his eyes. And then it all came flooding back, the images of Selene, the knife, and the blood—*so much blood*—threatening to overtake her.

Her body trembled as the memories crashed over her, and hot tears spilled down her cheeks. Without a word, Aurelia reached for him.

Levi swallowed hard and took her hand in his, his thumb gently tracing over her knuckles, his eyes locked on hers like he couldn't bear to look away.

He was here, and for the first time in days, she felt like she could finally breathe.

For the first time in days, she didn't *feel* alone.

Aurelia was discharged several hours later, after yet another round of exhausting interviews with the police about the attack.

Levi drove her home in silence. She didn't have the energy or the right mindset for conversation anyway. The pain medication they'd given her before she left the hospital left her groggy and emotionally exposed.

By the time they reached the house, the first light of dawn had begun to creep across the sky, as if the night itself were trying to erase all evidence of what had happened. Levi helped her inside with the gentlest of touches, settling her into their bed. She fell into a heavy, drug-induced sleep the moment her head hit the pillow.

When she awoke, it was late afternoon, and the house was quiet. After slowly meandering out of the bedroom, she was surprised to find Levi was still there, sleeping on the couch. At some point, he had changed into lounge clothes, though she had no idea where they'd come from, considering he had moved out as she requested.

He looked utterly spent, lips slightly parted as his chest rose and fell with deep, even breaths.

His thick lashes fanned across the dark circles under his eyes, telling her how little sleep he had gotten in the last few days. His usually neat hair was a mess, fanned across the pillow in waves, as if his hands had spent the night running through it in worry.

Aurelia let herself study him. The way his face looked peaceful in sleep, even as the weight of everything he carried etched lines across his features.

She was so lost in thought that she startled when a deep, gravelly voice cut through the quiet.

"Despite the overwhelming satisfaction of my wife ogling me in my sleep," Levi murmured, lips curving faintly into a smirk, "nature's calling. And I'd hate to ruin this moment by pissing my pants."

He hadn't opened his eyes, hadn't moved a muscle—except his delicious mouth.

Aurelia's face burned with embarrassment. She quickly schooled her expression before he could catch the flush rising in her cheeks. With forced indifference, she shot back, "I wouldn't call it ogling. More like...observing an unexpected house guest. There's a difference."

Levi's eyes snapped open, the teasing smirk fading as his gaze swept over her. Worry filled his expression, followed by something deeper, like raw sorrow and regret. Without a word, he stood and disappeared into the bathroom.

Aurelia exhaled, thankful for the brief reprieve to gather her thoughts. When he returned, she couldn't stop herself from looking at him. Her heart clenched painfully at the sight of him.

Yes, he was devastatingly handsome, but it was more than that. It was the way his grief and remorse showed plainly in his face; in the way his eyes couldn't seem to meet hers for long.

He sat back down on the sectional, this time close to her, elbows on his knees, hands clasped tight as if he were holding himself together by sheer will.

"I know that you wanted me out of your house," he began quietly. "After everything that happened...I obviously couldn't leave you alone. Not like this."

Aurelia frowned.

She opened her mouth to speak, but he held up a hand to stop her.

"Auri, please...let me finish," he said, his voice rough.

She nodded silently.

"I don't even know where to start," he admitted, nervously rubbing the back of his neck. "All I've done these past few days is think about this. About *us*."

He blew out a slow breath. "I put my house on the market. Been crashing at Isaac and Grace's."

That admission surprised her.

"After living here with you, I couldn't go back. That place...it was a prison before I met you. Now it's a tomb. Home is wherever you are."

Another crack splintered through the walls around her heart.

"This isn't an excuse—please don't think that. But I need to explain what went through my head when I saw you in that hotel room."

Aurelia steeled herself, the memory of that night flashing painfully behind her eyes. But this was what she had wanted, right? To understand him...to *hear* him?

Levi swallowed hard, his voice thick with emotion.

"I told you about my past relationships. How I've been used for my name, my money. How I've been cheated on over and over. I never told you the details...I thought if I didn't talk about it, it couldn't touch me anymore.

"But it did. It shaped me in ways I didn't even realize until I saw you standing there, in that hotel room."

His eyes went distant, trapped in the memory.

"I saw him first. Kyle. Lying there. Naked. Like he didn't have a care in the world. And then I saw you...wrapped in nothing but a sheet."

He choked on his next words.

"Suddenly, I wasn't in that hotel room anymore. I was fifteen again."

His voice dropped to a haunted whisper as he told her about the worst day of his life—coming home to find his mother storming upstairs, his father's car parked outside, and a stranger's car in the driveway.

"I followed her...right into their bedroom," he rasped. "My father...his mistress...both naked and asleep. My mother started yelling and woke them up, and the woman jumped out of bed naked, wrapping herself in my mother's bed sheet. Images from that scene have haunted me."

Aurelia gasped, a hand flying to her mouth.

"My mother threw the woman out, started screaming at him. My father was so angry that he had been caught, that he—he pushed her. She lost her balance and fell down the stairs. Hit her head on the edge of a step. Broke her neck...she was gone before even reaching the bottom."

He blinked rapidly, shoulders curled in.

"She wasn't perfect...but she didn't deserve that. And my father? He got away with it. Bought his way out of every repercussion and consequence. Told me I'd be next if I opened my mouth."

Aurelia's heart ached for the boy who'd lived through that nightmare.

"I never realized how much that moment shaped me. How every relationship after that felt like the same betrayal. I walked in on *every single one* of them cheating on me. And every time...it brought me right back to that day."

His eyes found hers again, full of anguish and regret.

"But none of that excuses how I treated you, Auri. You didn't deserve what happened to you—and you *definitely* didn't deserve what I said to you that night."

He dug his fingers into his scalp, gripping his hair like he needed the pain to keep talking, his whole body coiled with remorse he didn't know how to carry.

"I judged you through the lens of my trauma. I was a coward who ran away when you needed me the most. And I will regret that for the rest of my life."

He took a shaky breath.

"I'm not asking for forgiveness—I don't deserve it. I *am* asking for a chance to earn it...to show how much you mean to me. Because I'm done running. From myself. From this. From *us*."

Aurelia sat there, breathless. Charles's words again echoed through her mind.

Everyone comes with baggage, Aurelia. But sometimes...it's the way we carry it that makes all the difference. Don't let fear choose for you. And don't shut the door before he's even had the chance to fight for you.

Hadn't she done the same thing in the beginning? Physically ran away on their wedding day? Pushed Levi away when fear took hold?

She stilled, taking in every line of Levi's face, the raw sincerity in his eyes, and the fragile hope that she would let him fight for them.

Right then, Aurelia made the easiest choice of her life.

She would fight too. For herself and for the man who had become her home.

Levi

It was agony waiting for her to react.

Levi had opened up completely—his heart, his regrets, his broken past—and now all he could do was sit there and hope. Hope she wouldn't turn away. Hope he hadn't already lost her forever.

Then, at last, she moved.

Her uninjured hand gripped his hand, fingers curling tightly around his. The contact was so sudden, so sure, it stole the air from his lungs. He looked down at their joined hands in disbelief, not daring to hope too much, as his heart thudded painfully against his ribs.

She didn't say a word...but she didn't have to. That simple gesture told him everything. *It's a start.*

Slowly, cautiously, he lifted his gaze to her face, searching for any sign of hesitation.

He found none, and for the first time in what felt like forever...he let himself breathe.

Closing his eyes, he soaked in the moment. The feel of her hand in his. The faint, familiar, fragrant mix of florals and fruit enveloped him and calmed every frantic thought in his head.

When he opened his eyes again, she was still looking at him. Levi knew he had never seen anything more beautiful.

"I'm sorry," he whispered again, his voice raw.

Aurelia gave him a small, knowing smile.

"There's plenty of blame to go around," she whispered back. "Our relationship had cracks in its foundation from the beginning."

Then, with a soft sigh, she reached up and gently cupped his cheek. Her touch was warm, grounding him.

"I'm absolutely going to make you earn my forgiveness, though," she added, a wicked sparkle lighting her tired eyes.

Levi's heart gave a helpless, hopeless lurch.

He was definitely screwed.

Though this time, he welcomed it. He would fight like hell to prove he was worthy of her love—and of the honor of being her husband.

He knew it wasn't forgiveness. Not yet...but it was *hope*, and for now, that was enough.

There was so much work to do, so much to repair, if they were ever going to have the relationship they both deserved.

Looking back, it was painfully clear how quickly they'd rushed into this, especially the physical side of their relationship. He had fallen into old patterns again, letting work take over, staying late at the office instead of coming home to her, instead of prioritizing her and building something real between them.

The weight that lifted, however, was now replaced by a different one—the weight of the wedding rings still in his possession.

He hadn't given them back or dared bring them up, and she hadn't asked for them.

His ring remained on his finger, a constant reminder of the vow he refused to break, even when it felt like everything had fallen apart. But she deserved more. Their beginning deserved more.

A real wedding. Not the courthouse disaster Owen had thrown together. Not a day that existed only in the blurry snapshots of paparazzi gossip columns.

That memory didn't sit well with Levi, the residual anger from that day bubbling to the surface.

No...If they were going to rebuild, he wanted to do it right.

Which meant one thing: he needed to plan the perfect proposal.

To do that, he needed to solicit a little outside help from someone who could give him perspective.

His mind drifted to Estrella, remembering her earlier offer...

It was time to swallow his pride and schedule that appointment. No way was he leaving anything to chance, not if he was going to fight for her with everything he had.

CHAPTER 55

cAurelia

"I'd like to formally submit a request to the lady of the house to reconsider the terms of my atonement," Levi pleaded, panic lacing his voice as he stood behind the kitchen island like a man facing execution.

They'd slept in late after returning from the hospital, and though it was well past lunchtime, it was still too early for dinner.

Aurelia had agreed to let him start making amends. She had just told him what that entailed...and Levi was horrified.

"You're the one who begged for the chance to earn my forgiveness," Aurelia reminded him sweetly, barely holding back her laughter. "This happens to feel like a perfect first step. Request denied."

Levi looked absolutely betrayed.

"But...we *talked* about this..." he tried again, his eyes darting from her to the recipe lying on the counter like it was a death sentence.

"We did," Aurelia agreed, all innocent mischief as she tapped the recipe Levi now glared at like it had personally offended him. "And it would make me feel *so much better* if you made this for us to enjoy *together* tonight. I'll walk you through every detail—each ingredient, every step—so we can enjoy it *together*."

For one dramatic second, Levi gazed longingly at the trash can, clearly weighing his options.

Aurelia arched an eyebrow, her expression saying exactly what she didn't need to voice: *Are you serious right now? Stop being a baby.*

With a deep, soul-weary sigh, Levi dragged his eyes back to the recipe, shoulders slumping in defeat.

"I guess we're having *Braised Pea and Chouriço Soup* for dinner," he muttered under his breath, as if announcing the end of the world.

Aurelia burst out laughing.

For the next couple of hours, true to his word, but with the dramatic air of a man on death row, Levi prepared the soup as she read off the ingredients and instructions.

Aurelia sat propped up against the back of a nearby stool, her injured foot resting on the stool beside her, swaddled in blankets and surrounded by pillows like a queen overseeing her reluctant servant.

From the moment the ingredients hit the simmering pot, Levi eyed the concoction with blatant repulsion and suspicion, shooting it wary glances like it might leap out and attack him.

But the true betrayal came when Aurelia instructed him to add whole, cracked eggs into the broth.

His face went ashen.

In a cruel but completely fitting twist of fate, she had completely forgotten he also hated eggs.

Aurelia covered her mouth, trying not to laugh, as Levi stood there with the eggs in his hands like they were live grenades. She totally lost her composure when Levi gagged as he cracked the eggs into the pot.

In between his culinary suffering, their conversation became more serious. They talked more about everything that happened over the last several days.

"I've been thinking..." Levi began darkly, glaring at the package of chouriço as if it had personally wronged him. "If it's alright with you, I'd like to finish the second floor. There's more than enough space above the garage for three, maybe four small bedrooms and a full bath. Possibly use some of the space for that office you've been dreaming about...maybe even a drum set."

His mood visibly darkened as he tore into the chouriço with far more aggression than the task required.

"I've got a lot of time on my hands now," he muttered. "Might as well do something productive."

The mention of time—and what it had cost him—hit Aurelia like a punch to the chest, bringing back everything that had happened at Neuronix.

For days, everyone had been focused on her. On what had happened with Selene. On what she had survived. She hadn't even thought about what he and his friends had lost. Guilt twisted through her.

Quietly, carefully, she asked, "I saw what happened with Neuronix. How's everyone handling it? How...how are *you* handling it?"

Levi's mood darkened enough to cause the temperature in the room to drop. The knife in his hand turned into a weapon of vengeance as he hacked mercilessly through the sausage.

"I haven't had time to think about it," he said, his voice low. "Didn't have the chance before..." He hesitated. "Before you served me those papers."

Aurelia flushed with shame and winced, but Levi kept going, his tone distant, haunted.

"I sat on Isaac's couch for hours. Didn't move. Didn't see anyone."

His knuckles whitened as he gripped the knife.

"The only thing that snapped me out of it was hearing Isaac frantically looking for his car keys after Owen called. You know the rest."

He tossed the chouriço into the pot with a little more force than necessary, then leaned back against the counter, arms crossed tight over his chest.

His eyes, usually vibrant, were dull.

"The media made it out to be a grand scheme after the extra information I gave them," he smiled bitterly. "All of us—every founder—fired in one clean sweep. The one thing they didn't realize is that we planned for something like this years ago. The second we were fired, our shares were sold automatically. That's how we built it, as a safeguard. I never thought we would ever need it," he said angrily.

"The stock prices have tanked hard, but Tyler got exactly what he wanted. Now..." He gave a hollow laugh. "There's nothing we can do about it. The company's lost."

Aurelia stared at him, heart breaking all over again. The number of life-altering changes that happened over the last few days would make a regular person buckle under pressure.

"What's going through your head right now?" she asked softly.

Levi shrugged, but it was a miserable, defeated gesture.

"I let everyone down," he admitted in a broken whisper. "They trusted me to protect what we built, and I failed them. Failed you...failed everyone." The memories from the last few days settled over them both like a dense fog.

Aurelia felt like she couldn't breathe. One disaster after another. Her recent trauma was still a fresh, open wound. Their marriage teetered with fragility. His career and company were gone in a very public scandal.

The investigation at the Harvest Charity Ball was still open, and—then something clicked, like finding the missing piece of a complex puzzle.

Martin Strasburg works for Neuronix.

Her head snapped up, her mind racing back to that conversation at the event.

Martin had seen Levi there. Had congratulated her on their wedding. And mentioned so casually that he was a software engineer for Neuronix.

"He even let us keep partial rights to the technologies we helped create. That kind of leadership is rare. If Levi ever left Neuronix, I think half the company would walk out the door with him."

At the time, it hadn't registered as anything important other than a polite conversation with one of the featured charities. But now...now, it was everything.

Her heart thundered in her chest as she sifted through the recollections. There was something else—something she had seen in the paperwork from when they married. She couldn't quite place it, but it was there.

A wicked grin spread across her lips. Eyes flashing with purpose, she turned to Levi and said, her voice electric with excitement, "I think I know how you can take your company back."

Levi's head snapped up, his eyes locked on hers like she had dropped a live grenade between them.

Levi

A genius. His wife was an *evil, brilliant, drop-dead gorgeous* genius. Levi could only stare, absolutely awestruck by the brilliance of her idea.

With one simple question, she had flipped everything on its head. What had felt like an irreversible loss was suddenly a whole new ball game, and there was still plenty of time left on the clock for a comeback.

"Don't you, as an individual, still own partial rights and patents to your products?"

The answer hit him like a jolt of electricity.

He sure did...so did Owen and Isaac. Like him, they had never let go of their direct involvement in the development process, not even after the company went public. They hadn't wanted to become those executives who sat in corner offices and forgot how to code.

They had stayed in the trenches and kept creating and building. And because of that...they still owned the rights to the original code base. The foundation of *everything* Neuronix had become.

As Aurelia recounted her conversation with Martin Strasburg at the charity ball, her eyes practically glowing with excitement, the puzzle pieces snapped perfectly into place.

Martin had been there from the beginning. And if Martin was already talking about leaving Neuronix if Levi ever started something new...

Daring hope sparked to life in his chest.

"I can give you Martin's contact information if you'd like," she offered, her smile nothing short of luminous. Then she tilted her head, her expression turning sly. "Oh...and I might know someone willing to invest in a new venture," she added sweetly.

Levi barked out a disbelieving laugh and didn't waste a second. He rounded the island in two long strides and captured her mouth in a deep, soul-stealing kiss.

Because his wife didn't just save him—she had also handed his closest friends and most loyal employees back their future.

CHAPTER 56

Aurelia

Although Aurelia spent most of her time confined to the couch with her foot propped up, the days blurred together in a whirlwind of unexpected activity.

Somehow, the week had vanished right out from under her.

Now, the weekend had finally arrived, bringing with it the promise of laughter, teasing banter, and the much-needed comfort of the people she cared about most.

For the first time since everything fell apart, the entire gang was coming over for dinner.

The house was tranquil, offering a rare and fragile moment of peacefulness before the chaos descended.

Earlier, she had tried to help in the kitchen, but Levi had been an immovable wall of stubbornness, standing between her and anything remotely resembling productivity. His brows had drawn low with that perfect mix of concern and exasperation, his arms crossed as if daring her to try him.

The man took his role as Nurse Levi far too seriously. More than once this week, she had genuinely contemplated shoving him into the lagoon just to make a point. Though in the end, that fleeting frustration couldn't outweigh the quiet, aching gratitude she felt for his care.

Even if it did border on maddeningly overbearing.

For most of the morning, she savored the peace, the crackle of the fire Levi had lit for her a soothing backdrop to her wandering thoughts.

Autumn had settled over Joia City, the air outside crisp and tinged with the faintest promise of cooler nights ahead. Levi had left earlier for an appointment, undoubtedly connected to his mission to take back Neuronix.

To his credit, he had kept himself remarkably busy this week, pouring every ounce of restless energy into two things: his warpath to take Neuronix back, which Owen had dramatically and affectionately dubbed *The Reckoning*, and a second, equally unexpected project.

Owen had insisted the plan needed a name and had already decreed, *"Tyler will rue the day he took Neuronix from us! There will be a reckoning!"*

The name stuck, and so did the fire behind it. But when he wasn't plotting corporate revenge, Levi had thrown himself into a new distraction.

After barely surviving the dinner he had referred to as "Satan's Gruel"—and swearing never to cross Aurelia's culinary justice system again—he had come to her with an unexpected request: he wanted to finish the second-floor renovations.

She hadn't taken him seriously at first. But when he had mentioned she deserved a proper office, and that maybe they should think about those extra bedrooms...it hadn't taken long for her to say yes.

What she hadn't expected was the army of contractors who descended on the house the very next day. Sawdust still clung to the air, mingling with the smoke of the fire, while echoes of hammering and buzzing power tools seemed permanently etched into the walls.

And yet, true to form, Levi had kept it all running like a military operation. He stayed on top of the cleaning, ensuring the chaos never touched her little sanctuary downstairs.

Thanks to her injury and Levi's outright banishment from the second floor until it was finished, she hadn't seen any of it. For once, she hadn't fought him on it, deciding to let herself be genuinely surprised.

Remarkably, all that work had been finished in just over a week, and was completed only the day before. But what really caught her attention were the oddly shaped black cases carried upstairs yesterday. Levi didn't have to say a word; the steady rhythm echoing from above made it clear he had, in fact, set up his drum set.

Now, as she lounged in the warm glow of the fire, her thoughts inevitably drifted to everything that had led her to this fragile, quiet moment after a storm of violence and betrayal.

It had only been a week since her life had imploded.

Owen, working alongside Charles and the police, kept her informed as the investigation unfolded.

Selene's injuries—aside from various abrasions, a broken nose, bruises, and a concussion—would heal. But her arrest had been swift. She was being held without bail, facing an extensive list of charges that in Aurelia's eyes were still not enough.

Kyle had finally woken from his coma. The thought of him made her stomach churn with anger and disgust.

The silver lining was the moment he opened his eyes; he had folded like a deck chair in a hurricane, confessing everything and implicating Selene as the mastermind.

But that wasn't the worst of it. In his desperation for leniency, Kyle had thrown both Tyler Faulkner and Selene under the bus. He had admitted that Selene had given the compromising photos he had taken of Aurelia to Tyler—linking them both to her attack.

Aurelia's anger tangled into a bitter knot.

She didn't know who she hated more—Selene for orchestrating the whole plot and handing over the photos that almost destroyed her reputation, or Tyler for using them as a weapon against Levi and his—their friends. At that moment, Tyler was winning that race, having climbed to the top of her list with every deceitful thing he had done.

Yet...even through her justified anger, she mourned Selene's betrayal. How could she not?

She relived every memory, every moment of friendship, dissecting it under the harsh light of hindsight. Despite how much it hurt, she knew that wound would take far longer to heal than any of her physical injuries.

These thoughts continued to plague her until Charles had visited, carrying with him the crushing weight of Eleanor's legacy...which came in the form of an overwhelming stack of paperwork that would officially transfer her assets.

The scale of it all was staggering.

Much of it had already been liquidated. But Starhaven Manor...and several other properties...

The idea of living there was impossible.

It wasn't home.

But as she stared into the fire, a new vision took hold—one she hadn't dared think about since she first learned of the inheritance. How Starhaven could become something more.

A sanctuary. A place of *hope*.

A home for kids like her, aging out of foster care with nowhere to go.

The thought brought a soft, bittersweet smile to her lips. Her eyes fluttered shut as a desperate need for a nap overtook her, and for the first time in her life, she let herself dream.

Levi

That morning, Levi once again found himself seated across from Estrella in her comfortingly bright kitchen, where this journey had all begun.

The familiar aroma of brewing tea drifted through the air, but unlike that first meeting—when he had sat here composed and smug—today, he felt anything but put together.

His expression was tight, his posture tense, a hand unconsciously rubbing at the stiff muscles in his neck from yet another night spent on the couch.

So much had happened in the past few weeks, his thoughts were a tangle of regrets and what-ifs. Or maybe it wasn't confusion at all. Perhaps it was the unfamiliar discomfort of having to ask for help.

But Estrella, ever patient and ever knowing, simply sat across from him, those intense cerulean eyes watching, her hands calmly stirring a spoon through her tea.

"I must say," she began softly, her voice warm with maternal understanding, "I was both surprised and relieved to receive your call. Now...tell me, Levi. What's weighing on you?"

The gentle kindness in her voice cut straight through the storm in his head.

Levi exhaled slowly, his eyes dropping to the untouched mug of tea in front of him, as if the answers he so desperately needed might rise from its surface.

"I..." His voice cracked, forcing him to start again. "I screwed up. In the worst conceivable way."

He swallowed hard, the shame thick in his throat.

"I'm sure you saw the photos in the tabloids. The ones of Aurelia..." His jaw clenched.

Estrella's mouth pressed into a thin, disapproving line, but she said nothing. She didn't need to.

Levi dragged in a shaky breath and pressed forward.

"The way that night unfolded...when we found her..." His voice broke again. "I thought she had betrayed me. And I—god, I *reacted*. I was such an *ass*...I didn't even give her a chance to explain. I said things I can't take back. I didn't think. I didn't listen. I let every scar from my past dictate how I saw her at that moment. And now..." His eyes burned as he stared at the tea. "Now I don't know how to fix it."

Estrella's gaze softened, a knowing light flickering behind her eyes.

"Betrayal," she said gently, "even when it's only perceived, can rip open old wounds. But you've already taken the first step by acknowledging that mistake. Redemption doesn't start with grand gestures, Levi. It starts with accountability."

He gave a short, bitter laugh. "I've done that. And...mercifully, she's giving me another chance. But I don't know how to *deserve* it. I can admit now that we rushed into things—especially the physical side of our relationship. And I think...I think it made everything worse."

Levi swallowed hard. He couldn't remember the last time he had blushed over anything, but his cheeks burned now.

"She's become my greatest weakness," he admitted softly. "And that terrified me. It still does."

Estrella leaned forward, her gaze piercing straight through his defenses.

"Do you love her?"

The question slammed into his chest like a wrecking ball. He didn't hesitate.

"Yes," he whispered, voice ripe with vulnerability. "I love her more than I ever thought possible. But I'm not ready to tell her that. Not until I prove it. I want to ask her to marry me again...properly this time. Because she's the one I *choose*— not because of some contract, not because of obligation. Because she's it for me."

Estrella nodded, her expression softening into something almost proud.

"Then show her," she said simply. "With every action. Words are powerful, but trust is rebuilt through quiet consistency. Know her. Learn the things she loves, the things she fears. Listen more than you speak. And when the moment feels right—not because you're desperate or afraid—tell her. Tell her everything."

Levi swallowed the lump in his throat.

"I don't want to lose her," he rasped. "I've already lost so much. And without her...I'm nothing."

Estrella smiled, her voice low and sure.

"Then don't lose her," she said. "But remember, Levi—this isn't about *not* losing her. It's about becoming the man who deserves to *keep* her."

Levi left Estrella's home with his heart heavier but his path clearer.

No more empty promises. No grand declarations before he put in the work.

He would love her with his actions, not only his words. Actions that were quiet, steady, and unshakable.

And when the time was right, he would fight for the future they were always meant to have.

Together.

CHAPTER 57

Aurelia

Aurelia jolted awake at the sound of the front door bursting open, followed by the unmistakable thunder of Levi's footsteps charging through the house like an excited child on Christmas morning.

"It's time for the grand reveal, Auri!" he called, his voice booming with delight.

Blinking against the haze of sleep, she sat up straighter right before he appeared in the doorway, theatrically bowing at the waist and gesturing toward the stairs like some gallant knight.

She rolled her eyes, but the playful gesture couldn't hide the warmth spreading through her chest at the sight of him.

This was the Levi she had dreamed of.

Ever since their conversation that brought apologies and painful truths, he had been different. Whatever chains had bound him before had fallen away, leaving him lighter and happier.

This man—this smiling, vibrant, free man—was the husband she had fallen for.

A soft smile curved her lips as she lifted her arms toward him in silent request. Levi was at her side in an instant, his hands gentle and steady as he helped her rise and carefully guided her up the stairs.

And when they reached the top, her breath caught in her throat, and her eyes widened at the sight.

The space had been utterly transformed.

What was once a neglected attic was now a stunning, polished second story that felt like an extension of their hearts, not just their home.

Three modest-sized but beautifully finished bedrooms sat tucked beneath the charming, sloped ceilings, each thoughtfully furnished and designed, though one housed Levi's drum set. The new full bathroom mirrored their master bath below, but with the added indulgence of a separate soaking tub and double vanity—luxurious and perfectly suited for whatever future their home might hold.

But it was the final room that stole her breath.

The office. Or rather, *their* office.

She stepped through the doorway and felt the world stop.

It was simply perfect.

Positioned directly above their bedroom, the room opened onto a small private balcony overlooking the shimmering lagoon. Morning light would flood this space, and at night, the soft glimmer of water would cast rippling reflections across the walls.

Two long, dark wood desks sat opposite each other, flanked by built-in cabinetry and towering shelves that stretched toward the ceiling. Creamy upholstered chairs with soft turquoise accents waited at each desk, their placement so thoughtful she could practically see herself working there already.

The soft turquoise walls and natural wood floors flowed seamlessly with the rest of the house, and sheer ivory curtains framed the glass double doors that led to the balcony.

Every detail—down to the placement of electrical outlets and adjustable lighting—had been carefully considered.

She was overcome with emotion. Levi had done this for her...for them.

She turned, eyes ringed silver, and found him watching her with that open, vulnerable expression she had only recently begun to see and cherish.

Speechless, she crossed the room and threw her arms around his neck, ignoring the protest of her sore ribs and ankle as she pressed her face into the crook of his neck.

"Thank you," she whispered against his skin, her voice thick with emotion. "It's...It's flawless. More than I could have imagined. I...thank you."

Levi held her close, his arms strong but careful, his lips brushing against her temple.

"You're welcome," he murmured. His voice was rough, full of feelings too big to contain. "I meant it when I said I wanted to earn your forgiveness. This...this is the first step. The first of many."

He pulled back far enough to look into her eyes, his thumbs brushing her cheeks.

"You deserve the world, Aurelia," he whispered. "And this fool is going to spend every day proving that to you."

She smiled through the welling tears, her heart so full it ached.

Levi swallowed hard, his voice lighter now despite the intensity in his eyes. "I'm getting you a new laptop, too. Full setup. But for now..." His lips curved faintly. "I hope the lady of the house is pleased with her new workspace."

Aurelia looked up at him, her breath catching as the space between them shrank. His lips were so close she could feel his breath on hers, and in that moment—full of gratitude, love, and a thousand unsaid words—she gave in.

Closing the final sliver of distance between them, she kissed him, her lips saying everything she wasn't quite ready to say aloud.

Aurelia had never hosted more than one person in her home before, but any lingering nerves quickly vanished the moment their friends arrived.

The atmosphere was relaxed, with loungewear as the official dress code and no pretense of formality. In true Owen fashion, he declared that a potluck buffet of fast food was the only appropriate meal for the evening.

Now the kitchen island was a smorgasbord of pure, unapologetic chaos—fried chicken, tacos, burgers and fries, pizza, sandwiches, Chinese takeout, and even sushi, which had somehow sparked a passionate debate about whether it qualified as fast food.

Aurelia and Levi had at least attempted to contribute healthier options, represented by the tragically untouched fruit platter and a lonely house salad wilting in the corner.

"In no way is sushi fast food," Isaac declared, eyeing the suspicious rolls as he hovered over the pizza boxes.

Owen huffed, already halfway through a plate of fries. "Fast food means *food you can get fast*. I acquired sushi *fast*, which, by definition, makes it fast food. Took me less time than you did picking out your fancy pizzas."

Isaac shot him a flat look. "Fancy pizzas that you took two slices of and inhaled before anyone else could try them."

"I'm an equal opportunity food sampler," Owen retorted, pointing a fry at him like a weapon. "And don't you dare shame me! You're the one discriminating against sushi while happily hoarding spring rolls and lo mein."

"I'm too hungry to debate this nonsense," Isaac muttered, piling his plate high with his non-sushi selections.

"You're right," Owen agreed cheerfully through a mouthful of fries. "We need to fuel up first...so I'll have the energy to properly educate you on how wrong you are. *Again.*"

No one even bothered to sit at the dining table. Instead, they congregated in the living room, letting Aurelia keep her injured foot elevated in comfort. The fire crackled in the hearth, and—unsurprisingly—a POLmArK TV Romance was playing quietly in the background. Owen's doing, no doubt.

Aurelia had invited her new friend, Adelen, to join them, but work had tied her up. She promised to come next time.

Despite everything that happened, she was happy to have everyone gathered together like this. She waded through her thoughts until Grace's soft voice cut through them.

"Oh, honey...what's wrong?"

Heads turned toward her, concern instantly replacing the easy smiles. That was when Aurelia felt the wetness on her cheeks. Tears. Happy tears.

She laughed, wiping them away as she shook her head. "Sorry. I...I was thinking about how happy I am to know every one of you. How effortlessly you accepted me as one of you, and I guess that...snuck up on me. This whole 'not burying your emotions' thing is a wild ride."

Grace reached for her hand, her smile tender. "Time heals all wounds, my friend. But even when the pain fades, the scars stay. You're handling it beautifully."

Ivy smirked and raised her glass. "And if you don't heal like a delicate flower, you do it like a bad bitch. Either way, we've got your back."

"This," Owen declared dramatically, placing a hand over his heart, "this is what it means to have a squad. Just like in *Cheering for Love* when the cheer squad rallied around their coach after the kelp farmer she fell in love with broke her heart—"

Isaac threw his head back with a groan as Levi sighed heavily and muttered, "Here we go..."

Isaac's expression twisted in disbelief. "There's no way these are real movies. You can't possibly remember all this unless you're making them up."

Owen gasped like he had been personally attacked. "My brain holds multitudes, you peasant. Don't insult the sanctity of my knowledge!"

Isaac pulled out his phone. "Fine. I'm looking it up."

Owen crossed his arms and settled back, smug. Grace tried to hide her laughter by turning away, sipping her wine. Ivy made no such effort, openly laughing behind her hand. Levi shook his head and looked to the ceiling like a man praying for deliverance. Aurelia, for her part, was captivated.

She couldn't help herself. "You two really *do* argue about this all the time," she teased. "It's like...weird foreplay. Owen drops a POLmArK reference to get your attention. Isaac gets all scandalized and demands proof. Then Owen puffs up his chest and struts around with his endless movie knowledge. It's a full-on ritual. I've seen it in nature documentaries—it's a textbook mating dance."

Ivy choked on her fried chicken. Grace nearly spit out her wine. Levi's laughter rumbled through the couch where he sat pressed against Aurelia.

Owen and Isaac both gaped at her, stunned into momentary silence.

Right when worry began to creep back in that maybe she had taken it too far, Owen whispered in awe, "I've never felt so *seen*."

He sat up straight, eyes shining with excitement. "This is basically the plot of *Prickly Love*! How did I not make this connection before? It's exactly like when the nuclear chemist falls for the cactus costumer in the desert—"

"No. Absolutely not. *Do not finish that sentence!*" Isaac barked, but Owen was already on a roll.

"She's out there analyzing fallout, and she tells him not to mess with the cacti without protective gear. But *he's* building a portfolio of naturally bioluminescent cacti—but really, they're radioactive! And she rants about it, and he just...*swoons*. Like I do every time you argue with me, Isaac!"

With a gleam in his eye, Owen lunged toward him. Isaac dodged expertly, and Owen landed in a graceless heap on the floor.

Everyone lost it.

The living room filled with howls of laughter as Owen dramatically sprawled across the rug, one fist raised toward the ceiling.

"Mark my words, Isaac!" Owen shouted through the chaos. "Someday, I *will* star in a POLmArK Romance! And I will tell the epic story of our bromance for the *world* to see!"

Levi pulled Aurelia closer, his breath warm against her ear as he whispered, "You fit in perfectly, you know. The missing piece we didn't even know we were missing."

It made Aurelia feel...whole.

CHAPTER 58

Levi

Once everyone had calmed down and thoroughly gorged on the mountain of fast food, Levi stood near the fireplace, his expression serious.

"I have some important news to share," he announced.

All eyes quickly snapped to Aurelia, their gazes flicking from her face to her stomach and back again.

It took a beat for Aurelia to register what was happening. Then her mouth fell open in horror. She shot a sharp look at Levi and shook her head frantically.

He caught on a second later, his own eyes going wide. "Whoa—no! That's not— *that's not even remotely close to the news I'm sharing!*" He ran a hand through his hair, obviously rattled.

Aurelia crossed her arms, a knowing grin playing on her lips. Not that Levi would have been upset by such an announcement.

Clearing his throat, Levi tried again. "What I *meant* to say is that I have important news about Neuronix."

A collective "ohhh" rolled through the room.

"My insanely brilliant wife made a passing comment earlier this week," he started, his tone dramatic as he paced in front of the fire, clearly enjoying the building suspense. "And that comment has led to something...game-changing."

He paused long enough for everyone to get visibly twitchy with anticipation.

"Who wants to join me in buying Neuronix back and taking it private again?"

Silence.

Such complete silence that the crackle of the fire was the only sound in the room.

Levi shifted awkwardly. *Not exactly the reaction I was hoping for.*

Aurelia, always one step ahead, offered innocently, "Maybe you should explain *how* that's possible before the shock wears off?"

Ivy blinked. "Yeah. I'm going to need a little more than 'Hey, let's casually buy back a multibillion-dollar company.'"

Levi chuckled and nodded, grateful for the assist. "Okay, starting from the top. Remember those 10b5-1 trading plans we set up years ago? Every time we renewed them during our annual benefits enrollment, it automatically sold our stock at peak prices if we ever left the company involuntarily."

Isaac gave a low whistle. "Yeah, and have you seen the share price since? Between the data breach, our firing, and the utter chaos in leadership, it's tanked. A fraction of what it was."

"Exactly." Levi's grin turned sharp. "And guess who's been buying up those discounted shares?"

Grace's eyes narrowed. "Tyler Faulkner."

"Ding ding ding. The snake's now the majority shareholder."

Aurelia interjected smoothly. "But my exceptionally bright husband forgot something very important. Neuronix doesn't own the full rights to the intellectual property it's built on."

They both waited patiently as the realization settled over their friends like a slow-moving train.

Owen's eyes lit up first. "Oh my *god*. We still own the software rights."

Isaac leaned forward, grinning. "And if we refuse to license it—"

"—The company can't sell any products," Owen finished with glee.

"A *terrible* shame," Aurelia said, her voice dripping with mock sorrow, "if the entire software engineering team just happened to walk out and refused to transfer the IP rights."

Levi watched, satisfied, as their expressions shifted from shock to triumphant anticipation. *This* was the reaction he had been waiting for.

Grace clapped her hands together. "That would *devastate* the stock price. No team. No product. The company would collapse!"

"And we swoop in and buy the company back for pennies on the dollar," Ivy said with a wicked grin. "I'm all in."

Owen dropped the last fry into his mouth and wiped his hands with theatrical finality. "I'm only here for the chaos. But also—yes."

Levi snickered but raised a hand to calm them. "We need to think strategically. We'll need to guarantee that those engineers who walk out have financial security. If we can promise them job offers and bridge the gap in their salaries, they'll jump ship. I've already spoken to Martin Strasburg and he's ready...and so are a sizable number of the senior developers."

Aurelia's voice softened. "It's what Eleanor did. She guaranteed security for her staff to ensure their loyalty before she passed."

The room grew quiet at the impact of her words.

"This only works if we can financially sustain the fallout and secure what's left of Neuronix," Levi said quietly. "It's a risk. But it's a chance to rebuild it on our terms and better than before."

He looked at every one of them, his friends who had built this company by his side. Friends who stood by him through everything.

"So," he said, his voice low and even, "who's willing to take one last gamble on Neuronix?"

No one spoke. They didn't have to. Each one of them nodded, their grins slowly spreading like wildfire.

The Reckoning had begun.

CHAPTER 59

Harris

Harris Wilkerson lounged in his chair, a self-satisfied smile curving his lips as he surveyed his new office. *His* office. The corner office of the Chief Technology Officer of Neuronix. Finally, the position he deserved, where he would leave his mark on the world.

For a while, he had worried Tyler might not follow through on their deal. Especially after that humiliating day when someone uncovered the backdoor he had slipped into the Project DL code and ratted him out. Being fired and escorted out like some low-level nobody had been nothing short of a disgrace.

His smile faltered as the memory surfaced. That day in the HR conference room, his predecessor was already there, waiting with a glare full of contempt. Harris had seen that look from him too many times.

Tyler approached him soon after. Tyler cornered him in the elevator, bought him a drink, and offered him a deal he couldn't refuse. Sabotage the code, tank the project, and when the dust settled, there would be a nice little reward.

And here he was. Rewarded. Seated exactly where he belonged.

He had already begun tearing down the old systems, dismantling the pair programming structure first. Collaboration was for weaklings. Every man for himself; that's how real power worked.

Ping.

Harris glanced at his monitor as an email popped into his inbox.

Ping. Ping. Ping. Ping. Ping. Ping—

One after another, dozens of new emails flooded in.

Each one carried the exact same subject line:

MY LETTER OF RESIGNATION.

The smugness bled from his face.

Opening one email at random, his heart sank. Then another. And another. Each resignation was real—and every sender was a member of the IT or software engineering teams.

Panic and fear blazed through him.

The faint sound of footsteps sounded outside this office.

He sprang from his chair and yanked open his office door in time to see the wave of people moving toward him down the hallway.

One by one, they stormed into his office, each holding a single sheet of paper. Without a word, they set their resignation letters on the small conference table and walked out.

But it wasn't the resignations that stripped him—it was the looks. Some met his eyes with disgust. Others with cold disapproval. A few even laughed openly in his face.

And Harris...could do absolutely nothing about it. Frozen in that moment, he realized how powerless he truly was. A trickle of cold sweat started to slide down his spine.

Ping. Ping. Ping. Ping.

The emails kept coming.

Despite ascending to his precious throne, Harris Wilkerson witnessed what a real-life revolution entailed...and it was directed at him.

That was when he realized just how completely, utterly alone he was.

No one would be helping him out of the grave he had dug for himself.

CHAPTER 60

Tyler

Tyler Faulkner leaned back in his chair, inhaling the steam from his freshly brewed coffee, boots propped arrogantly on the hunter green executive desk in the CEO's suite. Exactly where he belonged.

It had all gone according to plan.

Lockwood had been a minor nuisance in the beginning...until that conveniently timed marriage to his fake fiancée. A distraction Tyler couldn't have orchestrated better himself. When those explicit photos landed in his inbox? That had been the real gift, delivered straight from the heavens. A few quick clicks and his media contacts took care of the rest.

Now, he had full control of Neuronix and its product roadmap. Government contractors were practically drooling over the technology, especially Project DL. If he played his cards right, he would make a fortune selling the technology to the military.

The smile on his face widened as he took another leisurely sip, savoring the rich flavor of the imported brew.

An unexpected knock sounded at the door to the office. His brows pulled together in confusion.

"Come in," he called, quickly planting his feet on the ground and straightening himself. He didn't bother to disguise his irritation over the interruption, however.

The door opened, and Harrington Perkins, Chief General Counsel, stepped in—grim-faced, a thick manila envelope in one hand and a neat stack of papers in the other.

"Well?" Tyler snapped, motioning impatiently. "What is this? Why are you barging into my office without an appointment?"

Without a word, Harrington dropped the envelope onto the desk with a heavy thud. The scratch of it sliding across the desk grated on Tyler's nerves.

"Neuronix has been served a cease-and-desist order. That's your copy," Harrington said coolly.

Tyler stared at the thick envelope, confusion clouding his features.

"What the hell do you mean by 'cease-and-desist'? On what grounds?"

Harrington allowed a slow, almost satisfied smirk to cross his face. "Turns out, Neuronix doesn't fully own the IP for its flagship products. The rights belong to the creators and developers." He let the unspoken implications of that hang in the air. "You're to halt all sales and use of those products immediately or face legal action. Effective immediately, Tyler."

Tyler gaped at him, refusing to believe what he just heard. "You've got to be kidding me. Fight it! That's *your* job!"

Harrington chuckled, the sound dark and humorless. "Correction. That *was* my job." He slammed another stack of papers down next to the envelope. "That's my formal resignation. Along with every single member of the legal department."

Tyler surged to his feet, his face a shade of red rarely seen in nature. "You—you can't just leave!"

"My loyalty was to actual leaders, Tyler. You? You're nothing but a pompous fraud who thought he could buy loyalty and respect." Harrington's eyes were cold and held no remorse. "This mess? It's yours now. Enjoy it."

Before Tyler could muster a response, Harris Wilkerson burst through the door, panting, eyes wide with panic.

"They resigned!" he gasped, nearly collapsing against the doorframe. "The entire IT department—every last one of them—resigned all at once!" His words tumbled out in a frantic stream. "They shut down the login portals, locked out customer sites—*everything*. There's no one to answer support calls. Customers are flooding us, and I don't have anyone left to—"

Tyler could only gape. His mouth opened, but no sound came out. He didn't know what to make of it.

Harrington snorted and clapped Harris on the shoulder with mock sympathy. "Oh, I wouldn't say that. You're still here."

Harris stared at him, horrified.

"You might want to head down and start answering the phones," Harrington called over his shoulder as he left. "That's what a real CTO would have done."

Harris turned back to Tyler, completely unravelling. "This isn't what I agreed to," he rasped. "This is a dumpster fire I *can't* put out. I quit. I—I'm done. I only wanted to be seen for my skills and the value I bring to the table at this company, not...*this*."

Tyler's eyes finally focused, as if seeing Harris for the first time.

"You're on your own, buddy," Harris said, already slowly backing out of the office. "I'm out."

And then Tyler was alone.

Alone in the office he had schemed and lied about to obtain, the silence inescapable.

Immobile and helpless as he watched everything he had spent months building collapse in a heaping pile of shit...and realizing there wasn't a damn thing he could do to stop it.

CHAPTER 61

Levi

Three weeks of relentless planning and sleepless nights were finally about to pay off. Levi couldn't stop smiling at his reflection as he ran a hand through his hair, making the final adjustments.

The past few weeks replayed like his favorite victory montage, each memory sweeter than the last.

The employee walkout was staged by Martin Strasburg and had been far bigger than anyone anticipated. What started as a symbolic protest turned into a full-scale exodus. Entire departments followed suit, crippling Neuronix from the inside out. But it was the IT department's grand finale that stole the show. Martin's call two weeks ago had been the highlight of Levi's year.

"No one should ever experience this level of workplace chaos," Martin had laughed, "but damn, was it satisfying. You should have seen Wilkerson's face when we all quit at the same time. He looked ready to wet himself. My only regret is not sticking around long enough to watch him realize we'd disabled everything—internally and for every customer too."

Levi couldn't stop laughing when he told the story to his friends. When the news broke later that evening, they'd all gathered at Aurelia's house for an impromptu watch party, celebrating with a mix of champagne and pure, unfiltered satisfaction.

The media called it "*the most epic mass resignation in corporate history.*"

And every time Levi thought about it, he smiled even wider.

After one last glance in the mirror, he left the bathroom, smoothing his sage green sweater over his dark jeans. Today was a big day, but he and Aurelia had agreed there was no need for suits or pretense. This wasn't about impressing anyone. This was about reclaiming what was his.

She was already in the kitchen waiting for him.

A vision in a soft violet sweater dress and brown leggings, her freshly colored signature rainbow highlights catching the light like streaks of spun glass. Even with that walking boot on her injured foot, she was the most beautiful thing he had ever laid eyes on.

She didn't need to dress up to take his breath away. She was his breath, the very air he needed to survive.

Levi crossed the room in three long strides, pulling her gently into his arms. He savored the warmth of her against him, the soft press of her body fitting perfectly into his own.

They had a meeting to attend—a showdown with Neuronix's desperate Board. Charles had already gone ahead, posing as the lead representative for the mysterious "buyers" circling the company's remains like vultures.

And what delicious remains they were.

Neuronix stock had fallen to a single digit, and the Board was scrambling, desperate to offload what was left before the entire ship sank. Tyler Faulkner, that arrogant bastard, had lost millions trying to secure control, only to watch it all burn to ash in his hands.

Greed. That's what took the Board of Directors down in the end. Their own unchecked greed.

Aurelia gave him a soft, lingering kiss before stepping out of his embrace. Slinging her purse over her shoulder and slipping on her sunglasses, she turned to him with a brilliant smile.

"Are you ready, my fearless leader?" she teased.

Levi smirked, savoring the spark in her eyes. "With that sass, you're going to steal the entire show today."

She turned toward the door, glancing back with a mischievous grin. "Well then...what are we waiting for?"

Levi stood straighter, his chest tight with purpose.

"Let's go get my company back."

Aurelia

The towering skyscraper loomed before them, an endless expanse of glass and steel that seemed to scrape the clouds.

Aurelia had only been here once before, for a lunch she would never forget. She pressed her thighs together at the memory that surged unbidden through her mind.

Levi must have been reliving it, too. His sidelong glance, eyes dark and glazed with the same hunger she felt, confirmed it.

That day...seeing him in his element, commanding from behind his massive desk...

She hadn't just surprised him with his favorite takeout. Behind that desk, she had dropped to her knees before him, her brand of dessert taking priority over the meal she brought. The way his head fell back, fists tangled in her hair, his barely restrained groans as she tasted him—

"You need to stop looking at me like that before we go in there," Levi rasped, his voice thick with longing. "If this goes the way we hope, you'll be able to show up for *lunch* whenever you want."

Heat crawled up her neck as she turned away, caught red-handed by his smoldering gaze.

"Don't get ahead of yourself, husband. You're still very much on probation," she teased, her voice light but her pulse pounding.

Levi sobered instantly. He held out his hand, palm open, his eyes searching hers with a quiet intensity that made her heart clench.

Sliding her hand into his, she gave him a small, confident smile.

"Let *The Reckoning* commence."

"Such a unique perspective, sitting on this end of the table. I have to admit, I understand the allure now," Levi mused, settling comfortably into his seat.

Across from him, Tyler Faulkner sat in the chair Levi once occupied as CEO, scowling like a petulant child. The rest of the Board wore equally sour expressions. Meanwhile, their side of the table—Aurelia, Charles, Owen, Ivy, Grace, and Isaac—stood united, a wall of calm defiance.

"But let's skip the pleasantries," Levi continued smoothly. "We've all been enjoying our newfound free time, only to be disturbed by news of how effectively you've run this company into the ground in record time."

Before Tyler could react, Aurelia began clapping...slow, deliberate, and mocking. Owen and Ivy immediately joined in, adding dramatic flair. Levi bit back a grin.

So much sass indeed.

"Imagine my surprise," Levi drawled, "when I learned Neuronix's stock price had plummeted from a steady $154 a share to—what was it yesterday? Right under $2?"

Aurelia leaned in, her hand slipping into Levi's as she spoke, voice honey-sweet and razor-sharp. "My dear husband, don't be so hard on him." Levi shot her a questioning glance, not expecting her to join in, but she continued, her sarcasm on full display.

"It's not every day someone orchestrates a hostile takeover only to spectacularly crash and burn as a leader."

Tyler's face turned an alarming shade of red, the veins in his neck pulsing.

"I can't imagine what you're going through right now," Aurelia went on, her eyes cold despite the faux sympathy in her voice. "Ousting the people who own the rights to the products you can't legally sell. Watching your employees stage a very public walkout because no one wants to work for a selfish tyrant. Not a single paying customer left happy. And now..." She slowly scanned the length of the table, meeting the eyes of each Board member before returning her gaze to Tyler.

"...you've all lost millions on the stock collapse. Such a difficult season for you all."

She smiled sweetly, while Ivy dabbed her eyes with a handkerchief—*where had she even gotten that?*—and Owen made loud, tragic *tsk tsk* sounds.

Tyler was visibly shaking, but Levi let them have their fun. After all, weeks ago, Tyler had planned for their public humiliation. It was only fitting they returned the favor.

"Well, in his defense," Isaac added with mock pity, "it's hard to run a tech company when you have zero experience or credentials. I always thought being CTO was easy *since I actually knew how to code*. But hey...guess that's just me."

"A PR nightmare!" Grace gasped dramatically. "Is it true even the marketing team walked out?"

Owen nodded somberly. "And the security team. And sales. And legal. Finance. Operations. Honestly, I'm surprised there's anyone left to turn the lights on in this drafty building."

Ivy let out a fake shiver. "Drafty *and* depressing," she sniffed into her handkerchief.

Levi almost laughed aloud, but now it was time for the grand finale.

"Luckily for all of you," he said, voice turning steel-cold, "we're a forgiving and benevolent group. We've come today with a proposal—a generous offer to buy whatever's left of this crumbling empire. As is. Assets and all. In cash."

That certainly got their attention.

Charles stepped in to lay out the details, but when a Board member blustered, "We'll lose complete ownership!" Aurelia's voice cut through the room.

"That's generally how buying you out works," she snapped. "Why would we *want* you involved after you ran this company straight into the ground? If you want to walk away with *anything* left in your pockets, you'll take the deal."

She gave Levi's hand a quiet squeeze. He had never seen this side of her before and fell in love even more.

Tyler slammed his fists on the table. "You think I'm too stupid to realize this was all orchestrated? The walkouts, the resignations—you *ruined* me! I should report you to the SEA!"

"Oh, I'm so glad you brought that up," Levi said smoothly. He glanced at Owen, who practically vibrated with excitement.

"We already filed a complaint with the SEA," Levi continued. "After Harris Wilkerson...shared some fascinating details with us."

Tyler visibly paled.

Owen stood, already uncapping a marker as he marched to the whiteboard. "Time for a story!"

"Wait! I can explain—" Tyler began, but Owen held up a hand.

"Nope. You're going to listen for once."

With dramatic flair, Owen began diagramming the entire scheme...from Tyler's stock grabs to his bribes, the planted backdoor in the software, and the final attempted data breach.

"And that brings us back to the start," Owen said with a satisfied grin, circling the final item on the list. "You were working with a foreign military group, planning to use our technology as a Trojan horse for a cyber attack."

Tyler erupted, shouting denials as chaos broke out—when the doors burst open. A swarm of National Bureau of Investigation agents flooded the room.

"Perfect timing, gentlemen," Owen called cheerfully, snapping photos of Tyler's arrest as he was shoved face-first onto the conference table and cuffed.

Levi and Owen looked at their friends, all wearing matching expressions of shock and disbelief, as the agents arrested Tyler. To his friends, Owen casually shrugged. "Turns out that the NBI has been watching him for a while now. Harris's betrayal simply helped speed up the process."

Through the pandemonium, Levi turned calmly back to the remaining Board members, casually pushing the paperwork Charles initially presented towards them.

"The SEA is about to launch its own investigation into securities fraud," he informed them coolly. "This deal is the only chance you have left to walk away from this mess with anything resembling dignity...and I want your greedy asses as far away from this company before I close every security gap you've helped expose."

They voted to sell what was left of the company and immediately signed the paperwork without hesitation.

As the group left the building, Aurelia leaned in close to Levi and whispered with a smirk, "That was quite a reckoning. At least life with you will never be boring."

Levi wrapped an arm around her waist, a rare, genuine smile lighting his face. "Never again."

CHAPTER 62

Aurelia

"Looks like you've healed beautifully," the doctor said, snapping Aurelia back to attention.

He was a short, slight man with tan skin and alert hazel eyes. His wide face was softened by a round chin and large ears, topped with tightly curled dark brown hair. She squinted at his name tag, already forgetting his name.

Dr. Pacheco. It rang a familiar bell now.

She sat on the crinkling exam table paper, her ankle propped up, having driven herself to this final appointment. Levi had been hesitant to let her go alone, but she assured him, multiple times, that she was fine.

Honestly, it was better this way.

In the blink of an eye, a month had passed since the Neuronix showdown, and Levi had thrown himself headfirst into the company's resurrection. The employees returned quietly, operations fell back into rhythm...except customer support.

Once the media exploded with news of Tyler's plot and his plans to weaponize their products, public trust crumbled. Grace had been working nonstop to manage the fallout—crafting careful messaging, overseeing public relations, trying to hold the bleeding line together.

Project DL was dead. Safer to erase it completely than try to untangle whatever malicious code Harris had buried in its depths.

"Aurelia?"

Dr. Pacheco's voice cut into her thoughts again. She blinked, realizing she had completely zoned out.

"S-sorry," she stammered. "Could you repeat that?"

He smiled gently, a look of knowing compassion in his eyes. "I said you're all cleared unless you have any questions?"

She shook her head and returned his smile. "No questions. Thank you."

He lingered for a moment, then tapped a finger against his temple and heart. "Remember...sometimes it's the wounds you *can't* see that take the longest to heal."

Aurelia swallowed hard. *Isn't that the truth?*

She hadn't told anyone about the new nightmares. Their intensity was far worse than the ones she had before the attack. They were near-nightly episodes that woke her screaming, soaked in sweat, Levi bursting through the door to comfort her with his warm hands and soothing voice.

She also hadn't told anyone that they continued to sleep separately.

"I'll include a therapist referral in your paperwork," Dr. Pacheco added quietly. "They specialize in trauma like this...just in case."

Her throat tightened. "I...thank you. I appreciate it."

He gave her a small, knowing nod and stepped out of the room, leaving her alone with the quiet hum of the fluorescent lights.

By the time she gathered her things and made it to the parking lot, the ache in her chest had only grown heavier. On the drive home, she let her thoughts wander.

It should have felt like a victory ditching the boot and air cast at last. But instead, frustration gnawed at her. Her thumb instinctively brushed against her left ring finger, expecting to feel the smooth band of her wedding rings.

There was nothing.

Her stomach clenched. She had done this exact same thing countless times in the last two months, and every time, it still surprised her to feel nothing there.

She never told Levi how much those rings had meant to her. That he had designed them for her, chosen a style that was everything she could have wanted without even asking. Simple, meaningful. Perfect.

She had always thought lavish jewelry was wasteful, preferring a handful of cherished pieces instead. And somehow, Levi understood that before she ever said a word.

The rings weren't the only thing missing.

There was still the matter of their sleeping arrangements.

They hadn't spoken about it, but Levi hadn't once shared her bed since moving back in. Night after night, he stayed upstairs in the spare bedroom, quietly keeping his distance.

He said he wanted to earn her forgiveness, and while she had agreed, she hadn't expected this.

She hadn't expected the separation between them to ache more than her physical wounds.

What is wrong with me?

The frustration boiled over. With a low, growling curse under her breath, she yanked the car over to the side of the road. She wasn't going home yet.

This...this needed to be resolved. Now.

With a fresh cup of tea in front of her, Aurelia let her eyes wander over the familiar kitchen, the soft warmth of the space seeping into her bones. She had almost forgotten how soothing this place was. How Estrella's presence could quiet even the loudest storm in her mind.

But not today. Today, the storm raged on.

"I must admit," Estrella began, settling gracefully across from her, "I was a little surprised to receive your call. But I'm happy you're here and looking well." Her sharp, knowing eyes swept over Aurelia with a look that saw far more than the surface. "Although you *appear* physically healed, I suspect there are wounds here—" she tapped her temple, "and here—" her fingers pressed lightly over her heart, "—that still need tending."

Aurelia swallowed hard. That wasn't an accusation. It was the truth.

She hated how hard it was to ask for help, how foreign it felt to even sit here and try to talk about this. But after driving aimlessly for nearly an hour, her hands seemed to steer the car here all on their own.

"I guess..." she began, fingers tracing the rim of her teacup, "I need help sorting through some things with Levi. But the truth is...I'm having a tough time figuring out what *I* want."

Estrella simply sat in patient silence, her eyes kind and unflinching.

Aurelia huffed out a breath. "I'm sure you remember how fabulously that wedding went," she deadpanned, earning the barest twitch of a smile from Estrella. "And everything that's happened since..." Her voice faltered, Estrella's expression darkening with a flicker of protective fury.

"When he moved into my house, it was...surprisingly easy. Weird, at first, but he made it easy. Even sharing a bed wasn't hard." Her cheeks flushed as she admitted, "We were intimate right away. I initiated it—on our wedding night. And it was..." She exhaled, her voice lowering. "It was like fireworks. Every. Time. And despite that, he never pushed for more than I could give. But after the hotel...after the kidnapping...we both made mistakes. And ever since, he's been different."

Lord, this is hard. Aurelia fidgeted uncomfortably in her seat.

"He's sleeping in the guest room. He hasn't touched me, hasn't even *looked* at me like he used to. He hugs me, he kisses me...but that's it." Her throat tightened. "And I hate how much it bothers me."

There. She had said it. *Finally.*

"I don't know what to do," she whispered. "I get it—I was hurt. He's giving me space. But it's like there's this wall between us now that I forced to be built, and I don't know how to break it down. And I hate that I sound so—so *needy* right now." She bit her lip hard, fighting the sting of tears.

Estrella was quiet for a long moment, then asked gently, "Have you told him any of this?"

Aurelia shook her head. "No. I don't know how to bring it up. I don't want him to think I'm accusing him of not trying hard enough...or worse, that I'm angry with him for respecting my space."

Estrella's lips curved, a sad kind of understanding settling over her face. "My dear, there is no perfect script for conversations like this. They're uncomfortable by nature. But the longer you avoid it, the more it festers. That's why you're here, telling me when you should be saying these words to *him.*"

The truth of that hit hard.

Estrella leaned forward, eyes unwavering. "Tell me, what have *you* done to fix things with Levi?"

The question hit like a slap.

Nothing, that cruel, honest little voice whispered inside. *You've done nothing.*

Aurelia's stomach turned as the truth washed over her. "I...I haven't done anything," she admitted, her voice cracking. "I've been so focused on how *I* felt, I didn't stop to think about how he must feel. I...I'm doing it again, aren't I?"

Estrella's expression softened, but her words didn't let her off the hook. "Put yourself in his shoes. You demanded a divorce without discussion. You gave back your rings. If the roles were reversed...would you feel safe to just pick up where things left off?"

Aurelia dropped her gaze, cheeks burning with shame.

"And ask yourself," Estrella said quietly, "why does the lack of intimacy matter more to you right now than rebuilding the foundation of your marriage?"

The air left Aurelia's lungs. That was it—that was the question she had been running from.

You know why that inner voice whispered again.

Estrella reached over and took her hand, squeezing it gently. "Find the answer to that, and you'll know what to do next. Until then...stop punishing yourself. And stop punishing him by keeping this all bottled up."

She gave her hand one last pat and rose to her feet. "Now...let's eat. You'll need your strength."

After lunch with Estrella, Aurelia couldn't bring herself to go straight home. Her heart felt too full, her thoughts too heavy to be confined within four familiar walls.

Instead, she found herself wandering downtown Joia City, a vibrant and lively stretch teeming with small artisan shops, eclectic cafés, and bustling sidewalks. It was the perfect place to get lost for a while, to breathe in the scent of roasted coffee and freshly baked bread, to let the cheerful hum of strangers become the backdrop to her spiraling thoughts.

She stopped in front of a quaint boutique, her reflection staring back at her through the glass. She didn't see the woman in the window. Not really.

She saw Levi.

Levi, who had waited on her hand and foot after everything. Who learned how to care for her without being asked and without complaint.

He had cooked for her. Cleaned the house. Done the laundry, despite his clear inexperience. He had even handled the groceries without the luxury of the apps he normally relied on, all while Neuronix was in shambles.

He had made sure their friends came over, filling the house with laughter and easy conversation because he knew she needed it—knew she couldn't ask for it herself.

He found ways to plan gentle, low-impact date nights where they simply talked. No pressure. No expectations other than being together.

He never once crossed a line she wasn't ready for.

The affection she alleged was missing...had never been missing at all. It just hadn't looked like the dramatic, sweeping romance she had convinced herself she wanted.

It looked like holding her hand for no reason at all. Like scooping her into his arms after a nightmare and rocking her back to sleep. Like the quiet, stolen kisses—on her temple, her cheek, her lips—when he thought she wasn't paying attention.

And what had she given him in return?

Her lips parted on a shaky breath. She had reminded him constantly that he was on *probation*. That he had to *earn* her forgiveness. She wielded that hurt like a weapon, as if punishing him could somehow undo the pain he had caused her.

She was punishing both of them.

It had to stop.

They'd rushed into physical intimacy before their emotional foundation had a chance to form. That was *her* mistake. And it was one she needed to own—tonight.

With renewed purpose, she pushed away from the boutique window and set off down the street, her mind clear for the first time in weeks.

She would fix this. Not with a grand gesture...but with honesty, vulnerability, and the truth.

Because if there was one thing she was certain of now...Levi was worth it.

CHAPTER 63

Aurelia

Aurelia sped through the streets of Joia City, mentally rehearsing what she would say to Levi the moment she walked through the door. She was done worrying, done waiting, and done with the distance Levi insisted on keeping between them.

She had never been shy about initiating physical contact before, mistaking it for genuine affection, so why should she hesitate now to initiate a conversation about what she wanted? About what she needed? About how much it hurt that he hadn't even asked if she wanted her wedding ring back.

It was a regular conversation. How hard could it be?

She had rushed into asking for a divorce out of fear and self-preservation, regretting it ever since. But stubborn, aggravating Levi still slept upstairs like they were polite strangers instead of two people bound by marriage. A marriage neither of them had wanted to end...unless she had read him completely wrong.

No. She wasn't going to overthink this. She wasn't going to fall back to believing she wasn't enough. She wasn't that caged bird anymore. She was done with self-imposed confinement.

It was time to be fierce and fight for herself, for him, and their future together. Time to spread her wings and *fly.*

The moment she pulled into the driveway, she flew out of her car and through the front door, determined to demand the conversation they had both been avoiding.

But before she could even get a word out, Levi appeared in the hallway, relaxed and looking absolutely mouthwatering. His dark green eyes locked on hers with something unreadable burning behind them.

"You're coming with me," he said, taking her hand without hesitation.

"Levi, I—"

"No arguments, Aurelia." His fingers tightened gently. "Come with me."

Levi gently tugged her forward and led her right back out the door.

Aurelia's hard-earned courage sputtered and died the moment Levi laced his fingers through hers and guided her into his SUV. The engine rumbled to life, and Levi drove in comfortable silence, his fingers drumming against the steering wheel in a slow, rhythmic beat that felt almost...nervous.

She studied his profile, trying to decipher whatever secret he was hiding, but he gave nothing away.

The silence stretched too long. Her resolve snapped back into place as she turned toward him, determined to say what needed to be said. If he thought he could avoid this conversation, he had no idea who he was dealing with.

"Levi, we need to talk," she blurted, before he could deflect.

He cast her a sidelong glance, a small, knowing smile tugging at his lips. "I know. We will. Once we get there."

She blinked. *What?*

"Listen, I—wait, what?"

"I said I agree," he repeated calmly. "We *do* need to talk, and we will. But after we arrive."

Confusion flickered through her, quickly followed by curiosity.

"Great. Awesome." She crossed her arms but couldn't hold the tension. "Where exactly are we going?"

Without answering, Levi reached across the console, lifted her hand to his lips, and pressed a soft kiss to her knuckles. His eyes gleamed with mischief as he whispered, "It's a surprise."

Aurelia narrowed her gaze but let him have this one...for now. She took in his outfit of worn jeans, sneakers, and a soft, long-sleeved crewneck. Simple and casual, ruling out anything formal, at least.

She thanked the universe for that small mercy, considering she was dressed equally as casually. Comfortable in skinny jeans, sneakers, and a lightweight Henley. Her hair was thrown up haphazardly and out of the way. Not exactly the kind of look she wanted for a life-altering conversation, but it would have to do.

They turned off the main road and onto a secluded path leading deep into the woods.

Had she not trusted him implicitly, she might have been somewhat concerned. The towering trees swallowed the sky, their shadows dark and foreboding, making the road ahead barely visible.

Finally, the woods gave way to a quiet clearing, and the sight before her stole every word from her lips.

Nestled against a steaming lagoon was a tiny, rustic cottage straight out of a fairytale. Its sloped wooden roof and natural stone walls were wrapped in delicate vines and glowing string lights. Warm lanterns flickered between the trees, bathing everything in soft, golden light.

A winding dock stretched out over the lagoon, leading to a cozy seating area outfitted with plush cushions and a woven rattan loveseat. A table for two was set under the canopy of lights, a picnic dinner waiting, the scent of roses perfuming the air.

Aurelia's breath caught, mesmerized by the scene.

Levi stepped out of the car, came around, and opened her door. His hand reached for hers, warm and steady.

Heart pounding, she let him help her to her feet, her eyes wide as she continued to take it all in.

"Levi..." Her voice was barely a whisper. "What is this?"

He said nothing at first. Then he took a deep, fortifying breath, then reached into his pocket and pulled out a small velvet box.

Aurelia's heart stilled, the world around them fading to the background as Levi slowly dropped to one knee.

"I know I've made mistakes," he began, his voice thick with emotion but unwavering. "I know I've hurt you in ways you never deserved. And for that...I'll never forgive myself. I let fear and my past dictate my actions. I didn't fight for us when it mattered most. But I'm here now and I don't want to spend another day without you by my side...not because of a contract, not because of circumstance, but because I love you, Aurelia. I love you in so many ways I never thought I was capable of."

Her vision blurred, tears welling in her eyes as he opened the box to reveal the rings she had once given back in anger.

"I've spent these last few months doing what I should have done from the very beginning—getting to know the real you. In doing that, I've fallen even more hopelessly in love. So, if you'll have me...this time, let's do it right. No obligations. No expectations. Only choice...because I choose *you*."

Aurelia pressed her trembling hand to her lips, her heart so full it felt like it might break under the weight of it all. Finally...*Finally* she let the tension go, her lips curving into a slow, radiant smile.

"Yes," she whispered. Then louder, stronger. *"Yes, Levi. I want to stay married to you."*

Relief and joy collided across Levi's face. Grinning like a fool who hit the jackpot, he slid the rings back onto her finger where they belonged and pulled her down into his arms, holding her like he never wanted to let go.

The night wrapped around them like a blessing, sealing a promise neither of them would ever break again.

Not just an arranged contractual marriage, but the beginning of something real. It was the beginning of forever.

Levi

After months of waiting and planning, Levi was finally ready to take the next step. He was going to propose to his wife...*tonight.*

Aurelia had her final doctor's appointment that morning, and he silently hoped she had been cleared from needing the walking boot and air cast. He had made sure she followed every recovery instruction to the letter, even resigning himself to sleeping in that damn guest bedroom all this time.

While his mansion sat on the market, he had held onto one untouched piece of property, a hidden gem his grandmother had cherished. The idea of proposing there had come to him weeks ago, remembering how his grandfather built that little cottage as a testament of love.

Levi's father was a bastard in every sense of the word, but he still remembered what a true gentleman his paternal grandfather was. Though his time in Levi's life was too short, he showered him with the love and attention his parents should have provided.

He shared many stories about Levi's grandmother and loved her deeply. This secret little getaway was built as a physical testament to his love for her. Now Levi understood what had driven his grandfather to do it. It felt only right to bring Aurelia there.

The place had fallen into disrepair over the years, and both he and his father shared blame for that. Determined to make it right, Levi spent weeks restoring the cottage and transforming it into a romantic hideaway. All those late nights and long hours had been worth it for this moment.

The joy in Aurelia's eyes was something he would remember long after his memory faded. She was etched into his very soul, and for the rest of his life, he would make sure she never regretted choosing to stay with him.

Remembering how insistent she had been about needing to talk, Levi gently pulled back and brushed away the tears on her cheeks. "Now that we've gotten *this* out of the way..." he teased, voice light but full of love, "what did you need to talk about, Mrs. Lockwood?"

Aurelia blinked at him, startled by the question. The joy on her face dimmed. She sat back on her knees, attempting to gather her thoughts. Levi readied himself for a potential setback.

"I wanted to talk about *us*," she began quietly, "about how much I hated you sleeping in the guest room. How much it hurt that you never mentioned the rings I gave back...or what was happening between us."

He opened his mouth to speak, but she held up a hand, stopping him.

"And...I've been a hypocrite," she admitted, her eyes shining. "From the start, you've been patient with *my* issues every time they came up. But I never gave *your* past the same attention or understanding. I'm so sorry, Levi." Her voice cracked as her eyes met his, full of raw, unguarded vulnerability.

"And there's something else." She took a measured breath. "I need to apologize for how fast I pushed physical intimacy. It was the only way I'd ever known how to feel...wanted. In control. Like I mattered, before people got bored with me." She winced, clearly uncomfortable with the confession. "Not that it wasn't *incredible* with you," she added quickly, cheeks flushed.

Levi's eyebrows lifted, surprised by the admission, but he didn't dare interrupt.

"I just...I still have things to work through. The doctor gave me a referral for a therapist this morning that I'm going to reach out to," she whispered. "But I *missed* you, Levi. I missed having you next to me more than anything. I miss *this*...because I love you too. I love being with you, in every way."

Levi's heart stopped at those four words.

I love you too.

Out of everything she had said aloud, those four words echoed through him. Over and over reverberating through his very being, embedding into his very essence.

There was so much he wanted to say, but the only thing that mattered was her...and right now she was too far away.

With a wide grin, Levi grabbed her by the waist and pulled her flush against him. His forehead dropped to hers, his breath warm against her lips.

"I love you, Auri," he whispered. "There's no scar too deep, no hurdle too high, that we can't overcome. Together."

Then he kissed her.

Deep, assertive, and utterly consuming, he poured every ounce of his love into it. His tongue relished the taste of her like it was the first time all over again, like he had found something precious he never wanted to lose.

When he finally pulled back, both of them panting, he buried his face in the crook of her neck and grinned wickedly against her. His hands slid down to cup her backside, pulling her closer still.

"Why don't we finish this conversation in the lagoon?" he murmured against her ear. "The water's nice and warm...and doesn't require any pesky bathing suits."

Aurelia arched into him, her body already aching for his touch.

"Warm and wet...like your wife," she breathed, threading her fingers through his hair.

Levi laughed low, dark, and sinful as he stood and swept her into his arms.

And with nothing but the quiet sounds of the night around them, he carried her toward the steaming water.

Aurelia

They barely made it to the edge of the dock and the picnic before their clothes vanished, discarded without a second thought. Levi was unable to wait another moment to taste her.

Before Aurelia could blink, she was sprawled across the cushioned patio loveseat, her legs draped over his broad, tanned shoulders. The carefully curated picnic lay forgotten on the nearby table as Levi buried his head between her thighs, his tongue on a relentless mission to rediscover every inch of her. Her cries echoed through the secluded woods, lost to the night as he worshipped her with every stroke and flick.

When her senses finally returned, she pushed him back against the cushions, her eyes gleaming with delicious intent. Levi sat back, watching her every movement like a predator in his element, muscles taut, waiting for her next move.

With a knowing smirk, Aurelia shifted to the table and bent over the picnic spread, intentionally lingering as she searched for the right selection. Levi hissed through his teeth at the sight of her arched back, her body on display, but he held himself still, anticipation thrumming through his veins.

She cast a sultry glance over her shoulder, her grin widening when she saw the raw hunger on his face. His body was hard, proud, and unabashedly hers. Her mouth watered at the sight, her desire spiking as she turned back to the table, plating the juiciest fruits she could find before placing them beside him.

Climbing onto his lap, she leaned in and kissed him deeply, her lips tasting faintly of sweet wine and promises.

"You look positively famished," she teased, her lips brushing his.

"I'm wasting away," Levi rasped, his voice rough with need as his hands slid up to cup her breasts, thumbs circling her hardened nipples, drawing a soft moan from her lips. "But right now, I'm far more concerned with feeding you."

Reaching for a piece of ripe pineapple from her plate, he held it to her lips. She laughed softly, biting into it as the juice ran down her chin and spilled onto her chest.

"Damn it," she gasped between laughs, the liquid trailing over her skin. "You stole my idea."

Levi growled low against her collarbone, his tongue already following the path of the sweet juice down her chest. "Oh, was that your plan?" he murmured against her skin. "Then allow me to execute it to perfection."

And god did he execute it...slowly and thoroughly until Aurelia couldn't bear it any longer, desperate to eliminate what distance remained between them.

Once they had polished off every piece of fruit on the plate, Levi shifted her over him, gripping her hips as he guided her down onto him, inch by glorious inch.

Aurelia's head fell back, a gasp leaving her lips as she took him fully. She didn't think she would ever tire of this—of the exquisite fullness, the way his body stretched and completed hers like no one ever had before.

She began to move, slow and unhurried, setting a sensual, torturously sweet rhythm. This time, there was no urgency, no desperate chase toward release. There was only connection, reverence, and love.

Beneath the twinkling lights and under the midnight sky, they took their time reacquainting themselves and their bodies, quietly rewriting their story.

One kiss, one stroke, one whispered promise at a time.

The stars glittered like diamonds against black velvet, casting silver light over the steaming lagoon. After Aurelia collapsed, boneless and satiated against Levi's chest, hunger eventually won out. They migrated to the edge of the deck, spreading the forgotten picnic across the floor within easy reach of the lagoon's natural stone shelf, which was a perfect swim-up bar in the hot, soothing water.

Remaining in the water—and completely naked—Aurelia indulged herself in a little of everything, delighted to find a chilled bottle of sparkling grape juice waiting in a bucket of ice. Levi hadn't forgotten her distaste for alcohol, a small, thoughtful gesture that melted her all over again.

Once their stomachs were satisfied, Levi wasted no time filling her in other ways; this time in the warm, mineral-rich waters. A different, more playful side of Aurelia had emerged when she lured him close...only to dunk him under the surface without warning. His sputtered outrage was met with her laughter—full, bright, and even punctuated by a few unflattering snorts.

She tried to swim away, but Levi was faster. He caught her waist, lifted her like she weighed nothing, and tossed her playfully into the water. This time, it was Aurelia who came up sputtering, and Levi who roared with triumphant laughter, loud enough to scare off any curious critters nearby.

When she tried to dunk him again, his arms wrapped tightly around her again, refusing to let go. What started as a teasing kiss quickly turned into something far more heated as she wrapped her legs around his waist and nipped his lower lip. Before she knew it, her back was pressed against the stone shelf, and Levi was buried inside her all over again.

Now, floating in the warm water, spent and utterly content, Aurelia lay cradled in Levi's arms. The tension that had gripped her for weeks dissolved under the stars and the security of his embrace. Her fingertips traced lazy circles across his chest, her cheek pressed against his shoulder.

"I have a confession," Levi murmured, his voice a deep rumble against her ear. His eyes twinkled with mischief.

Her suspicion deepened. "Spit it out."

"I...recorded the proposal."

Her brows shot up. "You did *what*?"

"I set up a camera on the roof of the cottage," he admitted, a sheepish grin forming. "High-quality, top-of-the-line. I wanted us to have a real memory of it, not something that fades or we remember differently for years down the road. I thought maybe we could even pull a few photos from it. Something tangible. A real memory, since..." he trailed off, guilt flashing in his eyes, "...since our actual ceremony was a disaster."

Something warm settled deep in her chest. "Levi..." she whispered, her throat tight. "That's...incredibly thoughtful. And sneaky—but wait." She sat up, her eyes wide with panic. "Was it recording the *entire* time we've been out here?"

He smirked. "You say that like it's a bad thing."

"Levi!" she gasped, scandalized. "You *better* have turned it off!"

He laughed, pulling her closer. "Relax, I'm kidding—mostly. I'll delete everything after the proposal, I promise. I wanted to start capturing our story...on our terms this time." He hesitated before cheekily adding, "Unless you want to watch everything we did in high definition."

She couldn't stop the snort that escaped as she fell deeper in love with this ridiculous, thoughtful man. She kissed him hard and fast, her lips lingering against his. "Thank you," she whispered.

His arms tightened around her. "Since we're already baring our souls..." His voice dropped into a serious, almost shy tone. "How many kids do you want?"

Aurelia blinked, then burst into soft laughter. "Wow. Jumping right into that one, huh?"

"I'm a planner," he said, his grin unapologetic.

She bit her lip, growing thoughtful. "I used to think I wouldn't be a good mother...that I'd become my mother. Now? I do want kids, a family. I want a real home—with you. Two or three kids, maybe? What about you?"

"Whatever you want is perfect," he said simply. "We can have a whole brood of little monsters, but not right away. I want us to have time first. Just us. Travel. Try new things. Make sure we're really ready when that time comes."

She smiled, threading her fingers through his hair. "I like that. But you're going to have to explain this 'extensive plan' of yours. What else aren't you telling me?"

He gave her a mock-sober nod. "It's a thorough list. Couples' curling tournament, learning to keep bees so we can make our own honey—oh, and taking you to your first metal concert."

She laughed outright. "Those are...ambitious options. How about we start with something simple? I want to travel. I've never been outside the city, never even been on a plane. And...I want a real wedding."

Levi's expression softened. "You do?"

She nodded. "Something small with only us and the people who truly love us. On the dock, maybe. With string lights. I want to walk down the aisle properly this time."

"Then we'll make it happen," he said without hesitation, pressing a kiss to her forehead. "Anything you want."

She settled against his chest again, then drew a deep breath. "There's one more thing I want. I...need your help."

Levi shifted to look at her. "Anything, Auri."

Aurelia hesitated, then let the words tumble free. "I want to use the inheritance Eleanor left me to make something meaningful out of it—help kids like me. Kids who age out of the system and have nowhere to go. I'm thinking about turning Starhaven Manor into a transitional residence. A safe place where they can figure things out."

Levi was quiet for a moment, his thumb brushing soothing circles on her arm. When she finally met his gaze, what she saw there wasn't surprise; it was pride.

"You are incredible," he murmured. "Funny story though...it's already in motion."

Her eyes went wide. "What?"

"I wanted to give you something real for our wedding, a proper wedding gift. I remembered you mentioning this idea at *Moonlit Buns*, so I had Charles start setting up the foundation. It's legally established, ready for you to take the lead whenever you're ready."

She threw her arms around him, holding on like she might never let go.

"You, sir," she choked out against his shoulder, "are going to be the death of me."

He laughed, tightening his hold. "I love you, Aurelia. I want to build the rest of my life with you."

She pulled back, searching his face. But before she could respond, a shadow crept across her features as thoughts crept in of Selene, Kyle, and the looming trial.

Her lips trembled. "Levi...there's still something I'm afraid of. It's hanging over us, and I don't know if I'm strong enough to face it."

His expression turned serious. "The trial."

She nodded.

"It feels like they still have power over me," she whispered. "I'm never really going to be free of them."

Levi cupped her face, his thumbs brushing away the tears threatening to fall. "I will be right there beside you for every court date and every hard moment. You'll never have to stand alone again."

She tried to laugh, but it caught in her throat. "I don't know how to be brave enough to face the source of my nightmares."

He leaned in and brushed a gentle kiss on her lips. "You *are* strong enough—you've always been. The only difference is that you now have me to remind you of that when you forget."

In his arms and under the stars, she felt her fear begin to loosen its grip, knowing that whatever came next, they would face it together.

From this point forward, Aurelia wasn't just surviving anymore; she was finally *living*.

EPILOGUE

Aurelia

The courtroom was cold and sterile, but Aurelia was unaffected. All she felt was fire pulsing through her veins as she walked in, her spine straight, her expression blank. Dressed in a sharp, understated maroon dress, she looked every inch the woman they hadn't managed to break.

After months of waiting, the air was thick with judgment, the final moments of reckoning for Selene and Kyle at last within reach.

Levi kept his promise. He was there beside her, as he had been through every agonizing moment leading up to this day. Clad in a deep gray suit, his hand gripped hers, a solid and unwavering reminder that she wasn't facing this alone.

Her gaze settled on Kyle first. His once-arrogant smirk was long gone, replaced by something hollow and broken. The sadistic man who once reveled in overpowering her now sat like a ghost of himself. A new scar cut across his brow—a permanent reminder of the day she forced him to kneel before her strength.

The restraining order violation had sealed his fate, and now, he was nothing more than a common criminal waiting to be told how many years he would waste behind bars.

Aurelia tilted her head, the faintest hint of a smirk curving her lips. *I hope the rest of your days are spent cowering under someone else's boot, a constant reminder of what you really are.*

Then her eyes landed on Selene.

Where Kyle was hollow, Selene was a barely contained inferno. There was no remorse or regret. Only seething hatred blazing in her eyes. Aurelia didn't bother hiding her rage—didn't soften her glare or temper the heat in her veins. She *wanted* Selene to see the depths of it and to remember exactly who she had underestimated.

But none of that mattered now.

What mattered was the judge's voice cutting through the tension like a blade. *Life in prison without parole for both Selene and Kyle.*

A slow, shuddering breath escaped Aurelia's lungs, her entire body trembling under the weight of release. Months of imagining this moment hadn't prepared her for the reality of it, of what it would feel like to finally *be free.*

Not caring who saw or if cameras were rolling, she threw her arms around Levi's neck, tears streaming down her face as she buried herself against him. He pulled her into his lap without hesitation, crushing her to his chest and kissing her hard. For long, quiet moments, she stayed there, letting the tidal wave of relief crash through her, not bothering to fight it.

When she was ready, she peeled herself from his embrace and stood. Levi followed, his eyes never leaving her.

With her head held high and her soul light for the first time in years, Aurelia turned on her heel and walked out of the courtroom. Levi held the heavy wooden door open, and as soon as she crossed the threshold, he wrapped her in his arms once more.

"It's done," she whispered into his chest, holding him tight.

"It's done," he echoed, pressing a kiss to her hair. His voice was thick with emotion but sure. "And now...we move forward."

Levi

The dock behind the house glowed beneath the golden hues of sunset, the lagoon reflecting the colors like liquid gold. A small circle of their closest friends gathered barefoot on the worn wooden planks—Owen, Ivy, Grace, Isaac, Charles, Estrella, and even Adelen. It wasn't extravagant or showy.

It was entirely theirs.

Aurelia smoothed the soft pastel aqua dress she had chosen, nothing like the dramatic gowns she once imagined brides would wear. It was simple, flowing, and effortless...exactly like her.

At the end of the dock, Levi waited, hands in the pockets of his tan linen pants, his gaze fixed on her with the kind of devotion that stole the breath from her lungs. He wore a crisp white shirt with a single hydrangea boutonniere pinned on the collar. Charles, their officiant this time, stood beside him with a wide, knowing smile.

Owen, ever the entertainer, had somehow talked them into letting him be the official "flower man" and was putting on an absolute spectacle, throwing petals with exaggerated flourishes as he strutted down the dock.

He caught sight of Adelen and—ever undeterred—tried to impress her with his petal-tossing prowess. Adelen was visibly unimpressed. Aurelia laughed as she began walking toward Levi, catching the determined gleam in Owen's eyes now set on Adelen.

That poor woman has no idea what she's in for, he thought with amusement.

A small, ornate wedding arch stood at the end of the dock, draped with flowing white fabric and adorned with tiny crystals that sparkled like stars in the fading light. Lanterns lined the dock's edge, guiding her path toward the man who had already owned her heart and touched her soul.

The reception area beyond was simple but beautiful. A long, elegant table was set with fine China, crystal glasses, and a vibrant floral centerpiece, surrounded by cushioned chairs. The quiet lap of water against the dock provided the only symphony they needed.

As she reached him, Levi took her hands gently and leaned in, his voice a low murmur meant for her alone. "No words exist to adequately describe how beautiful you look." He took pride in the blush that now crept over her skin, wishing he could explore just how far it spread beneath her dress.

Charles clapped his hands together, shaking Levi from his heated thoughts. "Alright, lovebirds. Let's do this before the sun sets completely."

The ceremony was intimate, filled with soft laughter and vows spoken with absolute certainty. This time, there were photos captured; Owen and Estrella made sure of that.

When Levi slid the wedding band back onto her finger for good this time, something settled deep inside him, down into the core of his existence. Something precious that intertwined his soul with Aurelia's.

It was the infallible knowledge that he was home.

Later, as they stood by the water watching the last traces of daylight slip beneath the horizon, Levi handed her a nondescript folder bound with a dark blue ribbon.

"What's this?" Aurelia asked, her brow lifting in curiosity.

"Open it," he said, his eyes gleaming with quiet anticipation.

She carefully untied the ribbon and flipped through the pages, then stiffened, surveying the various legal documents, charters, and deeds.

Levi had done it. He had made Aurelia's dream real. Starhaven Manor would become a sanctuary for kids aging out of foster care who needed a fresh start and a safe place. Exactly what she had once needed...she now could provide it to others.

Wrought with emotion, her eyes filled with tears as she turned to him. "Levi, this is—"

He wrapped his arms around her waist, pulling her close. "It's yours," he said simply. "It was always meant to be yours."

Tears slid down her cheeks, but for the first time in so long, they weren't born from pain. She pressed her lips to his, letting the warmth of their future—of *everything* they had fought for—wash over them.

A new beginning not born of luck or circumstance but forged by choice. By every heartbreak they survived, every wall they tore down for each other. This wasn't a love that simply happened; it was a love they fought for, bled for, and chose again and again.

Their lives were no longer separate threads but a single, unbreakable tapestry—one they were finally ready to live together. For the rest of forever.

ACKNOWLEDGEMENTS

I owe the existence of this book to my family who have supported me the entire way on this journey. For my children who have shown me that loving differently doesn't mean it is any less fulfilling.

But the backbone of this entire adventure is my amazing husband, who was and will always be, my number one champion that loves me as I am and supports me and my dreams...even those that I decided to pursue on a random train ride together during a weekend trip away.

From late night discussions about technology topics, to being forced to listen to me brainstorming different ways to allude to a penis, he has been my rock and steady force amidst the turmoil. I am lucky enough to know true romance in my life because of this amazing man who somehow willingly chose me as his forever.

There were so many others that helped me on this journey that I need to thank as well, like Melissa McGovern from Memos in the Margins who is not only my developmental editor, but an amazing friend that I was lucky enough to meet when she started our local moms book club. She did more than just editing but gave me a crash course on the world of bookish social media and introduced me to AK Cover Designs.

I can't forget The Inkwell Guild, my amazing author support group that has made this the rough patches more fun, and allowed us to learn from each other.

My fantastic beta readers Alex, Jen, Meghan, Louise, and MJ were instrumental in reading this book and not shy about giving me feedback. You all helped make this story better and I could not have made it this far without you.

I originally wanted to acknowledge my sister-in-law Heather, for contributing absolutely nothing to this book when she had demanded to be thanked in this section anyway. Unfortunately, she ended up being a beta reader as well and ruined this section of the *Acknowledgements*.